Romeo Redeemed

Romeo Redeemed

A NOVEL BY STACEY JAY

DELACORTE PRESS

Text copyright © 2012 by Stacey Jay
Jacket art copyright © 2012 by Elizabeth May/Trigger Image

Visit us on the Web! randomhouse.com/teens

Educators and librarians, for a variety of teaching tools, visit us at RHTeachersLibrarians.com

Library of Congress Cataloging-in-Publication Data
Jay, Stacey.
Romeo redeemed / Stacey Jay. – 1st ed.
p. cm.
Summary: In modern-day California Romeo is offered one last chance to redeem himself by switching sides and becoming an Ambassador–if he can prove himself worthy by making Juliet, as Ariel, love him in a reality with a different past than his own.
ISBN 978-0-385-74018-0 (hc) – ISBN 978-0-375-89894-5 (ebook) – ISBN 978-0-385-90827-6 (glb)
[1. Characters in literature–Fiction. 2. Love–Fiction. 3. Good and evil–Fiction. 4. Revenge–Fiction. 5. Supernatural–Fiction. 6. California, Southern–Fiction.] I. Title.
PZ7.J344Rom 2012
[Fic]–dc23
2011044333

The text of this book is set in 11-point Berthold Baskerville.
Book design by Angela Carlino

Printed in the United States of America

10 9 8 7 6 5 4 3 2 1

First Edition

For Carol.

All my love.

My only love sprung from my only hate!

Too early seen unknown, and known too late!

Prodigious birth of love it is to me,

That I must love a loathèd enemy.

—Shakespeare, *Romeo and Juliet*

Romeo Redeemed

ONE

Romeo

We reach the lonely hilltop just as the sun sets over Verona. Golden light bleeds to a crimson stain that spreads across the city, dipping into every secret place, marking every shadow. Just as her blood seeped from her chest . . . spread out to coat the stones of the tomb. Cold, mute stones. They will keep my terrible secret.

Juliet is dead, and her blood is on my hands.

I hide them beneath my cloak, but I can feel her death clinging to my skin. Warm, sticky, and slick, making it hard to hold the knife Friar Lawrence insisted I carry. This mess is all I have left of the girl I loved. The girl I destroyed. My heart writhes inside me, but I don't make a sound. I don't deserve to mourn her. I deserve this misery and more. I deserve to suffer for all eternity.

And so I follow the friar across the windswept hill, to the place where the poor and ungodly bury their dead. I follow, though I am certain now that the man I trusted with my love's life is a liar and a fiend.

Perhaps even worse. Perhaps I've struck a bargain with Lucifer himself.

"Move the stones. There is a body here that will suit your purpose." The friar grunts as he sinks into the damp grass by the grave. It's a peasant's grave, marked only by a pile of rocks that the dead man's family mounded atop his corpse to keep the animals away. "In the beginning, it's easier if the body is fresh."

I set the knife by his feet and begin shifting the stones, keeping my eyes on my stained hands as I work. Blood. Juliet's blood, drying to a dull brown that cracks and flakes as my fingers flex and release. The wind rushes across the hill, blowing a piece of her away, and the horror hits me anew.

How could I have done this? How could I have been such a fool?

The friar swore my betrayal would be a blessing. He promised Juliet would dance with the angels. She would see the gates of heaven open, and know my sacrifice had delivered her to that land of eternal spring. She would weep to go, but love me all the more for paying her passage.

I thought I was making a noble choice. Juliet and I were penniless, friendless. Death was waiting for us. If not on the road to Mantua, then in the paupers' slum in that unfamiliar city. We were born noble and knew nothing of how to make our own way. I've never filled my own bath, let alone earned a living. I have no skills, no guild, not even a goat or a plot of land to work. Death was a certainty. We would have starved to death, or been murdered in our sleep. The friar agreed that the greatest kindness I could show my wife was to end her suffering before it began, and leave her here to be buried with her family.

But I should have doubted, feared.

I didn't, not until I held her as she drew her last breaths. There was no bliss in her eyes, only agony, the sting of betrayal, and an ominous spark as hatred caught fire and began to burn within her.

Juliet died hating me, and only God himself knows where she is now. Since I was a small boy, I have been taught that suicide is a sin, and that those who take their own lives are damned. I should have listened to the teachings of the Church, not one mad friar who spoke openly of black magic and the end of times. How could I have taken such a risk with my love's soul? How could I have deceived her into thinking I was dead, into believing that driving a knife through her own heart was her only hope of joining me in the world beyond?

A part of me prays it will make a difference that Juliet was tricked into taking her own life. The rest of me knows praying is pointless. I am beyond the reach of anything holy, my lot firmly thrown in with the Mercenaries of the Apocalypse, the dark magicians sworn to bring chaos to the world.

I have made the blood sacrifice and taken the life of the one I cherished most. Now only the vows remain.

"Hurry," the friar says. "The prince's guard will pass through here after nightfall. We must be finished before then."

I reach for another stone. I am ready. I will become the

immortal abomination he's tricked me into becoming, and perhaps, in some small way, I will be able to make reparations for what I've done. It is what Juliet would want. She would want me to fight the darkness Friar Lawrence has awoken within me, and bring some small honor back to my life.

Or my death. I'm next to die. I will take the vows, make the mortal marks, and send my soul into another's dead body. It is the Mercenary way—to inhabit the dead—and one more thing the friar failed to mention until Juliet was gone and there was no turning back.

No turning back . . .

One, two, three, four . . . the pile of stones grows at the side of the grave as I uncover my destiny with shaking hands. The first layer is gone now, and the smell is horrific. The sickening sweetness of decay mingles with pungent burial oil and the stink of a long-unwashed man, driving me to the brink of sickness even before I lift the large, flat rock covering the head.

I gasp and pull my hands away.

The face is black with rot. Bloated, monstrous, and infested with insects. A beetle scuttles from what's left of the man's nose, and I stumble backward, bile burning a trail from my core to my lips.

The friar chuckles. "Come now, Romeo. It isn't as bad as all that. Once you've taken the vows, you'll have the power to return that body to its former glory." He leans over to peer into the man's face, nods. "Yes. That's the one. I vow the boy was handsome in life."

I swallow my sickness but can't take a step closer to the horror I've uncovered. "Did you . . . know him?"

"In a manner of speaking." He smiles. "I killed him." His

tone is easy, amiable, as if he's discussing what we'll have for supper when this errand is done.

My lips part, but no words come. I am dumbstruck, though I know I shouldn't be. He revealed his true nature in the tomb. How he delighted in Juliet's suffering, laughing as he pulled me from her dying body. Her pain was a pleasure to him, her blood a treat more tempting than wine. I wouldn't have been surprised to see him fall to his knees and lap her essence from the floor.

"I slit his throat five days past," he continues. "To be certain you had a suitable host."

Five days past. "That long? Even then, you knew that I . . ."

That I would betray the only beautiful thing I've ever known, that I would risk her eternal soul for a handful of promises.

"I knew the moment you came to my cell with the fever of yet *another* new passion burning in your breast." He meets my gaze, and I see myself through his eyes. I see what an easy mark I was, what a lovesick, lust-filled, selfish, gullible child.

He smiles again, confirming my damning vision, and motions me away from the newly opened grave. "That will do. You'll be able to cast off the last of the stones once you are inhabiting the body." He rises and comes to stand by my side, clapping me on the back with a familiarity that makes me cringe. "As a Mercenary you will be stronger than any mortal man who walks the earth. You will have the power to make the dead appear to live so long as your soul inhabits their flesh, and the power to mend all but the most grievous damage to your borrowed form."

I clear my throat, trying to remain calm as he bends and

takes up the knife. "So I will be able to die, then? I won't be truly immortal?"

He draws the sleeve of his robe up to reveal his darkly veined arm. "You will be as immortal as is required to perform your duties for the cause."

"And what duties are those?" The friar said that the Mercenaries bring pain and suffering to the wicked, paving the way for the final destruction of life as man knows it.

Life as man knows it seemed cruel and pointless to me once, but now . . .

I keep seeing Friar Lawrence's face as he watched Juliet bleed. She was not wicked, and yet how he relished her anguish. What if he has lied about my duties as well? If I'm to be given the task of murdering innocents, then the sacrifice of my soul will be for nothing.

"You'll have a special place in our ranks." The friar draws the point of the knife down his inner arm, and fluid closer to black than red swells to the surface of his skin. My own blood screams for me to run, to race for the city gates and throw myself upon the prince's mercy. Even if he kills me for violating the terms of my banishment, it will be a better end than this.

"Special in what way?"

"All in good time." The friar presses the knife into my hand. "Speak the vows, make the mortal marks, and all will be made clear."

My fingers are cold, numb. The knife falls back to the ground. "No," I whisper.

"No?"

"No." My voice is stronger, but I don't dare look at him.

"Need I remind you that your wife is dead?" he asks. "You

betrayed and murdered an innocent young girl whose only flaw was that she loved too greatly. You spilled her blood for the chance to join us, and now you have second thoughts? Now that she is dead and gone and no act of gods or men can undo what you have done?"

"I did this for her." I choke on the sob rising in my throat. "I am banished and she would have been ruined. I . . . I wanted her to be safe."

"And she *is* safe." He sounds so caring, so wise, the way he has these past weeks. I lift my eyes and find his earnest face inches from mine. "Or she will be, so long as you honor your promise. If you turn back now . . . well, I fear what will happen to Juliet without our magic to help her reach paradise. I fear her soul will be lost, and she will never understand the great sacrifice you have made for her happiness."

He's lying. There's nothing he can do *to* or *for* Juliet now. I feel that truth in my gut, deep down in my core, where regret rips me apart. I feel his lie, and I try to tell him so, but I can't move my lips, can't turn my eyes away from his. I am transfixed, mesmerized by the solace he offers. I want to trust in his gentle words, but there's a reason I shouldn't.

Some reason . . .

I close my eyes and see Juliet's hands on the hilt of the knife, driving it into her chest. I see her minutes later, after I've risen from the ground, proving I deceived her. I see her struggling to pull the weapon from her flesh with trembling hands. If she'd had the strength, she would have torn it from her heart and plunged it into my own. "But Juliet . . . she didn't . . ."

"Yes, my son?"

"She hated me," I say. "I could see it. And there was no

light in the tomb, no song as the angels welcomed her into heaven."

"Ah. I see." He nods sagely. "You have doubts."

I sigh. He understands. How could I have thought otherwise?

"Thomas had doubts. As did Job. Great men have always been tormented by doubt." The knife is back in my hand. I don't remember the friar stooping to pluck it from the ground, but he must have. Now the heavy handle warms my fingers, filling me with hope, purpose. "But there is no need to fear. Take the vows and fulfill the promise you made to your Juliet. And to me, the one who would be your brother."

"I had a brother." My voice is strangely distant, as if a part of me has already left my body behind. "He died when we were boys. My father was never the same."

"I understand." The friar rolls up the sleeve of my cloak with patient hands. "He was cruel to you."

"He will kill me if I return. He blames me for my mother's death two days past. He says my banishment stole her will to live, but it was him," I say, arms trembling. "He took it from her. Long ago. It wasn't my fault!"

"Shh." The friar's hand comes to rest on my shoulder, giving me strength. "Soon you will be beyond pain or regret."

I nod, and watch my right hand lift the knife. It's almost as if someone else is controlling my arm, but it doesn't trouble me.

"Soon you will feel nothing at all." The friar's voice washes over me, a warm, comforting wave.

Nothing at all. It sounds . . . wonderful. No pain, no shame. Not the ache deep in my soul in the place where Juliet was a part of me, the place that is dark and haunted now that she is gone.

Now that I have *killed* her, tricked her into taking her own life. *I* did this, and I will *never* be beyond the reach of that horrible truth.

The fog created by the friar's magic clears, and my mind is my own once more. My hand tightens on the hilt of the knife. This Mercenary is mistaken about me, and it will be his ruin. I will become one of them, learn their secrets, and find a way to use my new power for good.

And I will do it all for her.

Juliet. Her name echoes through my being as I draw the blade down my arm. Her face hovers in the air before me as I speak the vows. Her voice whispers words of strength into my ear as my soul is ripped from my body.

And then—suddenly—I am somewhere else.

Someplace dark and quiet that I swell to fill like poison gas, pushing at the edges of my new flesh, finding the boundaries that separate me from the world. But it is different. I am aware of arms and legs and belly and heart and all the other pieces that make up a man, but I can feel . . . nothing. Not heat or cold or the stones that lie heavy on my chest or the wind that blows across the hill. I pull in a breath, but it is empty too. The smell of the corpse is gone.

I open my eyes, blinking as the sky above Verona comes into view. It is purple, the red and blue merged together to create one last glorious burst of color before night takes hold. But even that is flatter than it should be, as if I'm staring at a poorly rendered painting instead of a vast canopy that covers the earth.

The friar appears above me, surrounded by a black cloud that hovers in the air around him. With my new eyes, I can see how dark and evil his soul truly is, and I am afraid, but it isn't fear as I've known it before. It is something bigger and smaller at the same time, a death cry encased in stone that no ear will ever hear.

"I can't . . . I can't feel. . . ."

"Of course you can't." With dispassionate eyes he watches me struggle to free myself from the last of the stones. "Didn't I tell you that soon you'd feel nothing?"

His meaning hits, and I'm certain my new heart skips a beat, but I can't feel that, either. I cry out and claw my way from the grave, but my true prison is inescapable. I am trapped in the body of a dead man. No matter how whole and alive the arm I hold in front of my face appears, it is still dead. Wrong. Rotten from the inside out. The magnitude of my folly settles around my shoulders, and I know my soul is doomed, but still I feel . . . nothing.

Nothing. Nothing. *Nothing.*

For decades, nothing, only ghosts of fear and pain and two-dimensional cutouts of the love I once felt. By the time I encountered Juliet's soul in another girl's body—fifty years later, when my mission for the Mercenaries was finally revealed and I was told I would fight my former wife for the souls of true lovers—the nothing had grown so big that I relished the chance to fight her. Hurt her. Make her weep when I convinced a man to slit his lover's throat and join the Mercenaries.

Her pain still touched something inside of me, made me remember the boy I was before I developed a passion for bloodshed.

Another seven hundred years, and dozens of battles with the warrior Juliet became, slipped by in a haze of wickedness, but still her misery reached me. Even when, between her missions, she left the earth and returned to the mists of forgetting, I could feel her out there, lost in the gray void, and it brought me pleasure. She was my bird in a cage, and I was a mad, damaged monster. But when I held her in my thoughts, I was strong enough to plot and plan, to conceive a way out.

I did not love her any longer, but I needed her. I'd stolen a spell from the Mercenaries and found a way for us to reclaim our true forms and escape the service of the immortal creatures who had deceived us. There is no heaven or hell, no ruling force but the cold logic of the universe that demands that all equations be balanced. The Mercenaries of the Apocalypse and the Ambassadors of Light knew that truth and made gods of themselves. Juliet and I could have done the same.

Could have.

If she hadn't fallen in love with that twenty-first-century boy.

If the friar hadn't discovered my plan and bid me turn Juliet to darkness.

If I hadn't been forced to kill my love a second time to protect her from a fate worse than death.

If the friar hadn't punished me by showing me that there are worse things than forgetting how to feel.

There is remembering.

TWO

SOLVANG, CALIFORNIA, PRESENT DAY

Romeo

I crouch in the shadows in the corner of the abandoned train station, watching the morning light creep into the birds' nests near the ceiling, clutching the blanket I've stolen from one of the crackheads who called the condemned building home. There were five of them, one a Mercenary, judging from the blackness hovering in his aura. They ran screaming when I crawled through the door, my skeletal hands scratching the bird-shit-covered boards, rotted flesh dripping a trail of horror behind me.

Even the Mercenary ran. He knew what I was, saw what

I've become, and feared that the curse I've acquired might be catching.

Cursed, damned.

It's true, and I've suffered greatly in the weeks since Juliet passed the second time. My senses have been returned to me, so that I might know I smell like a plague pit and look like a monster. So that I can feel pain slam into my chest, echo in my brain with every step I take. I am truly a thing of darkness now, a being so wretched I can do nothing but hide in humanity's corners, fighting to stay warm as the wind whistles through my bones.

The only thing that keeps me from taking what's left of my sorry life is the friar's warning that if I do, I will become a phantom, without voice or form.

How pleasantly do you think a few million years such as that will pass? When you are an invisible nothing and no one can hear you scream?

The greatest liars always tell the truth when they can. Everything else he said has come true. I have been cast out of the Mercenaries and forced into the specter of my soul, a cruel parody of my true body, ravaged by the atrocities I've committed.

What if the rest is true? What if my soul will remain even after this body is gone? Even *this* has to be preferable to *that*. *Something* preferable to *nothing*, to the torture of a voice without an ear, to existence without confirmation.

Even a scream as people run away is something. . . .

Hoarse sobs break the silence, a wounded animal keening at the sun streaming across the wall. I have cried more in the past weeks than in my entire life and afterlife combined. The ghosts that haunted me when I was a Mercenary rub against my insides, crowding me with remorse. Regret. Hate. Fear. Love . . .

I loved her all along. I didn't realize how much until I crept back to the place where she died the second time and touched her lifeless hand, cried over her wide, sightless eyes. Juliet. Her soul is gone forever now. I can feel the difference in the universe, the absence that is a world with one less spot of light. I tried to save her. I hope, in some fashion, I finally did. I hope she's at peace in the mist . . . or wherever it is good people go.

I hope that boy she loved is there with her. I didn't weep for him, but I felt sadness for his loss. For the first time in hundreds of years I wished I'd had some other choice, that I could have spared them both. But I couldn't overpower the friar, and their love wouldn't have survived his torture. The best I could do was kill them, and offer myself in their place.

Maybe someday I'll regret my decision, when these weeks of agony stretch into centuries and finally I am nothing but dust, and even the luxury of tears is denied me.

Best to cry while I still have eyes.

My sobs bruise the silence, stirring the birds from their nests. They leap into the air, wings snapping like sheets hung to dry in the wind, so loud I hunch lower in my blanket, letting it cover my ears. There are hundreds of them, so many the floor is mounded with waste, humming with flies.

This hole isn't fit for anything human to live in. It is perfect for me.

"There you are. I've been looking for you." The voice comes from the door, a melody of chipper notes that sting what's left of my skin. It's a woman, a beautiful redhead with flesh so pale the blue of her veins shows through at her temples and beneath her dark brown eyes.

"That's quite a trail you left." She smiles at me, the bow of her lips curving with hard determination.

So she's come to gloat. I'd thought the Ambassadors above such petty pleasures, but she's definitely one of them. One of the golden ones. Her aura is so bright, it outshines the morning sun, makes me squint as she crosses the room and squats down by my side.

"Now then, Romeo. How are you finding your retirement?"

I slit my eyes and hiss, squirming my blackened tongue through what remains of my teeth.

She laughs, a soft chuckle that assures me I am a very small, foolish monster indeed. "As good as that?" She nods. "I thought that might be the case. I didn't imagine this was what you had in mind when you tempted my Juliet with eternity on earth." So it's her, Juliet's nurse. I suppose I should be afraid, but what can she do to me now? Now that I am brought so low even the flies decline to lay their eggs in my flesh? "That's why I've come. To offer you a way out."

A way out. I haven't allowed the possibility to enter what's left of my mind. There is no way out. This is the way I will end. This is the inescapable pit at the end of the last road.

But perhaps . . .

"Why?" I rasp, as distrustful of Ambassadors as I am of their dark cousins. Ambassadors and Mercenaries are similar creatures in many ways. They both glean converts from the weak, both use the vital energy those converts generate with acts of goodness or wickedness to sustain their eternity in their alternate realms. Once they were members of the same coven, before the spell that split them in two.

This "way out" might very well be a "way in" to even greater trouble.

"The Mercenaries have been stealing our converts for centuries." Juliet's nurse tugs the edge of my blanket until my head pops free. "Some of my colleagues disagree, but I don't see why we shouldn't do the same. A complete reversal of allegiance generates great power. We need that now, when so many of our high ones have been lost."

Not lost, murdered. Slaughtered by Mercenaries who fight dirty, who kill for what they want, who will not stop until their fires are the only toxic light burning at the end of the world.

"Is that something you would consider?" she asks. "Becoming one of us?"

I know relatively little about the inner workings of the Ambassadors, but I know the Mercenaries. And I know they will win. The Ambassadors are weak, their hands tied by the goodness required of their magic. Becoming an Ambassador would be suicide.

I smile and nod, eager as a puppy. Yes, I will shift my allegiance. Yes, I will serve the Ambassadors. Yes, I will trade this misery for mindless years in the mist and long days in bodies that can feel. Yes, I will serve for however many hundreds of years they require, and then I will be free. To die as she died.

The Ambassadors didn't cast Juliet into the specter of her soul. When her service to them was finished and she refused to renew her vows, they let her die a natural death. It is more than I could have hoped for, if I'd dared let that feathered thing take roost in this cage.

"Excellent." She holds my chin in her hand as if I'm not vile, as if I'm something precious she's plucked from the water before the current carried it away. "But you must prove yourself true, Romeo. You must prove your commitment to us above all else. If you do so, I will come to you and administer the vows of a peacekeeper, one of our most valuable servants. If not, the magic I lend you will run dry and you will find yourself back in this body, without a single hope in the world."

My head bobs again, brushing against her hand, smearing my death on her clean fingers. I will be true; I will be faithful. I will serve as no Ambassador has ever served, because no Ambassador has ever known the horror of being what I am.

"Good. Here is what you must do." She leans in close, whispering in my ear, telling me impossible things, spinning an improbable scenario, tying it all up with a promise to come for me at the end when I have saved a life and perhaps even the world.

I. Romeo. *I* will save the world. Or at least, one version of the world.

A strange sound rasps in my throat. It takes a moment to realize it's laughter. When I do realize, I laugh again, to see if she will pull away, if she will recognize what a broken thing I am.

But she only pats my hunched back and tilts her face closer to mine. "You will do as I say? You will fight for me? Love for me?"

I smile. "When I am finished, the girl will believe she is the sun, the moon, the stars in the sky. She will think my name and ache with how wondrous it is to love. To be loved. To hold such a treasure in her hand."

{17}

Juliet's nurse laughs. "Good. Ariel will require all of your extraordinary charm."

Ariel. But she's dead. I killed that body, the one that hosted Juliet's soul. Put a bullet in her brain to put Juliet beyond the friar's reach.

Nurse stands, watching my face, somehow reading my fear in the scraps of skin clinging to my cheeks and chin. "I know what you did. That is why only you can undo it. Our choices create many realities. I can send you to a reality with a different past, give you the chance to make another choice and create a place for Ariel in the world."

I let the blanket slip from my shoulders. "I'm ready. Send me now."

"Patience," she says, even as she presses her hands together, summoning a light so bright it burns my eyes. "I must send you back to the body you wore when you killed Ariel, to a moment when Dylan Stroud's fate split in two different directions."

"Very well. He will serve my purpose." Dylan's body suited me well enough during my last shift. The boy is handsome, reckless, damaged—all the things young girls love before they grow wise enough to realize it isn't smart to play with fire. But Ariel is young. She will be drawn to him, seduced by the flames. I smile at the thought of her big blue eyes, her white-blond hair.

This might not be such a chore after all.

"Remember, you must make her believe in love," Nurse warns, moving her hands farther apart, building the knot of power she holds until the air hums with potential energy, with magic. "It doesn't matter what you feel or don't feel, but you must make her love you, instill in her the unwavering faith that the human heart is worth fighting for. Banish the darkness inside her and set her on her true path."

I wave one skeletal hand in the air. "Done."

Her lips curve again, but this time there is something predatory in her smile. "Then go and do well, Romeo. Make the most of your one and only chance." Her hands fall to her sides, and the golden ball flies at me, striking me in the face. The world explodes in a shower of sparks. I am on fire, dropped into a pit of flames, a torturous molten place where there is no air to breathe, no mercy to be found. I burn for what seems like hours.

And then, just as suddenly, it's over. I'm in another body, on a dark road, driving through a spring evening.

Cool air streams in through the open windows, carrying night smells—evergreen trees, freshly cut grass, rosemary growing wild on the hills, and the faint hint of cow manure. It is . . . glorious. My fingers curling around the warm steering wheel, the wind in my hair, the world popping outside—it is everything I thought I'd never have again. It is life. *Real* life, not the shadows I've been trapped in for so long. I pull in a breath and hold it until my lungs ache, before letting it out with a satisfied sigh.

From the passenger seat comes a sound close to a growl.

I'm not alone. I turn my head and catch Ariel Dragland's impossibly big blue eyes. She huddles in the seat next to me, glaring with thinly veiled hatred, her arms crossed, those long, spidery fingers rubbing at the collar of her shirt. I feel Dylan's memories of her swim inside me, a strange sensation after so many years dwelling in the empty bodies of the dead.

As a Mercenary, I lived in a hundred or more corpses, but

every one was the same. They were lonely prisons that kept me from the world. Now not only do I have senses that allow me to experience my humanity, I have access to the thoughts and feelings of the body I've borrowed. My last occupation of his body ended in death, but this version of Dylan is still alive, and will return to his physical form when my work is through. Until then, he'll wander the mists of forgetting, that place outside of time where I will dwell between my missions for the bringers of goodness and light.

If I please Nurse and the other Ambassadors.

I *will.* I can't go back to being a dead thing. I *won't.*

I focus, searching Dylan's memories.

He loathed Ariel for her weakness, for being such a willing victim, an easy target. But he thought the shirt she was wearing tonight made her prettier, made it less of a chore to fulfill the bet he'd made and seduce the school freak. He nearly succeeded too, nearly won five hundred dollars. If Jason hadn't texted him, if Ariel hadn't seen . . .

But she *did* see. And she was enraged enough to scare even a young villain like Stroud. He worried that Ariel might really be crazy.

I glance at her from the corner of my eye. Crazy is relative. From my perspective, Ariel is quite sane. But she's certainly angry.

And faster than one would think.

I barely have time to flinch before the wheel is in her hands. She pulls to the right and I curse beneath my breath, understanding the Ambassador's hard smile, as the car hurtles toward the ravine where another version of Dylan died and I first entered his body.

I've been sent back in time to woo a girl who hates the

body I've entered. Even if we survive this crash, I'm doomed. She'll never love me.

No, she'll never love Dylan. You're a different monster, one with soft words and gentle hands.

Sometimes gentle, sometimes not. I reach for the wheel, ripping it from Ariel's grasp, turning the car, offering just enough resistance to slow our spin. We hit the guardrail and bounce back onto the road, the tail end of the car skidding across the center line before we come to a stop on the deserted highway.

For a moment, the silence is broken only by our swiftly drawn breath, the narrowness of our escape stealing all our words.

Ariel is the first to recover. "I hate you. I will destroy you, Dylan Stroud. Just you wait and see!" And then she's out the door, running down the highway back toward Los Olivos, silver hair shimmering in the moonlight.

I watch her run in the rearview mirror, an unexpected smile creeping across my face. She is glorious in her hate. It's a shame I have to put out that particular fire, smother it with the sweet press of true love's kiss.

"True love's kiss. True. Love's. Kiss!" I turn the words into a song as I spin the wheel and pull around, heading after the girl who has no clue she's going to love me.

THREE

Ariel

Hate, him, hate, him, hate, him. My feet pound the beat and my thoughts scream the words. I *hate* Dylan Stroud. I can't believe I let him touch me. I should have known better. Things are never going to change. *I* will never change. I'll always be the Freak with the scars, even when I finally make it out of this town. Tonight proves it. I'm stupid. Crazy. Broken. And I always will be.

How else could I have thought I was falling *in love* with him?

I should have realized it was a joke. But I didn't, and by tomorrow the entire school will know that Dylan and I almost did it. Or maybe he'll tell everyone we *did*. I wouldn't be surprised. Then they'll have one more thing to pity me for, the girl who lost her virginity on a bet. Maybe Dylan will even tell his friends that I took the money he offered, and Hannah and Natalie and all the other girls who look at me like their worst nightmare come to life will think I'm a whore in addition to being the most pathetic loser on the planet.

Stupid girl, stupid freak, stupid girl, stupid freak.

I pull in a breath and choke on it. I wish we'd gone off the road. I wish we were both dead. I taste salt at the back of my throat. Tears burn my eyes. I want to stop running, lie down in the middle of the highway, and wait for some unsuspecting person to run me over. But I can't. Because the only car on the road is *his* car, and I won't give him the satisfaction.

If he wants to hit me, he'll have to pull onto the shoulder. The headlights behind me get brighter, a slow creeping glare that makes me feel naked. I want to crouch down and cover my head with my arms, but I don't. I keep running, facing forward. Even when Dylan's car putters up beside me and the passenger window buzzes down, I don't turn to look. I won't let him see that he's made me cry. Again.

"Why don't you get back in the car?"

Why don't you choke on your tongue and die?

"Please, Ariel. I just want to talk," he says. "I think there's been a . . . misunderstanding."

I stumble, but don't fall. That wasn't what I was expecting him to say. I was imagining angry words and threats and maybe something thrown from the car as he sped by. But whatever. Anger, fake apologies—what's the difference? It will all end the same way, with Dylan in control because he knows

I had a horrible crush on him and believed every false thing he said and did. I even believed he was as nervous about our first kiss as I was. I believed I made him ache and *want* the way I wanted him.

Stupid. Loser.

Not anymore. "Leave me alone."

"Ariel, please. Listen. I—"

"Leave me alone." I run faster. My eyes scan the woods at the side of the road. I wonder if it's worth running into the darkness to get away from *him.*

"No. I can't leave you alone."

I can't leave you alone. He says it in his sexy voice, the one he used when he called to ask me on this joke of a date. He's trying to lure me in again, and I hate him for it. Almost as much as I hate myself for noticing how lovely he makes everything sound. Listening to Dylan talk is almost as good as listening to him sing.

His voice is what pulled me in from the start, the way he sang "Bring It On Home to Me" like he knew what it felt like to love someone so much you'd give anything to be with them. Every time the choir members practiced for their performances during the spring formal, I'd have to stop painting the backdrops, close my eyes, and let Dylan's voice soak into my soul.

And then one day I opened them and found he was singing right to me.

Our eyes caught and held, and neither of us could look away until the song was finished. By the end, my heart was racing so fast I was afraid I might faint. He'd confirmed it. I just *knew* he felt the same way I felt. Compelled. Seduced. Enchanted. It was like I'd always dreamed falling in love would be.

Then I saw that text from Jason, and Dylan offered me fifty dollars to let him take what he wanted in the backseat of his car, setting my gauzy, romantic dreams on fire.

I wish I could set *him* on fire. I want to punish him. But how? What can I do to make sure he suffers? I've spent my entire life hiding my feelings, too afraid to show anyone how angry I am sometimes. Now I'm dying to show it. I want to scream and shout and rip Dylan Stroud apart with my bare hands. If I thought my crazy brain would let me, I might get back into his car and try.

But it won't. If I let myself get really angry, I'll have an episode. I always do. The cold will rush across my skin, my bones will lock and my insides turn to liquid, and all the angry, wailing voices will run wild in my head. They scream so loud I can't understand what they're saying, but I know what they feel. Despair. Despair so deep and wide that there's no hope of ever making it to shore. There is only misery that bleeds inside as the voices fill me up with their pain until the world goes dark. And when I wake up, my pants are wet from where I've lost control, and my bones bruised from thrashing on the floor.

It's not epilepsy; it's not a classical manifestation of any particular type of crazy; it's something the doctors don't know how to treat and not even the shrink I saw when I was younger wanted to talk about after a while. No one likes things they can't understand.

No one likes a freak.

That's why I hold it all in, especially around other people. I don't want anyone to see me like that. The one time was enough. It's been eight years, and still everyone who was on the playground in fourth grade remembers what happened.

They still look at me funny, and turn away when I walk past them in the halls. They still whisper the story to every new kid who moves into town, ensuring I'll always be an outsider.

Gemma's the only one who ever gave me a chance, and now my only friend is gone. She's run away. Or maybe she's dead. The missing person flyers her parents posted all over town make it seem like she could be, but I'm betting she ran away with one of her *many* boyfriends and simply didn't bother to tell me about it.

She must have finally realized how weird it was for us to be friends. Gemma's rich and beautiful and wild and fun and always has a boy or three dying to be with her. And I'm . . . me, the pale girl with the scars who's too shy to speak in class and had never even kissed a boy before tonight. I never mattered to Gemma. To anyone, really. I think even my mom would be relieved if she didn't have to worry about me anymore.

If Dylan's reflexes weren't so quick, I could have been out of everyone's way. I guess I still could be, but it will take so much more courage. It was easy to reach for that wheel. It won't be easy alone, and I hate him for that, too.

"Please. Let me give you a ride," he says. "You can't run all the way back to your house."

"Yes, I can."

"I wish you wouldn't." He sounds so sincere, so sad. "I really am sorry."

"No, you're not."

"I am. Stop running, and I'll prove it to you."

I don't answer. I run. I spend most of my time sitting at a desk drawing, or perched on a stool with my paints, but I'm not out of breath. I feel like I could run forever, just run myself out and vanish into thin air.

"Come on. At least let me give you your purse."

I slow. *My purse.* My keys are in there. My mom doesn't get off her shift at the hospital until eleven. If I don't get my keys, I'll be sitting outside my house for hours. And then I'll have to tell her what happened and see how disappointed she is that I've failed at being a normal kid. Yet again. And then there will be a lecture about trying harder and being confident and getting my head out of the clouds, and on and on until I want to scream. I'd do almost anything to avoid another one of those conversations.

I stop. Dylan brakes beside me. The car's putter becomes a rattle, and the smell of exhaust drifts to my nose. I sniff, wipe the tears off my cheeks with my sleeve, and brace myself. I'll grab the purse and start running again. I won't let him get to me. I won't fall for whatever trick he's trying to play.

I turn, walk the three steps to the passenger window, and hold out my hand. Dylan leans over the seat and presses my cell phone into my palm. I stare at it for a long second before realizing it's not what I came for.

"Give me my purse, please," I say, glad my voice remains steady and even.

"Not yet." Dylan looks up at me, his dark eyes glittering. "Get ready to record."

"Just give me–"

"Get ready to record. You're not going to want to miss this." He winks, grins.

Before I can think of how to respond, he's slamming the door shut behind him. He holds my purse in his hand as he jogs to the front of the car, and then drops it and backs away until the headlights cut him out from the darkness. The lights are so bright, I can see the outline of his T-shirt beneath his blue button-down. His skin is so pale, it glows. He's nearly as white as I am, but the dark brown hair that waves over his forehead and his almost-black brown eyes make him look dramatically pale, instead of washed-out and plain. If I were standing in his place, my hair and skin would blend together, and my blue eyes would fade to gray. I'd be even uglier than usual.

But Dylan is remarkably handsome. He is. There's no denying it, no matter how much I *hate* him.

"I'm starting." He props his hands on his hips.

I cross my arms and look at the ground.

"You said you wanted to destroy me," he says. "I'm about to give you everything you need to do it. If you don't hit Record, you're going to kick yourself."

I sigh, flip open my phone, and turn on the camera. I don't know what he's up to, but it's obvious he's not going to give me my purse—or my keys—until I play along.

I hit the Record button and stare at the smaller Dylan on the screen. It will be easier to get through this if I keep my eyes on mini-Dylan. I'll pretend I'm watching a movie, and the boy staring into the lens is an actor, not a liar who had his hands all over me. Not the boy who gave me my first kiss. Not the person who made me hope for things I'll never have.

"You recording?" he asks. I nod. I refuse to speak or react or do *anything* to make this new joke any more enjoyable for him. "Hi, I'm Dylan Stroud. Tonight I went on my first date with Ariel. And it might be our last date, because . . . I'm an asshole." He laughs, but it's not a happy sound. "I made a stupid bet with some other stupid assholes, and . . . I ruined something I didn't want to ruin."

The boy on the screen stops, swallows. His eyes shine with feeling.

I knew Dylan was a gifted singer, but I had no idea he could act. He's certainly putting on quite a show. If I didn't know better, I'd believe he was devastated over losing his chance with me. But I *do* know better, and his performance is disgusting.

I move my thumb to stop the recording, but he speaks again, and I hesitate.

"Ariel, I know what I did is unforgivable, but I . . . I just . . ." He takes a ragged breath. "I've been watching you for weeks, and I think about you all the time. About the way you smell like flowers and paint, and the way you tilt your head to the side when you draw, and the way you close your eyes when you're listening to a song you really like."

I press my lips together. Just because he's noticed things about me doesn't mean he's sincere. This is all part of his plan to get me back into the car, get into my pants, and collect his winnings tomorrow morning.

"I think about the way you hide behind your hair when you walk to class, and how much I want you to look up and see me next to you. Once, I almost brushed it out of your face, but I didn't. I wanted to, but . . ." His brow furrows and his chin lifts. "I'm a coward. That's why I let Jason and Tanner talk me into making that bet. But I didn't want to. I swear I didn't. And tonight, when I finally got to kiss you, I . . . I didn't want to stop."

His voice is husky, as if he's remembering all the ways we fit together when he was pressed against me. My cheeks get hotter, and it's harder to keep my attention on mini-Dylan. My hand is shaking. The temptation to look up and meet the eyes staring so intently into the camera lens is greater than I thought it would be. "And it wasn't because of anything or anyone but you," he says. "I like you. A lot. And I'd do anything for the chance to make you like me again too."

Wow. Give the boy an Academy Award.

Not only for saying all the right things in just the right way, but for hiding how smart he is, all the years I've known him. Not that I thought he was stupid—he makes decent grades, considering how little he tries—but I wouldn't have thought Dylan Stroud was capable of delivering a speech like that on the spur of the moment. He should consider acting if the singing career doesn't work out. Or maybe politics. That's a good profession for gifted liars.

He *is* a liar. I know it. I still don't believe him, but I could. If I listen much longer, I might, and prove I really am the dumbest girl on the planet.

"Are you finished?"

His shoulders sag. "I don't know. Am I? Do I . . . Can I have a second chance?"

"No." It's one word, softly spoken, but he acts like I've shot an arrow into his heart. He stumbles back a step, and his face gets even whiter. His expression is pained, fearful, desperate. Looking at him now, I'd believe he'd just learned he'll never sing again.

Dylan's after-graduation plan is to become a rock star. He and Jason Kim have a band and play at coffee shops and a few all-ages venues in Santa Barbara on weekends. They're going to move to Los Angeles together after graduation and get discovered. Gemma saw them once and said their guitar playing sucked, but even she had to admit that Dylan can sing.

"Please." He lifts his hands, palms up. "What do I have to say?"

But he's picky about what he'll sing in public. I heard him arguing with Mrs. Mullens, the choir teacher, about his song for the spring formal performance. All the other kids are doing musical numbers, but he wanted to do a rock-inspired cover of an old Sam Cooke song. He said he wouldn't be caught dead singing "Broadway shit."

"Ariel, listen. I'll—"

"I want you to sing."

His brows lift. "Sing?"

"I want you to sing that song from *West Side Story*. The one Logan is singing at the formal."

He stands up straighter, and his lips curve. I've seen Dylan smile before, but for some reason it looks different now. Softer around his lips and harder in his eyes or . . . something. It must be the headlights. "You mean 'Maria'?"

"Yes. That one. Sing it for me."

He opens his mouth and pulls in a breath, but I stop him before he can start.

"Naked."

"Naked?" The way he says the word makes me blush, but I ignore it. He can't see me. I, however, can see him. And so will everyone at school if I decide to show this video. He said he wanted to give me everything I needed to destroy him. We'll soon see how serious he was about that.

"Yes. Sing it for me naked," I say, surprised by how in control I sound. I've never even said the word *naked* out loud that I can remember. Let alone to a boy. But my voice doesn't waver. Even when I add, "And do a little dance."

"Sing and dance for you naked? Right here? On the side of the road?"

"Right here. And the dumber you look, the more I'll believe you're not full of crap."

I expect him to tell me that I'm crazy, to admit that everything he said was a lie and all he really wanted was to win that bet and collect his cash. I expect him to break and tell me the bet isn't worth it. *I'm* not worth it.

Instead, his fingers move to the top button of his shirt and he begins to sing. "Ariel. I just met a girl named Ariel."

My cheeks get hotter and my eyes close. He's using my name instead of Maria's. I almost tell him to stop, but when I open my eyes, he's already out of his button-down and pulling his T-shirt up to expose more of him than I've ever seen before. I've felt his body against mine, but looking at him is another thing entirely. He's even better-looking without clothes.

I forget how to speak. His shirt clears his head and falls to the ground as he hits a high, sweet, perfect note. His hips start to sway and his hands move to his belt buckle, sending my stomach diving into my guts. The hip swaying is over the top, and by the time he's out of his jeans and wearing nothing but his boxer shorts, the dance and the song are both beyond the realm of anything romantic or sexy. He's making a fool of himself, spinning around in circles like a ballerina, turning his back and spanking himself and adding in weird little grunts between the words.

Still, when he hooks his fingers into the top of his boxers, blood rushes to my head and the night spins. "Stop!" I shout, turning off the camera. "That's enough."

He turns, confusion on his face. "Wasn't I doing a good job?"

I clear my throat. "You did a great job."

"But I'm not naked yet."

"You're naked enough."

"Am I?" He smiles, a wicked grin that's unexpectedly . . . charming.

I bite the inside of my lip, refusing to smile back. No matter how he's embarrassed himself, I don't trust him.

"Put your clothes on." For the first time since our near dive over the cliff, I feel shy, uncertain.

He laughs. "Having a hard time resisting me after that dance?"

"That dance was . . ." I pretend great interest in my thumbs as I send the video file to my email and close the phone up.

"Irresistible? Sensuous? Seductive?"

"Nauseating?" Tough talk, but I sound like I'm flirting with him. I'm not sure I've ever flirted with anyone. Even him. The few times we spoke, I was too nervous to say much of anything beyond the required "yes" and "no," and we didn't do much talking before the kissing tonight.

He smiles and grabs his jeans, staring at me as he buttons and zips, making me drop my eyes to the ground, nervous all over again. "I don't think the dance is to blame." He steps into his shoes and reaches for his T-shirt. "You're probably hungry. Let's get something to eat."

I look up. "You want to get something to eat?"

"No, I want to take *you* to get something to eat." He pulls the shirt on and runs a hand through his hair. It's sticking up in a few places, but the messiness only makes him cuter. Or maybe it's the expression on his face. He looks so sincerely excited by the thought of spending more time together. "I want to woo you with food now that I've wooed you with words, song, and the magic of my interpretive dance."

I laugh. I can't help myself.

"The lady laughs," he whispers.

My smile vanishes, fleeing for safety as I tuck my phone into my pocket. This is crazy, but at least I have ammunition. If that video gets out, Dylan will never live it down. He's not the type of guy who's okay with making a fool out of himself. Not usually.

And maybe—if we break bread and declare a truce—he'll keep his mouth shut about what almost happened between us. At the very least, it's worth a try, and another hour or so in his company.

"Fine," I say. "Let's get something to eat."

He shrugs on his button-down but leaves it open as he grabs my purse from the ground and walks toward me. He doesn't stop until he's way closer than he needs to be to hand me the bag. I lift my chin, refusing to take a step back, not wanting him to know that his proximity matters. "Thank you." He leans down until his forehead nearly touches mine. "You won't be sorry. I promise."

I grab the strap of my purse, ignoring the way my stomach flutters. I don't care how nice he's being. There's no way I'm letting Dylan touch me. Ever. Again.

"Where do you want to go?" he asks. Headlights appear in the distance. He turns to look over his shoulder. We should get going. A lot of people from school are going to a party on the beach tonight, and I don't want to run into anyone who knows about Dylan's stupid bet.

"Wherever. The pancake house in Solvang is open until eleven."

He snorts. "You're too good for a pancake house. We're going someplace with real food. It's been far too long since I've had a steak."

"'Far too long'?" What's with him all of a sudden? When has Dylan ever said things like "far too long"?

"Far, far too long." He steps even closer. I stand my ground, fighting the urge to fidget.

"Okay," I say with a shrug. "As long as you're paying. I can't afford steak."

"Of course I'm paying. I want to do something nice for you." He tucks my hair behind my ear with a tenderness I haven't noticed in him before. The gentle touch surprises me, makes me hesitate when I'd usually hurry to flip my hair back over my shoulder to conceal the scars on my neck and jaw. "You're really pretty."

"You're really full of it."

"No, I'm not." Our eyes meet, and I *know* that he's thinking about kissing me again—it's written all over his face. For an insane moment, I think I might let him, but thankfully, the headlights get brighter, giving me an excuse to squint and lift a hand between us.

The approaching car pulls to a stop beside Dylan's. An older woman with hair dyed an unrelenting black leans out her open window. "You kids okay?"

"We're fine. Just checking one of the tires. But thanks, ma'am," Dylan says. "I appreciate you stopping."

"Okay, then." She smiles, obviously flattered by Dylan's show of good manners. "Have a good night."

"You too, ma'am." He waves as she pulls away, an enthusiastic wag of his hand that reminds me of the 1950s public service announcements we watched in political science. It's an innocent wave. A happy wave. A *weird* wave.

"'Ma'am,'" I repeat dryly.

"Yes, ma'am. I think I owe the world at large some respect after the way I behaved tonight."

I blink. He seems so sincere, but the notion that he might owe anyone anything is so *not* Dylan. I had it pretty bad for him, but I never imagined he was the type of guy who thought about other people even half as much as he thought about himself. At the time, that didn't bother me. It was flattering to have someone so good-looking and talented and, yes, full of himself, paying so much attention.

But now . . .

Well, it's nice to realize that he can at least *pretend* to care about other people.

"Good thing she didn't come by earlier." Dylan crosses his arms and leans against the car in a way that emphasizes how comfortable he is in his body. I can't help feeling envious, wishing my own skin didn't feel too tight and my bones too loose. "Or my little song and dance would have been even more embarrassing."

"Nothing could have made that more embarrassing."

He laughs. "That was the point, right?"

"It was." I hesitate before offering a careful "Thanks."

"You're welcome." He smiles—a sweet, almost shy smile. "I thought you deserved some good ammunition."

"Yeah, well. I . . . appreciate it."

If you're telling the truth, if you did it because you're actually sorry and not planning something even worse than what you did the first time, I silently add, my gut churning as my mind kicks around a few "worse" options.

I look up, searching his face for some clue as to what this dinner invitation is really about.

"I want to feed you, Ariel. No hidden agenda," he says. "What do you have to lose?"

Nothing. I have nothing to lose. Twenty minutes ago I was wishing I was dead. Who am I to be worried about what might happen in the next hour and a half? I'm living on borrowed time.

And so is he.

He opens the door, and I slide into the car, trusting he remembers that I almost sent him diving to his death, and that he will behave accordingly.

FOUR

Romeo

Meat. Glorious, glorious meat. Succulent, juicy, red, and bloody, seasoned with butter and herbs, every bite better than the one before. The myriad of flavors explode on my tongue, shimmy through my mouth, slap my taste buds and call them filthy little bastards, and I love it.

Love. I've died and gone to heaven, and it is this feast on my plate. I moan, and shovel in a forkful of cream cheese and chive mashed potatoes.

Beside me in our corner booth, Ariel laughs beneath her breath. "That good?"

"Better. I'm having a religious experience."

"God is a filet mignon."

"No. Filet mignon is God." I stab another bite and lift it to her lips. "Taste it."

She hesitates only a moment before opening her mouth and trapping the steak between her small, white teeth. I watch her chew and swallow, pleased to see her cheeks grow pinker the longer I watch. She really is lovely, and so much naughtier than I expected.

I certainly hadn't anticipated that I'd be dancing in the nearly nude tonight. She lost her courage there at the end, but not before proving herself a great deal more entertaining than her friend Gemma led me to believe the last time I inhabited Dylan's body. But maybe Ariel is a little different in this reality. According to Dylan's memories, several things are. Gemma has run away from home; it hasn't rained in weeks; and instead of performing in *West Side Story*, I'll be singing a solo at a school dance on Friday night.

I'm relieved. I don't know if I could go onto that theater stage again, to the place where I stabbed Juliet and stood over her as she began to bleed. It was Juliet's soul that suffered, but it was Ariel's eyes that closed in pain. We've only just met, but this girl and I already have a tragic history. It should hurt to look at her, but it doesn't.

Ariel is not Juliet, and she's alive. All I feel when I look at her is a desperate relief. A few hours ago, I was a damned creature without a hope in the world. Now I am a handsome young man eating a fine dinner with a beautiful girl. More proof that Fate is a capricious mistress indeed. Just in case the fickle bitch decides to change her mind again, I take a stab at the pasta on Ariel's plate.

"You like the steak?" I pop the gnocchi into my mouth

and shiver with pleasure. Ecstasy. I never appreciated what a gift it is to taste, until I couldn't.

"Yeah, it's really good."

"Good? It's orgasmic."

"Right," she mumbles, brushing her hair over her shoulder to hide her face. In the warm glow of the candlelit restaurant, her hair is honey-colored instead of silver. I'm tempted to run my fingers through it and tell her how beautiful it is, but I reach for a roll instead. All in good time. No one appreciates anything that's *too* easy to get, and I've already played the besotted young lover once tonight.

And a stunning performance it was. I took the few things Dylan's memories told me about Ariel and spun them into romantic gold. If Juliet's nurse had seen, she would have administered the peacekeeper vows on the spot. It would be madness to let a talent such as mine go unclaimed for the forces of goodness and light.

Goodness and light. The notion is still vaguely repellent. Luckily, I'm more skilled at seduction than I am at being a good boy.

"Are you two going to need anything else?" The waiter hovers at the edge of the table. The restaurant in Los Olivos was nearly empty when Ariel and I arrived. Now we're the only people still seated, and this man with the ponytail and patchy goatee is ready to call it a night.

"Anything else for you, darling?" I ask.

Ariel arches a brow, but I can tell a part of her enjoys the tongue-in-cheek endearment. "No, thank you," she says. "I'm stuffed."

"The lady is stuffed." I turn back to the waiter with a

smile. "And so am I. We'll take the rest of her dinner wrapped to go, and the check."

I wait until he disappears into the kitchen with Ariel's plate before sliding from my chair, crossing to the bar, and snatching an open bottle of red wine. Wine never hurt a new love, and I'm dying to see if it tastes as wonderful as I remember. I ease back beside Ariel, shove the bottle between my knees, and cover it with the tablecloth just as Patchy Goatee returns. Thankfully, Ariel doesn't say a word as I pull out my wallet and pay for our dinner.

"Everything was wonderful. Keep the change." I hand the black leather folder to the waiter and loop an arm around Ariel's shoulders. "Ready?"

"No," she whispers as Patchy heads back into the kitchen. "What are you doing?"

"Getting us something to drink. And saving someone from a rancid glass of wine tomorrow. It will be awful after it's left open all night."

"You're stealing."

"I'm *appropriating*."

"We're underage."

"Which is why I have to *appropriate* rather than *buy* this bottle. The shortsighted laws restricting teenage drinking have forced me into this," I say. "It's the Man you should be angry with, Ariel. *I* am innocent."

She lifts a wry brow. "*Innocent* isn't a word I'd use."

"What word would you use? Wait—" I hold up a hand between us. "Don't answer that. Not until you've had a glass of wine and think I'm pretty again."

She makes a sound—half growl, half nervous giggle.

"Seriously." She leans forward, anxiously watching the door where our waiter disappeared. "If you get caught, they might call the police."

"All part of the fun." I wink and slide the bottle under my shirt. "You go first, and I'll hide behind. In case the hostess is still in the lobby."

"You're crazy."

"So are you. We make a great team."

Ariel rolls her eyes, but when we leave the booth, she walks in front. We make it across the restaurant—past the hostess, who wishes us a good evening—and out into the cool air without being discovered. As we walk toward the car, Ariel nudges me in the ribs with one bony elbow. I turn to catch an unexpected spark in her eyes.

"What?" I ask.

"We did it."

"We did."

"That was . . . kind of fun." Her smile holds a hint of wickedness that makes me laugh.

"It was."

She glances over her shoulder before whispering, "I've never stolen anything before."

"You still haven't. But you should try it sometime. Great rush. No chemicals required."

"You're a bad influence," she says, a purr of approval lurking beneath the words.

"I'd promise to be good . . . if I thought you *really* wanted me to be."

Her smile wilts. "What's that supposed to mean?"

"A joke," I say, realizing I've taken the teasing too far for my sensitive silver-haired princess. "Just a joke."

"It's not funny."

"Sorry." I wrinkle my brow, doing my best impression of a decent person capable of deep *feeeeeling.* "Honestly. Sorry. Okay?"

"Okay," she says, but it takes a long moment for her to relax. As I move closer to her half of the sidewalk, I warn myself to be more careful.

"Pretty night," I say. Faint piano music drifts from the hotel across the street, but otherwise, the night is quiet. Still. Beautiful. I pull in another breath. Flowers and wood smoke and spring bursting out in the trees, and another dozen smells I can't quite place. "Gorgeous."

"It is," Ariel says, that cautious note still lingering in her voice. "I love spring."

"I love life." I reach for her hand, but she pulls away.

She stops; lets out a shaky breath. "Okay. Fine. I'm sorry, all right?"

"For what?"

"For . . . you know."

"I'm the one who should be sorry. And I am." I pull the cork from the bottle and sniff. Hm. Good stuff. Port. Stronger than wine, but just as delicious. My mouth waters, and I debate whether taking a swig will lessen the impact of my reassuring words.

"But I could have killed . . ." Ariel catches me sniffing and squints critically in my direction.

I let the bottle drift back to my side and try to act as if I'm troubled by things like homicidal/suicidal tendencies. "But you didn't." I drop my voice in a show of respect for the terrible *seriousness* of the topic. "And you won't do anything like that ever again."

She shakes her head. "No. I won't. I . . . No."

I resist the urge to laugh. "You *could* sound more convincing."

"I honestly can't believe I did it," she says. "But at the time, and right after . . . I was so angry, I really wished that we both . . ."

I slip my arm around her waist. She flinches but doesn't pull away. "I can understand why you'd want me dead." I lean down until her smell weaves its way inside me. She smells even better than the night. Lovely. Intoxicating. My arm tightens, her breath catches, and I whisper my next words inches from her lips. "But don't ever put yourself in danger again. Not for me. Not for anyone. You deserve a long, happy life."

"You think?"

"I know. You're a good person," I say, imagining how proud Juliet's nurse would be to hear me steering Ariel toward her better nature.

"Hm." The sound is skeptical. "I thought you said I was crazy." Her hands push lightly at my chest, but I don't set her free.

"You can be crazy *and* good. All the best people are crazy. I'm crazy, and I'm *very* fond of myself."

"Obviously." Her nose scrunches. It's adorable, and the curve of her waist feels nice. Very nice.

"So . . ." I urge her closer, smell the hint of our dinner on her breath and think about how long it's been since I've tasted a woman. "Think you'd be crazy enough to let me kiss you again?"

Before I can blink, she's twisted her hips and escaped from my arms. "Not tonight."

Well. Can't blame a long-deprived man for trying.

"Tomorrow night?" I ask with a wink.

She doesn't say a word, only crosses her arms and stares at me with those big blue eyes that seem so out of place in her young face. She's practically a child—all gangly limbs and rounded edges that haven't settled into the planes of adulthood—but her eyes are . . . old. As old as Juliet's, though not as ancient as my own. I have seen more than any creature ever should. I am an old, old, *ooollld* man.

If Ariel knew how old, she wouldn't let me near her. Even for a minute. This body might be eighteen, but my soul is old enough to be her great-grandfather's great-et-cetera-grandfather. She'd be repulsed.

Or maybe she wouldn't. Maybe she'd understand that my centuries trapped in the dead seem like a nightmare from which I've only begun to awaken. I betrayed Juliet when I was barely sixteen, and, despite all I've lived through, a part of me feels like a young man still. Ariel might understand something like that. She seems to know a thing or two about nightmares, this girl with the haunted eyes.

"No," she says, unimpressed with whatever she's seen in my face.

"Why not?"

"I don't trust you."

And you shouldn't. Not ever.

I nod. "Understandable. Lamentable, but understandable."

A wrinkle forms above the bridge of her nose. "Lamentable."

"Regrettable; sad; worthy of much lamenting, wailing, gnashing of teeth." I smile, ready to put the serious moment behind us.

"I know what it means. I just don't know where you've been hiding the vocabulary."

"In my boxer briefs," I say with a silly grin. "If you'd let me take them off, you would have seen for yourself."

Her laughter dances through the night, making the stars shine brighter. The happiness in it surprises me. I think it surprises her as well. She pulls in a breath, swallowing the sound.

The absence of her amusement makes the quiet seem . . . emptier than it was before.

"Yeah, well . . . So . . ." She gives the wine in my fist a pointed look. "Are you going to drink that or not?"

"Only if you'll join me."

"Sure," she says, surprising me again. After her lecture in the restaurant, I expected more resistance.

I pull the keys from my pocket. "Well then, shall I drive while you drink?"

"No. We shouldn't drink in the car. I know a place we can go. It's deserted at night," she says, then quickly adds, "but there are houses close by. People will hear if we talk above a whisper."

"Good." I nod thoughtfully. "So if you try to take advantage, someone will hear me when I scream."

"Ha ha." Her grin is wary, assessing, but still, a grin. "Funny."

"I'm even funnier after a few drinks."

She cocks her head and lifts a jaunty shoulder. "We'll see." I follow her across the street, away from the main drag. The antiques shops and gaslights disappear, replaced by normal streetlamps and an eclectic mix of houses—painstakingly restored Victorian homes, ramshackle boxes with toy-filled yards, and a bungalow with iron sculptures sprouting from the flower beds. After a few minutes, she turns left up a gentle hill. At the top is a playground, surrounded by a chain-link fence, lit by a single floodlight. Ariel pads up to the gate and reaches over to open it from the inside.

"Gemma and I used to come here," she says. "There's never anyone around after dark."

"It's perfect." I tip the bottle back as we crunch through the gravel toward the playground equipment. Ah, sweet and potent.

Ariel climbs the steps to a platform with an awning shaped like a rocket ship and sits down near the top of the slide. I settle in beside her and pass the wine, studying her profile as she takes a cautious sip. "Wow." Her tongue darts out to catch a drop escaping down the neck of the bottle. "That's really good."

"Oh, come on. You've had good wine before. Isn't Gemma's dad some sort of vineyard overlord?" I reclaim the bottle and tip it back.

"Yeah. But I've always been too nervous to drink at the Sloops'."

"Why?"

"Gemma's dad . . . He's pretty scary. Sometimes Gemma and I would steal a glass of chardonnay from the fridge at my house when Mom was working late, but it didn't taste like this."

There's sadness in her voice. It isn't difficult to guess the cause. I put on my troubled face and test my newly rediscovered empathy. "You're worried about her. Gemma."

"Yeah." She takes the bottle but doesn't drink. "Sometimes I think she's fine and just ran away to get back at her dad, but sometimes I'm afraid something happened to her."

"She's fine." I put my arm around her slim shoulders, wishing I could tell her that I have it on Ambassador authority that Gemma and her soul mate, Mike, are safe and deeply, disgustingly in love. "I bet she eloped with some dashing young man and is already halfway to happily-ever-after."

"Right." She takes a long drink and sets the bottle back on the boards between us. "Do you talk like this around your friends?"

"Like what?"

She shrugs. "I don't know. The vocabulary and the . . . old-fashioned stuff."

"Old-fashioned, huh? Well, I *have* been reading a lot of poetry lately."

Her big eyes get even bigger. "Poetry," she says, clearly dubious. "Like who?"

"William Cullen Bryant, Sir Walter Raleigh," I say, tossing out the first Gothic greats that come to mind. "And Shakespeare, of course. Sonnet 138 is a particular favorite. *Therefore I lie with her and she with me, and in our faults by lies we flattered be,*" I quote, savoring the words, rather surprised I can remember them. But then, "I've always enjoyed the poems written to his Dark Lady."

"I love all the sonnets," she says. "I like Shakespeare's plays a lot, but I *love* the sonnets."

"Me too."

"That's . . . hard to believe."

"Believe it or not." I scoot closer as she takes another sip. I suspect I should be trying harder to behave like Dylan, but Dylan is a shallow brute and about as charming as stepping in warm shit. Ariel enjoyed his pretty face, but in order to win her heart, I'll need more than looks. I'll need wit and charm—things that will be hard to come by if I stay completely true to Dylan's personality.

Besides, Nurse didn't tell me I had to successfully impersonate Dylan Stroud; she said I had to make Ariel believe in love, and I've never been one for going above and beyond the call of duty.

"Does my enthusiasm for poetry offend?" I ask, though I know damn well I've won several romantic bonus points.

"No! Not at all." She tries to cover her enthusiasm with another drink, but it's too late. I grin, and take the bottle when she offers. "I was just thinking about what your friends would say."

"My friends are idiots." I tip the bottle back, surprised by how light it feels. Ariel's sips must have been gulp-sized. I wonder if I should have warned her that port is stronger than table wine, but decide that a mellow Ariel could work in my favor. The looser she gets, the easier it will be for me to sneak past her defenses. "But you know what I mean. I'm sure Gemma's fine, and not spending her nights alone."

"Maybe."

I snort. "We both know she doesn't have trouble finding company."

Ariel's eyes narrow. "What's that supposed to mean?"

"Nothing." I know better than to say a word about Dylan's personal experiences with Gemma. According to his memories, Dylan and Gemma's "friends with benefits" relationship is one thing that's the same in this reality as it was in the other. Ariel, however, has no clue that her best friend used to enjoy slumming with Dylan Stroud on the mattress on his filthy bedroom floor last fall. Best to keep it that way.

"It was definitely something," Ariel says.

I hug her closer. "She has a reputation," I say gently. "You know that."

She turns to me, shrugging off my arm as she moves. "If she were a guy, you'd think that reputation was cool."

"I don't think it's cool or uncool," I say, not understanding why she suddenly seems so angry. I smile, hoping to defuse the moment. "I don't care if Gemma sleeps with sheep. You're the one I care about."

"Why? Because I'm the one you're betting on?" She stands, swaying on her feet, stumbling and grabbing hold of the slide railing for balance.

Sweet Dionysus. She can't be *that* drunk, can she? But then, she doesn't weigh much, and confessed to having little experience with alcohol.

"Ariel, we've talked about this," I coo. "There's no bet anymore. I promise." I stand and reach out to steady her, but she knocks my hand away.

"How did you know I was a virgin, anyway?"

In truth, Gemma told Dylan. They'd laughed about how strange Ariel was, and made bets on how old she would be before she got her first kiss, let alone her first anything else. It was that conversation that aroused his interest, made Ariel something he wanted to spoil.

But of course I can't tell her *that*.

I shrug. "Your lack of a love life is hardly a secret. And I know—"

"You don't *know*. You don't *know* me. I could have a whole other life. I could have secrets," she says, slurring the last word. "I could have dark, scary secrets."

"You could," I agree, amused. She's glorious when she's angry, but she's downright cute when she's drunk and belligerent. "Do you have dark, scary secrets? I'd love to hear them."

She points a wobbly finger at my nose. "Don't make fun of me."

"I'm not. I'm fascinated. Genuinely." I take a step closer. She trips and nearly tumbles down the slide, but I catch her before she falls and pull her close.

All the places where a girl is soft and a boy is not press together, and a new awareness crackles in the air between us. I feel it—the spark of genuine attraction—and I know she feels it too. Her lips part, my head spins, and I wonder if maybe I'm drunker than I thought.

But then again, I shouldn't be surprised that a pretty girl is affecting me the way pretty girls always did when I was alive. I should be taking advantage of Ariel's attraction and wine-lowered defenses. As heavenly as the wine tasted slipping down my throat, I know being skin to skin with Ariel, blood rushing as I lose myself in her, will make that heaven pale in comparison. With a little seductive pressure, I could have her, could sate the lust she inspires when her body shifts against mine.

I tip my head, letting my lips hover near the shell of her ear. "I have dark, scary secrets," I whisper, the thrill of the dare making my pulse race faster. "Let's share our secrets, shall we? I'll show you mine . . . if you'll show me yours."

She stiffens, and I realize too late that innuendo might have best been avoided.

"I can't believe you." She tries to pull away but stumbles again. "You thought you'd get me drunk and I'd do whatever you wanted!"

"I didn't." *At least, not at first.*

"You did!" She pushes at my arms, but I hold her tight.

"I'm not compelled to get girls inebriated in order to

convince them to sleep with me, Ariel. And I would never—"

"Oh really?" She stops struggling, but I can feel the tension still simmering beneath her skin. "So I guess you've had a lot of girls?"

"I've had . . . a few." My tone is cautious, but not cautious enough.

"Then why don't you go find one of them and—Leave! Me! Alone!" She throws her weight into me, pushing so hard I stagger off the platform, heels scrambling as I tumble down the steps. My arms fly out, catching the handrails halfway down, but it isn't easy to stop my momentum. My fingers cramp and the muscles in my arms tremble, and I barely avoid a backward swan dive onto the pavement.

I curse as I finally regain my balance. My heart slams in my chest, the unexpected moment of weakness making my blood race with fear. As a Mercenary, I had superhuman strength and an insidious ability to heal. I know that Ambassador converts aren't quite as strong, but Juliet held her own in a fight. She was definitely stronger than a normal girl, and even *she* hadn't been able to push me around like this.

A sour taste fills my mouth. That redheaded witch cheated me! Juliet's nurse sent me here without an Ambassador's true strength. How will I defend myself? What if I encounter Mercenaries? They'll see the golden light in my aura and know what I've become, and once they do, they'll stop at nothing to destroy me. How am I to fight off an immortal warrior of darkness with this puny human body?

"Shit!" I kick the metal stair, remembering too late that I have an audience. A very important, very angry audience.

"I knew you were lying." Ariel's voice shakes, and her eyes shine with unshed tears. "I knew it!"

"No. You don't understand. I—"

"I understand perfectly!" she shouts. "And I hate you!"

"Please." I hold up my hands in surrender. "Listen, I—"

"No. I won't listen. And I'll never—" She breaks off, eyes focusing on something in the distance. Whatever she sees stuns her motionless, into the hyperalert stillness of rabbits and other animals accustomed to their roles as prey. For a moment she is frozen, and then, just as suddenly, she curls into herself like a leaf set aflame.

Before I can turn to see what's frightened her, before I can ask her if she's all right, she dives for the slide. "Don't follow me!" She rattles down the metal, hits the ground at the bottom, and sprints for the gate like she's being chased by the devil himself. I spin, scanning the playground and the street beyond, but there's nothing, no one. We're as alone as we were a moment ago.

I rush down the stairs and across the yard. "Ariel, wait!"

"Don't follow me!" she screams again as she races down the dark road. A few houses down, a dog begins to bark and a porch light flickers on across the street. I ignore them both and chase after her. She's drunk and seeing things, and I can't afford to risk her getting run over. I need her alive and in love with me. I need her—

The headlights of a car parked on the street flare to life. I skid to a stop, lifting my arms, squinting in the harsh glare. I didn't hear a car pull up while Ariel and I were on the playground. Whoever this is must have been sitting here for a while. The car door opens, and I brace myself for an altercation with some concerned citizen who's seen Ariel running and assumed the worst.

I drop my arms and affect my most stricken expression.

I'll tell whoever this is that my girlfriend just found out she was pregnant, and that we were fighting over whether she should put the baby up for adoption. I want to keep it, but she says we're too young. *But is there such a thing?* I'll ask. *As being too young to love a child?*

The lie is already tickling my lips when the long, willowy silhouette circling the car becomes a person I can see. A person I recognize.

My jaw clenches. "What are you doing here?"

"I think I should be asking you that question." Juliet's nurse props her hands on her hips.

I ball my hands into fists, prepared to fight, though I know it will do no good. This woman has incredible magic. She could hurl another ball of light my way and I'd be done for, banished back to my monstrous body. But I won't go quietly. I won't make it easy for her. I've never made anything easy for anyone.

"Get in the car," she says.

I hesitate, some mad part of me screaming that I should run.

"Get in the car, Romeo," she orders again. "Or I will cease to be disappointed and begin to be angry."

"But Ariel is—"

"Ariel is presently beyond your reach. If you'd like that to change, come with me." She turns and walks back to the car. With one last glance down the road, I follow her. If I hope to win a place among the Ambassadors, I have no choice.

Taste and touch and newfound feeling aside, I am still a slave and I must obey.

FIVE

Ariel

I'm running again, but this time there are no words, no language but the language of fear: the *thump-thump-thump* of my pulse leaping in my throat, frantic gasps for breath, whimpers that vibrate my ribs as the thing I dread draws closer.

The stars spin, while below, the night is sharp-edged and terrible. I hurl myself down one dark street and then another and then out through an open field where stiff grass crinkles beneath my shoes. I stagger into a ditch and back out again, then down one row of a newly planted vineyard, stupidly thinking I can outrun my own crazy. But I can't. The monster is inside me, a product of my sick mind. That's the truth. No matter what I thought I saw on the playground.

Ripples in the air . . . invisible claws tearing holes in the night . . .

I must have imagined the ripples. I'm drunk. I'm not thinking clearly. It was a hallucination. A mirage. I'm not being chased; I'm being taken over. I didn't think I was angry enough to bring on an episode, but obviously I was wrong.

It's a night for being wrong, a night where every good thing turns awful.

I trip over something I can't see in the moonlight and fall to the ground. I smell dirt and the hint of fertilizer, and then it hits. The cold slams into my back, stabs into my skin like knives carved out of ice. My back arches, and every muscle pulls tight as my body tries to force out the pain, but it's impossible. The cold is already stealing up my spine on feet made of razor blades, bleeding into my brain, clearing the way for the things that howl and moan.

Not me. Not me. Not me!

Something deep inside me cries out, and for a second I wonder even crazier things. What if I really *did* see those ripples? What if the wine relaxed my defenses and let me spot something I'd never thought to look for before? Maybe the stories about people being possessed are true. Maybe the voices belong to someone else, some*thing* else. An evil spirit, or a ghost, or a demon, or—

The screams rush in like a hurricane hitting shore, drowning out my thoughts. Desperate cries echo off the walls of my mind, sounds of endless sadness that pour into me like a glass of water hurled into a thimble. I overflow and tumble into unconsciousness, taking the misery with me down into the dark.

Romeo

We drive in silence, up into the mountains, leaving the vine-yards behind. Past a lake and forests of gnarled oak trees, onto a narrow dirt road that winds up through acres of abandoned pasture. It's a road to nowhere, the perfect place to dump a body.

I would know. I've disposed of my share.

It feels as if we've been driving for hours, but I'm certain it's been much less. Maybe fifteen minutes, a half hour. It's hard to keep a hold on time. I keep seeing my ruined corpse, keep remembering the smell and the feel of my body rotting all around me. It was worse than hell. No creature should be forced to live through its own decomposition.

Not even a fiend like me.

"I don't understand," I say when I can't bear the silence a second longer. "I thought I was making a good start."

"By getting the girl so drunk she could barely walk?" The Ambassador's voice is glacial.

"I didn't intend to get her drunk. I thought the wine might help her relax."

"Altered states of consciousness aren't safe for Ariel. You've opened her to a great deal of pain, and lost what ground you might have gained."

"Exactly how troubled is she?" I wait for an answer that doesn't come, and finally begin to feel something other than fear. "If she's *that* delicately balanced, I should have been warned. It's hardly my fault that—"

The Ambassador slams on the brakes. My body pitches forward, but her hand flashes out before my head hits the windshield. She clutches my shirt and pulls me to her, into a cloud of vanilla perfume. It's a pleasant smell, but terrifying all the same. She might smell mortal—homey, even—but this woman is a supernatural creature of incredible strength. I can feel it in the way she lifts me from my seat with a crook of her elbow.

"Listen to me, and listen well," she whispers. "If you fail to win Ariel's heart and guide her onto the path of peace, it will be no one's fault but your own. You will have failed the world and made me a fool in the eyes of my fellows. If that comes to pass, I will be very, *very* displeased."

"I didn't mean—"

"And I *will* return you to your soul specter. Immediately," she says. "Don't think I will be softhearted and spare you that horror, because I will not." She pulls me closer, until her breath kisses my cheek. It's warm, but I fight the urge to shiver. "You poisoned Juliet's mind against me. I lost an Ambassador ready to ascend to the next level of service, and a girl I cared for. Despite my vows to harm no creature, I will not be troubled by your suffering, Romeo. I will enjoy it."

I cast my eyes down. I didn't poison Juliet's mind. I told the truth for once in my sorry existence, and I don't regret it. Juliet is free in death as she never was when bound to this woman's cause.

But I don't dare contradict the Ambassador. My desire to avoid suffering is greater than my need to tell any more truth. The promise of heaven is strong, but the threat of hell is always stronger.

"I understand," I say. "I will not fail you. Or shame you." I pause, weighing my next words. In the end I decide I must speak. If I'm killed because she has left me vulnerable, the job she's so eager for me to do will go just as undone. "But it won't be easy without an Ambassador's true strength."

"You don't require supernatural strength; you require supernatural charm." She tosses me into my seat with a flick of her wrist. "Your success with Juliet led me to believe you still possess that in abundance."

It was truth, not charm, that convinced Juliet to listen to me about the Ambassadors and Mercenaries, but Juliet's nurse isn't keen on truths that don't align with her opinions. I incline my head, letting her believe she's won the point, before adding, "But charm won't protect me if I'm attacked by Mercenaries."

"There are few dark ones in this valley." She returns her hands to the wheel and steps on the gas, guiding the car farther down the road. "And there are no Mercenaries at the school, where you'll be spending most of your time."

"Even a few is too many. If they see what I've become, they'll destroy me," I say, watching anxiously as she turns left onto a "road" that isn't much more than a pair of grooves in the high grass.

Where is she taking me? And why?

"They won't know you for what you are or what you've been," she says. "I've given you only a small portion of my power. You lack great strength, but you also lack enough magic to alter the color of your aura. You'll be safe enough." She pulls the car to the side of the road and shuts it off before turning back to me. "Unless, of course, you continue to fail as spectacularly as you did this evening."

"How was I to know that wine would affect her that way?" My tone is submissive, but I don't miss the tightening of her lips.

Apparently I am incapable of pleasing any female of the species this evening.

I cover my sigh with the slam of the car door and follow Nurse as she starts down a tree-shadowed path leading still higher up the mountain. "But I know now," I say, deciding assurances will serve me better than arguments. "I'll win her trust again. Things were going very well before the wine."

"Very?" she throws over her shoulder.

"Very, very."

"As confident as ever, I see."

"There's no reason not to be." I think of how Ariel let me hold her, how her heart beat fast in her throat when we touched. I had her close to surrender in hours. By the end of the month, she'll be mine. "She's ready to fall in love. I can feel it. You have nothing to worry about."

"Excellent. Then I trust three days will be sufficient?"

"Three days?" I stop dead, but she keeps walking, and I have to hurry to catch up.

Is this woman mad? *Three days?* Three blasted *days*?

"That's rushing things a bit, isn't it?"

"Perhaps." She lifts one shoulder and lets it fall. "Three days was enough for Benjamin Luna to win Juliet's heart."

I fight the urge to snarl. "Ariel *isn't* Juliet."

"Regardless. Three days is all I can offer. You have until Friday at midnight."

"And why is that?"

"In this reality, the soul mates you and Juliet were sent to protect have made their commitment, and the Mercenary and Ambassador sent to fight for them have departed." She lifts a low branch and holds it for me to pass under before continuing up the trail. "But Ariel is important to the fate of the world for both sides. If the Mercenaries knew how important, they would already be guarding her against our influence."

"But they aren't."

"No. Not yet. The dark ones can't see the circular nature of time the way we can. It's our best weapon against them. They won't sense how important Ariel is until her heart begins to open. It's only when they start to lose her soul that they'll realize how vital she is to their cause."

"You said that before, at the station," I say. "But how can one girl be so important? This war has been going on for millennia."

"And it will continue for many more," she says, "assuming you sway Ariel toward the light."

"And if not . . . the Mercenaries win?" My pulse speeds as I await her answer. I am a traitor. If the Mercenaries come into power, there's no doubt I will pay for my betrayal. I can't imagine a fate worse than being trapped inside the specter of my soul, but I'm sure the Mercenaries can. And they will. If I fail, I will experience torture that will make living in a dying body seem a sweet dream.

"Then no one wins," the Ambassador says. "If the Mercenaries succeed in eliminating light from the world, they will eliminate themselves. Without balance, there is chaos, and not even the purveyors of chaos will be able to rule it."

I believe her—the nature of the spell that created the Ambassadors and Mercenaries insists on light and dark. I've never understood why the Mercenaries believe they've grown powerful enough to ignore that all-important fact. Still, I need to know if there will be a period of Mercenary rule before the world goes to hell in the proverbial handbasket.

"But if I fail, the Mercenaries take control?"

"For a time." She turns down a wider path. We're able to walk abreast without tree limbs tugging at my shirt, and soon the trail opens into a clearing. A hundred feet ahead, at the top of the mountain, a cabin huddles amidst a gathering of stones. "If the Mercenaries win Ariel to their side, they will eventually cry victory over all the permutations of reality."

"And this is the moment that tips the scale in their favor."

She nods, confirming my fears. "Humanity would already have been doomed, but the first time the conditions were ripe for Mercenary victory, Ariel was killed before she could commit her future atrocities."

I try to imagine Ariel committing "atrocities," and fail. She's angry and confused, but she's only a girl. Just one sad, mixed-up girl out of hundreds of thousands of girls just like her. And even in the short time we've spent together, I've heard her laugh, seen mischief in her eyes, and tenderness in her smile. It's hard to believe someone who made Dylan pay for his cruelty with something as benign as a naked serenade is capable of true evil.

"Hard to believe," I mutter, echoing Ariel's words from the playground.

"Believe. If left unchecked, Ariel's acts of darkness will make the world's cruelest dictators look like naughty children."

Well then. Ariel. A surprising girl, on all fronts. "Then, I suppose I did you a favor the last time around. When I put a bullet in her brain."

"It was better for her to die than to live to become a monster," she agrees, surprising me. Ambassadors are sworn to preserve life, and yet this woman is ready to deign murder a necessary evil. More than anything she has said thus far, the pronouncement finally convinces me that Ariel's fate will determine our own.

"Assuming I win her heart," I say. "Will that be enough? If, as you've said, there are dozens upon dozens of realities, then—"

"Not for this girl. Her birth was difficult. In all but two versions of the world, she died before she could draw her first breath. If she's taken care of here, the danger Ariel Dragland poses will be eliminated."

Taken care of. Danger. *Eliminated*. "If I didn't know better, I'd think . . ."

"I pray it won't come to that," she says, slowing as we approach the abandoned homestead. "It is ultimately *best* for her to live and become an advocate for peace."

I stop, holding my ground when Nurse continues around the side of the cabin. Now that we're closer, I can feel a troubling energy emanating from this place. There is something unnatural here, something that makes the food and wine in my stomach churn.

The Ambassador turns, waiting for me to follow. "Come."

"But . . . there's something . . . I feel . . ."

"There's nothing to be afraid of. Not yet." She motions for me to join her. I do, but slowly, each step a battle won against the increasingly demanding urge to run, to flee this place like Ariel fled the playground. I don't know what Ariel saw earlier tonight, but I know what I sense right now. I sense Mercenary magic, the cold pricking of evil across my skin.

But I must be mistaken. Juliet's nurse needs me. She wouldn't deliver me into Mercenary hands.

"What happens after?" I ask, trying to keep my mind off

the dread making every hair on my borrowed body stand on end. "When Dylan's soul returns?"

"I'll address that concern. When the time comes."

"He's cruel. He doesn't care for Ariel. He'll undo all my hard work," I say, seeing an opening. A few hours of life have made me greedy for more. "Perhaps it would be better if I stayed with her on a more permanent basis. I could be her . . . protector."

Nurse smiles, amused by my obvious ploy, but I can't smile back. The energy is even worse behind the cabin. Leafless trees and knotted brown vines squat in the grass, gnarled sentries protecting the black face of a cliff that rises another fifty feet before the mountain ends in a thick bald knob. I falter again, not wanting to go a step closer to that seething rock.

"You can't stay." She takes my hand and urges me on. I want to pull away but curl my fingers around hers instead, letting her lead me through the brambles at our feet. "If you do your job well, there will be no chance of Ariel's soul turning to darkness, and the Ambassadors can't waste magic on a soul already won. When your work is finished, I will administer the peacekeeper vows and you will go to the mist until you are needed to serve the cause again."

"But—"

"Ambassadors are Mercenary targets. You know that, Romeo. As soon as you take the vows, your aura will mark you as one of us and you will be vulnerable. But without the vows, you will return to the specter of your soul and rot."

I sigh at her inescapable logic.

"The Mercenaries will want their revenge," she says as she picks her way around a petrified tree, bringing us close enough to the cliff for me to see a dark slash in its middle. A cave. The evil threading through the air is coming from inside. I can practically smell it. "Any Ambassador still here when they arrive will be at risk."

"And what about Ariel?" I pull my hand from hers, unable to take another step.

"What about her?"

"The Mercenaries will kill her before they'll let her live on to become a force for love and light," I say, spitting the last words. "If I turn her heart and leave her, I'm setting her up to die."

The Ambassador places a hand on my shoulder. "Do you care?"

Do I? The angry knot in my gut, the way my fingers want to wrap around this woman's throat and squeeze as punishment for failing to think her plan through, make me think I might. At least a little. My appetite for murder has vanished, making me wonder if it was ever *mine* to begin with. Perhaps it was the Mercenary magic inside me that craved death and destruction, and not my own soul at all.

"I already killed her once," I say finally. "I don't want to be the reason she dies a second time."

Nurse cocks her head. "I'm surprised. Pleasantly."

"I live to please, my lady."

Her lips curve. "Save it for Ariel, my boy. I am immune to your charms."

I sigh. "I only want to make sure she's—"

"I will take care of the girl."

"But—"

"I appreciate your concern," she says sharply. "But your focus should be on doing whatever it takes to win Ariel, heart and soul."

"Whatever it takes," I repeat, apprehension tightening the back of my neck.

"Lie, cheat, steal. Even kill if you must." The bite in her tone makes my eyes drift to her sharp little teeth. "That's why you're here, Romeo, instead of some worthy Ambassador. You can do things we cannot."

I stand straighter, clench my jaw, steeling myself against the revulsion rising inside of me. I've killed before. If I have to, I can kill again. I *must.* "Who would you have me kill?"

"Anyone who stands between you and your goal."

I shake my head, banishing from my mind the image of Ariel with a bullet hole between her eyes. That was another reality. This reality doesn't have to end in the same bloody fashion. "I doubt that will be necessary."

"Most likely not. But it's important that you understand how far I'm willing to go to protect the future."

I look over her shoulder, unable to keep my eyes from the opening to the cave. The evil energy still whispers there. The cave is a monster, and we're close enough to hear it breathe. "But I . . . That isn't why we've taken this drive."

"I think it's important that you see something as well." She reaches for me again.

I clench my hands into fists. "Whatever's in there, I don't want to see it."

"What you *want* doesn't matter. Just as what you *feel* doesn't matter," she says, her voice all the crueler for its calm, patient tone. "No one cares about you, Romeo. You are a means to an end. If you fail to be useful to me, you will fail to matter to anyone, save those who will torture you for their entertainment."

I bare my teeth in a horrible smile, hoping there's still

enough Mercenary in me to frighten her. "I assume you're nicer to your other converts."

"I've given you a chance at salvation. I don't know that I can be much nicer. Except perhaps to provide you with the proper motivation." She snatches my arm and pulls me along as if I'm a child who has wandered into the street.

She means to hurt me. I have no doubt of that now. I was a fool to believe the Ambassadors would be any different from the Mercenaries. For nearly a thousand years I was ruled by pain and fear, and my new master is just as cruel as my old one. The bringers of light simply have better benefits.

Though taste and touch and smell can be their own punishment. . . .

I learned that much in the weeks I was trapped in the specter of my soul. In that feeling-rotting-stinking nightmare of a body that taught me new ways to suffer. Just the smell of it was enough to drive a man mad.

The smell. The *smell.*

The stink floods over me at the entrance to the cave, making me choke. I try to rip my arm free, but the Ambassador grips me, forcing me inexorably forward, toward the thing growling in the darkness, the beast she has imprisoned with her magic and brought me to visit. To remind me how easy it will be for her to take away what she's given, to assure me that I am her creature and that I must play by her rules . . .

Or not play at all.

INTERMEZZO ONE

VERONA, 1304

Juliet

The afterlife is a nightmare. Hell is knowing that you might *never* wake up.

The stone beneath me bruises my spine; my fingertips pulse from where I've ripped my nails trying to claw the lid of the sarcophagus away. I draw in stale air, pungent with the stink of Tybalt's body rotting in his own deathbed a few paces away, but I lack even the luxury of gagging at the stench.

I'm back in my sarcophagus, buried alive, trapped and dying in the dark. Again.

Again.

I tell myself it's only a dream, but I can't open my eyes. I can't move, can't lift a hand to push against the marble slab that covers my face, can't part my lips to cry out for help.

I feel the poison the friar gave me to help me fake my death pulsing wickedly through my veins, writhing into my brain like a maggot feeding, leaving madness in its wake. I'm dimly aware of my heart beating, of my skin sweating feverishly despite the cold in the tomb, but my soul remains separate from my body, lost and wandering in a terror-filled world from which I may never return.

Maybe this is Nurse's work. Maybe she cursed me to this hell for refusing to rejoin the Ambassador cause. Perhaps I will remain here—believing myself buried alive and dreaming darkly—until the end of time.

I fight my way through dreamscapes peopled by feral corpses with black teeth bared, a hundred dead Romeos, each more rotted and wrong than the last, all hungry for a taste of my heart. He lunges at me from the shadows, rises from the mud beneath my feet, eyes burning red like a demon sent to pull me into the flames.

His clawed hands grab my ankle and drag me down, drowning me in liquid earth. Mud flows into my nose and rushes down my throat, cutting off any hope of breath. My heart slows, my fear-sharpened thoughts go fuzzy, and something deeper than sleep draws me close.

For a moment, I believe I am truly gone, at peace, beyond the reach of Romeo and the Mercenaries and my nurse, who betrayed me, and the pain of knowing that Ben is dead.

Ben. The memory of his face at the end—battered and bruised by Romeo's fists—threatens to shatter what's left of my heart. My Ben, my beautiful, sad boy whom I believed for one breathless moment I could make happy and whole. But there is no happiness in the world, and soon I won't know the meaning of *whole*.

My heart sputters to life and the nightmares begin again, even more horrible this time. I watch Romeo's corpse transform, becoming beautiful and filled with light. I watch him take the Ambassador vows and move on to find peace in service while I remain here, lost and alone, and somehow I know that it's real. I have been punished for my refusal to serve the Ambassadors any longer, while Romeo—the most wicked being I have ever known—is rewarded.

Will be rewarded. It hasn't happened yet. But it will. I *know* it will. This is a vision, not a dream, and it makes me want to scream until blood flows down my throat.

Life was never fair. I don't know why I thought the afterlife would be any different—but I did. God help me, I did. But it isn't, and I am proven the most tragic, tortured breed of fool.

I try to close my eyes, to open them, to force my dreaming self to turn away from the vision of Romeo's golden beauty, or force my sleeping self to wake. But I can do nothing. I *am* nothing. I am more lost and powerless than I was before. Even as an Ambassador. Even in the mist.

Something breaks inside me, a fissure up the center of my being that allows the nightmares to sink their claws in deeper. The monster Romeos return, accompanied by every horror mankind has ever imagined, crawling on blood-soaked claws, dragging bodies bloated with evil through fields of death and decay. I run, bare feet squishing in the rot, howls of pain from the living dead becoming a roar that rushes inside, emptying me of everything but pure, unadulterated fear.

There are whispers in the air. They drift from the bleeding sky, floating down to feather against my skin. It's Nurse's voice, trying to soothe away my terror, but I'm too far gone. Lost. Mindless. Her promise to come for me, her insistence that time is a circle, not a line, her assurance that my fate is entwined with Romeo's but I can escape and find salvation, make little sense to me. Words are only sound, drumbeats inside my skull that confound me with their irregular rhythm.

I run until my dream self pitches forward in exhaustion, and then I fall. And fall and fall, through seemingly endless inky space until I land with a jolt inside my body.

My *real* body, not some borrowed shell, not the body of Ariel Dragland. *Mine.* I am thirsty and shivering and sweating out poison, and am weaker than I can remember being in my life or afterlife, but I am myself. And I feel . . . *alive.*

My sticky eyelids fight their way open. There is still only blackness, but I know it's not the twisted dark of my dreams. This is real. I am *truly* in the tomb. God . . . how is this possible? *How?* Have I traveled back in time? And if so, how far back? How long have I been here? And most important—how long do I have until Romeo and the friar come for me, the way they did the first time I lay in this pit?

I don't know. But it isn't long enough.

I have to get out.

I run my swollen, aching tongue over dry lips. I pull in a gulp of air to scream, and then I hear it—a voice. Calling my name from a distance. The Capulet tomb is large, with twenty steps leading underground and room for generations of Capulets to lie side by side in their giant stone beds, but I can still make out the words the man speaks, and I *know* that voice.

"Juliet! Are you there?" He's doing his best to sound kind, but I'm not fooled for a moment.

It's the friar, the Mercenary in possession of Friar Lawrence's body. He's come for me, and I am so very weak. I'm no longer an Ambassador, and even if I were, I wouldn't have the strength to fight one of the high ones and win.

He is one of the strongest, most ancient Mercenaries. And he will kill me. Now.

I shiver, bite my lip, feel my tongue cramp at the back of my throat as my empty body tries to be sick and fails.

No, he will do something worse than kill me. Much worse. Even Romeo knew that, and pitied me enough to attempt to make my death a swift one. But he failed to grant me even that small mercy. The friar will have his torture, my slow death to relish, and I can do nothing but lie here and wait for him to do it.

Wait. Helpless. Helpless. *Helpless.*

Fury, blinding in its intensity, burns in my chest. My eyes roll back and my lids close and I slip gratefully back into the world of nightmare. It's better. It's better to sleep and dream of horror than to stay awake to greet the real-life evil creeping into the tomb, hungry for blood and pain.

SIX

Ariel

I don't know how much time has passed, but when I wake up with my face in the dirt, it feels late. Too late.

My mom is going to *kill* me.

I tell my hands to push into the ground and get me up, but all I manage to do is trigger a round of thrashing. My nerves scream, and vertigo turns my stomach to liquid. It's like every time I've dreamed about falling but a hundred times worse. I'm messed up. *So* messed up. I always am afterward, but this is worse than ever. I feel hollowed-out, like the screaming things ate my insides and left a shell behind. A jack-o'-lantern without a candle, no spark to light me.

My chest gets tight. Maybe this time is the last time. Maybe this is the crazy I'll never be able to climb out of. Maybe the damaged piece of me has finally destroyed the part that can imagine a better life, and now I'm finally, completely broken.

I feel wetness on my cheeks and give up trying to move. I lie still, inhaling the comforting smell of grass and earth, trying to allow my mind and body to connect on their own. I'm going to be okay. I'm still thinking straight. I can still worry about getting in trouble with my mom and be embarrassed over the way things ended with Dylan.

I can't remember what I said to him, but I'm guessing I made a fool of myself. I'm pretty sure he deserved whatever I dished out, but I wish I'd had more control. I just got drunk so fast. One second I was fine, and the next, everything was spinning, and deciphering the meaning in his words was like trying to translate a foreign language. *Stupid.* I should have been more careful. Even a sip or two is usually enough to make me feel loose and silly. I should have realized that sharing a nearly full bottle was a bad idea. I obviously can't handle my liquor.

You can't handle life.

I close my eyes, too tired to disagree with myself. Besides, the voice in my head is right. I can't handle life. I can't even control my body. I'm lying on the ground with my face in the mud, and my legs are cold and clammy from where I've wet myself, and I can't even talk my hands into helping me stand.

No. I can. I have to. Because there's no one here to help me.

A part of me is grateful—at least Dylan didn't see me this way—but the other part is stupidly disappointed. Why didn't he follow me? He was trying so hard to act like he cared—or at least cared enough to keep me alive until he won his bet.

Shouldn't he have made sure I got home safely? He had to know I was drunk. If the gossip around school is to be believed, Dylan has enough experience with controlled substances to know when someone's messed up.

But maybe he *did* try. I remember him running after me, calling my name, but then everything gets blurry. I don't remember running out of Los Olivos or how close I was to home before I collapsed. I know I'm in a vineyard, but there are dozens of vineyards close to town. I could be anywhere. Hopefully I'm not too far from El Camino Road. I have to get home before my mom goes crazy and calls the police. She's working late, so at least that's in my favor. She doesn't get off her shift until eleven, won't make it home until eleven-thirty, and probably won't get really freaked-out until after midnight.

We've never talked about a curfew—I've never dated, and Gemma and I usually hung out at my house on nights when Gemma wasn't out with whoever she was dating—but I know my mom well enough to know that she won't be cool with my staying out later than midnight on a school night. I was surprised she let me say yes to Dylan's Tuesday-night invitation in the first place. But she probably would have given me permission to ditch school, take roofies, and have kinky sex with Dylan all day in my room if I'd asked. She was *that* thrilled that I was finally doing something normal.

It was pathetic, really, how thrilled she was.

I know Mom blames herself for the lack of romance in my life. She dropped a pot of grease when I was six years old and gave me the scars she believes caused my "tragically low self-esteem." I told her I forgive her. I even hinted that there are reasons I'm repulsive to boys that have nothing to do with my messed-up skin. But she doesn't believe me, and

I know she thinks I'm going to be alone forever if something doesn't change.

I'd thought the new Dylan might be the start of that change. He used to make fun of me in junior high, but he certainly hasn't acted like I'm repulsive lately. Not before and not after.

Before and after. *Before* I tried to kill him, and *after* he chased me down the side of the road and made a fool of himself for the chance to take me to dinner. Which is the real Dylan? The one who agreed to take the Freak's virginity for money or the one who said I was a good person and deserved a happy life? The one who stripped and sang for me or the one who inferred my best friend was a slut?

I have no idea, but I want to find out, and that's not going to happen if I don't get home soon. Mom will never let me out of the house again if I drag in after midnight.

I try to communicate with my arms again. This time, my fingers twitch and curl, and finally, inch by inch, I drag my palms through the dirt and lift myself up on shaking arms. By the time I get to my feet, I'm trembling all over and feel like I might be sick, but I stay upright. I lift my chin, inhale cool, stomach-soothing air, and take a look over the tops of the vines. It takes only a second to spot the turrets of the Castle Playground.

Finally. Some luck. The playground's only a few blocks from my house. I'll be home in ten minutes if my legs hold out.

Stumbling only a few times, I make it down the row of vines and cut through the soccer field near the playground. The towers and delicate bridges leading from one piece of equipment to the next look magical in the moonlight, and I'm struck by the idea that I should have taken Dylan here instead of the rocket ship park in Los Olivos. But I have bad memories of this place, ghosts that scream and point at me as I hurry toward the road.

Mom brought me here when I was little, a few months after the accident, when my skin was bright shiny red and my hair only a few inches long. It had melted on one side when Mom spilled the grease, and it had to be cut off. I had nothing to hide behind, no curtain to pull when the kids stared and one girl screamed that there was a troll under the bridge.

I think she was trying to start a game, pretending more than being cruel, but my mom still lost it. She yelled at the girl, and then the girl's mom yelled at my mom, and then Mom pulled me away. We never went to the playground during the day again. She made me wait until after supper, when there were hardly any other kids at the park. She said she wanted to protect my scars from the sun, but I knew better. She was overwhelmed by the task of mothering the monster. I was already having the episodes by then, already spending two to three afternoons per week with a child psychologist. My mom couldn't handle more negative interaction. It was easier to hide at home than to go out and face the big, bad world.

I decide right then not to tell her about the bet. I don't want her pity, and I don't want to be protected from Dylan the way she protected me when I was a kid. Bad news or not, Dylan is . . . interesting to me. I think I might still hate him, and there's a chance I'll end up avoiding him like the plague for the rest of senior year, but that's a decision I want to make for myself.

The thought makes me feel stronger, more in control, and

by the time our blue house comes into view, I'm feeling good enough to take the last fifty feet at a jog. Mom's car is already in the carport. I don't know how long she's been home, but hopefully I've gotten here in time. At least there aren't any police cruisers in the driveway. That's a good sign.

I hurry up the stairs, but then slow down, opening the screen door carefully. The lights are on in the kitchen. I'm not surprised to find Mom waiting up, but I thought she'd be catching up on her TiVo'd episodes of *Grey's Anatomy* or something, not lying in wait right by the carport door. I take a second, smoothing my hair and brushing some of the dirt off my shirt. There's no helping the pee drying on my jeans, however. Or the smell.

The screaming voices don't take me over often anymore—and when they do I'm good about making sure I'm alone in my room—but Mom knows why I used to wet myself when I was little. She had to come pick me up the day I embarrassed myself at school, and she used to sit with me when I'd get angry at the psychiatrist's office and slip into an episode. She'll guess what happened, and I'll be back at the shrink again before I can say "Let me explain."

My throat clenches. I back down the steps. Maybe I can sneak in my window. Maybe if I shove my clothes under my bed and get into the shower before—

"Ariel? Is that you?" Mom sounds worried but not freaked out. It must not be that late. Not that it matters now. *God.* Why didn't I think about what I look like? Why didn't I have the sense to go around back as soon as I saw the kitchen light?

"Ariel?" Mom appears at the screen door, looking narrow and faded in her white robe with the gray flowers. "Why are you standing outside, honey?"

"I . . . I thought you might be asleep."

"I wanted to wait up and hear about your date." She smiles. "Come inside. It's getting chilly."

I trudge up the stairs. There's no avoiding it now. Might as well take my medicine. As soon as I'm in the door, Mom's nose wrinkles and her attention drops to my legs. I close my eyes and imagine my body wadding up into a tiny ball and rolling down the hall into my room, my ears and face and everything all mashed up together so I can't hear whatever she's going to say.

"Oh, Ariel. What happened?" she asks as she closes the door behind me. "Where's Dylan? Where's your purse?"

"I . . ." What to say? A lie or the truth or something in between? Or do I dare tell her to mind her own business for once? That it's my life and I'll bear the pathetic weight of it on my own?

"You what? Talk to me."

"I lost my purse." I look at the ground and rush on before she can start lecturing me about losing my cell, a capital offense in her "we're on a budget" handbook. "Dylan and I got drunk on the playground in Los Olivos, and I started walking home because I didn't think he should drive," I say, deciding that's close enough to the truth, while hopefully saving me from the psychiatrist. "I had an accident before I could get home. I didn't want to go to the bathroom outside, and I tried to hold it too long."

"Oh my god." She sighs, but she doesn't sound angry. I risk looking up. "Why didn't you call me to come pick you up?"

"I thought you'd be mad. I lost my purse. I would have had to call collect."

"You can call collect anytime. And I'm *not* happy that you lost your purse, and you'll be paying for a new cell phone yourself out of your savings, but . . ." She shrugs, and the frustration I heard in her voice when she mentioned the cell phone seems to drain out of her. "But I know kids your age drink. You're eighteen, and that's old enough to have a glass of wine every now and then. I'd just rather you do it here at the house and keep it responsible. Like one or two glasses, not enough to get you drunk and making reckless decisions."

Wow. That was unexpected. I don't know what to say. She's being so . . . cool. I know she'd do about anything to see me acting "normal," but I didn't expect her to be so understanding about my mistake. "I . . . I didn't know that."

"Well, now you do," she says with a soft look. "So how did the date go? Other than the obviously not-so-great ending?"

"Okay, I guess."

"Okay?" Her brow wrinkles. "Then why did Dylan let you walk home alone?"

"He just . . . had to get home." I stare at the windmills painted on the cabinets and shuffle my feet, resisting the urge to tell her more about my confusing night. No matter how cool she's being, that still doesn't seem like a good idea. "I'd really like to take a shower and get changed, Mom. I feel gross. And stupid."

She nods and takes a step back, but then reaches out to pat my shoulder, a quick *pat-pat-pat* that's awkward but kind of nice. "Don't feel stupid. But don't get drunk and wander around by yourself again either. Something horrible could have happened, and I would never have forgiven myself. I worry about you since . . . you know."

Since Gemma, she means. She mentioned the flyers,

but we haven't talked about it much. I don't really want to talk about it now either, but I appreciate that she's worried about me.

Even if her worry won't do a thing to keep the crazy away.

"I'll be careful," I say, and then find myself unexpectedly adding, "but if something happened, it wouldn't be your fault, you know. I'm eighteen. I'm old enough to take care of myself."

"I know, but I . . . I love you. You're the most important person in my life. You know that, right?"

"Yeah," I say, even though—until that very second—I wasn't completely sure. But suddenly it seems so clear, a glaring truth that I've somehow managed to ignore.

It's like the pink tiles on the wall in the bathroom. I never noticed they had flowers on them until Gemma made fun of them for being tacky. I grew up in this house and used that bathroom several times a day for *seventeen years*, and I never noticed. Now I can't go in there without staring. Once you've seen something, you can't un-see it. I stare at those flowers a lot and wonder what other obvious things I might be missing.

I never imagined that how much Mom loves me was one of them.

"I'm sorry if I haven't said that enough," she says, making my throat tight all over again.

"You say it plenty."

"Are you sure? I worry I haven't, that I haven't been the kind of mom you need me to be."

A weird sense of déjà vu crackles in the air between us. I know she's never said anything like this to me before, but it *feels* like she has. It's unsettling and makes my voice tremble when I promise, "You've been fine. I'm okay."

"Really?" she asks, doubt in her eyes.

They're a lighter blue than mine, but otherwise Mom and I look like sisters. Same long white hair, same scrawny build with elbows that are too big for our arms, same thin lips that we bite when we're worried. She had me when she wasn't much older than I am now. All alone, after my bio dad told her to get an abortion and bolted. For the first time, the reality of that settles inside me, scary and heavy and awe-inspiring. I can't believe I almost destroyed the person she worked so hard to keep alive. How could I have thought that killing myself was something Mom would be relieved about?

Maybe I *should* head back to the shrink. Maybe I'm even crazier than I thought.

"You've been great," I say, pressure building behind my eyes. "I love you, Mom." I reach for her, wrapping my arms around her shoulders as she grabs me around the waist. We hug each other tight for a long time. Long enough for me to realize that the top of her head comes only to my cheekbone. I'm taller than she is, by a couple of inches. Another obvious thing I've missed.

Finally she pulls away with a smile. "Good talk."

"Yeah." I look at the floor, feeling awkward, but not in a bad way. "Thanks."

"All right, why don't you go get cleaned up," she says. "Leave your clothes in the hall and I'll start a load of laundry."

"No, that's okay." She hasn't done my laundry since I was twelve, and I'm way too old for her to have any obligation to touch my pee-soaked jeans. Besides, I know she must be exhausted. "My jeans are gross. You don't have to—"

"I'm a nurse, honey. I handle much worse every day,

and I have to do a load of scrubs anyway. I'll get everything washed and in the dryer, and we can fold tomorrow."

"Okay." I start out of the room, but she stops me before I reach the hall.

"Wait a sec," she says, snapping her fingers the way she does when she's forgotten something. "I wanted to tell you: Wendy's going to give me a ride to work tomorrow. So you can sleep a little later and take the car to school if you want."

Gemma used to drive me to school. In the ten days since she's been gone I've been getting up early to walk to avoid the horror of the bus. No one over the age of sixteen rides the bus, and I couldn't stand the thought of all those rows of junior high kids staring at me as I climbed aboard.

I didn't think Mom had noticed my early departure, but I guess she has.

"Thanks." I hope she knows I mean for more than the car.

"You're welcome." She smiles. "Just try not to wake me up on your way out. I might have to work a double tomorrow, so I'm going to sleep in until nine or so."

I nod and hurry down the hall to the bathroom. I start the shower and strip off my dirty clothes, dumping them outside the door and closing it again. Then I stand there, waiting for the steam that will signal that the water is finally warm enough. It takes a while. Like always. I spend the time staring at the pink tiles and their flower decorations.

Forty minutes later, after a long, hot shower, I wrap my towel around my chest and tiptoe to my room. The dryer is running and mom's doorway is dark. She's probably asleep, as I should be soon. It's nearly one in the morning. I'm only going to get six hours, and that's if I fall asleep the second my head hits the pillow. After everything that's happened, I know I should be exhausted, but I'm not. I'm wired, and even after I've changed into my striped pajama pants and a cami, I don't turn off the light.

Instead, I walk to my easel and check on the canvas I prepped this afternoon. It looks good. I'll be able to start tomorrow on the fairy I've been sketching. Or maybe I'll do something different. I've been on a mythical-creature kick, but I'm starting to feel like it might be time for a portrait. Maybe that self-portrait I've never been brave enough to attempt. I didn't think I could stand to look at myself in the mirror that much, but maybe I can. Maybe I'll even see something in myself that I've missed.

Things I've missed.

The thought hits me strangely. I feel a tug at the back of my brain, the nagging suspicion that I've forgotten something important. Something I saw, something I heard? I can't remember. But it's there, lurking below the surface of my mind.

I turn from the canvas to my gallery wall. All the best things I've painted since I was twelve are hanging here. It's the one sight that always makes me feel hopeful, and it's my best thinking place. If I stand back and let my eyes track from the tree on the mountain, to the boy on the hill, to the unicorn dying by the water, my mind calms and I think more clearly.

Usually. Not tonight.

When I get to the unicorn, I get a sick, spinning feeling, like the déjà vu in the kitchen but a hundred times worse. Something's wrong. I move closer, lift my fingers to the unicorn's face—the one I spent hours getting just right—and shiver. Nothing looks different, but somehow I *know* that someone's been in my room, looking at this painting. Not Mom. A stranger. Someone I don't know has been in here, touching and searching and poking their nose into the most private parts of my life.

I whirl away from the wall, scanning the rest of the room. Everything's still in the place it was when I left. My homework is stacked on my desk, my closet door is half-open, and my comforter explodes in horrible ruffles except for a dent on the right side, where I sat while I was putting on my shoes. I cross the room, check out the closet, open my dresser drawers, even get down on the floor and peek under the bed. Nothing's different, but the feeling that someone has been here only gets stronger. I know I'm being weird, but I can't seem to calm down.

Finally, after a fruitless search of my backpack and desk, I force myself to turn off the light and crawl into bed, but the irrational fret-fest only gets worse. I could swear someone else has been sleeping in my bed, lying her head on my pillow, dreaming her own dreams in this place that's supposed to be mine.

Mine. *Not* mine. The voices . . . What if they're not what I've always thought they were?

It's the thought kernel I've been waiting to pop open, and it calms me. I reach for the journal by my bed, the one I use to write and sketch things that I dream and don't want to forget before I wake up. I turn past a quick line drawing of the high school crumbling into ruins beneath a night full of menacing stars, and find a blank page.

Ghost, demon, some kind of possession, I write. *Ripples in the air, claws tearing the world open to find a person who will listen to the voices scream.*

I close the book around the pen and set it on my night-stand before curling under the soft flannel sheets. I've never been able to listen to the voices. They overwhelm me before I can even think about trying to understand them, but maybe I haven't been trying hard enough. If they really are ghosts or something, they might want me to listen. Ghosts in stories always need the living to intercede on their behalf, to pursue justice or right a wrong or do something that puts their soul to rest.

Things that scream like that are beyond rest.

But I'm not. Not yet. I'm safe, my eyes are heavy, and my muscles are aching with exhaustion. Finally even the disturbing feeling that someone's been in my room isn't enough to keep me awake. I sleep, and dream of the boy from my painting, the one on the lonely hill where the sky bleeds like night is murdering the day.

The wind is punishing and the boy's brown curls blow around his head, flying into his dark eyes, but I know the stinging hairs aren't the reason for the tears streaming down his cheeks. He's miserable, as sad a person as I've ever seen, as sad as my own reflection on the days when I wonder if I'll make it through another day.

Still, he's beautiful. Like an angel fallen from heaven. When he lifts his eyes to mine, I can't breathe. His pain and beauty wrap around my ribs and squeeze.

I forgive you, *I want to say, though I don't know for what. But before I work up the courage to speak, a man in a brown robe appears behind the boy, and the grass between us splits.*

The earth opens like the mouth of a hungry baby bird, and the man shoves the boy between the shoulders. The boy falls into the newly formed pit, and I scream, but there's no sound. There's nothing but the wind and the hungry ground gobbling as it rolls over the boy like water. I fall to the ground and claw at the grass, but it's too late. He's gone. I feel it like a knife shoved into my heart.

"I forgive you," the man in the robe says to me, the echo of my own thought making me lift my eyes. His are a blue so pale they look watered down, but that doesn't make gazing into them any less terrifying. This isn't the first time he's killed. Or the second, or the third, or the hundredth.

"Come with me." He reaches for me, but I scramble away. His hand is too clean. It should be caked with dirt and blood. It should be marked by what he's done.

My thoughts take hold of the dream and dig deep. I watch with horrified satisfaction as the man's flesh peels away from his fingers. I see muscle and bone and all the hidden things I've stared at in my anatomy book to learn the truths of the bodies I draw, and soon his hand is nothing but raw tissue that sends blood raining down onto the grass.

But the man in the robe seems to feel no pain.

"And neither will you, dear," he says. "Peace will be yours if you put yourself into my keeping."

He reaches for me again, but this time his hand is a giant's hand. His fingers reach out, out, out, until they arch over me like the beams of a house built of nightmares. The blood rain falls onto my face, slips between my lips, and I fall to the ground screaming. But not because I'm scared or horrified. Because the blood is sweet and I want more. I want to tilt my head back and let it flow down my throat.

I want to laugh and dance and celebrate the safety of becoming one with the darkness.

I wake up in the middle of a deep breath and barely hold in the scream pushing at my lips. I swallow and shiver and try to calm my pounding heart.

Morning light shines in my window, and the yellow ruffles

on the bed are soft cotton-candy sunshine floating in the middle of my room. There's nothing to be afraid of. It was just an awful dream. There's no blood, no evil monk or whatever he was, no dead boy.

I rub my eyes and turn to look at the gallery, taking comfort in seeing the boy standing on his hill, thinking maybe I'll paint him again. But up close this time. Up close with something in his eyes other than pain. Maybe hope or laughter or . . . love.

The thought makes me blush and look away, as if the boy's a real person who might be able to read on my face the silly things I'm thinking. I'm ridiculous, but it feels good to smile, so good that the secret silliness is still wrinkling my lips when I look out the window.

And see Dylan's face. And scream the scream I thought I'd swallowed.

SEVEN

Romeo

Damn! Caught. I wave my hands and hold up Ariel's purse, trying to stop her scream before her mother comes running. I should have ducked down the second she opened her eyes, but I couldn't resist the urge to watch her wake. She was strangely compelling, all soft with sleep, hair fuzzy and tangled, smiling that smile. . . . *That smile,* the one that makes her look so young and innocent and good.

Standing there with the dew soaking through my shoes, I was possessed by the desire to make sure that she stays that way, that she never knows what it's like to be poisoned by her own mistakes. The need came from a genuine place, separate from the fear that kept me awake most of the night, reliving every terrifying step into the cave.

Now the fear is back.

I have only three days. Three days to transform the sight of me from something that makes Ariel scream to something that makes her smile *that smile*. It might be impossible, but I have to try. I have to do more than try. I have to succeed, or I am lost, and the world along with me.

Screw the world, I think, but the thought doesn't feel as true as it once did. I don't want the Mercenaries to win, I know that much.

"I came to bring your purse. I only want to talk," I whisper, hoping Ariel can hear me through the window. The glass looks thick, but I don't want to shout and risk disturbing her mother if she hasn't already been disturbed. "I'm sorry," I mouth.

She presses her hand over her lips and glances at her bedroom door, watching it for a tense moment before throwing off the covers and stepping out of bed. She's wearing a tight white shirt with thin straps that reveal the scars on her arm, and loose striped pants. The pants ride low on her hips, exposing a strip of pale skin and the curve of her stomach. The bit of skin mesmerizes me. I can't keep from imagining what it would be like to run my hands over her sleep-warmed body, over those long arms—one perfectly smooth, one beautifully damaged.

She really is beautiful. Despite the scars. Or maybe . . . because of them. She's a walking reminder of how precious and fleeting life can be. No one lucky enough to be pulling in breath should take that for granted. No one should hold back when they can reach for what they want with both hands.

Want. I'm suddenly drowning in it. I want to touch her

so badly that it hurts, that it makes my tongue sluggish, and I sputter when she throws open the window.

"What are you doing here?" she demands.

"I–I . . ."

I want to touch you. I want to curl into bed beside you and see if you can teach me to dream something that won't make me wake up screaming.

"I . . ." I shake my head, hoping to jostle free a few words I can actually speak. "I–I–"

She grabs the purse from my hand and sets it on the floor inside. "My mom will freak if she sees you outside my window," she whispers, casting another anxious look over her shoulder before turning back to me. "There's a lock on the fence gate. How did you get over?"

Breathe. Concentrate. "I climbed." I stare at a spot over her shoulder and tamp down the last of the ridiculous weakness. I can't remember ever feeling so damned needy, even when I was a child and my father set fire to the nursery after my brother's death.

The plague doctor told my parents that boiling sheets and possessions in hot water might keep the infection from spreading. Instead, my father burned everything. Every piece of furniture in our shared nursery, every article of clothing, every wooden whistle and block and all my brother's carved animals. Even the blue blankets our mother had embroidered. We'd gone to sleep with them every night since the day we were born. How I ached for that blanket when it was gone. Almost as much as I ached for my brother. I went to sleep each night after the fire with my tiny fists pressed to my chest, wondering if I would die from the aching.

But even *that* wasn't as strong as this desire to wrap my

arms around Ariel's waist, press my face into her stomach, and beg for some kind of comfort.

Pathetic. Weak. I'm losing what's left of my mind.

I have to focus. I can't let this sudden need for human connection distract me from my course. There will be opportunity for connection in all its forms at a later date, in another body, after I've won my place among the Ambassadors. I know Juliet was careful not to use her borrowed bodies for selfish pleasures, but I don't have to do the same. As soon as I'm safe, I can find a dozen girls as lovely as Ariel—lovelier—to hold me in their arms. The thought should offer solace, but it doesn't.

I lick my lips, taste my own desperation, and hope she can't see how close I am to the edge. "I needed to see you."

"Why?"

"I was worried you might not have made it home."

"I did. Obviously. I . . ." Her eyes drop to the wet grass at my feet. "Everything's fine."

Everything's not fine. You hold the fate of the world in your hands, and the person sent to help you is being eaten alive by his own fear. Damn Juliet's nurse. I was fine before she forced me into that cave. Her "motivation" has only brought me closer to failure.

"No, it's not," I say. "You're mad at me."

"I'm not mad at you." She doesn't sound convincing.

"Are you sure? You weren't very happy with me when you left last night."

"I . . . can't really remember." Her eyes meet mine, apprehensive, uncertain. "I know we argued, and I have a feeling I should still be mad at you for something, but . . . it's fuzzy."

I take a breath, finally feeling it's safe to smile again. She doesn't remember. Thank mercy for small favors. "I'm sorry. You *should* be mad. This is my fault," I say, pouring on the charm that seemed to be working before I made the mistake of introducing alcohol into the equation. "We were drinking port. It's fortified, a lot stronger than normal wine. I should have warned you."

"Oh." Her fingers tug at a tangled lock of hair. "I didn't know."

"Again, my fault. Forgive me?"

The edge of one lip curves. "You didn't hold a gun to my head and make me drink."

"I also didn't chase you down and make sure you got home." I brace my hands on the windowsill and lean in, tipping my head back to look up at her, struck by how much this moment reminds me of the night I stood beneath Juliet's balcony.

Maybe that's why I'm such a useless mess. That was one of my last nights as a *relatively* innocent boy in love. The friar and I spoke the next day, and the slow seep of poison into my heart began. Even now the effects linger, forcing me to lie and deceive, to pretend a love I don't feel for a girl who deserves better than this.

Better than me.

"Are you okay?" she asks. Her fingertips brush the back of my hand, inciting a wave of pleasure-pain that skitters across my skin. Pleasure to be touched, pain to know I am so unworthy of her compassion.

"Fine." Not fine. But I can't remember the last time fine was a word that applied to my existence.

"You must be cold." She peeks over her shoulder one last time. "Come inside."

"Thanks." I pull myself up on the sill and hop down beside her, close enough to feel the heat of her body, to smell the lavender lingering in her hair. "I really am sorry," I whisper, not wanting to frighten her away. "I could hardly sleep. I was worried about you."

"It's okay," she says, swaying closer. I hold my breath, the possibility that she might brush against me making my heart beat faster. "I'm sorry too."

"For what?" I ease her hair over her shoulder, letting my fingers hover near the skin at her neck. I hold her gaze, waiting for permission to touch her again.

Her throat works and her lips part and her mouth drifts closer to mine, and for a dizzying moment, I think she might kiss me. Instead she lets out a breathy laugh and shakes her hair back around her face. "For being weird." She steps back, crossing her arms, as if suddenly uncomfortable in her thin top with the thinner straps. "Let's just forget about it."

"Forgotten." I drop my hand and force a friendly smile. "Want to go get breakfast?" Hopefully getting Ariel out of this bedroom will help me pull myself together. "I'm craving something deep fried and covered in sugar, maybe with some syrup on top."

"Sounds healthy."

"We're young. Who cares?"

Her mouth curves again. "I could eat. Where do you want to go?"

"Wherever. Your choice."

"I don't care, just not the Windmill." She captures the same lock of hair and gives it another tug. "I don't want to see anyone who might know about . . . you know."

She doesn't want to see anyone who might know about

the bet. I nod. "We'll go someplace else. And before the day's over, I'll make sure everyone understands that the bet's off and I'm an idiot. Especially the idiot part."

Her smile tries to stretch, but she traps it with her teeth. "Sounds good."

"Then let's go eat."

"I need to get dressed first. Do you want to wait for me out—"

"No." I don't want to be apart from her for a moment, not until I know we're firmly back on course. "I'll turn around, I won't look."

She lifts a dubious brow, but I see the spark of trouble from last night in her eyes. "You promise?"

"Do you . . . *want* me to promise?"

"Yes," she says, while her eyes flash "no." "I want you to promise."

"You trust me enough to take my word?"

She cocks her head to one side, considering me down the slope of her button nose. "About this. Even if you break it, I've already seen *you* naked, so . . ." Her shoulder lifts, a seductive roll of bone that hints at the sensual nature she's been too guarded to indulge since discovering her date with Dylan was a prank.

"You've only seen me *nearly* naked," I correct, wishing I had more than stolen memories of being tangled up with Ariel. "But I won't break my word. Even if you *beg* me to."

Her lips twitch. "I'll try to control myself."

I grin. "You have a sarcastic streak."

"I do."

"I like it."

"I thought you might." Her playful tone makes me want

to grab her and tickle her until she squeals. I haven't tickled a girl in centuries, and it's such a nice excuse for getting your hands where they aren't usually supposed to be. . . .

"Dylan?"

First her ribs. Then, when she leans forward, I'd circle her waist with my fingers, find the ticklish spot right where—

"Dylan?" She props her hands on her hips.

"Yes?" I blink, banishing my comparatively innocent fantasy.

"Are you turning around?" Her smile makes me suspect she's guessed the direction of my thoughts. It's a smile of discovery, timid, but with a burgeoning sense of power, the grin of a girl learning the influence she has over a boy. It wasn't what I set out to achieve this morning, but I'll take it. Ariel could use some empowerment, and I can use anything that makes her want to keep me around long enough for her to fall in love with me.

"Turning, turning." I offer her my back, giving her privacy, distracting myself from thoughts of dressing and, more important, *un*dressing by studying the paintings on the wall. The bold color and deft line make my brain squirm agreeably. Her work is technically excellent, with a whimsical, slightly morbid subject matter that I, for one, find charming. "These are wonderful."

"Thanks." She sounds nervous but pleased. "Some are really old, from when I was twelve. They stink, but I keep them up there. They remind me of how much I've learned."

"I like them all." I knew Ariel was an artist from my last turn through her life, but I didn't remember her work being so evocative. My Mercenary eyes functioned, but did they see?

I'm guessing the answer is no. If they did, I wouldn't have

overlooked the painting on the lower left. I remember it from when I was in this room before, skulking in the shadows, waiting for Juliet, but I wasn't drawn to it the way I am now. I cross to stand in front of the landscape, the familiarity of the windswept hill hitting me like a fist in the gut. It looks so much like *my* hill, the one where the human Romeo died and the monster rose in his place.

And the boy . . .

I lean closer, inspecting the delicate swirls of paint that form his hair and simple cloak. The face is too small to be recognizable, but it could be mine, the one I was born with, the one on the body that is at this very moment trapped by Ambassador magic in that mountain cave, rotten and raving with its bones showing through its rapidly deteriorating skin.

Now that my soul has left the specter, he is once again driven by the need to hunt me, to take my hand in his and reunite my body and spirit. He is a part of myself, left over from what I would have been, influenced by what I've become, and compelled by primal forces beyond human understanding to balance the cosmic equation I unbalanced when I became a Mercenary. The specter is a wretched thing because my soul is wretched. I never expected to see myself any other way, ever again.

But now . . .

"Who is this? In the painting?" I turn to find Ariel buttoning her jeans. Our eyes meet, and awareness thickens the air between us before I spin back around with a quick, "Forgive me."

"It's okay. I know you didn't . . ." She clears her throat. "He's no one. Just a boy I imagined."

A boy she imagined. A boy in a period cloak on a lonely

hill, shoulders bowed by shame and grief. It's probably a co-incidence. What else could it be? Still, it's hard to look away, even when a knock comes at the door and Ariel urgently orders me, "Under the bed. Hurry!"

"Tell her you're sick. Get her to call the school," I whisper, inspiration striking. "We'll go to the art museum in Santa Barbara."

"What?"

"Play sick, and we'll play hooky. I want to look at beautiful things together."

She shakes her head, but I can see that she's tempted. "I can't. I—"

"Ariel," her mom calls from out in the hall. "Are you awake? It's seven-fifteen."

"Just a second, Mom," Ariel calls. "Under the bed. Please!" she mouths to me as she backs away. I hit the floor and roll onto the dusty carpet beneath the bed just as the door opens and a sleepy-sounding Ariel wishes her mother "Good morning."

"Good morning."

"I thought you were going to sleep late, Mom."

"I was, but something woke me. I felt rested, so I decided to get up." She pauses before letting out a surprised, "Your purse! I thought you said you lost it."

"Um, no." Ariel's feet shift as she presumably turns to look at the purse lying in a saggy brown lump by the window. "I found it on the floor last night. I must have forgotten to take it with me."

"Well, that's good news." Her mom sighs. "Now I won't have to call the phone company during my break. One thing off the list."

"Yeah," Ariel says with a cough.

"So how are you? You look pale. Tired after your big night?"

"Yeah, a little. Tired and . . . kind of sick to my stomach."

Under the bed, I smile. The more time I spend with this girl, the more I like her. She's full of surprises. Even considering that some of them aren't pleasant, I'll take surprising over predictable any day.

"You're probably hungover," her mother says.

"I don't think so. I feel sick. Like the flu or something."

"That's what a hangover feels like, Ariel. That's why you should have one glass of wine, not four." The mother doesn't sound amused, or particularly sympathetic. "There won't be any more going out on school nights if this is what happens the day after."

"I know, Mom. I'm sorry." Her voice is so small and remorseful that I'm certain she's decided to give up on our adventure. But then she coughs. And clears her throat, and sniffs a sickly sniff. "I just . . . I really don't feel good. Could I stay home today? Just this one time?"

Her mother sighs, a tired exhalation ripe with defeat. I grin, sensing the battle is won. "All right. Since you haven't missed a day all year."

"Thanks so—"

"But if this happens again, there will be no more dates on school nights and we'll have to talk about a curfew."

"I understand. Thanks, Mom. You're the best."

"Right, right." She laughs beneath her breath. "Go ahead and get back into your pj's. I'll call the school and tell them you won't be there today."

"Okay."

"And I'll call Wendy and tell her not to pick me up since you won't be needing the car." I watch the mother's feet move away before pausing in the doorway and turning back. "Is there anything you need before I leave?"

"No," Ariel says. "I'm going to go back to sleep. I can warm up some soup if I get hungry later."

"All right. Since I'm up, I might as well head out and grab a few things at the store. Call my cell if you think of anything you want me to bring home tonight. Just remember I probably won't be back until after eleven."

"Right. Thanks, Mom. I . . . I really appreciate this. And last night."

"You're welcome. Call me later. I love you."

"Love you, too."

My next breath feels sharp in my lungs. *Love you.* The words are sweet when she says them, but a part of me is already dreading the day she'll say them to me. I need her love, but lying is becoming harder than it used to be, especially not knowing what will happen when I've fulfilled my mission. Juliet's nurse said she would take care of Ariel, but how can I trust her? The woman who spoke so easily about the fortunate nature of Ariel's murder in another reality?

Ariel's upside-down face appears to my left, peering into my hiding place. I rush to banish my scowl.

"I feel awful," she whispers. "I don't like to lie."

"It's for a good cause." I stay where I am, watching as she lies down on her belly and scoots under the bed beside me. I imagine how different this would feel if we were both on top of the bed instead of underneath it, how easily something childlike could grow adult possibilities. I clear my throat.

"Besides, a museum is twice as enlightening as anything going on in that school."

"True." She smiles. "And I've been *dying* to go. I haven't been in almost a year."

"I've never been. This will be my first time."

"Don't worry. I'll be gentle," she says, with a blush that makes her joke almost unbearably cute.

"Naughty."

Her blush deepens. "Yeah, well. I figure if you can't beat 'em . . ."

I laugh, a real laugh that soothes away the sharp feeling in my chest. "That's okay. You don't have to be gentle. I like it rough. Just don't make any bets involving my virtue. Only wastes of flesh do things like that."

"You're not a waste," she murmurs.

"Just stupid?"

"You're not stupid, either." She considers me with an intensity that makes me glad I'm hidden in the shadows. "That's what makes it so hard to understand."

"Understand what?"

"Why you made the bet in the first place."

I shrug. "Maybe I *am* stupid."

"Or maybe you're a different person."

I lie perfectly still but for the curl of my fingers into the dusty carpet. Could she know? On some level does she realize the truth?

"I mean, you're one person at school with your friends. You practically ignored me last week except at rehearsal," she says. "And then, when we're alone, you're completely different. Even the way you walk is different."

Ah. Not the truth, but she's getting warmer. "You're right."

"So which one is the real Dylan?"

Neither. The real Dylan has left the building. You're stuck with me, the thief of hearts, and I'm sorry for that. More than I thought I could be.

"I don't know," I say instead. "But I'd like more time as the person I am when I'm with you." I meet her eyes, but can't muster up a sappy smile. Pretty lies sound so ugly this morning. "Thank you for forgiving me."

"Thanks for forgiving me back."

There's a crawling feeling in my throat, a skip in the rhythm of my pulse. I feel . . . guilty? Yes, I think that's it. I know I should reach out, take her hand, make the most of this moment hiding in the shadows beneath her bed, when she's happy and open to a romantic gesture. But I can't. I can only nod and ask, "When do we leave?"

"Thirty minutes. Maybe an hour. As soon as my mom leaves for work."

She crosses her arms and lays her cheek on top. I do the same, forcing myself to watch her watch me, to whisper and plan, and to pretend the warmth growing between us isn't fueled by deception.

EIGHT

Ariel

I can't believe this. Any of it.

The past fourteen hours are a dream that keeps getting progressively more bizarre. First finding out about the bet, then the near disaster in the car, then Dylan acting as if he likes me—maybe even a lot, maybe even for real. And now this easy escape from my crushing routine. I can't believe it.

I can't believe I *undressed* with Dylan in the same room. I can't believe I've been flirting like it's my new job. I can't believe I conned my mother or that I'm skipping school or that I called the office and pretended to be Dylan's dad's girlfriend to keep him from getting detention. I can't believe Dylan and

I shared a large coffee and three sticky pink donuts, or that we listened to his favorite playlists and talked music the entire way down to Santa Barbara, or that he's made me smile more in a few hours than I have in months. Maybe longer.

If it weren't for the episode last night and the nightmare this morning, I'd think this was all some pretty dream I'm going to wake up from any second.

But it's not. It's real.

I'm really standing here in the Works on Paper wing. Dylan Stroud is really hovering over my right shoulder, staring at an Egon Schiele painting of a gaunt man with sunken cheeks and footless legs. He's really close enough for me to smell the detergent on his tight gray T-shirt. Close enough that his breath kisses my neck when he speaks.

"I like this." His voice is hushed. It's as if he feels it, that charge straight to the heart I get whenever I look at something by a master. Who would have imagined?

I guess *I* would have. Back when he sang that song for me at the spring formal rehearsal, I *did*. I believed he felt the way I felt, that books and music and art dug into his guts and rearranged his molecules and seemed more real to him than real life ever does. And maybe I was right. Maybe the way he acts at school is a cover to hide that part of himself that other people wouldn't understand. Because most people don't see the world the way we see it.

We. Could we be . . . we? Maybe. Today I say . . . maybe.

I still don't trust him. Not entirely. He's too different. He watches me like a stranger, like someone who hasn't sat across the aisle from me since first grade. We're having a great time, but a voice in my head warns me to be careful, to keep my distance. Still, distance isn't easy. Looking at art alone has always been a transporting experience, but looking at art with Dylan is completely . . . sexy.

I close my eyes, and my entire face starts to burn. I've never even *thought* that word, but since the moment Dylan crawled through my window this morning I've been *feeling* it. All my senses are heightened and conspiring against me. The sunlight slanting across the room, the warm, soapy smell of Dylan mingling with the old-book-and-older-paint smell of the art, the hint of coffee floating up the stairs from the café, and all the raw emotion hanging on the walls.

It's sensual, heady. Sexy.

It makes me want to turn around, wrap my arms around his neck, and press against him the way I did last night. I want him to kiss me again. I know it would be better than it was the first time. More authentic. Maybe even the most authentic thing I've ever felt.

"What do you think?" he asks.

"I love it." I turn my head and find his lips only inches from my cheek. I don't know whether to hold my breath or breathe deep, to pull back or give in.

"You don't think it's ugly? Disturbing?" His dark eyes flick to my lips. I know he's thinking about kissing me, too, and I start to worry that my heart might injure itself from all the slamming it's doing behind my ribs.

I shake my head. "No. It's real. It's beautiful."

"You're beautiful."

I tuck my chin, letting my hair fall over my ruined cheek. For a second I'd actually forgotten about the scars. I never forget about them. Never. That's why I'm wearing a billowy long-sleeved blue shirt and jeans even though I know it will get warm today. I always cover the scars on my arms; I always keep my hair arranged to conceal as much of my face as I can. I can't believe I let my guard down. Even for a second.

"Don't." His fingers trail up my throat, and my breath shudders out in a way that leaves no doubt about what he makes me feel. A part of me is ashamed, and demands I run before Dylan laughs and confesses this is all a prank.

But another part wonders . . .

I look up. He isn't laughing. "Don't hide. There's no reason to."

"Yes, there is," I whisper. "People stare."

"Have you ever thought they're staring for a different reason?" His fingers curl around the back of my neck, and my body hums like he's touched me everywhere, all at once. "Because you're too beautiful *not* to stare at?"

"No." I swallow, keenly aware that his lips are slowly moving closer. "I haven't."

"Well," he whispers. "Maybe *you're* dumber than you seem too." And then he kisses me, a soft brush of his lips against mine. It's feather-light and fleeting, and he's gone before I can even think about kissing him back, but it doesn't matter. It still feels like my soul is going to explode, like I'm going to shatter into a thousand pieces and all of them will grow wings and fly wild through the room.

"Come on. I want to see more." He takes my hand. After only a moment's hesitation, I let him. "Let's check out the special exhibit."

"We can't. It doesn't open until this weekend." I'd been both disappointed and relieved when I'd read the dates on the sign downstairs. I love Schiele's work, but a lot of it is on the . . . erotic side.

I stop walking at the closed door to the exhibit, holding

still when Dylan gives my arm a tug. "Really. It's not open to the public."

"And?"

"We'll get in trouble if we go inside. They might have an alarm on the door."

"They might." He looks over his shoulder, eyes glittering. "We'll never know unless we open it."

Something in my chest rumbles, like a motorcycle revving up. Exciting, wild, and *way* too similar to what I felt last night when we stole that bottle of wine. Daring is exhilarating, but it can also be dangerous. "The last time we broke the rules, I ended up drunk and forgetting things."

"No, the last time we broke the rules, we ended up having a lovely drive and eating some pink donuts with extra sprinkles," he says, urging me closer to the door. "We agreed to forget about that other time that I can't even remember because I've forgotten about it so completely."

He reaches for the handle, and the rev inside me builds to a roar. I look over my shoulder, noting the lack of cameras near the ceiling, half wishing the museum guard we saw in the other room would wander in and keep me from giving in to this reckless side of myself. But he doesn't, and when the door opens with a squeak—and no alarm—I let Dylan draw me inside the softly lit room.

The door snicks shut behind us, sealing us into a silence more private than that of the rest of the museum. This is ours, not to be shared. It makes the air taste better.

"See? Nothing to worry about." Dylan keeps hold of my hand as we walk toward the first set of paintings, older works that resemble that of Schiele's mentor, Gustav Klimt. There's a beautiful woman with red hair and piercing eyes, and several moody twilight landscapes. I take them in, trying to act like this is normal, holding hands with a boy, being one of two.

"And these are . . . very nice," he says.

I laugh at his disappointed tone. "They are." I lead the way deeper into the room. The exhibit is arranged in chronological order, and I know Schiele's darker work came later. I'm still nervous, but now that we're inside, I'm also excited. Looking at art up close and personal is so much better than seeing it in a book. "But I think you'll like his later work more."

"Why do you think that?"

I shrug. "Just a hunch."

We stop in front of a series of portraits of women. One is holding her skirts bunched in her hands, revealing a long stretch of thigh. Another sits with her legs spread and chin propped on her knee, both provocative and innocent at the same time. The last is of two women—one nude, one in a red dress. They're embracing, obviously lovers, but it isn't sexy. It's sad. Furtive and lonely. I can feel the ache the woman in the red dress feels. Her life has been hard, and now her heart is in danger. This could be the last time she ever holds the person she loves in her arms. I take a shaky breath, heaviness building behind my eyes.

"Your hunch is right." Dylan squeezes my hand. "They remind me of you."

"Really?" I turn to him, surprise banishing the rush of emotion. "Why?"

"I don't know." He angles his body closer to mine. "Why are you afraid? Why are your eyes so old and sad, pretty girl?"

My lips part, and for a second I think about lying. But I can't, not when he's gone to the trouble of really seeing me. I can't remember the last time anyone did that, if anyone ever has. "I guess I've seen more than I should." Or *heard* more, felt more. I swallow, trying not to think about the screaming things or my wrecked mind. I don't want to be broken and strange today. I want to be happy, a girl holding hands with a boy.

"This isn't just about the accident when you were little, is it?" He looks down at me with concern, but not pity. I'm glad. Concern is hard enough to handle.

I glance back at the paintings. "Not really, but it's related, I guess. The other stuff started right after the accident, when I was in the hospital trying to get better."

"Other stuff."

"I started . . . hearing voices. That no one else could hear. The doctors thought I was having a bad reaction to the morphine, but even after they took me off the medicine, the voices didn't go away." I cross my arms and stare at the girl with her head on her knee. She can't be more than fifteen, but she's seen her share of bad things. I can tell. She knows how I feel and gives me the courage to say, "I still hear voices sometimes, if I get really angry."

"What do they say?"

"I don't know. I can't understand them." I'm uncomfortable—very—but I can't seem to stop telling the truth now that I've started. "They just scream. They don't sound human."

I risk a glance at him from the corner of my eye, expecting to see him backing away from the crazy girl. But he's still close. Too close. I catch another whiff of his Dylan smell, and things begin to ache inside of me. I could get used to this. I could come to count on him being next to me, on having someone I can really talk to. I could come to care and need and maybe even love, and then, when he finds out how messed up I really am, the pain of losing him will be horrible. Unbearable.

Better to clue him in to the fact that I'm the Freak the kids at school think I am, and get it over with.

"I call them my episodes," I say, voice brittle as I force myself to break this fragile thing I want to cling to so badly. "I had one last night. I thought I saw something on the playground, like a ghost or . . . something. And then I got cold the way I do before I start to hear the voices. So I ran. I made it to a vineyard before the screaming started. I fell down and passed out in the mud, and when I woke up . . ."

My eyes slide closed. I feel like I'm going to throw up, but I'm not finished. I'll tell it all, and then I can walk to the bus station and start trying to figure out how to get my stupid, freakish self home.

"When I woke up, I'd wet my pants." I spit the words out like seeds. Swift. Efficient. "Just like in fourth grade. You remember that, right? Everyone knows the story of how the Freak became the Freak."

He doesn't say anything. Not a word. *Nothing,* for so long that the nothing feels like a weight that will crush me into Ariel juice on the floor. I open my eyes, braced for a sneer or a laugh or words that will make me feel smaller than I do already. But he doesn't say a thing. He just stares at me, a look on his face I can't pin down. Maybe disbelief. Maybe fear. Maybe a really bad case of déjà vu.

I'm having some of that again today. As wonderful as this morning has been, it has also been eerie. It's like I've lived it all before, and a part of me knows that Dylan and I aren't going to end well. That's why I made myself say what I said.

I *know* something's going to go wrong, and better that it happens sooner than later.

I wait for Dylan's eyes to give me a better idea of what he's thinking, but it's like he's a museum exhibit—frozen in time, never to change. Finally I have to break the silence. "So I guess you think I'm crazy for real now."

He flinches, runs his tongue between his lips, and then does the last thing I expect. He takes my hand again, and holds on tight. "I don't think you're crazy. I . . ."

"You what?"

"Screaming things." He says the words like he'd say *chair* or *car* or *donuts,* like something he could point out in a picture, something he understands.

I cling to his hand, the feeling that something is about to be born in the space between us making my heart race. What will he say? Is there any way that he could understand? No one ever has. I assumed no one ever *could,* but maybe . . . His eyes meet mine, and I don't know whether to laugh or cry, to celebrate that I've found a similar creature, or to mourn the fact that there's a person alive with eyes sadder than mine.

"I want to tell you something." He licks his lips again. "But I . . ."

"You can tell me." I take his other hand, and wish I had the guts to put my arms around him the way I want to. "I won't think less of you."

He shakes his head. "Yes, you will. You—"

Before he can finish, the door to the exhibit squeaks open and an impatient voice demands, "What are you kids doing in here? This is a closed exhibit."

It's a man with gray-streaked brown hair wearing a browner suit. He isn't the museum guard we saw earlier, but he's obviously someone official. And angry. I pull away from Dylan, dropping his hands, as if not touching him will somehow reduce the amount of trouble we're about to get into.

Dylan edges in front of me. "Sorry. We didn't realize."

"The sign on the door says No Entry." The man narrows his eyes and takes another step into the room. "Why aren't you two in school?"

"We go to the college?" The terror inspired by the possibility of getting caught ditching makes my lie come out as a question.

The man snorts. "You look like you're twelve years old."

"We're freshmen," Dylan says, his lie smoother than mine. "Art history majors. That's why we wanted to see the exhibit."

"So you're some of Professor King's kids?"

"Right." Dylan nods. "The professor's a big Schiele fan."

The man smiles, a smug, condescending, old-person grin that makes me feel about three years old. "There is no Professor King. And I'm calling your parents."

My stomach turns to lead, and I think I hear Dylan cuss beneath his breath, but I can't be sure. My heart is beating too loud in my ears. My mom is going to kill me. *Really,* kill me. She was cool last night and this morning, but she will *not* be cool with the fact that I lied to her and played sick so I could skip school and go to Santa Barbara.

I'm a walking dead girl. All that's left is for my mom to come retrieve my body.

The man waves us toward the door. "Follow me to the office. We'll call your parents and–"

"Run!" Dylan grabs my arm and hauls me in the opposite direction. I trip, but he helps me along beside him until I find my balance. When I do, I don't hesitate. I sprint, keeping pace with him as he dashes for the emergency exit on the other side of the room. Suit Man shouts for us to "Stop!" but we don't. We dart around glass cases displaying some sculpture I wish I could have looked at—I didn't know Schiele sculpted—and behind us I hear dress shoes begin to slap the wood floor. I have a split second to wonder what will happen if Suit Man catches us, and then Dylan is lunging for the door with the red and white stripes on the handle.

An alarm blares, but I don't hesitate. Who cares about the alarm? We're already caught. We can't get into any worse trouble, and we might just get away. These stairs have to lead somewhere.

Dylan grabs the black railing and swings around the first landing, looking over his shoulder to make sure I'm close behind before pounding down the concrete steps with a *bum-bum-bum-bum* that echoes in the stairwell. I follow him, letting my feet fly without thinking about the next step, carried along by adrenaline and the delicious rush of running from something I actually have a chance of escaping. It's exhilarating, a high that makes me want more, more, faster, faster.

I catch up with Dylan and pass him on the second landing. He laughs as I beat him to the main level, and I giggle like a madwoman as I lead the race down a shiny, tiled hallway, toward a set of glass double doors with sunshine and green grass on the other side.

Dimly I hear Suit Man shout again, but his voice is far away, and we are nearly, nearly, almost—

"Free!" I shout as I burst into the light, another laugh bubbling up as I spin to see Dylan dashing through the door behind me. He grabs me around the waist and swings me in a circle, pressing a breathless kiss to my cheek. My feet hit the ground again, but on the inside I'm still floating.

"Come on." He pulls me toward State Street. "Before he sends someone in better shape."

I jog after him, holding tight to his hand, his kiss burning through my skin and setting me on fire as I realize that—for the first time in my life—I'm not running alone.

NINE

Romeo

"And a Coke, please," I tell the man working the snack shack by the beach.

He passes over the drink and four fish tacos with extra salsa, and I press the last of my money into his hand, happy that I've spent all of Dylan's cash on pleasures of the soul and the flesh.

Food and art and a beautiful girl. It is . . . good.

I scan the beach, and find Ariel spreading out the sleeping bag we pulled from Dylan's trunk. She looks up at me and smiles, and I have to pause to catch my breath. She is . . . She just . . . She shines. Her blue eyes are bright and clear, and the late afternoon sun catches her hair and spins it into gold. The tip of her nose and her mouth are pink from our walk down to the pier and back, and when we kissed with our feet in the water, I could taste the sun on her lips.

She is also . . . good. More than good. And I am wooing her, winning her.

Barely one day down, and she's already *so close* to loving me. I can feel it when she holds my hand, when she watches my face when she thinks I'm watching the road, when she reaches up to take the box of tacos and our fingers brush and she smiles that easy smile that looks so good on her. I swear I can practically feel the love bubbling up inside of her.

"Thanks." She scoots over, making room for me on the slick green fabric.

"Welcome." I settle beside her, close enough that our knees touch. Even that small contact is enough to make my blood rush faster. Sometime between this morning and our early dinner on the beach, I've gone from the seducer to the seduced. I don't know if it's because hers are the first lips to touch mine in seven hundred years, or if she's the idiot savant of kissing, but Ariel's allegedly unskilled lips are quickly becoming an addiction. A compulsion.

I steal a kiss as I grab a taco from the box, surprised to feel electricity jolt through my core in response. I keep thinking I've imagined it, the way she affects me. "I only had enough money for one drink," I say as I pass the Coke over. "Hope you don't mind my germs."

"I don't mind," she says. "I think I have your germs by now."

My smile slips, and I almost drop my taco into my lap. Juliet said something so similar when she was wearing this body.

And then she kissed me like we were young and in love and there was nothing in the world but the two of us and more raw feeling than two bodies could hold. In that moment, the misery of my dead flesh cut deeper than it had in centuries. I would have sold my soul for lips that could feel. Even if the kiss was a lie to protect the boy Juliet really loved. Even if I had no soul left to sell.

"Dylan?" Ariel touches my wrist, her fingers cool despite the warmth of the day. "You okay?"

"Wonderful." I glance up, and try to look it.

She lifts her chin, squinting against the sun as she considers me. "No."

"No?"

"No." She unwraps my taco, rewraps it so only one end is exposed, and places it back in my hand, and I suddenly want to cry all over again. I duck my head and laugh instead, but my laughter sounds desperate, sad.

Ariel turns back to her supper, carefully peeling the silver wrapping, giving me a moment before she says, "You never told me what you were going to say in the museum."

"No, I didn't." I take a bite, focusing on the burst of lime and the earthy taste of smoky fish. I don't want to think about things that scream and scream without ever being heard.

Well, the Mercenaries assume they can't be heard. But Ariel hears . . . something. Maybe she's right and the voices in her head are a product of madness. Or maybe the lost souls have found an ear that can hear. According to the friar, I wasn't the first Mercenary outcast to be banished to the specter of his soul. There have been others throughout the ages. Many of their bodies must have turned to dust by now, leaving nothing but their spirit behind. The friar assured me that to become a lost soul was to be without any way to interact with the world. But what if he's wrong? What if . . .

"Are you going to tell me?"

"Maybe." I take another bite, savoring the taste. "If you'll play too."

"Play what?" she asks, caution edging into her tone for the first time in hours.

"Tell Me True. We take turns telling each other things we've never told anyone else," I say, inventing the game as I go along. Nothing brings people together like a good secret. "And the last person to run out of secrets is the winner."

"What will I win?"

I laugh as I pluck my second taco from the box. "I wouldn't be so sure of yourself. I have a *lot* of secrets."

"Okay. Then you go first," she says. "I already told you a secret at the museum."

"You've never told anyone about the . . . screaming?"

She shakes her head. "No. Not if you don't count my mom. Or my psychiatrist."

"Moms and psychiatrists never count." I lick a drop of salsa off my thumb, and wonder which of Dylan's secrets I should share. I pick one at random that I think will suit the occasion, but when I open my mouth, something unexpected comes out. "I used to have a brother."

I blink. Where did that come from? Until this morning, I hadn't thought of Nicolo in . . . centuries. If you'd asked my Mercenary self if I ever had a brother, I don't think I would have known for sure. I certainly wouldn't have cared. But now . . . Thinking of that lost boy makes my food stick in my throat.

"Really?" Ariel asks. "I didn't know that."

I take a moment, checking Dylan's memories, making sure my story won't disagree with any history Ariel might be aware of. No. Dylan and his father didn't move to Solvang until Dylan was in first grade, and since then Dylan and Ariel haven't spoken more than a few times. They certainly haven't shared any family secrets. It's safe for me to tell Ariel about Nicolo, though I have no idea why I want to.

I guess I simply want to tell *someone.* Before it's too late. I've never spoken about my brother to anyone, not even Juliet. By the time I met her, Nicolo had been dead ten years, and I'd learned to pretend that I didn't miss him like some necessary part of me that had been cut away.

"Really." I stare out at the frothy sea, not sure I can look in Ariel's eyes while telling this ancient story that suddenly feels so fresh. "He was my twin brother. He died when we were five years old."

"I'm so sorry." Her cool hand finds mine. "What happened?"

"He had a fever." I close my eyes, and I swear I can see him, the way he looked at the end, red-faced and glassy-eyed and rambling about monsters no one else could see. "Nothing could bring it down. He was dead in two days."

She squeezes my hand. "What was his name?"

"Nicolo." I pull in a shaky breath. It's so wonderfully awful to say his name out loud. How could I have forgotten him, how could I have betrayed his memory for so long?

"What was he like?" she asks, as if sensing how much I need to talk about him.

"He was wonderful, my father's favorite. We were both so little, but it was already clear who the better brother was going to be. Nicolo was brilliant and good. Even when no one was watching." I bite the inside of my cheek, refusing to lose control. I don't deserve to. "He would give me his dessert anytime I asked for it, and let me ride the pony we shared first even though the animal hated me. I dug my heels in too hard and tugged at Nissi's mane. She only tolerated me out of love for Nicolo." I pause before adding, in the closest thing to a joking tone as I can manage, "My father had a lot in common with that horse."

"So things were bad after?" she asks. "With your dad?"

I nod. "He hated me. For living, when I should have been the one to die." I take a deep breath. Let it out slowly. I wish I could tell her more. I wish I could tell her how cold Father was to Mother after Nicolo's death, as if he blamed her, too. I wish I could tell her how—after a decade of Father's cruelty—my mother became a shade of her former self, how she died the day I was banished, how Father blamed me for that as well.

But I can't. There are aspects of my story that don't mesh with Dylan Stroud's life. And there are truths too painful to speak.

We're quiet for a moment, both of us staring at the sea and the white birds swooping up and down on the salty wind. Finally she whispers, "I'm sorry."

"You're not going to tell me that I'm crazy? That of course my father doesn't wish I were dead in my brother's place?"

"You could be crazy." She sets the box of tacos on the ground, her second one untouched. This game has killed my appetite as well. I toss the last of my uneaten dinner into the box beside hers. "I mean, I know I've underestimated how much my mom loves me, so I'd like to think . . . But . . . I've heard some things about your dad."

Dylan's dad is a drunk with eager fists, but I'd take him over my own any day. Dylan has some good memories of his father—trips to the beach when he was little, shared beers on the couch watching the Stanley Cup, his sixteenth birthday, when his dad gave him a car and the freedom he knew Dylan craved. My own father was simply brutal.

He taught me to fight by nearly killing me with his sword. I survived living with him by learning to be quick with a lie, to say whatever he wanted to hear before he banished me to my room for a day or more, with orders forbidding my mother or the servants to bring me food. He taught me that hell could be a place on earth and that the devil was a man with a thick brown beard and eyes that relished my pain.

I loved Juliet, but I would be lying if I said the fact that she was the daughter of my father's sworn enemy wasn't part of the reason I fell for her so quickly. I knew marrying a Capulet would drive my father mad. Juliet and I fantasized about her cold mother and my wretched father dropping dead from shock when they found out what we'd done. We imagined how much better life would be when it was only her father left; the way my mother's heart would heal when I was the new lord of the Montague estate. If I hadn't killed Juliet's cousin, maybe our dreams would have become a reality.

Instead I betrayed her and proved myself as monstrous as the man who sired me.

"I'm sorry. For saying anything about your dad," Ariel says, making me realize I've been silent too long. "Are you mad?"

"Of course not." I shrug. "Word gets around in a small town."

"Yeah. It does." She scoots closer, presses a kiss to my

cheek, and whispers, "If you need to get away, you can come to my house. Anytime. No matter what."

Before I realize what's happening, before I can talk them down, tears prick at my eyes. It's a little kindness, but it feels like so much more. It feels like being brought in from the cold. It's proof that Ariel is the person I see when I look at her, someone good. The Ambassador is wrong. This girl could never be evil. Never.

I turn to her, full of some emotion I can't name. Gratitude? Respect? Kinship? My lips part, but I can't think of the words to let her know that I feel . . . something for her. Something real. As impossible as it seems.

"Are you crying?" Her eyes open wide. "I'm so sorry. I didn't mean to—"

"Don't be sorry." I take her face in my hands and pull her to me, kissing her with all that feeling I can't name.

My tongue slips past her lips, and I taste salsa and something sharp and sweet that is Ariel's taste, and then I'm beyond taste or smell or even touch. She wraps her arms around my neck, pulling me in tight, and I swear I feel my soul brush against hers. I expand beyond the boundaries of Dylan's body, out until I am the waves crashing on the beach, the sun shining in her hair, the wind that sweeps over our skin. I am everything and nothing and exist only because this girl presses her heart to mine.

My chest is unbearably tight, and for a breathless moment— as Ariel shifts her thighs and slides into my lap—I feel I might die from the beauty of being so close to her, from the beauty of her fingers threading through my hair, her weight settling into mine, her lips moving to my throat, where she kisses the place where my pulse rushes beneath my skin.

"God, I love you," I whisper, and come crashing back into my body with a suddenness that makes me gasp. I don't know what's more shocking—that I've called on the god I don't believe in, or that the lie I told felt so much like the truth.

At least, in the moment, it did. Now, staring up into her face, watching suspicion banish the flush from her cheeks, I'm keenly aware of my deception. I feel some soft feeling for her, but I don't *love* her. I don't love anything, not the way a real person does. I am a selfish, bitter, nasty creature out to save his own skin. Whatever I'm feeling, it's undoubtedly born from selfishness and fear, with a hearty dose of lust thrown into the mix. And Ariel is too clever to believe my lie.

She slides off my lap, swiping the back of her hand across her lips to wipe the taste of me away. She shakes her hair around her shoulders and tips her chin down, drawing the curtain between us as her hands fist in her lap and squeeze.

I curse myself beneath my breath. I should have waited; I should have been careful to pace myself and the progression of our false romance. Now I could have ruined everything, all because I let pleasure overwhelm my purpose. I'm like a hormone-addled boy, swept away by a kiss.

"I'm sorry," I say, knowing I have to say something.

"Why are you doing this?" She hunches her shoulders, and for a second I think she's going to cry. Instead, when her words come, they are cold and hard with edges that will cut me if I listen too closely. "Why did you come to my house this morning? Why are we here right now? What do you *want?*"

"I want to be with you."

"Why? Why now?" She looks up, and her eyes make me breathless again.

She is so completely . . . herself. I stared at this face for hours when Juliet was inhabiting Ariel's body, but it's like looking at a different person. I never realized how much difference a soul could make, though I should have. No matter what body she wore, I always knew Juliet on sight. I didn't need the golden light hovering in her aura to point my former love out in a crowd. I'm beginning to think it would be that way with Ariel, that even if she looked at me through different eyes, in a different skin, I would know her.

And fear her a little, even if she didn't hold my future in her hands. There's something about her that makes me feel like I'm not nearly as clever as I'd like to believe. The girl . . . gets to me.

"Why?" she demands again.

"Because I like you." I do. I like her. I like the way she kisses my cheek so softly one moment and pins me with her ruthless stare the next. I like the way she makes me certain she's a fragile thing in need of protection, then turns around and fills me with giddy laughter and nameless dread.

"That's not what you just said," she whispers.

"I know." I reach for a napkin, buying time wiping my fingers while I think of what to say. I need a pretty lie, but the only thing that comes to me is the truth. "I like kissing you too much. My lips got away from me."

"So you don't love me."

"Maybe not. I don't know. I . . . I've never felt this way before." I meet her eyes—trying to gauge if the confused-lover routine is buying me back a degree of trust—and find her studying me with an intensity that makes me fight the urge to squirm. "What about you?"

"What *about* me?" she asks, as wary as she was last night on the playground.

Shit. I wet my lips and try to laugh, but fail and end up covering my awkwardness with a shrug. "Nothing. Never mind." I force a smile. "I just wanted to know if you'll go to the dance with me on Friday."

Now it's her turn to blink. "You want to go to the dance?"

"I want to go to the dance with *you*," I correct her. "It could be fun, right?"

"But I thought you . . ." She studies her hands. "I heard you talking to Jason at practice. I thought you two were going to leave right after you sing your solo. Don't you have a gig?"

"I'll cancel it. If, you know . . ." I watch her, but she gives no sign if I'm on the right track. I take a breath and soldier on, not knowing what else to do. "I'd be happy to cancel it if you can put up with me stepping on your feet for an entire night."

She narrows her eyes. "This isn't a *Carrie* thing, is it?"

"Who?" Carrie? I search Dylan's memories but can't find any information on a girl named Carrie. But he's had his share of casual encounters. There's a chance he was with a Carrie and doesn't remember her name. *Shit again.* I shake my head, having no choice but to confess my ignorance. "I don't know Carrie. Is she a friend of yours?"

"No, she's– You really don't know *Carrie*?" Her lips thin and curve. I'm so glad to see her smile that I couldn't care less that I'm the source of her amusement.

"No."

"*Carrie*," she says, as if repetition will penetrate my thickness. "You know, the Stephen King book about the freak girl who goes to the dance with a cute guy, but it's all a joke and the popular kids dump blood all over her and she ends up killing people with her mind powers?"

"I never read it."

"Really?"

"I stopped reading books a while back." Like, two hundred years back, when my ability to empathize with man's condition deteriorated to the point where I couldn't understand why the characters were making the choices they did, or why I should care if they lived or died or found their happy ending. For me, happiness was the electric moment before a new Mercenary convert drew his or her knife across their loved one's throat, that shining instant when I wasn't the most dreadful creature in the room.

"But it sounds good." I push the dark memories away. There's nothing I can do to change my past. Dwelling on it is a waste of time.

"It is good. Sad, but good," she says. "There's an old movie, too. I've got it at my house. My mom and I watch it every Halloween. You can borrow it if you want."

"Let's go watch it now." I grab the taco box and stuff the last of our trash inside. "We still have time before your mom gets home." I stand, but Ariel stays seated, peering up at me in confusion. "What?"

"You never answered my question," she says.

"You never answered mine, and I asked first."

She licks her lips, and then presses them together. For a second I think she's going to say no, and unexpected disappointment flashes through me. I asked her in order to deflect attention from our love talk, but I can't deny I like the idea of swaying in the dark with her. It would be a nice way to spend the last hours before I leave my borrowed body.

"Okay," she says.

"Is that a yes?"

"Yes. I'll go to the dance with you," she says. "But if it's a joke, I swear I—"

"It's not a joke." I come to my knees beside her and stare deep into her eyes, making sure there's no way she can miss the truth I'm about to speak. "You are not a freak. You are beautiful and clever and very enjoyable to be around. When you're not mad at me."

She rolls her eyes. "Right, but you—"

"And I'm not one of the shining people," I say, refusing to let her brush me off. "I'm a choir dork who wears a lot of black and drives a crappy car."

"No one thinks you're a dork."

"No, they think I'm a bad boy with a dad who knocks me around and the front man for a band named Demon Biscuit. And that was *my* idea. I thought that was cool," I say, smiling when she laughs. "I'm a bigger freak than you'll ever be. I honestly don't know why I'm not ostracized by humanity."

"I do. You're confident and a great singer . . . and the hottest guy in school."

I sit back down, the need to be next to her a compulsion I don't want to resist. "You think I'm hot?"

"Duh," she whispers, then adds with a blush, "And you're an amazing kisser."

"Takes one to know one."

"Right." Her laugh puffs at my lips, making me ache, but I don't close the distance between us. The only thing better than kissing Ariel is waiting to kiss her, those moments of delicious anticipation when I know she's about to sweep through me and empty me of everything but light and desire. "I'm an *inexperienced* kisser." Her lashes spread across her pink cheeks, and I barely resist the urge to kiss her eyelids. I want to kiss

{127}

her everywhere, taste every inch of her skin, memorize every knobby elbow and gentle curve. "Last night was my first kiss."

"Is that your Tell Me True?" She nods, and I lift my hand to her hair, running a lock through my fingers, marveling at how soft it is. "So it's my turn again." She tips her head back, a silent invitation to kiss her. I bring my mouth to hers, but stop just before we touch, to whisper my lie against her lips. "I don't care if I ever kiss anyone else," I say, refusing to feel guilty, knowing I'm making her happy. "You are . . ."

"What?" she whispers.

"A revelation." And that part is not a lie. She *is* a revelation.

When she kisses me, I taste truth and beauty and all the good things I was certain were beyond my reach. But they aren't, not with her. With her, I am . . . better. Still not good, but farther from evil. I wrap my arms around her and pull her close, and for the first time, I wonder if maybe . . . if I had the time . . . and the chance . . .

Maybe I could actually be worthy of her love.

INTERMEZZO TWO

V<small>ERONA</small>, 1304

Juliet

The nightmares rend my sanity with tiny demon claws, but still I fight to stay asleep. I fight, but even in dreams the smell reaches me—the sweet, musty, mineral scent of salvation. Water. *Water.*

I wake with a start that sends agony shooting through my stiff muscles.

The world inside the tomb is still as black as pitch, and my aching bones howl as I roll to the right side of my prison, but I don't let fear or pain distract me. I reach out, find the trickle of water through the marble with shaking fingers, and press my mouth to the stone. I am so weak, my soul clinging to my body by a few rapidly unraveling threads, but the water is an inspiration.

I run my tongue across the rock and taste hope. I purse my lips and suck, greedy and shameless, until the silence outside my grave is broken by a chuckle near the source of the life-giving water I drink.

Life-giving . . . if the friar hasn't poisoned it.

I scuttle to the far side of the tomb, pressing my hands over my mouth, stifling the scream swelling inside me. I pull my legs into my chest, scraping my knees as I move. There is just enough room for me to ball my body into the fetal position, to seek protection in the most primitive, helpless way a human being can.

"Juliet?" My name becomes a filthy thing when he speaks it. His evil permeates the stone, washes over my body in oily waves that make me tremble. "Speak to me, my dear. Let me know that you are well."

I tuck my head, squeeze my eyes closed, and pray for sleep. But sleep is far from me now. The water set things moving in my mind that won't be so easily stilled.

"I thought you would be thirsty. I've tried to move the stone, but it is too heavy for one old man," he says. "We must wait for Romeo."

Romeo. The first time I lived through this day, the friar pulled me from the grave to witness Romeo's seemingly life-less body crumpled on the floor in the hall of the tomb. The friar said the messenger had lost his way on the road and Romeo had never received our letter. Romeo had had no knowledge of the plan to fake my death and had assumed I had truly drunk poison rather than be wed to Paris. That's why he had taken poison as well, and lay dead on the cold earth.

I can remember the rage and pain and misery and helplessness I felt. I can remember how empty the world seemed without the light of my love, how easily the decision was made, how smoothly his dagger slipped from its sheath. I shoved the blade into my breast without the slightest hesitation. The agony of my heart bursting inside of me was a cruel blessing. Then, death had seemed the only choice.

Is that still their plan? For Romeo to play dead and trick me into committing suicide? If so, then why is the friar here now? Why does he pretend he lacks the strength to move the stone? He is a Mercenary. He has the strength to lift my entire sarcophagus off the floor. So why . . .

"Juliet. Please . . . I know you are awake. I hear you crying." I bite my tongue, stilling the sobs I hadn't realized were escaping. "I fear for you, my girl. I fear your mind has been touched by this terrible risk we've taken."

I pick at the flaking skin on my lips, the sting as I pull a strip of dead flesh free helping me focus through my fear. The plan must have changed. He and Romeo must have a different plot. But this time I will be ready for them. I won't go quietly. I won't go at all. I will live to bring what goodness I can to the world. It's what Ben would want. Ben, who would never hurt or deceive, who loved me so well in such a short time, whom I will hold in my heart when terror threatens to overcome me.

I pull his face to the front of my mind, and imagine I am looking into his eyes as I whisper, "I am awake." My voice is hoarse and small, but the friar hears me. I know he does.

"Juliet?"

Who else would it be, you monster? How many other girls have you buried alive this week? I dig my fingernails into my palms and let out a shuddering breath, shocked by how close the words came to leaping from my mouth.

I can't let him realize I know what he is. I must let him assume I'm still an innocent young girl and he my trusted confessor, for as long as possible. I must use his ignorance of my true experience to my advantage. It's my only weapon, my only hope.

"Yes, Father," I say, trembling. "I am so afraid."

"Don't be afraid, my child. I am here. I will stay with you and be certain you emerge from this misery." He says the right words, but I hear the caution in his tone. He senses something isn't right; I can feel it.

I'm an Ambassador no longer, but there is something supernatural left inside me. I pull my knees in tighter, imagine myself a nut with a shell hard enough to protect my secrets.

"Please," I whimper, trying to think nothing but what I thought when I was in this place the first time. I am terrified that my duplicity will color my voice. "Get me out. Please."

"I can't. I lack the strength. But Romeo will help me. He should be here soon. Unless . . ."

"Unless what?" I sob, heart racing. This is it. Whatever he says next, it's my clue as to how to avoid death in the tomb a second time.

"Did you communicate with him, Juliet? After I left you with the sleeping draft?"

"No," I say without a second's hesitation. It's the truth. I spoke to no one after my final confession to the friar. I went to my room, changed into the blue gown I wore the day Romeo and I were married, said one final prayer, and took the poison.

The friar grunts. A sound of dismay? Or disbelief?

"I didn't. I swear it. What has happened? Is he well?" I ask, knowing Romeo's welfare would still be utmost in my mind, even now, when *I* am the one buried alive.

After a brief pause, the friar says, "I don't know. We were to meet at dawn on the road outside Verona. But when I arrived, he wasn't there."

"What?" It's a lie. Isn't it?

"I waited for several hours," he says. "But Romeo never came. I asked about him at the tavern and on the plaza where his friends often stand idle, but no one had word. I sent a second messenger to where he said he'd be hiding, bidding Romeo to come straight to the Capulet tomb, but it has been several hours now, and . . . I fear something has happened to the boy."

"Oh no. No!" I bury my face in my hands, the tears coming easily. My mind and body are fragile, and I have plenty of things to cry about, though I couldn't care less if Romeo has abandoned the friar.

If Romeo has come to his senses in this new version of the past and fled the Mercenaries, it's best for everyone. Well, everyone . . . except me. But I will find a way to escape. I must. Because even if Romeo is gone and the friar's mission to convert another Mercenary has failed, he won't set me free. He'll let me die here. For his own entertainment, if nothing else.

"I'm sorry, child. But there may still be hope. Perhaps—"

"No, there is no hope," I say, bitterness thick in my voice. My plan is half-formed and impulsive, but there's no time for second-guessing. "He's gone. He regrets our marriage. He told me so the morning after . . . The morning we . . ." I break down, sobbing hysterically. There's barely enough water left in my body to make tears, but I don't let that stop me. I weep as one betrayed, one violated in the worst way a lover can violate another. I weep as if Romeo has stolen my heart and tossed it onto the side of the road, a thing of such little value, it isn't worthy of the space it takes up in his saddlebag.

"Shh, shh, my girl. Surely you are mistaken. Romeo loves you. Truly. With all his heart and soul."

"No, he isn't ready for marriage. He confessed it to me," I say. "I thought he would come to his senses when he saw I was willing to tempt death to stay faithful to our vows, but . . ."

"This is true, Juliet?"

"It is." I make a desperate sound—part scream, part sob, part cry of pain. "And I wish I could kill him for it!"

I dissolve into tears again, but more quietly this time, straining to hear the friar's response, wondering if he will take the bait. He's been courting Romeo, believing Romeo to be, between the two of us, the most easily swayed to murder. But I could serve his purpose just as well—if I am willing to kill my soul mate, to slay Romeo and swear myself to the Mercenaries.

In order for me to do either, he must set me free. And when he does, I will find a way to safety. I can do it. If I keep myself surrounded by people, he won't have the opportunity to kill me. Mercenaries won't reveal themselves in a public place. They prefer to conduct their business—and their torture—in private.

"It is a sin to even think such things," he finally says.

"I don't care." I summon as much passion as possible, though my body shakes with exhaustion. "I don't!"

"Juliet, quiet. You will hurt yourself."

"No. *I* will hurt *him.* Find someone to lift the stone. I will hunt him down and—"

"Silence." The sudden hatred in his tone makes me flinch. "I feel you, girl. I feel your lies."

My skin goes cold. "Wh-what?"

"Where is he? You *know* where he is," the friar hisses. "And if you want to live to see another sunrise, you will tell me. Now."

I cringe, wishing I could seep into the stone beneath me and disappear. Because I have nothing to tell him, nothing but a scrap of a nightmare that threatens to dissolve completely if I examine it too closely.

But it's all I have. My only chance.

And so I make another confession to this dark priest. "I've seen Romeo in a vision," I whisper. "He's betrayed you. Nurse is making him an Ambassador."

TEN

Ariel

I'm half awake, half asleep, floating in that in-between place when you're awake enough to know you're dreaming but asleep enough that the dream seems real. I'm with the beautiful boy on the hill again. This time we're alone, lying side by side, holding hands, bare legs tangled in the tickly grass. The sun is warm on our faces and the air is sweet and fresh, and I'm so happy, I'm not sure I'm capable of being happier. I want to stay here forever, on this hillside, our little piece of heaven.

Or hell.

The man in the robe, and his giant, bloody fingers, flash through my mind. I remember the way the ground opened up and pulled the boy under. Fear tries to break through the bliss. I know I should warn him, but my lips won't move. I'm frozen, mesmerized by the feel of his toes curled around my calf. I've never touched another person like this, so easy and relaxed, but sensual at the same time.

I wonder if this is what it's like to have a lover, and my belly flutters.

I tell myself it's just a foot and a leg, not that big a deal, but my body won't listen. My skin hums, and my insides melt as his thumb rubs back and forth across the back of my hand. I hold my breath, praying he'll roll over and kiss me, press me into the grass with his weight until we're even more tangled up in each other and I forget that terrifying things exist.

"I love being with you," I whisper. "I never want to leave."

"I love you." The words make me roll my head his way. When I do, I'm not surprised to see Dylan's eyes in the boy's face. My mind is mixing them together. The boy's hand feels like Dylan's too, and his voice is the same husky mumble. "I do, you know. Even if I don't know it yet."

I smile. "You're a dream."

"Am I?" he asks, a twinkle in his eyes. "Maybe you're the dream."

"I don't care who's dreaming, as long as we never wake up."

"Agreed." He shoots me a look that makes me shiver, and I suddenly can't wait for him to come to me. I roll over, my hair spilling around his face as I find his lips. I kiss him, and he moans into my mouth as his hand slides down my back, lingering at my waist, squeezing my hip, making me wish I were brave enough to let the need I feel when he touches me lead the way. I want to pull my soft, gray dress over my head while he looks up at me from his place on the ground and decides what part of me he's going to—

"Ariel? Are you awake?" A distant voice echoes across the mountain.

The dream world goes fuzzy around the edges. The grass and sun fade away, until there's only the black behind my eyes. I expect to feel sad to leave the boy, but it's hard to feel sad when I'm so warm and my blood is rushing so fast and I wake up to find Dylan's lips on mine.

Or I guess *my* lips are on *his*.

He's lying on the couch, and I'm halfway on top of him, our legs entwined, his hand at the small of my back, my hand sliding under his shirt. I feel his bare skin hot against my fingers and break off the kiss with a wobbly breath. The room is dark, and a few feet away the credits are rolling at the end of *Carrie*. We must have fallen asleep.

"Are you–"

"Yes," I whisper. "I'm awake."

"But you weren't a second ago."

I pull my hand from under his shirt, my face so hot I'm afraid I'll catch fire. "No. I wasn't."

He smiles. "You were sleep-kissing."

"I guess." I'm hyperaware of how close we are, but uncertain how to gracefully disengage. If only I had more experience waking up on top of a gorgeous boy. Or more experience being this close to a member of the opposite sex, *period*.

"I *know*," he says. "I kept saying your name and you didn't answer, and then . . ."

"Then what?"

"Nothing." He shrugs. "It's no big deal."

"Tell me. Or I'll be even more embarrassed."

"You shouldn't be embarrassed." He wraps his arms around my waist, holding me tight when I try to pull away.

After a moment, I relax. His body feels too good to fight,

and beneath the awkwardness, there is an unexpected . . . familiarity. We fit, Dylan and me. "Please, I want to know."

"You bit me," he says, voice husky. "Just a little bit. On my neck."

"Ohmygod." I glance down to see the faint imprint of teeth marks on his skin, and humiliation steals my breath away. Or maybe it's the way he's looking at me—with that light in his eyes that tells me I'm not the only one who thinks we fit together *very* nicely—that makes it hard to breathe. "I'm so sorry."

"I'm not." His hands slide beneath the hem of my shirt. "You can bite me anytime."

"You like being bitten?"

"I like anything you do to me."

Oh my. I lick my lips. "I was asleep. I've never bitten anyone before."

"So you don't think you have any latent sadistic tendencies?"

I let out a shaky laugh as his hands slide from my waist to the base of my ribs. "You sound disappointed," I murmur, my mouth drifting closer to his.

"Well . . ." His wicked grin makes my nerves sizzle. "I told you I liked it rough, didn't I?"

"Excuse me?" comes a shocked voice from the kitchen, killing the joking response on my lips. My mom. She's home. *Oh god!*

"Ariel? What's going on in here?"

I peek over the back of the couch and try to look innocent as I subtly unwind my legs from Dylan's. "Hi, Mom. You're home early." I sound guilty, and the way Mom's arms are crossed and her fingers are digging into her yellow scrubs isn't a good sign.

Beside me, Dylan drops his feet to the ground and tugs his gray T-shirt back around his waist. A quick hand through his hair, and no one would guess he's been doing what we've been doing. If only I could say the same. I can feel my hair fuzzing around my head, and my lips are still hot and puffy. My mom doesn't date much, but I'm sure she remembers what a girl who's been making out looks like.

Oh man. This is going to be bad. What do I say? How to explain what she heard?

I pull in a breath, but before I can speak, Dylan stands and circles the couch with an outstretched hand. "Hi, Mrs. Dragland. I'm Dylan. Ariel and I went out last night. Sorry I didn't come inside to meet you before."

Mom takes his hand, but she doesn't look happy about it, and ends the shake after a barely polite second. "I remember you, Dylan. You're the one who got my daughter drunk and let her walk home by herself."

"Yeah. I . . . messed up." He ducks his head. "I got worried when Ariel wasn't at school. That's why I came by to check on her. I wanted to make sure she was okay, and let her know how sorry I was."

"And she obviously forgave you." Mom's brow arches in my direction. I stand, debating whether I'm feeling brave enough to cross to the other side of the room.

"I had to crawl on my belly across your kitchen floor, but it was worth it," he says. "And your floor's a little cleaner now, so . . ."

He smiles, but Mom is not amused by clean-floor jokes. I gather my courage and hurry around the couch. "It's my fault," I say. "I was lonely after being by myself all day, so I asked Dylan to stay and watch a movie. We were watching *Carrie* and fell asleep."

"You *sounded* like you were asleep," she says, reminding me I come by my sarcastic streak honestly.

I open my mouth, but nothing comes out. I'm too embarrassed. I look down at the floor and squirm my toes into the carpet, wishing I had my shoes on. I'd feel so much less vulnerable with shoes. And maybe a sweater, and a suit of armor with a Mom-glare-deflecting force field.

"We just woke up," Dylan says. "We didn't do anything wrong, I promise."

"My definition of wrong and yours might be different, Dylan. I'd like you to leave, please."

"Okay." The hurt in his voice makes me want to strangle my mother. Why is she doing this? In front of the first boy who's ever dared step foot in the Freak's house?

"Is it okay if I pick Ariel up for school tomorrow?"

"I'll take her to school." Mom shoots another narrow look my way. "If she's feeling *well* enough to go, of course."

"Oh . . . all right." Dylan takes a step toward the door, but then turns back to my mom with a sigh. "Listen, I know you're angry, and I know you probably heard us joking, and it wasn't the kind of joke a mom wants to hear, but I care about Ariel. I really do."

"I'm sure you do." The condescension in Mom's voice makes me cringe.

If she keeps treating him like a little kid, I'm going to die. Or wish I were dead if I get too angry. I can't handle another episode tonight, not two nights in a row, not after this beautiful day that has me dreaming things I've never dared to dream before. Dylan doesn't think I'm a freak. He knows about the screaming things and all the rest of it, and he still kissed me and held me and acted like I was a normal girl. Maybe I can *be* normal. With him.

If my mom doesn't ruin everything by laying down the parental law the one time I don't need her help.

Instead of backing away, Dylan steps closer. "I'm sorry we've gotten off on the wrong foot, Mrs. Dragland, but I hope you'll give me a chance to prove that I'm good for Ariel. I promise I would never do anything to hurt her."

Mom's brows draw together, but she doesn't say anything right away. I can't decide if that's a good sign or a bad one. Usually she's pretty quick with a comeback. Maybe she's actually *thinking* about what Dylan said. Or maybe she's thinking about how long it will take her to grab my grandfather's .22 from her closet. Dylan has danger written all over him. But then, that's part of what I like about him.

What I *more* than like . . . ?

No. It's barely been a day since I found out about the bet. I'd be an idiot to trust him completely. Even when he's saying the right words, there's something off in the way he says them. I don't think he's lying, but I don't think he's telling the whole truth, either. I want to know what he's hiding. What he's holding back when he's been so open about other things. His honesty was painful today, but even the story about his brother didn't break through that final wall between him and the truth.

Still, when he looks my way, I don't see anything false in his eyes. He wants to be with me. And he wants it badly enough to stand and talk this out with my mom when it would be so much easier for him to walk out the door.

"That's a big promise, Dylan," Mom finally says. "Especially for a seventeen-year-old boy."

"I'm eighteen," Dylan says, a daring hint of playful in his tone. "December baby."

Mom doesn't smile. "I'm sure you know what I mean. Sometimes we hurt people without meaning to, especially when we're young."

"I know. But I meant what I said."

Mom considers him for a moment before nodding, just once. "All right, but we're going to have some ground rules." She turns to me. "No company if you're supposed to be home sick. Got it?"

I bob my head. "Yes, Mom. Sorry. I didn't even think about that."

"And from now on you have a midnight curfew on weekends and eleven on school nights," she says. "I talked to the girls at work, and that's the time their teenagers have to be in, so don't tell me I'm being unfair."

I nod again, so glad that she's not going to forbid me to see Dylan, that I don't even stop to think about what's fair or unfair.

"And if it becomes an issue," she says, "I expect you two to use birth control. Birth control pills *and* a condom to protect against disease."

Oh. My. God.

My eyes squeeze closed, and my heart shrivels like a shame-scorched raisin. If I didn't know what embarrassment was before, I *certainly* do now. How *could* she? Right here, right *now*? *In front of Dylan?*

"Yes, ma'am," Dylan mumbles. He's staring at his feet, his face bright red. Great. Now he's mortified too. I shoot Mom a wide-eyed "What in god's name are you doing!" look.

"I'm sorry." Her casual shrug makes it clear she's *not* sorry. At all. "I'm a nurse, and I don't believe in leaving things unsaid that could affect you both for the rest of your lives. I've seen too many pregnant high school girls." She hangs her purse on the hook by the door and kicks off her shoes, proving how comfortable she is with this line of discussion. I swear, I think she's *enjoying* making us squirm. "Those girls are almost always alone, and the boys who promised not to hurt them are long gone."

Dylan looks up. "I understand."

"I don't think you do." Mom props her hands on her hips. She doesn't sound angry—only matter-of-fact—but that doesn't make the atmosphere on our side of the room any less stressful. "I had Ariel when I was nineteen, but I want her to have time to learn who she is before she has to learn how to be a mom."

"Me too," Dylan says, his voice soft, almost . . . wistful.

He has that sad look on his face again, the same one he had when he talked about his brother. I wonder if he's thinking about him now. Or maybe he's thinking about *his* mom, who, according to the rumors, ran off and left Dylan and his dad right before they moved here. Either way, I wish I were beside him, holding his hand.

Then do it. He put himself out there, and all you've done is stand and watch.

Right. I force my wobbly legs to move, crossing to Dylan and slipping my hand into his. He glances over at me, surprised. Then he smiles, and suddenly I don't feel awkward or embarrassed or unsure anymore. Whatever his secrets, Dylan needs me. Maybe as much as I need him. Maybe even more.

"Well then. I guess we're all on the same page." Mom

sighs a funny little sigh. I look up to see her leaning against the archway leading into the family room, watching us with a faint smile. "You have all your homework done for tomorrow?"

I nod. "As far as I know."

"Okay. Then you two can watch some more TV if you want. But Dylan should be gone by ten-thirty, and you in bed by eleven, Ariel. You need to get some rest."

"Okay."

"I'll be in my room with the door cracked, and I'll be able to hear *everything*," she says. "Nice to meet you, Dylan."

"Nice to meet you, too, Mrs. Dragland. Thank you."

She smiles. "You're welcome."

After she's gone, Dylan and I stand in the darkness holding hands, the soundtrack from the menu screen of the *Carrie* DVD playing softly behind us. Despite the creepy music, I suddenly feel like laughing. We did it. We survived.

And Dylan is still here.

But when I turn to him—expecting to see him as relieved as I feel—his smile has slipped and gone sad again. "What's wrong?" I ask.

"I'm . . . afraid."

"Of what?"

"I don't want to mess this up," he whispers.

"You didn't. She's not mad anymore, I can tell."

"I don't mean that. I . . ." He pulls his hand from mine. "I don't want to hurt you."

"Then don't," I say, feeling stiff and nervous now that we're no longer connected.

"Things aren't that simple." He props his hands on the back of the couch, his shoulders hunched. "There are things I can't control."

Oh. I see. I should have known we couldn't go on like this, so easy and comfortable. We'll be back in the real world tomorrow, and my life there is still as crappy as it's ever been. Still, there's no reason Dylan has to get down and wallow in it with me.

"Is this about school?" I ask. "Because if it is, I . . . We don't have to act like . . . you know." I was about to say we don't have to act like we're together, but we haven't talked about being together, and I hate the idea of pretending he means nothing to me, that *I* mean nothing to him. I bite my lip. "I mean, if you're worried about what your friends will think, I—"

"No." He turns, shaking his head. "I told you, I don't care about my friends. It's . . . something I can't talk about." He looks away, focusing on a spot over my shoulder the way I've noticed he does when he's nervous. I know so much more about him than I did this morning, but I want to know more. I have to know what he's hiding.

"Why not?" I ask. "We've talked about a lot of things."

"Nothing like this. You'll think . . ." His eyes meet mine for a second before shifting away again. "I don't know what you'll think."

"Try me," I whisper.

He stares into the kitchen, like he's searching our faded cabinets for the answer to some unspoken question. "Maybe I will," he finally says. "But not right now."

I sag, feeling like I've failed a test. "Give me a hint?"

"A hint?"

"Yeah. Just so . . ."

So I know you're not keeping something awful from me. So I know I'm not going to find out that everything I think about you is wrong. So I can keep falling for you and know it's okay, because at this point I'm not sure I can stop.

"I'll sleep better," I say instead.

"I'm not so sure about that." He hesitates, and I'm starting to think I've heard his final word on the subject when he asks, "Do you believe in magic?"

"What kind of magic?"

"The kind that has the power to change the future. Spells that make people gods and slaves and monsters. That kind of magic. Real magic."

He isn't joking. I can tell. "I don't know," I say, seriously considering what he's said. "I've always wanted to believe in magic, but . . ." I think about my life, about pain and monotony and unfairness broken only by moments when I'm too lost in my art to care. I think about my missing friend with her miserable excuse for a dad, and Dylan's messed-up home life, and the cliquey people in this town who never gave my mom a chance to fit in. I think about crooked politicians and global warming and greed and selfishness and apathy and hate and my increasing assurance that there is no way out to a better place from these dark times, and sigh. "No, I don't."

"Really?" he sounds surprised.

"I don't see much evidence to support believing in magic."

"You don't find your life magical?"

I almost laugh. He's *got* to be kidding. "No, I don't. Is there something about my life that *you* find especially magical?"

"More than you know."

"Like what?"

"More than I can tell you right now," he says, still frustratingly vague. "But I will say this: I believe in magic. I *know* it exists, and I know that some of it is good, and some of it is unreservedly evil."

The way he says evil makes my skin itch, like I can feel all the bad things in the world circling around me, drawing closer and closer. I think about my dream and the man in the robe, and shiver. "How do you know?"

"I'll tell you. Soon." He lifts a finger and traces the place on my cheek where soft becomes bumpy. Even this morning I would have cringed, but now his touch only makes my heart beat faster. He *really* thinks I'm beautiful. That alone is almost enough to make me consider the existence of magic. "But in the meantime, be careful," he says. "And don't get angry if you can help it."

"Why?"

"I don't think you're crazy." He tips his head, bringing his lips closer to mine. "I think those things you hear are real, the result of some bad magic, and connected to some very dangerous beings."

"Don't joke," I say. "Not about that."

"I'm not. I'm serious. Just in case I'm also right, it's safer if you don't attract their attention."

I shake my head, too overwhelmed to know what to think, or which of the dozens of questions racing through my mind to ask first. Before I can decide, Dylan stops me with a finger on my lips. "I promise I'll tell you more. Right now you need some rest."

"You think I can rest? After . . ." My hands scoop the air, gathering up everything he's said. "You just told me you think I'm cursed, or something. You're either joking or crazy or—"

"Or right."

I pause, assessing him. "There's no such thing as magic."

"I wish you were right."

My skin prickles. I'm getting close to his secret. I can feel it. "How do you know? Where did Dylan Stroud learn so much about the supernatural?"

"A better question would be, what if I'm *not* Dylan Stroud?"

What? What the *heck* does that mean?

"Haven't you heard you shouldn't judge a book by its cover?" he asks. "Especially if all the words inside are different?"

His words skip across the surface of my brain, leaving disturbing ripples behind. If I ignore common sense, I can almost see the image the ripples are forming, a flowing map to guide me from the changes I've noticed in Dylan to the reason for them. But I can't. It's too far to travel. If I start down that road . . . if I even let myself consider . . .

"That's crazy," I whisper.

"Yes. But something to think about." He smiles. "Think your mother will let me drive you to school tomorrow? Now that we're all friends and united by a belief in the careful use of contraception?"

My cheeks burn, the memory of my mother's mortifying behavior distracting me for a moment. "Yes," I mumble. "I think so."

"Good. I'll pick you up tomorrow morning. Seven o'clock. We'll get breakfast." He kisses my forehead, and moves toward the door.

For a second I think about begging him to stay, but I don't. I stand and watch him slip into the night, wondering which of us is crazier—him for introducing such an insane possibility, or me for thinking about believing it?

ELEVEN

Romeo

When I swing into her driveway at six-forty-five, Ariel's already waiting outside, backpack slung over one shoulder.

"You're lovely this morning." She is—gauzy white shirt, dark jeans, and long white braids tied with leather at the ends. "Like a very pale Indian princess."

She smiles and says "Thank you" as she slides into the passenger seat. "You're early."

"Couldn't sleep. I needed to see you again."

"I couldn't sleep either." She closes her door, and I pull out of the driveway, aiming Dylan's car toward downtown.

"I've been up since two working on a new painting. I think I might actually need coffee for once."

"That can be arranged," I say, waiting for her to bring up the subject that *must* be plaguing her mind.

But she doesn't say a word about my cryptic warnings last night. She remarks on the uncommonly beautiful day, reminds me that the homework for English—which I haven't bothered to complete—is due, and asks if I'm ready for the last rehearsal for the spring formal performance after school.

"Of course."

"Of course," she echoes with a roll of her eyes. "You aren't nervous at all, are you?"

"I don't get nervous unless it's a matter of life or death," I say, the words coming out heavier than I intended. Two days. Just two more days. Two, two, two, *two*. I banish the disturbing mantra with a grin. "Besides, it's a low investment performance. One song—on and off the stage in five minutes—and I'll have the rest of the night to spend with you. We get to wear our own clothes, so I won't even have to change out of costume." I reach out, turning down the heat. It suddenly feels warmer with Ariel in the car. "Which reminds me—I need to go shopping. Up for a trip to the thrift store later this afternoon?"

"Sure."

"I'm thinking a vintage tuxedo. Something in pastel if we can find it."

"Okay," she says with a laugh. "Sounds like fun." And then she takes my hand and holds it all the way into Solvang, and I am . . . torn.

Is it best to pretend I never hinted that I'm another soul

in Dylan's body? The change in Ariel after only a day of undivided romantic attention is remarkable. Maybe continued commonplace, banal romantic pressure will be enough to save my skin. But can I trust "maybe" at a time like this? When less than forty-eight hours remain and hell awaits me if I fail? Or should I follow my instincts and tell Ariel the highly abridged, creatively edited, and largely false version of my sad tale?

My gut tells me that Romeo Montague—one of the most famous, most tragic lovers in history—will have a better chance of winning Ariel's heart in the time we have left than Dylan Stroud will. I've used my real identity countless times in the past, to twist the human heart and bend a potential Mercenary convert to my will. It's amazing how quickly an otherwise perfectly rational human being will believe the extraordinary in the name of being part of an epic love story.

And the nagging worry remains—what will happen to Ariel when Dylan's soul returns, if I don't tell her *some* version of my truth? How can the Ambassadors trust that Ariel will continue to believe in love if the person who's touched her heart reverts to his old, nasty ways?

Yes, Dylan will retain some of my memories of seducing Ariel—minus the details about the Ambassadors and the Mercenaries—but he won't love her. I'm pretending to care to save my own skin. Why will he believe he was pretending? What story will his sick mind create to fill in the gaps made by having his body inhabited by another person's soul? And will that story destroy Ariel's faith in love's power?

Or will her faith stay strong and her light be snuffed out by Mercenaries once she's no longer useful to their cause?

Who cares? The Mercenaries might kill her, but at least she'll be free to die a normal death. You can't say the same. Keep your head, or you'll find it filled with rot before the sun rises Saturday morning.

"Dylan?" Ariel gives my arm a gentle shake. "Are we going to breakfast?"

"Yes," I snap, then realize what I've done and gentle my voice. "Yes. Can't face a day of learning on an empty stomach."

"Okay." She sounds cautious, guarded, leaving no doubt she heard the anger in my voice. "Well, you passed the pancake house two blocks ago, so . . ."

"I thought we'd hit the bakery, have coffee and a chocolate croissant or five. My treat." I pull into a parking spot on the street, only a few doors down from the Windmill Bakery.

"No, I want to buy," she says, hesitation in her tone. "You got dinner the other night and everything yesterday."

I wave her concern away and jump out to open her door. "I scored a couple twenties from my dad." I take her arm and help her out of the car. "I'm a rich man."

"Won't you need that later?" she asks, dragging her feet as we step onto the sidewalk. "For the thrift store?"

"No worries. I've got everything under control." I do. I won't let fear or worry or anything else divert me from my course. I must catch this girl any way I can, the way a spider catches a fly. And the spider doesn't let concern for the fly divert it from its course; the spider does what it must to survive.

"Wait," Ariel says, stopping abruptly at the entrance to the bakery, pulling her arm from mine. "I can't."

"Why? What—"

"I just can't. I told you yesterday I didn't want to come here." She backs away as the door behind me opens with a tinkling sound. I glance over my shoulder, and see precisely what has my fly so terribly upset.

"Aw, man! No way. I already spent that sixty bucks." The loud male voice is followed by a chorus of louder, meaner male laughter. "You suck, Stroud."

Three lanky boys and a shorter, more solid boy with spiked black hair and a cruel smirk emerge from the bakery. They prowl across the sidewalk, jackals smelling easy prey. I stop, frozen in place as I meet the pitiless eyes of the shortest boy. Jason Kim. Memories of the way he laughed as he tortured me for betraying Mercenary secrets rush inside me, filling my mouth with the taste of blood and fear.

My maker, Friar Lawrence, inhabited this boy's body during my first go-round in this time. It was his fault I was forced to kill Juliet and her new love. He left me no choice, and then he left me no way out, banishing me to my soul specter, condemning me to more misery and horror.

My fists ball, and something inside me curls into a poisonous knot. What if it's him again? What if he's still lurking in Jason's body? Will he know me? And if he does, what will he do? Will he take me now, banish me to my specter, and steal away my second chance and Ariel's future? If it is him, he will try to turn her. And if he can't turn her, he will kill her, and I will be helpless to prevent him.

Helpless, a dog snapping at the ankles of those who hold the power.

I decide right then that I must tell Ariel whatever it takes to keep her safe. I must make her believe my lies before anyone else can hurt her with theirs. My lies will protect her. Theirs will steal her immortal soul and make her a monster. Like me.

"Why didn't you call me yesterday, dude? I thought the Freak cut your junk off or something." Jason's voice is higher than I remember, and his grin makes check marks in his plump cheeks. Soft cheeks, with no memory of what it feels like to have an ancient evil working the muscles beneath. And his eyes . . . They're cruel, but not malevolent.

My maker isn't in that body. It's not the friar; it's just a boy. I take a deep breath, coming back to myself enough to realize Ariel is no longer by my side.

"Five hundred dollars, bro," Jason continues. "That's pretty sweet. Once everyone pays up, we can get those new amps." He reaches a hand out for Dylan to clasp in victory. I stare at his white palm and thick fingers—thinking I'd like to cut them off—and then turn my back on him. He doesn't matter. Ariel matters.

I find her already a block down the street, blond braids swinging as she retreats. I'd been pleased that she'd pulled her hair back this morning, and eliminated the shield she hides behind. But seeing her now—hunched and broken and seething in pain—I am pleased at nothing. Damn Jason and the other boys. Damn Dylan.

Damn myself.

"Ariel, wait!" My cry is echoed by the mocking voices of Jason's three minions, pathetic shadows with names like Craig and Tanner and Brodie, names that mean nothing to me. But they mean something to Ariel. I can see it in her expression when she turns, in the mix of fear and despair and anger pulling at her face.

These boys have treated her as subhuman fodder for their own amusement. They're the ones who never let her forget that she's damaged, who have told again and again the story of her scars and the day she wet herself on the playground, until she became a living urban legend that the stupid children laugh at and the smarter children fear.

They have locked her in an invisible cage with a warning not to feed the Freak, and she hates them for it. She hates them and fears them, and is denied even the pleasure of unleashing her anger because of the screaming things that will be summoned by her rage.

It is . . . hell. They've put her through hell.

And I hate them for it. *Hate*. And it feels wonderful—sharp and hot and blissfully uncomplicated. This is what I know. Tender feelings and concern are foreign emotions I can't manage. But I know exactly what to do with hate.

I spin with my fist raised at the perfect angle, my centuries as a dealer in violence and bloodshed serving me well. I catch the redheaded Craig in the jaw with a satisfying thud, and the boy in the green flannel shirt—Tanner or Brodie, I don't care enough to search Dylan's memories to figure out which—above his left ear. The second boy howls in pain, and someone on the other side of the street cries out for us to stop, but I barely notice.

This is perfect, magical.

The darkness that was my constant companion in my Mercenary life surges to the surface, a friend I welcome with open arms and tight fists. I rush forward, punching the third boy twice in the back as he runs away, *thud, thud*—right above the kidneys, where I know it hurts like hell. He falls to the ground—groaning, writhing—and I spin to look for Jason with a smile on my face. This will be a pleasure, a skin-bruising, teeth-smashing pleasure.

It takes only a moment to find him. He has lacked the sense to run down the street. Instead, he's cowering in the doorway of a closed toy shop a few storefronts away, whimpering, maybe even—

"Tell me you aren't crying!" I shout as I stalk down the sidewalk. I catch Ariel's eyes for a moment—see the faint curve of her lips and the straightness of her spine—and a rush of satisfaction lifts me even higher. I've pleased her, defended her. She'll love me now, save me. She'll have to! "You should be ashamed of yourself," I growl. "You pathetic excuse for a—"

A hand grabs my elbow. I spin with a clenched fist, expecting to find that one of the other boys has come back for more. Instead, I see . . . a ghost.

My arm falls to my side and my face goes slack.

No, not a ghost. He's alive. His fingers are warm, his eyes flash with anger, and I can hear him draw breath before he tells me to "Back off, man."

"Benvolio?" I croak, disbelief tightening my throat. How can this be? *How?* My cousin died hundreds of years ago.

But despite the modern clothes he wears—jeans and a black T-shirt—there is no doubt this *is* Benvolio, not some twenty-first-century look-alike. I know my cousin. I grew up with this boy, spent fifteen years of my life with him as my closest friend.

He releases my arm with a cautious flick of his wrist. "Do I know you?"

"It's me. Romeo," I whisper. "Benvolio, I—"

"Ben," he says. "Just . . . Ben."

"Ben."

"Ben Luna."

No. No, this can't . . . This isn't . . .

"I started school here last week." He casts a glance over my shoulder. "I have gym with that guy." I turn to see Jason scuttling across the street, taking advantage of my distraction to escape his beating. I think I should be angry. I think I should follow him. I think I should make sure Ariel's okay. But all I can do is shift my gaze back to Benvolio, and watch his lips move, and fight the wave of panic surging inside me. "I get why you'd want to pound his face, but none of those guys were doing anything to you," he says. "And my brother's going to be here in a few minutes to meet me for coffee. He's a cop, so . . ." He shrugs. "I figured you'd rather avoid getting arrested."

"Yes. I would. Thank you . . . Ben." Not Ben. *Benvolio.* This is my cousin, not the boy who fell in love with Juliet. He lacks the morose sincerity that made me want to stab Benjamin Luna in the gut a few dozen times—just to give him something to be so goddamned tragic about. This *is* Benvolio. From his soul to his skin to the way he props his hands on his hips in a vaguely menacing fashion.

But he seems to *believe* he's Benjamin Luna. What does that mean? What the *hell* does it mean?

And where is the real Ben?

"No problem," he says. "What was your name again?"

"Dylan."

His eyes narrow, and I see my savvy cousin peeking out, suddenly suspicious. "That's not what you said the first time."

I never could fool Benvolio. I can't fool him now, though he's obviously fooled himself. Or someone has fooled him. Someone or something.

The Ambassador sent me back in time to a different reality. Perhaps some supernatural force has sent Benvolio forward in time? But why? To what purpose? If Benvolio were here to hurt me, he would hurt me. Right here, right now. Benvolio is nothing if not straightforward and to the point. So perhaps there is no point. Perhaps this is simply a strange, cosmic coincidence.

I force a laugh. "I mistook you for someone else, a friend I did theater with last summer. He played Benvolio. I played Romeo."

"Yeah?" He knows I'm lying. "What play was that?"

"The one with Romeo in it," I say, losing my patience. "*Romeo and Juliet?*"

He acknowledges my smart-ass tone with a lifted brow. "Never heard of it."

"You've never heard of *Romeo and Juliet*? Do you live under a rock?" I sense movement out of the corner of my eye. It's Ariel creeping cautiously to my side.

Shit. I'd practically forgotten her, a mistake I can't afford, no matter how mind-bending it is to have a conversation with my cousin six hundred and something years after he should have turned to dust.

I smile, and wrap an arm around her waist.

"You okay?" she asks.

"Perfect. You?" She nods and shoots Ben a nervous look. My arm tightens, pulling her closer, wanting there to be no doubt in Ben/Benvolio's mind that we are together. The other Ben Luna definitely had a thing for willowy blondes—this one in particular. "Ariel, this is Ben. Ben, Ariel."

"Nice to meet you," he says with a warmth that makes

me want to smash in his toothy smile. That's not Ben Luna's smile; that is Benvolio's smile, the one that would have won him more than a few hearts when we were young if he hadn't been too honorable to tamper with a girl's virtue.

"Ben was telling me he's never heard of *Romeo and Juliet.*" I drop a kiss on top of Ariel's head, marking her as mine.

"Oh." She sounds distracted, tense. Probably wanting to talk about the fight, to thank me for defending her. "What's that? A band?"

"A play," Benvolio says. "Don't feel bad. I didn't know what it was either."

Didn't know what it was either. What the . . .

Suspicion, sick and insidious, churns in my gut and I wonder . . .

And then I wonder some more. . . .

And then I know I have to make it to a library. Immediately.

"So sorry, Ben, but we have to go. Pressing business at the school library," I say, pulling Ariel back toward the car.

"Okay." His gaze shifts between Ariel and me, as if trying to judge if she's a willing companion or a captive. I barely resist the urge to bare my teeth and hiss at him.

Instead I grin and say "See you around" before turning back to Ariel. "I'm sorry. I know I promised you coffee and breakfast, but I—"

"It's okay." She pulls her hand from mine, crossing her arms as we walk. "I'm not hungry anymore."

I pause by her door, forcing myself not to rush her into the car. She seems upset, and I can't afford to lose any ground. "Why? Did I do something wrong?" I hang my head, trying to look properly ashamed. "I'm sorry if I scared you. I couldn't control myself. I wanted them to know they aren't allowed to hurt you anymore."

"I wasn't scared. I . . . loved it." She looks up, her wide, anxious eyes meeting mine. "I loved watching you hit them. I was sad when that other guy stopped you." She swallows, then adds in a horrified whisper, "I wanted you to make Jason Kim bleed. A lot."

I blink, surprised. And pleased, though I know I shouldn't be. I'm supposed to be turning Ariel away from her dark side, not indulging her taste for bloodshed. But then, I didn't really believe she had one. She seems so *good* to me. At least, most of the time. When she isn't trying to commit murder/suicide by driving a car off the road or proclaiming her undying hatred.

"It's okay." I draw her close, tucking her beneath my chin. "I think it's normal to feel that way about someone who's hurt you."

"Is it?"

I sigh. "Well, maybe not normal. But . . . I understand."

"I know you do." She rests her cheek on my chest, and lets out a long breath. "Thank you."

My arms tighten. "Don't thank me. I'm . . . sorry."

She tilts her head back. "What for?"

"I don't know. I . . ." I can't meet her eyes. I look over her head and scowl. Ben is still standing there, watching us though he pretends to watch the street. I pull away and reach for the car door. "Let's go. We'll talk in the car. I don't need an audience."

"Me either. There's something weird about that guy," she whispers as she slips into the car, bringing an unexpected smile to my face.

Ah, Ariel. Some might say she has poor taste, but I can't help but be flattered.

Take that, *knight in shining armor. This lady prefers the knave.* I give Benvolio my nastiest smirk as I pull the car out and drive away, bound for the book that will put my fears to rest.

TWELVE

Ariel

I cling tight to Dylan's hand as he hurries up the walkway toward the cluster of hunkered brown buildings that make up Solvang High. It's another beautiful day, and most of the school is out on the grass eating breakfast or hanging on the benches that line the path, soaking up the morning sun before heading for homeroom. Everyone seems to be in an unusually cheerful mood, but the loud conversations and bursts of laughter fade as Dylan and I rush by.

Heads turn, and voices drop to a whisper. It's obvious people are shocked to see us together—the school bad boy and the shy, strange freak. I can feel their attention like fingers poking into my skin, leaving tender places behind. I risk a peek at our audience from behind my braids. Most people look curious, or skeptical, or amused, but a few of the girls are smiling with melty looks in their eyes. They seem happy. For me.

It's crazy. Impossible.

I can barely believe this is real, that twenty minutes ago Dylan bashed in the faces of his friends for me. That he defended me, and kept his promise to make sure everyone knows I matter to him. It boggles my mind, makes me feel dizzy and off center as he veers off the path toward the library.

Even in my most secret, cheesy, romantic imaginings, I never let myself whip up anything like this.

I tip my head down, hiding a smile I can't control. This is nuts. This is a fairy tale. This is *my life*. I hold the knowledge tight inside me, letting it burn until it feels like my heart is catching fire. But in a good way. I can't imagine being cold or lonely or scared again. Not so long as Dylan's hand is in mine and we are we.

We *are* we. I don't think there's any question about that after what just happened, but we might as well make it official.

"So," I whisper as Dylan pushes into the library and stops to scan the shelves. "I guess we're . . ." Boyfriend-girlfriend? Dating? Maybe just "Together?"

Dylan makes a vague sound beneath his breath as he crosses to the drama section. My smile curdles. He's been so distracted since we left the Windmill. He said he forgot about a homework assignment and needed to hit the library before class, but it's hard to believe that homework has inspired such urgency. Earlier he acted like he couldn't care less about blowing off our English assignment, and he's never been what anyone would call a diligent student.

As if sensing my worry, he reaches out and gives my braid a gentle tug. "I'll only be a second." He drops his backpack onto the ground and runs one hand over the spines of the worn library bindings until he comes to an especially fat book that he snatches out with a grunt.

I have time to see that he's chosen *The Collected Works of Shakespeare* before he flips the book open to the table of contents. His finger traces down one column of plays and then the other, pausing at the last title on the list. His face falls, and I know that something awful has happened. I just can't imagine what. I touch his back, but he flinches and shoots me the strangest look, as if he isn't sure who I am.

I drop my backpack beside his. "Are you okay?"

He flips through the pages, turning them so fast, they snap. "This is impossible. There must be some mistake."

"What is it? What's wrong?"

"Complete works, my ass." He slams the book closed and shoves it back onto the shelf. "You're certain you've never heard of *Romeo and Juliet*? The Shakespeare play? The most tragic love story ever told?"

I bite my lip. "I love Shakespeare, but I haven't read *every* play. I might have missed—"

"No. You wouldn't have missed *Romeo and Juliet*. They've made dozens of movies, and books, and musicals inspired by—" He breaks off and turns to me, pointing a finger at my chest, a slightly manic smile on his face. "*West Side Story*! You've heard of that. It's based on *Romeo and Juliet*. The character of Tony is Romeo and Maria is Juliet." His hopeful tone becomes a touch impatient. "You remember. 'Maria.' It's the song you asked me to sing the night we met."

"We met in first grade." The words are true, but they feel

like a lie. I may have known Dylan almost my entire life, but I've only known *this* Dylan a couple of days.

Maybe that's why I'm not entirely freaked out when he takes my hand in his and whispers, "We both know that isn't true. You know me, Ariel, and you know I'm not him."

I have no idea what to say to *that*. The only thing that comes to mind is "*Tristan and Isolde*."

"What?"

"*Tristan and Isolde*. That's the legend *West Side Story* is based on."

The last hint of hope drains from his face, until he's so pale he looks sick. "*Tristan and Isolde*. The Irish story, about the knight?"

I nod. "The knight who's taking the princess, Isolde, home to his king. She's supposed to marry the king, but she and Tristan drink a love potion on their way back and fall in love forever. That's when Tristan, Tony in the musical, sings the song about Maria."

His hand falls to his side, and my fingers slip through his. The loss of contact shakes me, but despite my nerves, I go to him, the same way he came to me when I was upset after the fight. I'm not going to let fear keep me from him. He wants me. He *needs* me; I can feel it.

I wrap my arms around his neck, drawing him close. For the first moment he stays stiff, and my fear threatens to turn to terror. What if I'm wrong, what if this is still just some enormous joke? I'm so accustomed to expecting the worst that it's almost impossible to relax and believe. Hope is dangerous, a hole in my soul's armor. I can feel the vulnerable place pulse and ache, begging me to seal myself up before it's too late. But then, slowly, Dylan's arms come around my waist.

He drops his head into the curve of my neck and exhales, his breath warm on my skin. I feel his relief. It's my relief too. My arms vibrate with it.

"Ariel," he sighs. "I'm in trouble, I think."

"Why?"

"I . . . I'm not sure I exist," he mumbles into my hair. "Or if I did, things didn't happen the way they did before. I don't know what it means."

I pull him closer. He sounds crazy, but then, I know what it feels like to be labeled a nut without my story being heard.

What could he mean? Is his twin brother still alive? Has he somehow stepped into Dylan's place and taken over his life? It sounds like the stuff of soap operas, but there's no denying that the Dylan I hold in my arms is very, *very* different from the one I knew up until nine o'clock Tuesday night.

"I don't understand," I say. "But I want to. You can tell me . . . whatever it is."

"You really won't believe me now," he says. "You've never heard the story. There might not *be* a story."

"You told me the screaming things I hear might be caused by magic, and I still got in the car with you this morning. And I'm here with you now, and I . . ." I lick my lips, but find I'm still afraid to say out loud how much I care, no matter how real the emotion is starting to feel. "I want to help. Just . . . try me. I think it's obvious I'm not your average skeptic."

He stares down at me for a long moment, his defenses dropping until I'm looking straight into his soul. Finally. This is it; the walls are down. I'm about to find out the truth.

"Once upon a time, in the city of Verona, Italy, a long, long time ago, there was a boy named Romeo," he says, the catch in his voice telling me this is no fairy tale. This is a closer story, one that tears at him on the way out. "He was sixteen years old and very angry with his father, and the world, and god, though he'd been raised to fear the Church too much to confess that, even to himself.

"He was from a wealthy family and had more than his fair share of leisure time to devote to dwelling on his anger. And when Romeo wasn't angry, he was heartsick. He imagined himself quite the tragic lover." He laughs as he scans the row where he shelved Shakespeare's complete works. "He fell in love at least once a fortnight, and it always ended desperately. No girl was ever as perfect as he imagined, until the one girl who captured him completely. She was from a very strict family."

"What was her name?" I ask, more curious than I probably should be.

"Rosaline," he says. "She and Romeo got along very well. They talked for hours and took long walks in the country, accompanied by her nurse, a giantess with an infected leg who breathed heavily and reeked of vinegar and killed even the thought of romance." His nose wrinkles, but the grin on his face fades quickly. "One day, Romeo convinced Rosaline to meet him behind her father's stables. But instead of the heated kisses the boy was expecting, Rosaline told him she had vowed to remain chaste and was planning to devote her life to the Church. She asked the boy not to call on her anymore, and denied him even a single kiss."

"So," I say, sensing that the story isn't finished. "What did the boy do?"

"He went out with his cousin Benvolio and got very drunk, and crashed the party of his father's sworn enemy. It was a costume ball, and easy to hide in plain sight. He and his cousin drank their enemy's wine, ate his food, and danced with his women. And then the clock struck ten and a girl of unimaginable beauty appeared on the stairway, and Romeo fell in love again. Just like that. The girl was . . . the sun, and she blinded him."

He stares into the distance, like he's seeing the girl again and finding her beauty as painful as ever. Something inside me—the childish part that thinks fairies and unicorns and all kinds of magical things could be real if we believed in them the way we believe in bombs and the Internet—knows that this story is truth. Dylan's truth. Or . . . someone's truth.

Maybe the truth of a boy named Romeo.

"Her name was Juliet," he says. "She was the daughter of Romeo's enemy, but it didn't matter. Being with her was magical. She was so good and passionate and sweet and lov-ing and . . . *his,* in a way no one ever had been. He should have been happy." Now the words come in bursts, forced out. "But he wasn't, and he made the biggest mistake of his life. He betrayed her. His intentions were good—at least he convinced himself they were—but he was a coward and . . ." He pulls in a breath, but it only seems to make him more upset. "He was cursed, destined to wander the world for eternity doing ter-rible things. There was no love in him, and he was sure there never would be. And Juliet . . . died. And it was his fault."

"I'm so sorry."

"I don't deserve your pity," he says, voice cracking.

"I don't care." I stand on tiptoe to press a kiss to his sad lips.

For a second he's still, but then he kisses me back, deep and desperate, like my mouth contains the oxygen he couldn't find in the air. His arms wrap tight around me and squeeze, and I can feel his heartbeat echo in my chest. He kisses me until my lips bruise and my head spins and my pulse races and I start to feel . . . *dangerously* close. It would be so easy to slip out of my skin and seep into his. I could lose myself in him, step through the door he holds open and never find my way back through. I could—

"Dylan? Ariel?" Mrs. Lorado sounds more shocked than scandalized, but her interruption still has the same effect.

Dylan and I jump apart, breathing deep, hands shaking. I turn to Mrs. Lorado, but it's hard to focus on her milky face with its puckered lips. All I see is a blur of white swimming before me, and an explosion of color below her neck. She's famous for wearing obnoxious sweaters with cartoon characters or googly-eyed puppies or Santa Claus and his reindeer, months after Christmas is over.

When I first met her, I thought the sweaters were a sign that she was lovably quirky, like my sixth-grade teacher, who handed out unbirthday cards every Friday. But Mrs. Lorado isn't lovable, and doesn't realize she's quirky, and I get the feeling she hates kisses in the library as much as she hates beverages and food and talking above a whisper.

"This is unacceptable," she says when the seconds stretch on without a word from me or Dylan. "What do you have to say for yourselves?"

"Sorry?" I think I should add something else, but I can't think of what. All I can think of is Dylan's story about Romeo and Juliet and magic and unimaginable possibilities that I can nevertheless imagine. Pretty easily.

"Sorry is inadequate, Ariel. It's this sort of thing that leads to the library being closed until the librarian is here to open it," she says, gearing up into full lecture mode. "And you know that there are no public displays of affection allowed anywhere on campus. It's in the handbook. Twice."

"Does anyone actually read the handbook?" Dylan asks.

"Don't sass me, Mr. Stroud." Mrs. Lorado crosses her arms, making the eyes of the Persian cat on her sweater narrow threateningly. "Consider this your warning. Next time I catch you doing anything but reading in the library, you'll be marching straight down to the principal's office. Now get to homeroom."

Dylan and I mumble "sorry" a few more times, grab our backpacks, and hurry toward the library door as the first bell rings. We emerge into the sunshine, but it doesn't feel as warm as it did, and the happy cloud that carried me along the path has blown away. I aim myself toward my locker but can't muster the speed walk that's required if I'm going to make it there and back to building four before the second bell. This world doesn't seem as urgent, not with Dylan's story lingering in my mind, so big and unfinished.

"That was a true story," I say, breathless, though I've barely reached strolling speed. "Wasn't it?"

"It's my story. I know it sounds crazy, but—"

"Is that how you learned about magic?" I ask, letting him know I won't waste his time with talk of how crazy things can also be true. I know all about crazy. And true. And I know a crazy truth when I hear it. "Were you really cursed?"

"I was. A man tricked me into signing away my soul, and I spent hundreds of years trapped in my own private hell." I make a sound, but he cuts me off. "Don't. I meant what I said. I don't deserve pity. I was . . . very selfish. And a coward."

I take his hand. A couple of girls rush by on our left, but their hurry doesn't infect us. If anything, we walk slower. "You're not that person now."

"I don't know. Maybe I am." He stops and turns to me.

"But I *do* care about you, probably more than I've cared about anyone since—"

"Juliet," I finish, surprised that I'm not jealous. Not even a little. I'm . . . dizzy. He hasn't said he loves me, but he might as well have.

"Yes. Since Juliet."

"So you're . . . Romeo." He nods. "But how? And why? And . . . Shakespeare?"

"I knew him."

"You knew Shakespeare? *The* Shakespeare." My god. He's ancient. His story made me think he might be, but . . . Shakespeare. It's mind-numbing to think about how old that is.

"I told him a version of the story I told you, and he turned it into a play. He'd heard the legend before; I simply drew his attention to its dramatic potential." He stops outside a darkened classroom, one of the resource rooms that aren't used until later in the day. "I told him the easy part. The rest is a longer story." He glances down the path before reaching for the door.

A voice in my head whispers that I can't stay here with him—my mom will *not* be happy if she gets a call about me skipping class—but I ignore the voice and let him pull me into the shadowy room. I'll get home before Mom and catch the recording.

Even if I don't, who cares?

There is *magic* in the world.

There are cursed boys and dangerous secrets and maybe answers and hope and happy endings. For all I know, there might be unicorns and fairies, too, and there's no way I'm going to let real life stick its ugly, wart-covered nose into this moment.

THIRTEEN

Ariel

As soon as the latch clicks shut behind us, Romeo leads the way to a dark corner that can't be seen from the rectangular window in the door. He settles down cross-legged on the tight blue carpet. I sit down beside him, feeling like a little kid again. It's like circle time, when we'd go around and share whatever we'd brought for show-and-tell, but a thousand times more exciting, with none of the terrifying pressure of having to speak when my turn comes.

He reaches out and takes my hands. "This isn't a happy story," he warns, staring down at the places where we're linked. "I knew I was joining a dark group of people. As I said, I wasn't the nicest boy. I was angry and selfish and thought there were a lot of people in the world who deserved to suffer."

I think about Jason and the real Dylan and all the other boys who made the bet. I think about Hannah and the girls who've avoided me like my scars are a plague that's catching, and I shrug. "You were probably right."

He shakes his head. "No one deserves what these people do. They are utterly evil. I had no idea how evil until I vowed my allegiance to them. As soon as I did, I knew I'd made a horrible mistake, but it was too late. There was no way out. The way they force their converts to live . . ." He tries to pull his hands from mine. I hold tight, wanting him to know I'm with him. "I lived inside the dead."

"What do you mean?"

"My soul entered the corpse of my choosing, and the magic of the people I served made it appear lifelike. But it was still a dead body. It still felt . . ." He looks up. I try to keep thoughts of zombies and horror movie monsters from my face. I manage, but then another fear zips through my mind.

"Is Dylan dead?" I ask. "Is that why you—"

"No. His body is alive, and his soul is resting in another place. This shift is different. This is my first time in a living, feeling form in hundreds of years. Before Tuesday night, I couldn't taste or touch or smell. And I did terrible things. Unspeakable things, but . . . I could speak of them. If you want me to."

I want to tell him it's okay and I don't need to hear it. That who he is now is all that matters. But I know it's not that easy, and he doesn't really want it to be. "How terrible is terrible?"

"I was a monster." He lays the words down like a verdict.

Blunt. Inescapable. He means murder and things worse than murder that I don't even want to think about, but for some reason it doesn't change the way I feel.

"But you would take it all back if you could," I say. "You're different now."

He nods, relief flooding into his eyes. "I am different. I swear to you."

"What changed? Why are you here? You're not here to do something terrible to me, are you?"

He hesitates for a second too long. "No."

"Are you sure?" I feel like I have to ask, but I'm still not afraid. Not of him. I'm still haunted by this feeling that Dylan and I—*Romeo* and I—are going to end badly, but I no longer think it will be because of anything he'll do.

"I didn't set out to hurt you. A short time ago, I did something marginally noble that drew the attention of a different magic. Good magic." He wrinkles his nose. "Or better magic, at least. I was given a chance to . . ." He sighs. "This is difficult."

"I haven't run away yet."

"I . . . You've heard the story of *The Little Mermaid*."

I nod, not surprised by the abrupt change in course. At this point, I'm not sure anything he says could surprise me. "Yeah. I have the same name as the character in the Disney version. But my mom named me after the archangel."

"The angel of wrath and creation. Suits you." He does a decent impression of his amused smile. "Then you know that the mermaid traded her voice for legs, and was unable to tell the prince why she washed up on the shores of his kingdom, or what she required in order to be able to stay."

"So . . . you're saying you can't tell me why you're here."

He nods. "And you can't tell me what you need from me to

stay." He nods again, making my empty belly burn. "But you need something. And you . . . want to stay."

"I would give anything to stay," he says. "But the play worries me."

"What does the play—"

"I've never lived in a world where there was no Romeo and Juliet. I don't know what it means. The play is gone. Does that mean I simply never spoke with Shakespeare in this reality, or is it something more?"

My mind sputters, hiccupping over the latest piece of his puzzle that he's tossed out so casually. "You mean there are . . . other realities?" The cells in my brain move farther apart, spread like the expanding universe, leaving me wobbly and less solid inside. "Like . . . things going on at the same time, but in different . . . spaces?" I'm not sure I've made sense, but he seems to understand.

"There are," he says, confirming the existence of something I find harder to believe than the story of his curse or another soul living in Dylan's body. But magic has always seemed more real to me than science. Just thinking about how our bodies are composed of tiny, racing particles with their own internal life is enough to give me a bad case of the creeps if I dwell on it too much.

"I've only experienced two," he continues. "But I've been assured there are more, the world branching off into parallel versions of itself as people make choices that alter the course of the future."

"That's . . . wild." The same people. Different business. It makes me wonder . . . What if there's a reason his story isn't as impossible to believe as it should be? What if . . . "Have we . . . Did I know you before? In another reality?"

His eyes meet mine and I feel him struggling, but I don't know if it's because of the things he's forbidden to say or his own reluctance to answer the question. "Yes," he says, making my heart stop. "And no." It picks up beating again, with a jerky *thu-thump*. "I saw you, but we never spoke. I was in that world on a mission for the dark magicians who owned me for more than seven hundred years."

"But you're free now."

"I'm enjoying a reprieve," he says. "But I may have been tricked. The woman who lent me the power to borrow Dylan's body . . . I don't trust her."

"She's a sorceress?"

"More like a witch," he says, a wry smile lifting one side of his lips.

"A witch." I know he means more than her ability to work magic. "Like the sea witch in *The Little Mermaid*." It sounds silly when I say it out loud.

In this darkened room, hunched together on the carpet, it feels like we're playing some elaborate game of pretend. But this isn't pretend. This is Romeo's life, and maybe his death if I'm understanding him correctly. In the original story of *The Little Mermaid,* she turned to sea foam because the prince didn't have the sense to love her.

I think I love Romeo, but it's so hard to know for sure. I've never felt anything like what he makes me feel—this overwhelming mixture of terror and joy, bliss and foreboding.

And there's something else that bothers me. A lot.

"You said that Dylan's soul is somewhere else, and that you're borrowing his body." He sighs, and I know the answer to my question before I ask it. "He's coming back. Isn't he?"

"Yes."

Oh god. Dylan. Not the Dylan who loves me or stands up for me or kisses me like I'm the heroine in an old 1980s movie. The other Dylan. The one who took bets on whether he could get me to sleep with him and thinks I'm a loser-freak-joke.

"I'm sorry." Romeo tugs the end of my braid. "Do you hate me?"

I look up. "Why would I hate you?"

"We don't have much time. Maybe it would have been better . . ." His eyes scan my face, as if trying to memorize every part. "I don't want you to think I'm using you. I'm here because I care, but maybe it would have been better if I'd left you alone."

"No." The strength in the word surprises me. "How long do we have? To figure out what to do?"

Romeo pulls my hand to his lips and whispers against my skin, "If the witch keeps her word, until Friday at midnight. Three days from when I arrived in Dylan's body."

Three days. That means it could all end tomorrow night. If I don't figure out how to help him, then . . . what happens next? I don't know. But I can guess it will be bad. Heartbreakingly bad.

The thought has barely flashed through my mind before I'm reaching for him. I can't speak. I can't think about him dying or worse. I can't think about being alone without him. I need him close while he still has a body to show me how he feels.

He comes to me, moving over me as I lie back on the carpet. His hands cup my face and his lips meet mine, and he kisses me with all the pain and love and desperation that I'm feeling. My heart is so full I feel I might explode, but the particles inside of me are still spreading, reaching out, finding space that wasn't there before. Finding hope that feels more like a peephole into another world than a chink in my armor.

"I'll figure it out," I whisper. "I'll find a way. I won't let you go."

"Just promise me one thing." His fingers brush my cheek, even that small touch enough to make my heart race faster. "Promise me you'll never forget how this feels."

"I promise." It would be impossible to forget. If he's gone by tomorrow night, I'll spend the rest of my life replaying every second with him, this person who fits me more perfectly than I imagined possible.

"And I want . . . If we can't be together, I want you to find someone else. Let someone else love you as much as I wish I could."

Love. He said it. Or at least he said he wished he could love me, which is practically the same thing. Isn't it? I don't know. I only know that, "I don't want anyone else." Tears rise in my eyes, a stinging flood I refuse to set loose. "And no one wants me. I'm nobody."

"You're not nobody," he says. "Not to me."

And then he kisses me again, and I kiss him back, and keep kissing him. Even when the bell rings, signaling the end of homeroom, and the halls outside fill with the sounds of people talking and laughing and slamming locker doors. All of that is distant and unreal, another world. I've entered my own alternate reality, one where I'm brave and not afraid to fight for what I want.

Romeo

Mission nearly accomplished. I should be pleased.

Ariel is *so close* to loving me. I can feel it in the way her lips move against mine, in the eager hands that pull me close. I've almost won her heart and paved the way for my departure. When Dylan comes back to this body, she won't be surprised or hurt. She'll be able to hold on to the memory of our time together and weather the fallout. I've even planted the seed for a love-filled future, with my noble request that she find someone else if I'm not able to stay.

Even with the strange absence of *Romeo and Juliet* in this world, I know I should be congratulating myself. Giving myself a mental high five and an exploding fist bump and tossing off the worry that has felt as if it will eat me alive.

Ariel is a sure thing. I won't ever have to go back to my rotted corpse. I will be an Ambassador. The world is saved—at least for the time being—and the Ambassadors and Mercenaries will continue to duke it out for control of however many realities there are, for however much time is allowed them. It's exactly what I hoped for, and if I had to color the truth to win Ariel over to the light, who cares? It's best for everyone if she never learns her capacity for evil.

So why does her touch fill me with pain? Why are her lips the most bittersweet thing I've ever tasted?

Because she's a dead woman. No. A dead girl, *and you know it, you worthless, faithless coward.*

It's true. But I've known from the beginning that what I was sent here to do would put Ariel's life at risk. In the beginning, the Ambassador's promise to "take care of her" was enough to set my guilt aside. But suddenly it's not. Not nearly.

Look at how that Ambassador "took care of" Juliet. She enslaved her in ignorance for centuries and then abandoned her to be killed by the Mercenaries. How can I risk leaving Ariel to a fate like that? How can I justify what I've done, no matter how much good will come of it?

I don't know. All I know is that here, in her arms, with her bones resting on mine and her pulse racing beneath my lips, I can't imagine anything worse than a reality without Ariel in it.

Then do something. Take action, before tomorrow night.

I will. I must. At the very least, I can warn Ariel more specifically, make sure she's as prepared for Mercenary evil as a human being can be. Perhaps knowledge can save her. And if not . . .

Then I'll do what I have to do. Like the Ambassador said, I'm not one of them yet. I can still lie and cheat and kill to get what I want, and what I want is Ariel alive.

FOURTEEN

Ariel

His voice is still beautiful—even more beautiful, though I wouldn't have thought that possible a few days ago—but it isn't Dylan's. It's higher, sweeter, and so pure it makes my bones tingle and the hairs on my arms stand on end. Listening to Romeo sing is a full body experience. It would be even if I hadn't spent the day dreaming about how I want to spend what I pray *isn't* our last full night together.

My toes curl in my shoes, and my hands shake as I load my paint supplies into the cart I'll wheel back to the art room tomorrow morning. I can hardly wait for him to come down off the stage, take my hand, and run with me until we find someplace where we can be alone. Together.

Together together. Me and Romeo. Tonight.

Just thinking about it is enough to make me want to spin in giddy circles. I can't decide if I'm more terrified or excited, but everything I know about fairy-tale curses points to this as a potential solution. In the stories, love is always the answer. Love breaks the spell and turns the frog into a prince, the beast into a man, and would have kept the Little Mermaid on land with legs and the man of her dreams if the stupid prince hadn't fallen in love with someone else.

Romeo and I have certainly shared true love's kiss—shared it well into first period, in fact, and got yelled at by Mr. Stark for coming in late to English—but I still haven't said the words. I can't. Not yet. There's a part of me that refuses to believe this is real, a snarky voice inside that insists I've finally gone off the deep end. But I know how to silence that voice. Tonight, when Romeo is as close to me as another person can get, when I look up into his eyes and see straight into his soul, I'll know there's no reason to hold back. I'll tell him then. That I . . . love him. Because I do, I really think I do.

Being with Romeo makes me feel more alive than I've felt in my entire life. Before I met him, it was like my skin was completely made up of scars, a numb shell too afraid to give pleasure a chance. But now my skin is awake and wild and as determined as the rest of me.

I lift my eyes, find him standing center stage, commanding the attention of the room. His last note hangs in the air, filling the cafeteria, catching and holding every listener captive.

The rest of the choir stands motionless at the base of the

stage, the cafeteria ladies have stopped their after-school cleanup in the back rooms, and the teachers and students working the decorations committee for the dance are frozen—tissue flowers and gossip forgotten. In the silence after the music fades, we're as quiet as residents of a graveyard for one breathless moment before first one and then another person sighs in relief. It's awful that it's over, but in a way we're glad. It can be painful to listen to something so perfect for too long.

The silence gives way to enthusiastic applause and a "whoot, whoot" from someone in the choir, but Romeo either doesn't realize the effect he's had or doesn't care. He just slips the microphone back into its stand, glances at Mrs. Mullens—who gives him a shaky thumbs-up—and grabs his jacket from the floor of the stage. He hurries down the steps as I tuck the last clean brush into the cart.

"Hey." His voice is full of the same wonder that has made me feel like I'm floating a few feet off the ground all day.

"Hey." I smile.

"You ready?" He holds out his hand.

"Completely." I twine my fingers through his and let him lead the way out of the cafeteria, feeling more sure of my decision with every step. His hand feels so right in mine. I know everything else will feel just as right. Perfect. As magical as Romeo himself.

Romeo

"Maybe we should hold off on shopping. Are you sure you even want to go to the dance?" Ariel asks. She dawdles at my side as we cross the parking lot, as decidedly *un*-thrilled by our errand as she was ten minutes ago when I aimed the car toward the Goodwill store over by Highway 101. "We don't have to go, you know. I don't–"

"Of course we do," I say. "Dances are fun."

"No, they're not," she deadpans, the flatness in her tone making me laugh.

I grab her hand and loop it through my arm. "Have you ever been to a dance?"

"No."

"See there. You don't know if they're fun." I stop in front of the store and turn to her, smile faltering at the look in her eyes. It's the same look she had the entire time she was painting, the one that leaves no doubt what she's thinking about. And knowing she's thinking about *that* makes it impossible for me to keep from thinking about *that.* About her long fingers on the buttons of my shirt, my hands pulling her blouse over her head, her lips on mine as she starts to work on unbelting and unbuttoning and–

"So. Yeah." I clear my throat and scan the parking lot, pretending I'm checking where I parked the car while I pull myself together.

Just yesterday I was determined to enjoy myself with Ariel if the opportunity presented itself, but it's different now. No matter how much I want to be with her, it doesn't feel right. I'll be gone by tomorrow night. That's the truth, no matter what false hope I've allowed her to cling to in the name of making our short time together happier.

And when Dylan comes back, I don't want him to be in possession of any of *those* types of memories. I don't want him to have ammunition he could use to hurt Ariel. Even more important, I don't want to share. I don't want another boy, even one whose body I'm using for my own purposes, to know Ariel in that way. I'm sure it will happen for her eventually—when our days together are a dim, surreal memory—but I'll be in the mist by then, awaiting my call to service from the Ambassadors, safe from the knowledge that she's found someone else.

"Besides," I say in a falsely upbeat voice. "I want to go to the dance."

"You want to go," she repeats. "I don't—"

"I want to go *with you*," I correct her, wrapping my arms around her waist. "I want to hold you close and inhale the magical scent of hot-glued felt flowers and old burritos and boys wearing too much cheap cologne." She rolls her eyes, but I can feel her relaxing. "And I want to remember you being as beautiful as I know you'll be tomorrow night."

She drops her chin to her chest. I can tell she's thinking about tomorrow night being our last night, but thankfully she doesn't say a word. If she asks me about it again, I might tell her the truth, and the truth isn't good for anyone.

She'll hate me if she learns that Juliet didn't simply die but was tricked into killing herself. That *I* am the one who did the tricking, and that I was sent here to deceive her in much the same way. She'll be angry, horrified. It certainly won't make her love me or turn her heart toward the light. Unburdening my conscience would be an entirely selfish act.

So why do I feel so compelled to tell her everything?

I don't know. But a streak of madness deep in my bones urges me to pull her back to the car, drive her up to the mountain cave where the specter of my soul raves in his prison, and confess every sordid, shameful detail of my past. I suppose a part of me thinks she *might* be able to forgive me. And if she can forgive me, then maybe . . . maybe . . .

You don't deserve forgiveness. Your own, or anyone else's.

"Okay," Ariel says, calling me back from the dark corners of my mind. "But I don't know if I'm going to find a dress here. They usually don't have much in my size."

"We'll find something. Don't worry." I urge her toward the entrance. "In addition to my killer charm and haunting singing voice, I happen to have an eye for fashion."

She smiles. "Of course you do."

"Undeniably." I motion to the ensemble I pulled together from Dylan's sad little closet—dark jeans, a khaki button-up rolled at the sleeves, and a burgundy sweater vest I found in a box. I suspect the vest was his mother's, but I put it on anyway. "I mean, look at me."

"Gorgeous." She pinches my stomach as she walks by. "And so modest."

"Modesty is for lesser men." I hold the door open as she steps through. Inside, the air is warm and pungent with the smell of dusty old clothes. It's strong, like the scent lingering in a barn, and I can't keep from wrinkling my nose.

Ariel giggles beneath her breath. "Powerful, isn't it?"

"We'll wash everything twice. Three times if we have to."

"Right. But you know . . . Well, I wouldn't want to *wear* it, but I kind of like the smell." She leads the way to the back of the store, past aisles of faded blue jeans and circular clothes racks stuffed with sagging sweaters. "It reminds me of when I was little. My mom and I didn't shop anywhere else until I was in junior high. We still come once a month or so."

"So you know the lay of the land."

"I do." She smiles, and reaches back to claim my hand. "Don't worry, I'll show you the way."

Her words send a sizzle of electricity across my skin. I try to ignore it, but it's damned difficult. All I want to do is touch her. Being near her has become frighteningly imperative. I stand too close as we flip through a rack of hideous suits. My fingers nip her bare waist when she reaches up to slide a red dress from its hanger, and I squeeze her hips through her jeans when she grabs shiny white leather boots from the floor.

By the time we make it to the dressing room—arms full of smelly clothes in various shades of obnoxious—I can barely resist the urge to pull her into the curtained partition with me. There's a girl's curtain and a boy's curtain, but the old woman working the cash register has glasses an inch thick and a hearing aid the size of a piece of cauliflower sticking out of each ear. She won't notice if Ariel slips in with me.

And watching her getting dressed and undressed, and knowing you can't touch her, won't be torturous. Not at all.

"I do enjoy a little torture now and then," I whisper, visions of my fingers tugging zippers up and down for Ariel making my mouth run dry.

Ariel turns, hand lingering on the curtain of the girl's room. "What?"

"I said you have to come out and show me everything."

"You too. I especially want to see the plaid one." She smiles that wicked grin that makes her thin lips even thinner. The one that makes me want to kiss her. But then . . . what doesn't?

Damn. I have to stop dwelling on temptation, or there will be no doubt about *if* I'll give in, only *when.*

I duck into the dressing room, determined to achieve some level of control. My choice of wardrobe helps. The suits I've picked are deliberately awful. My motto for fashion: If you can't afford to make an elegant statement, make a ridiculous one. Hence the plaid suit jacket, the pleated olive-green pants with the camouflage sweater, and the skin-tight acid-washed jeans with the "Jesus Rocks My World" T-shirt. All of them get a laugh from Ariel, but when I come out in the robin's-egg-blue bell-bottom tuxedo with brown piping and the ruffled collar, I know I've found a winner.

"You're kidding me." Her laughter bubbles up from deep inside her, and a silly grin blooms on my face.

Her laughter. It makes me so *stupidly* happy. Like a small child. Or a dog. I should be ashamed of myself—enjoying her so much when all I've done is lie and put her life in danger—but I'm not. I need this, just an hour or two to relish the innocent pleasure of her company.

"It's only sixteen ninety-five," I say with a flutter of my lashes.

"You're serious."

I prop my hands on my waist and stick out a hip, striking a pose worthy of a supermodel. "Look at me. Don't I look serious?"

She collapses into the chair outside the dressing room in a fit of giggles so cute they make my insides fizz. "No! You must be stopped," she says.

"Why?" I strut down an aisle of yellowed lingerie, swiveling my hips, batting bras with flicks of my fingers. "I will be the king of the disco. I will be—" I spin and strike another pose. "An inspiration."

She sniffs and swipes at her eyes. "The real Dylan would die before he'd be seen in public in something like that."

"The real Dylan is boring." I brace my hands on the arms of her chair and lean down until our faces are a whisper apart. "And he's not one fourth the kisser I am."

"Is that right?" Her lips quirk.

"You know it is."

Her smile melts, and her breath comes faster. "Yeah. I do."

"So don't even think about kissing him again after I'm gone." I manage to hold on to my playful tone, but only barely. "You'll be very disappointed."

She exhales, and the last of her merriment floats away. "I don't want to kiss anyone else. I don't want you to go."

"I don't want to go." My voice is as rough as the scars on her face. I dip my head and press a kiss to her cheek.

Her arms loop around my neck. "Please . . . can't you tell me something? Help me help you."

"I wish I . . ." I duck my head, knowing the lies will come easier if I'm not looking her in the eye. "I can't say a word, or the magic keeping me in Dylan's body will vanish."

Her cool fingertips dig into my skin. "I hate the woman who did this to you."

"Don't hate her. Don't hate anyone." I kiss her other cheek. "You're too beautiful for hate."

"You realize you're the only one who thinks I'm pretty, right?"

"I didn't say pretty; I said beautiful. And I wasn't talking about the way you look. I'm talking about who you are." She looks up at me, lips parted, but this time I know she doesn't want a kiss. She wants to know if I'm serious.

I pause, stare deep into those naked blue eyes and realize . . . I am serious. "I've told a lot of lies in my time," I say, hoping she can see that I'm speaking from what's left of my heart. "And I'm really, *really* good at making people believe them. But I'm not lying about what I see in you. You are unique and wonderful and powerful, and, if you let yourself, someday you'll be fearless. You'll change the world. Make it better."

And I wish I could be there to see it.

"If I do," she whispers, "it will be because of you." She kisses my forehead, and I die a little. I'm not worthy of her respect or affection, and I never will be. "Okay." She runs a fond hand through my hair, making the hurt a little worse. "I'm glad you're wearing this monstrosity."

I swallow, fighting to keep the self-loathing from my expression. "Why?"

"It's hard to be completely sad when you're wearing so many ruffles." She flips my collar before standing and crossing to her dressing room. "So you've picked out your . . . statement. Now you have to help me find something."

I plop down in the chair, cross my arms, and affect a pout, determined to recapture our playful mood. "How can I? When you didn't model any of them for me?"

"I couldn't. The red dress was way too big, and I won't have time to alter it before tomorrow night. The pink one was too short, and really ugly, and made me look like I was ten. The plaid skirt and sweater were okay, and they would have matched the plaid suit coat, but with you wearing the blue tux . . ."

"Hold on a second." A memory of the store window flickers through my mind. "Get in there and get naked," I say, heading toward the front of the store.

"Now, that's what I've been waiting to hear." The words are softly spoken, even a little shy, but there's no missing the sultry note in her tone.

FIFTEEN

Romeo

I turn to find her watching me with *that* look in her eye, the hungry one that makes me even hungrier. Innocent girl, *my ass.* I don't care if she did have her first kiss only two days ago. Ariel is a temptress, and I am . . . weak, weakening, weaken-est.

I walk back to her, feeling the danger increase with every step. "What is that supposed to mean?"

"I think you know," she says. "But I can tell you if you don't."

"No," I say, not sure I can take hearing her say the words aloud. "I don't think that's a good idea. Dylan will be coming back to this body."

"Maybe."

"Most likely. And I don't know what he'll remember. If—If we— He may remember he was with you because he fell in love with you. Or he may remember he was with you for some other reason. Including that bet."

"I don't care what he remembers."

"I care," I say. "I don't want you hurt."

"You'll hurt me more if you don't listen to me." She lays her palms over my heart, making it beat faster. "I want to do everything I can with you in the time we have left. I want to go to my first dance, and cook my first dinner, and go skinny-dipping, and everything else we can fit in."

Skinny-dipping. What's she trying to *do* to me? "It's cold outside."

"I know a hot spring, way out in the country near where my grandparents used to live. It's warm all year, and very private." She tips onto her toes, bringing her lips closer to mine. "We'll bring a picnic. And towels and blankets to wrap up in. After. It will be perfect."

Blankets. After. Perfect.

I close my eyes, but open them immediately, finding no strength in the images flashing behind my closed lids.

"I was serious this morning. I've walked the earth for more than seven hundred years. Most of that time is a blur, and I still feel like a young man, but what I *feel* doesn't matter. The reality is that I am *repulsively* old."

She cocks her head, as if I've said something stupidly adorable. "I don't think you're repulsive."

"You don't know everything about me. In many ways, I'm still a monster."

"Are you trying to scare me?"

Am I? I should be encouraging her love/lust in all forms, not frightening her away. But I don't want to lie anymore, and I don't know if I can keep from telling the truth if we're skin to skin. "Maybe. Maybe you should be scared."

"Your curse doesn't scare me; why should your age?"

"Because, I'm . . ." I sputter and try again. "It's . . . I'm . . ."

She takes my hand. "When I look at you, I don't see a monster."

"You don't see *me*. You see a body I've—"

"I see *you*," she says, with a surety that shuts me up for a moment. "And I care about you. Isn't that all that matters?" Her fingers link through mine, making my throat feel tight.

Care. She still hasn't said she loves me. I need to finish the job of winning her, no matter what it takes. I can't afford to keep pushing her away, but I can't seem to stop.

"Care matters. But what if the woman at the register were a man? An old man with hair in strange places and sagging skin and a giant red nose and ears that touch his shoulders and that nearly-dead smell people get after a lifetime of eating too much meat? What would you say then?"

"I'd say that's pretty gross."

"Exactly. Now multiply that times ten and you'll have some idea how truly undesirable I—"

She stops me with a kiss that turns into a smile and another kiss. By the time she pulls away, I'm smiling again. I can't help myself. She . . . *does* things to me. This girl.

"You're so romantic," she says.

"I'm not trying to be romantic." I scowl.

"Which is very romantic. In its own way," she says. "But pointless. I want what I want, and you don't have the words to convince me that I don't want it." And then her arm is around my waist and she's kissing me again, a long, lingering kiss that makes my body hum and my soul ache, and makes Longing lift its fist and knock out the much weaker Reason with a single blow.

I sigh into her and give up the fight. My fingers thread through her hair, pulling her closer, knowing I'll never get enough of her. She intoxicates me, but not in the way that leaves a man senseless. She lifts me up like a breath of sweet air, like sun on my skin, like . . . god.

No, not god. Like the *idea* of god, the one I imagined when I was a boy, before my father broke my mother's faith and spirit, back when she told stories of the merciful lord who loved me and my brother no matter what. Through her eyes, I saw something bigger than myself, bigger than any trouble that would ever find me. It was intoxicating, the thought of being loved so much, to have been given such a gift.

To *give* such a gift.

Could I? Maybe? Could I . . . *love* Ariel? Is that why she makes me feel this way?

Liar. Such a grand liar, you've deceived yourself.

I wince, and the rhythm of our kiss falters for a moment. Right. I don't love her. I never would have so much as spoken her name if I didn't need her to save me from a fate worse than death. This isn't love. It's gratitude.

And lust, of course. It's lust that makes something primal inside of me insist that this girl is mine and no one else's. It feels like more, but it isn't. Juliet found a second soul mate, but were I able to see my own aura, I know it wouldn't be blushing the pink of true love. I am a damned thing in limbo, of neither the light nor the dark, and my soul is too tainted to ever feel anything innocent or true.

But still . . . I *need* her, and the need cuts so deep, it makes me dizzy. I don't know why. I don't know anything anymore. I'm lost and confused and drowning in my own thought vomit.

I pull away, breath coming fast. "I don't know what's right." I shake my head. "You make me feel . . ."

"Like you're eighteen?"

I gaze down into her peaceful face, considering her all over again. Every time I think I've got a complete picture of Ariel drawn in my mind, she does something to surprise me, to smudge the edges into something new, an image more complex and intriguing than what it was before. "I guess so. I never made it to eighteen, but . . ."

"And you make me feel normal." She rests her head on my chest, and my arms go around her. There's no question that they will. "I've never felt normal, and I don't know how long it will be until I feel this way again. If ever. But with you, I am, and it's . . . perfect. So just go with me. Okay?"

I'm not sure what I'm promising, but I find I don't really care. I don't want to think; I want to feel. Like her, I want to feel normal, even if only for a stolen moment that will have to last me eternity. Besides, I've never been the "good guy." No reason to start now, especially when Ariel is practically begging me to be bad. "All right," I say.

She looks up at me. "Yes?"

"Yes."

Her smile is the loveliest thing I've ever seen. "Good."

Not good. But it's too late to turn back now. "Go back to the dressing room. I'm going to bring you something perfect."

"And then we'll get out of here," she says.

"And then we'll get out of here."

"And go wherever I want to go."

"Wherever you want to go."

"And do whatever I want to do."

I take a breath. "Whatever you want to do. Whatever."

She smiles and walks calmly into the dressing room. I take a moment, appreciating every step, keenly aware of how I hate to see her go.

Ariel

At first I think he's joking. "That's a wedding dress," I say, pulling my hand away from the hanger like the skirt is concealing a poisonous snake in its ruffles.

"I know." He sticks his face through the curtain, looking disappointed that I'm still in my shirt and jeans. My eyes meet his, and my lips tingle, wanting to kiss him again already. "Try it on."

"But—"

"It will be perfect."

"But I—"

"Trust me?"

Yes. I do trust him. I *do*. I trust him with my heart and soul. So I take the dress and fight my way through the crinoline and twist myself into knots hooking every hook and zipping every zipper.

And when I'm finally through, I'm so, *so* glad that I did.

I stand before the full-length mirror in the dressing room, mesmerized by my reflection. The deep V of the neckline is pretty scandalous, but it emphasizes what little I have on top in a way I never thought clothing could accomplish. The narrow waist fits perfectly, and the ruffles that start on the left hip and swirl in a half circle around the skirt aren't ridiculous at all. They're gorgeous, and give the dress a feeling of movement even when I'm standing still. It already seems like I'm dancing. I can only imagine how beautiful it will look when I'm spinning around the floor in Romeo's arms.

His arms. I want to be in them. *Right now.* I reach for the zipper and drag it down.

"I hear a zipper," he says from outside the curtain, making me jump. The realization that he's hovering makes me smile, and my skin feel hot all over.

"It fits. I'm going to put my other clothes back on."

"Aren't you going to show me first?"

"Not until the wedding day," I tease, pulling at another zipper.

"But I want to see!"

"Tomorrow night." I undo the waist hooks and let the dress puddle to the ground around my ankles as I reach for my jeans. "It will be more fun if it's a surprise."

"You have a cruel idea of fun." He sniffs. "Fine. I don't need to see it. I'm sure it looks as good as *I* knew it would." He sounds genuinely upset. He really does love clothes. If I let myself, I can imagine us making this a regular thing, imagine him teaching me how to dress, like the shopping buddy I never had. The buddy who makes me understand the meaning of lust for the first time in my life.

I do. I *lust* for him. It's like a brain-and-personality-altering drug. I can't believe half the things I've said in the past thirty minutes, but I don't regret any of them. I'm ready. I can't wait.

I grab the dress and push through the curtain, but my grin fades when I see that Romeo isn't standing outside. I scan the store, thinking he must have gone to pay for his tux, but he isn't at the cash register, either. He isn't by the shoes or the suits or the—

I spot his dark head in the section with the dishes and pots and pans. His back is turned and it looks like he's talking to someone. But who? It's not like any of Dylan's friends would come to the Goodwill. Tanner's parents are loaded, and Jason Kim's family is flat-out *stinking* rich, almost as well off as Gemma's. The Kims own the property next door to the Sloop compound, fifteen acres with a hobby vineyard and a mansion with an indoor basketball court. Allegedly.

I've never been there, but Gemma has. Her parents used to make her tag along to barbeques at their neighbor's house when she was younger. She told me all about the basketball court and Jason's loft room that's as big as my entire house.

Gemma. I haven't thought about her all day. It's strange. Ever since she disappeared the week before last, I've been so worried that I haven't been able to go long without imagining the horrible things that could have happened to my best friend. It's been a scary distraction. But today I've been distracted by other things. This is the first time she's crossed my mind, which only makes it that much more shocking when I get close enough to see Romeo talking to a girl with shiny brown hair that brushes her shoulders, bright red lipstick, and a ball cap pulled down low over her face. Even with the hat, I know her immediately.

It's Gemma. Here. In Solvang. Alive! Home!

I'm so excited, I drop the dress and run. "Gemma!"

She turns to me, the anger in her expression transforming to surprise of the not-totally-pleasant variety. A funny feeling flutters inside me, but it's too late to adjust my course. I'm already practically on top of her.

The hug is brief—only a few seconds—but it's enough to make me feel really, *really* stupid. She's rigid and tight, and I can feel her wanting to pull away. I unwrap my arms as fast as I can and step back, covering my awkwardness with a smile. "I'm so glad to see you!"

"You too. You just . . . scared me." She tugs her cap lower and glances nervously around the deserted store before knotting her arms across her chest. "What are you doing here?"

"I'm here with Rom—Dylan."

"You're here together?" She raises a skeptical eyebrow, and shoots Dylan an even more skeptical look. I glance at Romeo, but he's staring at the ground. Guess he wants me to handle this. It makes sense. She is *my* best friend.

"Yeah. We're shopping for the dance."

"You're kidding." A bubble of shocked laughter pops from her lips.

"No. I'm not," I say, angry before I finish the last word.

Why am I the one answering questions? Why is she doing her best to embarrass me? And more important, why is she acting like everything's fine and this is any other time that we've run into each other in town? She's been a missing person for what feels like forever!

"Forget about me. Where have you been?" I don't try to keep the irritation from my tone. "We've all been so worried. I've been crazy wondering if you're okay."

She purses her lips and widens her eyes, as if I'm the one who's behaving irrationally. "It hasn't even been two weeks, Ree. I'm sorry I didn't call, but I've—"

"No one knew if you were dead or alive!" I cross my arms too, feeling the need to brace myself against this conversation.

"Your parents have posters up all over town. They think you've been kidnapped or murdered or—"

"My parents are full of shit," she says, the same heat in her voice that always accompanies mention of her mom or dad. "They know I'm fine. So do the police. Haven't you wondered why there's nothing on the news about a Sloop being kidnapped?"

"I . . . no. I didn't . . ." I swallow against the acid rising in my throat. "They really know you're okay?"

"Yes!"

"Then why—"

"I'm sure they're hoping someone will see me if I come back into town, and report back like a good Sloop minion," she says, with another anxious survey of the store. "That's why I'm staying away from the town center. I haven't graduated yet, so there's a chance my parents could force me to come back if they find me. But I called them the first night I left. They know I'm never coming home again."

"What?"

"I don't belong to them anymore." She lifts her left hand in the air and holds it there. For a second I think she's going to give me the finger or something, and I am entirely, furiously confused. Then I see it. The rings. There are two. One a simple silver band and one with a tiny little diamond poking proudly into the air.

"You . . ." I shake my head. I can't even say the words. I was freaked out by trying on a wedding dress I plan to wear to a dance. I can't believe that Gemma's actually—

"I'm married," she says, erasing any doubt.

"To who?"

Her eyes flash as she takes a peek toward the door. "You'll

see. He's getting gas, but he'll be here in a second. He needs some jeans for our trip, and we're trying to save money. But he's over eighteen and I'm eighteen, so it's completely legal. My parents are going to have to live with it. I talked to a lawyer in LA. As soon as I get my GED, they will *never* control my life ever again." She smiles, but it's different from her usual smile. There's no anger or meanness lingering beneath, no hint of the sarcastic smirk that's been the only smile in Gemma's repertoire since the seventh grade.

She just looks happy. A little manic, but still . . . happy. Free.

No matter how upset I still am, I can't help but feel happy for her. Even if I have a hard time believing that getting married was a good idea. Gemma bores easily. I've never known her to date the same guy for more than a couple of months. I can't imagine her content with one person for a *year,* let alone until death do them part.

"So how's that working out? Your happily ever after?" Romeo asks, speaking up for the first time.

I cut my eyes his way, silently warning him not to ask Gemma any questions. Maybe he doesn't know that Gemma and Dylan hate each other.

As if on cue, Gemma curls her lip and snarls, "It's going great, psycho. How's the sociopath thing going? Skinned any small animals lately?"

"Not lately. I've been trying to cut back."

Gemma falters, surprised by the comeback. I pounce on the moment. "So where are you going to live?" I ask. "Are you going to get an apartment in town or—"

"No way. We're out of here as soon as possible. Which reminds me . . ." Gemma casts another meaningful look Dylan's way. "Could you disappear? I need to talk to Ariel without being overheard by the criminally insane."

Romeo slides an arm around my waist. For the first time, his touch makes me feel awkward. "Anything you say to Ariel, you can say to me."

Gemma laughs. "Come again?"

"You heard me."

"I don't know who you think you're fooling, Stroud," she says, her voice pure acid, "but I—"

"Hey, Gemma. Sorry. I was—" A breathless man wearing a short-sleeved black shirt—the better to show off his many tattoos—hurries up the aisle behind Gemma. He slows when he sees she's not alone. "Oh. Hi, Ariel. Dylan." He offers me a grin, but his expression grows chilly when he nods to Romeo.

He knows Dylan is in trouble a lot. Mike worked at the school for almost an entire semester, and probably had Dylan in detention at least once or twice. Mr. Stark always makes his student teachers do the things he hates to do. Like run detention and grade papers and tutor the kids who are having trouble writing a persuasive argument. Mike was tutoring Gemma until he took a leave of absence twelve days ago. Mr. Stark said he had family problems and had to take some time off. Now I know that was a lie. Mike wasn't having family problems; he was eloping with one of his students.

Wow. Gemma. And Mike, the *student teacher*. It's . . . scandalous.

Which is probably why she did it. Gemma loves anything with shock value. I'm sure she'd have her own collection of tattoos if she didn't have a fear of needles.

"How are you, Ariel?" Mike asks. "Did Gemma ask you to meet us here?"

"No, she just *happened* to be here." Gemma wraps her arm around his waist, mimicking Dylan's possessive gesture. "It's a sign, don't you think?"

"I do." He smiles down at her, his eyes soft.

Aw. At least one of them got married for the right reasons. Mike's clearly in love. Crazy in love. It makes me hope Gemma feels the same way. If not, he's going to be really, really hurt when she decides to dump him for the next flavor of the week. I look back at her, searching her face for some clue as to how she feels, but she's not looking at Mike, or me. She's still glaring. At Dylan.

"Will you please leave?" she asks. "Mike and I need to talk to Ariel, and you are not welcome."

"Please, Gemma," I say. "I–"

"It's all right." Romeo steps away and scoops my dress from the floor. "I'll go pay for our things. Call if you need me."

I nod, but I hate the feel of him easing away from me. I don't want to be apart. Our time is running out, and I don't want to miss a moment. Even for Gemma. I love her, and she's been my best friend since we were little, but her complete lack of concern for how her disappearance would make me feel has soured this reunion.

"What a freak show." Gemma rolls her eyes. "I thought he'd never leave. What are you doing with him, Ree? He's twisted."

"He's nice to me."

"I'm not exactly sure what you think *nice* means, but Dylan isn't–"

"I know what nice means," I say, interrupting Gemma for the first time in our friendship. "And I know it isn't *nice* to disappear and not even *think* about how worried your best friend will be. I was really scared. You should have called me."

Gemma's mouth falls open, and she stares at me for a long, long minute. "I'm . . . sorry," she finally says, glancing up at Mike before she continues. "I didn't think."

"I'm sorry too," Mike says. "We called the police, and faxed over our marriage license to Gemma's parents and the police department. We thought everything was okay. We had no idea Gemma's parents had posters up until we got into town this morning."

"We seriously didn't," Gemma agrees. "But . . . I . . . You're right. I should have called."

"Yeah. You should have."

"I'm really sorry." She sounds like she means it, and there's a shine in her eyes when she asks, "Forgive me?"

"Forgiven," I say, amazed by how easy that was.

Jeez. I should have called Gemma on her bull *years* ago. But I was too grateful to have a friend to risk standing up to her. I wouldn't risk it now if it weren't for Romeo. His words from earlier still knock around inside me. He thinks I'm strong, that I could change the world. He has certainly changed me. If he can touch me this deeply in a couple of days, think how I could touch the world in a lifetime. Maybe there is a way out of the dark present to a brighter future.

It would be a nice thought, if the possibility of facing the future without Romeo weren't tearing me apart. I turn, and find him still at the checkout counter. Gemma has five more minutes, and then I'm out of here.

"Are we okay?" she asks.

"We're good." I smile. "What did you need to talk about?"

She takes a deep breath. "I need a favor. Kind of a big one."

"Okay." I look between her and Mike, but their hopeful expressions don't give me any clue what the favor is going to be. "What's up?"

"Mike and I are headed to Seattle, to stay with some friends of his for a while until my dad calms down," Gemma says. "When I talked to him, he said he was going to force me to have the marriage annulled."

"But you're eighteen. You're legally an adult."

"He says since I'm still in high school it doesn't matter. Their lawyer said they have the right to force me to live under their roof until I graduate. Or get my GED, which I obviously haven't had time to do yet."

"Maybe if you talk to them, they'll change their minds?"

"Since when have my parents listened to anything I say?" She's right. Her mom and dad have never been big on caring about what Gemma wants. "There's no point in talking to them. We wouldn't have even come back here if we didn't need cash. Mike's savings are running out, and we need something to hold us over until we can get jobs in Seattle. I've got a thousand dollars and a bunch of jewelry hidden in a box in the back of my closet. If we hock the jewelry, that should last us until we get money things figured out. The only problem is . . . getting to it."

"We have to lay low," Mike says. "I shouldn't have let Gemma get out of the car and come in here, but there was hardly anyone in the parking lot, and–"

"And the lady who works here is blind," Gemma says. "And deaf. And I didn't think anyone who knew me well enough to connect my face to that poster would be at the Goodwill."

"Never underestimate the allure of the Goodwill," I say, earning a smile from Mike and a grunt from Gemma. "Okay, so you want *me* to go get your stuff." The thought of walking into the Sloop home without Gemma makes my heart race. Her mom is a supersnob, and her dad is plain scary. His eyes don't look like they're connected to a soul. "But how will I get inside?"

"Tell them you left a few things in my room the last time you spent the night. Go right after school before my dad gets in from work. My mom will be back from her morning shift at the tasting room and will have had her first couple glasses of chardonnay by then. She'll be too buzzed to walk you up the stairs. She'll send you up, and you can stick the box in the bottom of your backpack and pile some of my T-shirts and pajamas on top. She won't check your bag, and even if she does, she doesn't know what my stuff looks like anymore. You can just tell her they're yours, wish her good luck finding her long-lost daughter, and head out the door."

I think about it for a few seconds before nodding. "Okay."

"Okay?" She sounds surprised.

"I'll do it. What about Saturday? Your dad works at the tasting room until three or so, right? I could—"

"Could you go tomorrow instead? Please?" Gemma wheedles, obviously seeing the reluctance on my face. Tomorrow could be my last day with Romeo. "It won't take more than half an hour. You can just grab the box, swing it by our room at the Knight and Day Motor Lodge, and we'll be on our way and out of your hair."

I know she wants to get out of town before someone who's seen those posters spots her and reports back to her mom and dad. "All right." It shouldn't take long. And I can always ask Romeo to drive me. "I'll go tomorrow. Right after school."

"You will?"

"Didn't you think I would?"

"Well . . . yeah." She cocks her head. "But I thought you'd need a lot more convincing."

"No." I glance over my shoulder. Romeo is waiting by the door, his suit and my dress flung over his arm. I don't need any more convincing, and even if I did, I wouldn't stick around to get it. I have my own drama to live for once. "It sounds doable. I'll take care of it and meet you at your hotel at four."

Gemma smiles and lunges for me, wrapping me in a fierce hug. "Thank you so much, Ree! You're a lifesaver."

"Really, thank you. We're in room fifty-three. Around the back," Mike says, a little uncomfortably. I can tell he doesn't like the thought of needing Gemma's money to get by, but I imagine he's strapped for cash. It's not like you make any money being a student teacher. "We appreciate your help."

"Consider it my wedding present," I say when Gemma finally sets me free. "I hope you'll be really happy together."

"We will be." Gemma beams up at Mike. As far as I can tell, she loves him more than she's ever loved anyone else. Which doesn't necessarily mean a whole lot, but still . . . I hope it will be enough.

"Okay," I say as I back away. "Then I'll see you at—"

"Wait." Gemma's eyes shift to where Dylan stands by the door, then back to me. "I honestly don't mean to be a jerk, but you should think twice about dating Dylan. He's not a nice guy."

"I know what I'm doing. I promise. But thanks for worrying about me."

"But, Ree, I—"

"I've got it under control," I say, as firmly as I've ever said anything to Gemma. "Trust me. I'm not stupid."

For a second I think she's going to keep arguing, but then she nods. "Okay. Just . . . be careful."

"I will. See you tomorrow." I wave, and then turn and hurry toward the door. When he sees me coming, Romeo's face lights up. In that moment, I swear I can see past the skin he's wearing to the person inside. And I don't care what he's done, or who he used to be. He is beautiful.

"Hey. The woman gave me the suit *and* the dress for forty, if you can believe that." He looks so happy to see me, like he was worried I'd forget him in the few minutes we were apart.

As if that's possible. As if I'll ever forget.

I wrap my arms around his neck and kiss him, squashing the clothes between us. He makes a surprised sound, but it doesn't stop him from kissing me back, a deep kiss with a little bit of rough that leaves my entire body buzzing by the time I pull away. "Let's go."

"Yes," he says, his voice promising that everything I've been dreaming about this afternoon is about to happen.

I take his hand and walk out the door without looking back.

SIXTEEN

Romeo

The magnitude of the near future hums between us as we swing by Ariel's house to say hi to her mother and make a quick picnic, and gets louder and more distracting as we drive to the other side of town for blankets and towels. Dylan's dad will still be at work—or at the bar down the street—and even if he catches me walking out with a few towels and a comforter, he probably won't ask any questions. Unlike Ariel's mom, who was quite curious about our picnic plans, and even stole a peek into our basket when she thought we weren't looking.

Luckily that was *before* Ariel slipped into the bottom the protection we purchased at the gas station.

Protection. If only it were so easy to protect her from all the dangers in her life.

"You okay?" she asks.

"Fine," I say, pushing my fears to the back of my mind, doing my best to keep up my end of the conversation.

We talk a bit about the dance and about Gemma and Mike and what Ariel has promised to do for them tomorrow, but soon silence falls again. Our preparations are almost complete. The moment is nearly at hand, and the moment is too momentous for small talk.

Seven hundred years of thinking and longing and remembering is about to come to an end. It's been seven hundred years since I've been with a girl. There's been no one since Juliet. I tried once or twice early in my Mercenary afterlife, but the inability to feel made it impossible. Pressing my skin against another's and feeling nothing was far, far worse than feeling nothing on my own. It only made the loneliness worse. Even the seductions I performed as a Mercenary stopped well before reaching the bedroom door.

Not that Ariel wants a bed. Or a door. She wants skinny-dipping in the moonlight, all of her bare to all of me, naked and covered in little water droplets and—

"You're *sure* you're okay?" The lightest touch of her fingertips on my arm makes my breath rush out with a strangled sound.

"I don't know." I park the car on the street a few houses down from Dylan's and cut the engine, but make no move to get out. "I'm . . . It's been a long time since . . ."

"Since . . . Oh. Really?"

I nod, but can't bring myself to look at her. "A *really* long time. I'm not sure I'll . . ."

"Are you joking?"

I shake my head, wishing I were, wishing I didn't feel like a kid on his wedding night. Worse, on my actual wedding night, I'd been too stupid to be nervous.

She kisses my cheek. "You'll be perfect."

"Aren't I supposed to be the one reassuring you?"

"I don't need any reassuring, but if you do . . . We can just go swimming. If that's what you want."

"It's not what I want. I want you." I do. I want her. "But I—"

"No buts."

"But—"

"No. Buts."

"Oh there will be. Have you ever seen a man's butt in real life? Hideous. Especially Dylan's. Pale, fish-belly-colored skin with hair like patchy grass and—"

She laughs, that high, pure laugh of hers that sets things sailing inside me.

"I'm serious," I say.

"You're funny," she says, laughter warming her eyes. "And I'm not afraid of any part of you."

I want to tell her I am. I want to tell her that I'm afraid of the dark and the past and the lies and the evil in the world. I'm afraid of her beauty and kindness and the way she holds my hand like I'm worthy of her touch. But most of all I'm afraid of leaving her defenseless. I'm afraid of the fingers that twine through mine being bent and broken as some Mercenary tortures her while I can do nothing to protect her.

Nothing. It's what I'm known for. I've been nothing for so long. How can I change that now, when the course of my destiny was determined so long ago?

All I know is that I have a hard time denying her, especially when I want her so badly I can hardly remember what I'm supposed to fetch from Dylan's room.

So I don't say a word. I just kiss her, and promise to "Be right back."

I step out into the rapidly cooling air and cut through the neighbor's yard, heading around the back of Dylan's small, run-down house, where the door is always unlocked. Why bother locking up? It's not as if the Strouds have anything worth stealing. Their television has seen better days, and the rest of the furniture is too shabby for the Goodwill to take on donation. Even their computer is an ancient thing that takes forever to start up and even longer to connect to the Web.

But still . . . there might be enough time . . .

I haven't been able to get to a computer all day, and I'm still troubled by the disappearance of *Romeo and Juliet*. Maybe it's nothing. Maybe Shakespeare simply decided against dramatizing the story a troubled young man told him in a pub late one night. Juliet and I lived and died hundreds of years before Shakespeare was born. It wouldn't have been strange for our story to fade into obscurity without the Bard's influence keeping it alive. But our tale was a popular one among the traveling minstrels of our day. There might still be some mention of the story of Romeo and Juliet in history if a person went looking for it.

And then there's the boy who thinks he's Benjamin Luna. I should discover what I can about Ben/Benvolio. That mystery is too strange to be ignored.

As I make my way through the living room, I see that the computer is already on. My decision is made. I set it to connect, and by the time I fetch two mostly clean towels and grab the comforter off the bed, the search engine has launched. I slide into the chair, type in Benjamin Luna, and wait the end-less thirty seconds it takes for the search results to load.

When they do, there isn't much to see.

No Facebook page. No juicy gossip or confessional blog. Just an honorable mention in a soccer tournament and a brief cameo in his mother's obituary. I shift the results to show im-ages only, and am rewarded with crappy school pictures pro-vided for newspaper articles about his athletic endeavors. He still looks like the Benvolio I remember so well.

"Lame," I tell the boy. The old Benvolio was much more interesting. I type in *Romeo and Juliet* and hit enter.

There doesn't seem to be anything to worry about where Benjamin is concerned. The real issue is, why does Ben look like Benvolio? And more important—

"No." My voice is loud in the otherwise silent room. I scroll down the first page of search results and then the sec-ond and the third. There is nothing. *Nothing.* I try adding *Ve-rona* into the search, and then the year *1304,* but still nothing.

Heart beating in my throat, fingers stiff, I type in *Juliet Capulet,* and am rewarded with a single mention on a geneal-ogy website: *Juliet Capulet, 1290–1304, buried in Verona, Italy.* No mention of why she died at the tender age of fourteen, no drama surrounding her death. I try *Romeo Montague,* and *Verona, Italy* and wait and wait, forcing myself not to panic as I scroll through the search results. At the bottom of the fifth page, I am finally rewarded for my patience.

"There," I whisper, clicking the link. But the relief I feel at finding mention of myself fades quickly. The website is in Italian—not medieval Italian, the modern version that isn't as familiar—but I can decipher it well enough to know that what I'm reading isn't good.

It's a walking tour of some of the more obscure Verona historical sites, including the church and burial ground where Juliet was interred. My name is mentioned only once, in a paragraph beside a picture of the church:

In 1304, the original church caught fire. The flames were contained before they spread to the churchyard, but a significant portion of the nave was destroyed. It was reconstructed in 1306 with donations from Benvolio Montague, a wealthy landowner whose cousin, Romeo Montague, was killed in the fire, along with the parish priest. A statue of the benefactor stands at the edge of the yard, keeping watch over the tombs. After leaving the church, turn left at the central sarcophagi and proceed north fifty paces to see the statue, as well as the oldest markers in the cemetery and . . .

I can't read any more.

I close the browser window and shut down the computer, as if that will somehow make this new story go away. It has to be a story. Fiction. Just like Shakespeare's play. I didn't die in a fire any more than I died on the floor of Juliet's tomb. I didn't die at all. I'm here, in this boy's body. That alone is proof the story is false, or at least operating under false assumptions.

It was an empty shell those ancient people discovered; my soul had already moved on. That would explain why the friar's body was found as well. That form had outlived its usefulness and the Mercenary abandoned it to find another.

But why were the two of us found together in the church? Did he carry my body there after we parted ways on the hill? After I stumbled into the countryside; walking day and night for weeks; struggling to escape my inescapable prison; to die, though I was already dead; to exhaust myself into sleep, though I had begun to realize sleep would also be denied me . . .

"It doesn't matter." I shove the chair with more force than necessary. "It doesn't change anything."

But it does.

The story of *Romeo and Juliet* is gone, and this one-line mention in a travel brochure is all that remains of me. The Mercenary I was would *never* have allowed such a thing. If Shakespeare wasn't interested, I would have found another bard to immortalize my tragedy. I needed my fame, took perverse pleasure in generations of young people being forced to study me in school. Knowing every soul in the Western world knew my tale—or a version of it, anyway—was my only comfort. It gave me a connection that didn't require touch or taste or smell. It kept a spark of sanity alive in my diseased mind.

I would not have allowed this to happen. I wouldn't have let my short human life fade away.

As I gather the towels and blanket and slip out the back door, I can't stop thinking about the fire in the church, about what it would feel like to burn to death. I can almost smell the smoke, feel the heat on my skin as I hurry back to the car. I'm so distracted that I don't see the truck in the driveway, or realize who's come to greet me, until Dylan's father steps into my path.

"What the hell do you think you're doing?" The flat of his hand hits my sternum, shoving me back, making me cough as I pull in my next breath.

"Going to a friend's house," I say. "Sleepover." I try to walk around him—figuring the less said, the better—but he stops me with another shove. This one is hard enough to make me stumble. The towels and blankets fall to the ground as my arms swing out to regain my balance. Before I find my feet, he's slamming me against the garage door.

"I know you took my money, you little shit. I want it back. All of it." His face is red, his eyes glittering and bloodshot. Even if I still lacked a sense of smell, I'd know he's been drinking. With a working nose, the whiskey on his breath is enough to make my gut pitch.

Or maybe my gut is simply anticipating the discomfort that meaty hand will inflict when it slams into my middle.

Dylan's father "vented his spleen" on me once during my first visit, but at the time I hadn't been able to feel a thing. His punches only made me laugh like that mad creature I was. Now both my body and spirit would rather avoid a scuffle. Ariel is in the car. I don't want her to see this.

"I didn't take your money," I lie in my most soothing voice.

"Bullshit." His open palm curls into a fist.

"But if you need some cash, I've got some in my backpack," I rush on. "I can go get it and be back in a minute."

"I don't want 'some cash.'" His sneer is meant to be mocking, but his slurred *s* ruins the effect. He's a joke, and if Ariel weren't a few yards away, I'd tell him so and make a run for it. Dylan's usual safe places will be off-limits now that I've alienated his friends, but—

You can come to my house. Anytime. No matter what.

Ariel's words on the beach. She said them before she knew I wasn't Dylan, before she knew I wasn't the person who'd turned her heart into a joke. And still she offered sanctuary, compassion. Most of the time, she's a good person. Truly *good,* in a way most people aren't.

But some of the time . . .

I catch sight of her over Dylan's father's shoulder. She's standing at the end of the drive with the lug wrench from Dylan's trunk in her hand and a dangerous expression on her face. Her blue eyes burn with cold fire. I've seen that look only once before, in the moments before she dove for the wheel of Dylan's car and tried to pull us both to our deaths.

If I don't defuse this situation, Ariel's going to show Dylan's father her bad side, maybe even her murderous side. Not that he doesn't deserve it, but it's my job to turn her toward the better part of her nature, and the last thing I want is to see her this angry. If I'm right, and the screaming things she hears are lost souls, it's best not to attract their attention. I don't think the lost souls report back to the Mercenaries—they've been cast out, punished, hence the *lost* before the *soul*—but there's no reason to take stupid chances.

"Okay. I'll get the money." I lift my hands in surrender, looking him straight in the eye, hoping he won't turn around. I don't know what he'll do if he sees Ariel. My gut says Mr. Stroud wouldn't touch another person's child—especially a girl—and that his fists and frustration are reserved for his own offspring, but I'm not ready to put my gut to the test. Just the thought of Ariel bloody and bruised makes me want to leap at this man and rip his nose off with my teeth. "Let me get my backpack. It's in the house."

"Not *the* house, *my* house," he shouts while Ariel creeps closer, and I shake my head as subtly as I can, willing her to go back to the car. Instead, she tightens her grip on her weapon.

"I pay for everything, while you sit on your skinny ass."

"I get paid for my gigs with the band," I say, hoping to calm him down. "I can pay you back in a few—"

"I don't want to get paid back. I want you to get off your

ass and get a real job," he bellows, face flushing redder with every word. "By the time I was your age, I was supporting my parents!" Redder, redder, and the fist at his side begins to shake. "But I let you stay here for free. And how do you thank me for it? You *steal* from me!"

Everything happens at once. He winds up for the hit, my arms move to block the blow, and the wrench falls from Ariel's hand with a piercing clatter. Mr. Stroud spins, staggering around in time to see Ariel's eyes roll back and her knees buckle.

"What the hell?" he shouts.

I shove him aside and run, reaching Ariel seconds before her head hits the pavement. I pull her shoulders into my lap, planning to scoop her into my arms and escape to the car, but then I feel it. The cold.

Under her skin, a cold that seeps into my bones and freezes so hard I think I might shatter. It's the cold of the ice at the poles, blue and ancient with pieces of mammoth hair stuck in the cracks, the cold of things that have been frozen so long they can't remember being fluid. So cold it burns, scalding away love and hope and happiness in a creeping ice floe of terrible.

Dimly I hear Dylan's father asking "Is she okay?" and cursing as Ariel begins to shake and twitch, but I can't respond.

I'm no longer in Dylan's body. I'm lost in the cold, so shocked by the misery seething inside Ariel that all I can do is stare into Mr. Stroud's frightened face as he kneels beside me and shoves a stick from the yard into my limp hand. "If she keeps shaking, shove this between her teeth. I'm going to call nine-one-one."

He turns and stumbles toward the front door. I want to tell him to stop, that an ambulance won't help her, but when I open my mouth, all that comes out is a scream. A long, lonely scream, like the ones wailing inside her. The lost souls are screaming, and I must scream with them, because I am their brother. My borrowed magic and living body don't matter. Down at the core, where the real Romeo is curled up in the corner, I am still a creature of darkness. And I will never escape. This is the way I will end, as one of the screaming things, lost and alone except for these brief moments when I can rush inside someone like Ariel and—for a few precious minutes—have my misery be heard.

SEVENTEEN

Ariel

No. No. No! Get out!

My eyes squeeze closed and my body thrashes as I fight the monsters shredding my insides with their jagged teeth. There's no doubt about it now. The things screaming their banshee shrieks in my mind aren't coming from me. I *know* I saw them this time, ripples in the air with gnarled fingers that reached for me seconds before the cold hit, as fierce and frightening as ever.

More frightening.

Romeo is out there. In trouble. I tried to force the anger down and hold it tight, but when Dylan's father lifted his fist, I lost it. In that moment, he was every bully who'd ever pushed someone around, and I wanted to punish him. I imagined the crunch his bones would make when I brought the wrench down on his head. I thought about the way the blood would gush out to coat the driveway, and something inside me screamed with satisfaction, a scream so familiar I knew it was only a matter of time.

And now pain rules my body and the screaming things howl in my brain. It's misery, torture . . . but not unbearable. For the first time I hold on, clinging to consciousness after I would usually tumble into the dark. There's something different. A sound. Not one of the screaming things, but not—

I'm here. Here. Here.

The chanting is soft, but once I hear it, it's impossible to ignore. I focus on the truth in the voice that repeats the word over and over again, like a mantra holding the world together. It's Romeo. He's here with me, and he really does care. As much as I care for him. Maybe more. Because he knows what it's like to be so lost that he's certain he'll *never* be found.

But he's wrong. *I* will find him. I will—

Forgive. I forgive you.

I don't know why those are the words he needs to hear, but they are. I feel it. And I know the moment he hears me. His soul shudders and then he's gone, taking the screaming things with him. It's like a wind that sweeps through my being, carrying the cold away.

My eyes open to a dim blue sky with the hint of night creeping in at the edges. Romeo holds me in his lap with his head bowed. "You can't forgive me."

"You heard . . ." I lick my lips. "You heard me?"

He nods but doesn't lift his eyes. "But you can't."

I brush the hair from his forehead with trembling fingers. "I do." My voice is rough, but I can talk and move, and for once I've made it through an episode without losing control. It's because of him. Somehow, he held the things back. If I needed more proof that he has magic inside of him, this is it.

"No. You don't know everything," he whispers. "If you did, you never could forgive me." His shoulders bow a little deeper, and I'm suddenly struck by how much he reminds me of the boy in my painting.

The boy I painted years before I met Romeo. The boy in my dreams, whose portrait I've been working on when I should be sleeping. But I'm afraid to sleep. Sometimes I dream of the boy, but more often I dream of the man in the brown robe. He says he'll forgive me and grant me peace. He's terrifying, but in the dreams, I need his forgiveness. I've done something so horrible that I don't think anyone will ever forgive me, and I know I'll never forgive myself. It's only a dream, but I understand what it feels like to believe you're beyond redemption.

I wrap my arms around Romeo and pull myself up, until I can whisper into the crook of his neck. "Whatever you did, you can't change it. All you can do is be better, and I believe you are. I forgive you."

He doesn't say a word, only kisses my shoulder before easing me from his lap and rising unsteadily to his feet. "I need to stop Dylan's father from calling the paramedics." He clears his throat, runs a shaking hand through his hair. "No need to waste time in a hospital when there's nothing they can do."

"No," I say, coming to my knees. "He's dangerous. I–"

"I'll be fine. Stay put." He strides across the brown grass, up onto the porch, and through the open front door. I stand, determined to follow and make sure he's safe, but before I make it to the steps, he's back.

He stops in the doorway, surveying me with a raised brow. "That doesn't look like staying put."

"I'm not leaving you alone with him."

"My hero." He closes the door and shuffles down the steps with the ghost of his usual wicked grin. "He's passed out. Doesn't look like he made it to the phone. We're fine to go." He grabs the towels and blankets from the driveway and starts back to the car.

I snatch the tire iron and follow, holding the question rising inside of me, until Romeo has pulled away from the curb. "You felt them, didn't you? The things I hear."

"I felt them. I should. I come from the same source."

"What?" I ask, sure I must have heard him wrong.

"If I fail to accomplish my mission, I might be one of them someday," he says, the certainty in his words making my stomach lurch. "They're lost souls. They were cursed to roam the human world until their bodies turned to dust, and now they're trapped forever in the earthly plane with no way to express their misery. Humans can't see or hear them."

I twist the bottom of my shirt until the fabric scratches my skin. "*I* hear them." I can't think about the first part. Romeo becoming one of the things that haunt me is too horrible to imagine. "Why? Why me?"

"I don't know." His lips twitch. "Maybe you're just lucky."

"Right." I let out a breath that holds an impossible hint of laughter. I can still laugh. Minutes after an episode, and I can laugh. For me, that's good enough reason not to give up. "Screw luck. We'll make our own luck."

"How will we do that?"

"Let's go back to my house. I want to show you something. I think it might be important. My mom should have left for work by now, so we won't have to worry about her eavesdropping."

"What is it?"

"It's better if I show you."

He readjusts his grip on the wheel. "Okay."

"It *is* okay." I put a hand on his leg as he turns back toward my house. "We'll make it okay."

He sighs, but the silence that follows is comfortable. I find myself enjoying the drive through town as night falls and the antique streetlamps flare to life. Even the silhouette of the Castle Playground, black against the dusky sky, doesn't make me upset. I smile, and turn to find Romeo watching me with a soft look on his face. "You amaze me," he says.

My cheeks heat. "There's nothing amazing about me."

"I beg to differ."

"You don't have to beg." I lean in and press a kiss to the place where his heartbeat pulses at his temple. "And you don't have to go home. Just park a few blocks from the house. My mom won't be back until late. She won't notice your car, and we'll be sure to lock the door to my room."

His eyebrows lift. "Are you asking me to sleep over?"

I shrug, suddenly nervous. "That's what you told your dad you were doing, right?"

He turns onto El Camino, his expression darkening as he parks in front of the house with the ceramic cows in the window. "I didn't like seeing a weapon in your hand."

"I wasn't going to let him hurt you." I slam the door behind me, taking the hand he offers before starting down the street. "Even if it had been the old Dylan about to get his face smashed, I couldn't have just sat there and watched it happen."

"You could have called for help."

"I've called for help before. No one can help me. It's time to help myself." I don't realize how much I mean the words until they're out. It *is* time to help myself. And Romeo. I won't stand by and be weak or afraid anymore.

"Then help yourself." He stops before we reach the empty carport. "Don't worry about me. Or Dylan."

"I'm not going to worry," I say, urging him toward the house. "I'm going to win."

Romeo

I follow her inside. I know that there's nothing she can show me that will change my fate or give us the storybook ending my fairy-tale-loving girl is after, but still . . . something's changing inside me.

Something she said . . . about helping herself . . .

The answer is there somewhere. Hidden in a few simple words and stubborn determination. I can't help myself, but maybe . . . if I'm willing to do whatever it takes . . . if I love her . . .

God. Do I love her? Do I? Maybe . . .

"It's in here." She stops at the door to her bedroom, hand hovering over the knob. "It's not finished yet—it's barely even started—but I want you to see it."

"All right." Even knowing that this thing she wants to show me can't change our fates, I'm intrigued. *She* intrigues me. I want to learn everything about her. I want all her secrets;

I want to banish her shame; I want to let her banish mine. I know it's hopeless. But still . . .

As she opens the door and flicks on the light, illuminating her private gallery, I'm struck again by how much I wish I had more time. I want to see what she'll paint next month, next year. I want time to prove I can make her happy for longer than a few days, to prove to myself that I remember how to do this.

Or that I've finally learned how to do it. For the first time.

I loved Juliet, but I wasn't good to her. Even before I betrayed her. But I have been good to Ariel, *for* Ariel. And it no longer feels like something I'm doing to save my own skin. It feels like something I do because I have no other choice. I pulled her into my arms and held her close while the lost souls raged, because I couldn't imagine leaving her. Because I . . .

I . . .

"I . . ."

"What?" Ariel glances over her shoulder, one eyebrow raised. I stop in the door, stunned that her face has become so beautifully familiar, the face of someone I—

I open my mouth, close it, but before I can speak, Ariel motions me over.

"Here. Look at this." She lifts the easel in the corner and carefully spins it around. "I turn them to the wall when I'm not working, because I can't stand to look at them too long until they're finished, but . . ."

I know she's still talking, but all I hear is the whooshing of blood in my ears. I stare into the boy's face, mesmerized. She has captured him perfectly, from the dark, troubled eyes, to the strong nose and the particular olive of his skin. She even caught the scar above his brow, where his father's sword came too close the first time he and the boy sparred in the yard.

How? How has this . . . *How?*

"Romeo?"

I flinch. She's at my side, but I don't remember seeing her move. "Where . . ." I try to keep my voice even. "How do you know this boy?"

"I don't. He came to me while I was working. I painted him on a hill a few years ago." She points to the painting that gave me chills the morning we went to the museum. There's no doubt, then. It *is* me. On my hill. Incredible, unimaginable, but as real as this girl slipping her hand into mine. "I've been dreaming about him lately. So I decided to paint him."

I shake my head. This is *impossible.*

*Living in dead bodies and traveling to different realities and spending perfect days with a girl you shot in the head—*that's *impossible. But you've done it. Magic made it possible.*

"Love has its own magic," I mumble beneath my breath. I said the same words to Juliet the first time I lived through this time, but I didn't believe them. But maybe there *is* magic in the world that has nothing to do with Mercenaries or Ambassadors. Could this girl, could the way she feels . . .

The way *I* feel.

There's no denying it now. No denying the way everything inside of me melts when she leans closer, when her arms slide around my waist and I am no longer alone.

"It's you. Isn't it?" she asks, palms smoothing up and down my back, her touch as perfect as it's been since the first time she let me take her hand.

"It is. I don't know how, but . . ." My chest aches, but not with fear or sadness. With hope. With love. I love her. I *love* her, and it is better than anything else I can remember. "You found me."

"I'll always find y—" Her last word is lost in my kiss. I hold her so tight, I can feel her heart race in perfect rhythm with mine, faster and faster until we fall onto her bed and her fingers find all the buttons and zips keeping us apart. And it is perfect and right. Because I love her. How I love her.

"I love you," I murmur against her lips.

"I—"

I cover her mouth with my hand, whisper against my own knuckles while our noses brush. "Don't. If you say it, I could be taken even sooner." She might not need to say the words—the Ambassador has great magic, and ways of finding out the truth that don't require speech—but there's no reason to tempt fate. Not tonight. Tonight I want to be with her, to memorize every moment of our first and last and only night together.

She kisses my palm before peeling my fingers away. "But I do. And I will. Forever."

"Forever," I echo, and for the first time, I know that forever is a promise I can keep. I will love her forever, until the world crumbles and this memory is the only thing keeping me sane.

Our lips meet again, and the last of our clothes land on the bed, the chair in the corner, the floor.

And then there is nothing but the magic of her touch.

We talk late into the night—she tells me of her nightmares of the man I knew as Friar Lawrence, and I warn her never to trust him. I tell her about my life as a boy—more about my brother and my mother—and my afterlife as a Mercenary, before words give way to kisses and the whisper of cool hands on warm skin.

Her mother comes home around two in the morning, and we fall silent, lying on our backs in her bed, fingers threaded, legs entwined. I stare at the ceiling and replay every moment of the past few hours over and over, until I can't help but roll over and press a kiss to her bare shoulder. She is so beautiful. Perfect. Mine.

No. Not mine. I am hers. I belong to her, this girl who has dreamed of me, pulled my lost face from the past and brought it to life. She's saved me, made me a good man for the first time. And now I will save her. I know how to do it. The answer was always there, waiting for love to bring it to light.

Juliet's nurse said I would be cast into the body in the cave if I failed her. I can only trust that that means I'll stay in this reality, where Ariel is alive and in need of my protection. Come tomorrow night, when the Ambassador offers to administer the peacekeeper vows, I'll refuse. I'll go back to my wasted body, and spend the decades before I turn to dust protecting the girl I love.

I'll stay far enough away that she'll never see what I've become, but close enough to defend her against the Mercenaries who would harm her. I know their tricks, and in my soul specter I'll be able to see their black auras. The instant one of them starts sniffing around my love, I'll sever the bastard's head from his body. I'll surely be caught eventually, but until then, I'll buy Ariel as much time—as much life—as I can.

I pull her closer. "If I can't stay, know that I'll be watching over you in whatever way I can," I whisper into her hair. She lies heavy in my arms, finally close to sleep.

"You're going to stay."

"I'm going to try. But if I can't . . ." I don't want to speak the words aloud, but I have to. "Remember what you promised. Love someone else."

"Could *you* love someone else?"

I pause. Could I? Loving someone else isn't an option, and I can't see any face but Ariel's when I close my eyes. But that isn't what she needs to hear.

"I've already loved someone else."

"Do you love her now?"

"Not the way I love you." I can't lie. Not about that. The place in my memory where Juliet lives has changed. I feel for her, but nothing rises inside me when I think of Juliet's pretty face, except guilt and regret.

"How is it different?"

"It was . . . selfish with Juliet. I spent a lot of time composing love poetry that I thought made me sound clever, and dwelling on how much our romance would hurt my father. When I was with her, *I* was always in the way. I couldn't stop thinking about Romeo long enough to know Juliet. But with you . . .

"Even that first night, you surprised me, made me think and feel and . . ." I take a breath and let the words go, trying to trust the truth. "Yesterday was one of the best days I've ever had. But I still didn't think what I felt was real. And then, today, it suddenly became so clear. I love you. More than I've ever loved anything else. I love you enough that I want you to love someone else when I'm gone."

She sighs, a sweet, sad sigh that assures me I've said the right things. For once, the right things and the true things are the same. Maybe they always would have been with Ariel.

"But you're not gone, and I can't imagine feeling this way

about anyone else." She seals the words with a long kiss that sends fractures zigzagging through my heart. "Promise me you'll try to stay."

"I'll do everything I can."

"Me too." Then she lays her head on my chest and falls asleep. Almost instantly, like a child without a care in the world. I lie still and listen to her breathe, try to memorize the feel of her ribs expanding as her breath comes in and out, the smell of her hair spreading out on the pillow next to mine. I don't want to sleep, to lose a minute of this time with her, but my borrowed body is human, and exhaustion finally pulls at my mind. I'm half-asleep by the time I turn to the window, so close to oblivion that for a moment I think the face behind the glass is a dream.

But then she lifts one golden, glowing hand and crooks her finger, sending a jolt of power surging up my spine. I'm instantly buzzing awake, my heart pounding as my eyes home in on her eyes, not at all comforted by her pleased expression.

For almost a thousand years, Ambassador pleasure has been my pain.

I know this time will be no different.

EIGHTEEN

Romeo

If I could have feigned sleep and turned away, I would have, but the Ambassador's magic calls to me, makes my blood itch in my veins. After only a moment, I slip my shoulder free, slide my leg from beneath Ariel's, and ease off the bed. She mumbles in her sleep and curls tighter under the covers, but soon grows quiet. I take a moment, soaking in the sight of her, fighting the horrible feeling that this is the last time I will ever see her sleeping.

Maybe even the last time I'll see her at all.

I steel myself as I walk to the window, determined not to let Juliet's nurse know my secret until I'm certain my time is truly up. She won't be happy when she learns I'm planning to refuse her offer. She said the shift of my allegiance would bring the Ambassadors great power. My decision to return to a rotted corpse rather than swear myself into her service is *not* going to go over well.

The thought makes it easier to return her smile as I raise the window, letting the smell of the spring night and her vanilla perfume drift into the room. "To what do I owe the pleasure?"

"You truly have no shame." Her gaze flicks down and back up again, reminding me that I'm as naked as the day Dylan was born.

I grin wider, propping my hands on my hips. "If you're uncomfortable, I can put something on."

She laughs beneath her breath. "I'm thousands and thousands of years old, Romeo. I remember a time when all humans went around without clothes."

"That many thousands." I tuck the information away for later. "I always thought you and the Mercenaries were younger. The legends say you were Greeks."

"Legends evolve. They change to suit the needs and understanding of the people who listen to them."

"Like lies."

She tips her head, conceding the point. "I suppose."

"So what lies are you here to tell me now?"

"Ambassadors don't lie, Romeo. You know that." She crosses her arms, cozy in her dark green sweater, the golden light still shining from her hands making her look like she's huddled over a camp fire. "I've come to congratulate you. You've succeeded in record time. Ariel is in love. I felt the change in her spirit this afternoon, a dark weight being lifted."

My heart drops. I knew it. I *knew* Ariel's silence wouldn't matter.

"Her heart is secure," she continues. "She will never become a force for darkness. You can come with me now, and take your place among the Ambassadors."

I step away from the window. "But I . . . I have to stay and protect her."

"You know that's impossible." Her voice is gentle but firm.

"Nothing is impossible."

"All right. Not impossible, but criminally unwise. If I were to allow you to stay in Dylan's body, you and Dylan would both be dead within a few days. His life would be unnecessarily wasted."

"You can't know that. I might be able to escape them, outsmart them. I–"

"This isn't up for discussion." Her expression hardens. She's done humoring me. "You must come with me. Now."

"But I . . ." I look over my shoulder, gut twisting at the sight of Ariel curled under the covers. "I love her."

"I know. I have to admit, this is quite a surprise. You're an extraordinary creature, Romeo Montague. The change in you will make you an even more valuable asset to our cause."

I turn back to her. "I'm not a creature or an asset. I'm a man, and this is what my face used to look like." I point to the portrait in the corner, and watch a hint of unguarded emotion flicker in the Ambassador's eyes. It's only there for a moment, snapped away as quickly as a knife from a child's hand, but I see it. She didn't expect this. I don't know whether to be encouraged or afraid. "Ariel painted that. Not from anything I told her but from what she saw in a dream. This is the second portrait. The first she finished years ago." I pluck the painting from the wall and hold it up to the window. "It's my old body, on the hill where I took my Mercenary vows."

I watch her, waiting for her to see that this changes everything, but she only stares at me with that same calm, collected, slightly amused expression. It makes me want to strangle her more now than ever before. "How do you explain this?" I ask through gritted teeth.

She lifts one shoulder. "I can't."

"Aren't you even going to try?"

"I don't see any reason to. We've accomplished what needed to be done, and no one—human or immortal—has ever fully understood the magic of dreams."

"Well, you might want to try," I snap as I hang the painting back on the wall. "Because the friar has come to her in her dreams as well."

"What?"

"The friar. He comes to her in her sleep." I take cold satisfaction in the furrowing of her brow. Stupid Ambassador. But as gratifying as it is to shatter her smug assurance, it's equally chilling. This woman is the only thing standing between Ariel and pure evil, and she's woefully unprepared.

"He's promised to forgive her and grant her the peace she's been seeking," I continue. "I warned her not to trust him, but I can't say with any certainty that she'll be safe from his influence. She suffers from these strange attacks. She believed she was mentally ill, but I held her when she was struck down today. She was full of Mercenary power. I don't know how, but the souls of the Mercenary outcasts are able to enter her mind. Usually when she's angry, but I'm sure the friar could arrange for the attacks to become more frequent."

"I'm sure he could," she says after a moment. "Once

certain barriers are broken, many unusual things become possible."

"What kind of barriers? Can they be rebuilt?"

"Not that I know of. People who are open to our magic have usually experienced significant trauma. The trauma erodes the natural barriers that keep the mind protected. Without those shields, humans are vulnerable to all types of invasion. The lost souls are only one of many things that might find their way into a delicate mind like Ariel's. That's why it was so important for you to—"

"Her mind isn't delicate. It's under attack," I say, unable to hide my anger. "She's being tormented by things she can't even understand. She deserves—"

"Exactly. She can't understand, and even if she could, it would be pointless to explain. There's no way to give back what she's lost. Her mind has opened a door that should have remained closed, and once some things are known, they cannot be unknown." She casts a significant look in my direction, and then over my shoulder to where Ariel lies on the bed. "I'm sure you understand that. After this evening."

"If you're trying to make me feel guilty, you'll fail," I say. "Being with Ariel wasn't a mistake. The only mistake would be leaving her undefended."

"And how do you think you've acquired a conscience after all these years?" She curls her glowing hands over the sill and narrows her eyes, showing me a hint of the cruelty hidden beneath her beauty. Her expression accentuates the fine lines around her mouth, making me guess for the first time that her body's age is closer to forty than thirty. "Because of magic *I* gave you. You are nothing better than you were before. Without my help, you would have never had the chance to care for this girl, let alone be outraged that she's not being cared for as you see fit."

"She's not being *cared for* at all!" I grip the window, mimicking her battle stance. "When I leave, they will kill her. You say you'll watch over her, but I don't see that anything you can do will–"

"You're right," she says, shocking me into silence. "I wasn't aware that the friar was coming to her in her dreams. I'm only able to touch the sleeping minds of my own converts. I didn't realize such a deep connection was possible with a human untouched by our magic."

"It is," I assure her. "She described him perfectly."

She sighs. "If so, if he's already entering her subconscious mind, then he'll eventually–"

"Drive her mad," I finish, blood chilling when she nods, confirming my fear.

"And the mad are incapable of real love. One must have possession of one's mind to have possession of one's heart," she says.

"No . . ." I shake my head, refusing to believe I've understood her correctly. "That can't be. We have to stop him. This can't have been for nothing!"

"Shhh," she warns when Ariel moans in her sleep before growing quiet once more. "This hasn't been for nothing," she whispers. "You have been brought to the light."

"I . . . It's not enough." My entire body sags. It's the moment by the tree all over again, when Juliet and Ben were at the friar's mercy and there was no hope but to destroy them before he could. But I can't destroy Ariel. Not even to save her from a fate worse than death. I love her too much. What's more, I respect her. This is her life, and there are some decisions that no one should make for another person, no matter how noble their reasons for lifting their weapon.

The realization hits hard. Maybe the Ambassador is right. I know I didn't do Juliet any favors by tricking her into killing herself the first time, but what if I was wrong to take her life under that tree as well? What if I wasn't seeing clearly? What if there were possibilities for her future that I couldn't comprehend?

Possibilities . . .

"*Romeo and Juliet,*" I say, suddenly reminded of the changes in this world. "The Shakespeare play has vanished. Juliet is a one-line obituary, and I've become a mention in a tourist brochure. They say I died in a church fire."

The Ambassador doesn't look terribly surprised–by the change of subject or my revelation. "This is a different reality. Many things will be changed."

It's what I suspected, but for some reason the explanation still doesn't sit well. "Benjamin Luna is certainly changed. I saw him today. He isn't the same boy."

"As I said, choices made in the past will–"

"He looks like my cousin Benvolio Montague. *Exactly* like him."

She hesitates. "You remember his face so well?"

"He was like a brother to me after my own brother died. He was seven and I was five. We grew up together. While I was alive, I spent more time looking at his face than I did my own. It was Benvolio I spoke to today, though he believed himself to be Benjamin Luna." I pause, waiting, but she says nothing. "I swear to you," I insist. "It was Benvolio, body and soul. Here in this town, seven hundred years after my cousin lived and died. How is that possible?"

She gives me a pitying look. "You were very close to him?"

"He was the only member of my family who wasn't cruel, insane, or after my father's money. But that doesn't matter. I know what I saw."

"Sometimes what we *want* to see can be a powerful–"

"I wasn't seeing what I wanted to see." I clench my jaw, fighting to keep my frustration in check. "I saw what was there."

"I'm sure many people look like your cousin. He was an average boy, if I remember correctly. But you . . ." She turns back to the picture in the corner. "There is no doubt that that is your handsome younger self. Ariel has a talent."

And that's it. My concern has been dismissed. But I won't let her off that easily. "Whether it was Benvolio or not, don't you understand what this means? If we'd been summoned to this version of the world, Juliet would never have met the real Ben Luna, or fallen in love with him. She might still be an Ambassador, working for your cause."

"Yes, she might still be alive," she says. "You might not have shot her, or stolen a precious soul from the world."

My chest tightens as Juliet's wide, dying eyes rise in my mind. The pain is worse now. It was Juliet's soul, but those were Ariel's eyes. Now that I've looked into her face and seen love unlike anything I thought I'd know again, it's even harder to stomach what I did. Even if I felt I had no choice.

"Yes," I whisper.

"She might even be here instead of you." Nurse's voice is hard, merciless. "But she's not. You are. And confusing coincidences aside, the most important thing is to prevent Ariel from being turned."

"I can't kill her," I choke out, throat aching. "I can't."

Her hand comes to rest on mine. "It might be the only way to save her."

"Please, no," I beg, knowing she'll find someone else to do the job if I refuse. "Please. There has to be another way."

"There may be something . . ." She casts another glance toward the bed. There's a softness around her mouth that gives me some comfort. Maybe Ariel isn't simply a means to an end or a way to save the world. "Let me consult the other Ambassadors. If the Mercenaries can enter her dreams, there *may* be a way we can as well. If so, we can offer her protection."

"I'll help. Any way I can."

"There's nothing for you to do. There may be nothing that *can* be done," she warns. "But . . . in light of this news, I don't think it's safe for you to leave Ariel just yet."

My breath rushes out, the force of my relief making my arms shake. "Thank you."

"Stay with her; don't leave her side. I'll contact you to-morrow." She steps away from the window, and the light emanating from her hands dims. "If you don't hear from me by sunset, meet me at the cave on top of the mountain at mid-night."

"Could we meet somewhere else, closer to town? I prom-ised I'd take Ariel to the dance." She lifts a disbelieving eye-brow. "I know it sounds ridiculous, but it's important to her. And to me. I know I can't stay, but if we could have one more night, a few hours to share something at least, *she* may remember . . ."

"She will remember you. And you'll remember her if you want to badly enough," she says. "Juliet chose to forget certain things, but you *will* have a choice. We are not cruel, Romeo.

Unlike your former masters, we care for our converts and would not send them to the mist if we had the power to keep them on earth. We won't steal your mind or your memories. You will guide your own destiny as much as any soul who serves a higher purpose."

A higher purpose. A few days ago the thought would have made me laugh. But now I intend to serve one. Just not the one Juliet's nurse has in mind. . . .

"That's good to know," I say, pretending to be grateful for her kind words, though I know I won't need them. I won't be going to the mist. I will be staying here. With Ariel. "In that case, another memory of her would be even more appreciated."

"Very well." She reaches out. Light leaps between us. Her magic stings as it surges beneath my skin, but not nearly as badly as it did the first time. When it's over, I feel recharged, as if I've slept all the hours I spent staring at the ceiling, memorizing the feel of Ariel's body against mine. "The power I've given you will keep you in this body until midnight tomorrow. Not a moment later. If you haven't taken your vows to me by then, you will be returned to the specter of your soul and live out the rest of your days in a rotted corpse."

"Midnight. Like Cinderella," I say.

"You've always reminded me of Cinderella." Her dry tone makes me smile in spite of myself. "Do you understand me?"

"I understand."

Her lips curve. "Good."

Good indeed. I nod and promise to meet her at eleven-thirty in the woods behind the school, even as I begin to plan my escape from the mercy I was willing to kill for a few days ago.

Nurse disappears into the night, and I turn back to the bed and climb in beside Ariel. The covers are warm and her scent weaves through me, soothing all my hurts. I will never forget the smell of her skin. Even when my nose burns with the stench of my own decay.

As soon as I lie down, she shifts in her sleep, her head finding my shoulder, her hand smoothing across my chest until it rests over my heart. I can feel the love in her touch, even when she is far away from me in whatever dream she's dreaming. I hold her close, kiss the top of her head, and hope that her dream is a sweet one.

And then I lie staring at the ceiling, working out the details, trying to ignore the crushing pressure as my new heart learns how to break.

INTERMEZZO THREE

Juliet

"My nurse is going to make Romeo an Ambassador," I say again, knowing my fate depends on whether or not the friar believes this lie I'm not entirely sure is a lie. I *did* see something in my dreams. I saw Romeo bathed in golden light, filling with Ambassador magic. "She's going to steal him from the Mercenaries."

"Impossible." But I hear him stop walking away. He *stops,* and I tremble. If he leaves, I will die in this hole. But not until I suffer for another day or two before dehydration claims my life. "How do you know about the Ambassadors?"

"Does it matter? I know, and I had a vision of what Nurse is planning."

"Only the high Ambassadors have true visions of the future," he says. "And you are *not* one of those, girl. You have been touched by magic, but—"

"My nurse is able to reach me. In my dreams." I would swear I heard Nurse's voice while I was sleeping, echoing through the skies of my nightmares. "She showed me what will come to pass."

"And why would she do that?"

"To punish me." Maybe it's true. Maybe it's not, but there's enough doubt in my mind to make it sound like I'm stating a fact. "She wants me to suffer. That's why she sent me here."

"You came to the tomb in the back of a cart. I witnessed it with my—"

"No, not *here*. Not the tomb. This time. I was in the future. I was an Ambassador. For more than seven hundred years." I can feel the change in the air as I speak. He's intrigued, finally wondering if I might be worth fishing from his trap. "Romeo and I *did* live on to become enemies. For centuries. And then you captured me and he defied you. He tried to spare me from torture, but he failed, and somehow my nurse sent me here."

"You're lying," he says, but his certainty is slipping.

"You said I was a bad liar. You should know I'm not lying now." I pray my mix of fact and fiction is working to my advantage. "Nurse sent me here to die for refusing to renew my Ambassador vows, but I would rather live. I will kill for you, swear my allegiance, whatever it takes to survive to make her pay for giving Romeo a place in her world when he deserves nothing but pain."

"Hm." It's almost a laugh, but it's not. I don't know what to make of it, so I remain silent, waiting until he speaks again. "*If what you've said is true,*" he says, his voice becoming clearer as he moves closer, "if your vision is sound and you are from the future, then Romeo is beyond our reach, safe in another time. Mercenary magic is bound by time and place. I'd thought it was the same for the Ambassadors, but . . . that's neither here nor there." He grunts as he leans down to whisper through the notch in the stone. "The sad truth is that I can't send you into the future to fetch Romeo with your knife. So . . . what have you left to offer me? As sacrifice?"

"My father." I ignore the lump that rises in my throat. "He isn't as dear to me as Romeo was, but I love him."

"Your father," he repeats, unimpressed.

"I haven't seen him in centuries. I want his arms around me more than anything else in the world." The lump in my throat grows, becomes a fist that feels as though it will cut off the air to my lungs. "But I will rip him apart," I choke. "If you will let me out."

He's quiet for what feels like forever. In the silence I have time to seriously consider my words. I am trapped in the dark in my own filth, with thirst and hunger and terror wrecking my mind. Would I kill to be free? Would I violate my belief that no good can come from murder? *Any* murder? Even the murder of the friar, a man who has done nothing but spread evil across the earth for hundreds of years?

No. I can't. Ben was right. Killing won't make anything better; it will only make me worse. But lies . . . I am at peace with lies. And I will tell as many of them as I must to escape this hell.

"You would like to become a Mercenary," the friar says, his tone flat, emotionless, unreadable.

"No, I wouldn't. But I will, if it's the only way to have my revenge."

He hums beneath his breath. "You would do that? You would fight the Ambassador that Romeo will become?"

I nod in the darkness, ball my hands into fists, and whisper, "Yes."

"Very well," he says after a moment. "I suppose your father will serve our purpose."

I flinch as the rough scrape of stone on stone fills the air, vibrating the walls of what would have been my deathbed. The gray light of the tomb pricks at my eyes, the slightly less stale air of the mausoleum wafts over my face, and my weakened blood rushes with relief. Even the arms of the monster reaching in to pluck me from the darkness are better than the long, torturous death that awaited me.

And I will escape these arms. I will find a way.

"Are you ready?" The friar's fingers dig into the bruised flesh at my hip. I try to pull away, but my knees buckle and I'm forced to lean my weight against him. I'm not strong enough to stand on my own. But I will be. Soon. He has to revive me—I couldn't kill a gnat in my current state, let alone my father—and when he does, I will run, hide.

"I'm ready." I turn my face toward the stairs leading up to the churchyard, desperate for a breath of truly fresh air.

"Then I hope that everything you've said is true," the friar says with a sharp thrust of his arm.

Fire ignites in my belly and spreads with a ruthless intensity. My hands fly to my middle to feel the sticky heat of my own blood spilling through my fingers. I have a split second to realize what he's done, and then I'm falling. I crumple to a heap of stinking skirts at his feet, the last of my hope burned away by the time I hit the floor.

He knew I was lying. He wins. Again. Always. Forever.

He kneels beside me. I close my eyes against his vile face. "If she sent you here, she will come for you," he says. "Your nurse isn't cruel. She'll be wanting to give you another chance. But when she arrives, she will discover you dead and me waiting. Then I will find out if time is as easily traversed as you think, my child."

I open my eyes, wanting to tell him he's wrong, that Nurse doesn't care what happens to me now that I'm no longer one of her slaves, but he's already gone, moving swiftly through the mausoleum and up the stairs, out into the night. Or the morning. I don't know which, and now I never will. I watch him go, watch his feet step out of sight, as I struggle to breathe past the agony spreading through my core.

This is it. After all the centuries, after all the struggle and sacrifice and lessons learned, and now—

She comes from the shadows on the far side of the tomb, emerging from behind the most ancient of my family's sarcophagi, shuffling across the space between us with a quick glance over her shoulder to where the friar disappeared. Her cloak is pulled tight around her gray hair, and her face is paler than I remember, but I recognize the old woman immediately.

"Nurse," I gasp.

"My sweet girl." Her work-roughened hands find my face, brush the hair from my eyes. "There isn't much time," she whispers. "You must renew your vows. Let me save your soul a second time, Juliet."

Not Nurse. The Ambassador inhabiting Nurse. She's been here the entire time, watching the friar torment me the way she watched Romeo trick me the first time I was pulled from my tomb.

"No." I bat her hand away with blood-slick fingers. "Sending me here hasn't changed my decision."

Her lips part in surprise. "I didn't send you here. I swear I didn't."

I don't respond. She's as much of a liar as Friar Lawrence.

"I think perhaps the universe itself sent you, certainly a power greater than any Mercenary or Ambassador." She leans close, brushing her lips across my forehead, making me shudder with disgust. "You are meant to walk this path, Juliet. You are meant to be something greater than a mortal girl living one mortal life. I am so happy I found you."

"How?" I lick my lips, fighting to speak past the pain twisting through my gut. "How did you find me?"

"After you left Ariel's body, the fabric of reality was altered. The places where you and Romeo touched the future and the past changed. I'm able to see the possibilities of our planet, keep track of time and space as it is altered by man's decisions and by supernatural influence. There was a dramatic change in all versions of the world shortly after your final shift. It wasn't difficult to see what caused those changes and, from there, to realize what I had to do to bring you back to your true place."

"So it's true. You've made Romeo an Ambassador."

"You saw. . . ." She sighs. "I didn't mean to reveal that to you. I meant only to send comforting thoughts while you slept." She looks away, over her shoulder, as if checking to see if the friar is creeping back down the stairs, but I can feel her hiding from me. "But no. I haven't. I've only given him a chance."

"Why?"

She turns back, a strange glint in her eye. "Don't you think people deserve a second chance?"

"Not him."

She smiles. "I agree, but your fate and his are intertwined. I had to remove Romeo from the equation in order for your destiny to be fulfilled. If I hadn't put him on a path to existing outside of time, you would never have become one of us again."

"I will never be. . . . Never."

"Juliet. Please . . ." Nurse takes my hand, casts a sad look down to where the blood soaks my dress. "You're dying."

"I was dying before," I whisper, finding it harder to speak. "And then I woke up here. I'll see where I wake up the next time."

"There won't—" She casts another nervous glance toward the entrance to the tomb. "It's different now. There won't *be* a next time."

I close my eyes, wishing she would go away, wishing the friar would come back and give her something real to worry about.

"Look at me!" She jostles my shoulder, sending a sharp stab of pain flashing through my stomach and into my spine. "*I* did this."

"I thought . . . You said . . ."

"I didn't send you here, but I changed things when I put Romeo on a different path." She cups my chin and leans close, until I can feel her breath on my lips. "You were sent here to have another chance at life, and if I hadn't interfered, you would have found it. You would have found a man to love and made a family. You would have died when you were sixty-three of an infection in the blood. I saw it all, the tragically short human life you would have lived if I hadn't taken action."

I shake my head. What is she saying? If that . . .

"Then . . . why . . ."

"In order for you to live that life, Romeo was also brought back and given happiness," she says. "A long life with a woman he loved. A child. Five grandchildren. *Twenty* great-grandchildren, *twelve* of which he lived to see brought into this world. In that possible future he was nearly a hundred when he died *peacefully*. In his *sleep*."

Her lip curls. "You clearly think an eternity of service to the Ambassadors is too good a fate for the likes of him. Can you imagine the alternative? All the blessings he would have reaped if I hadn't stepped in? While you died without a chance to change the world for the better?" Her laughter is one of the harshest sounds I've ever heard. "I couldn't allow that to happen."

"So you . . . took my happiness away?" My eyes sting, but I'm too empty to cry. "To prevent Romeo from finding his?"

"No, my darling." She strokes my hair like I'm a favorite pet. I wonder if that's all I ever was to her. A pet. If I'd been anything more, she wouldn't have played with my heart the way she has. "I haven't taken anything away. I've given you a chance for so much more. Any girl can get married and have children. Not any girl can change the course of history, save the world, further the cause of love and light through the ages. You are special."

An impossible tear slips down my cheek. "No."

"Juliet, some of us are called to serve a higher cause."

"There is no higher cause than love." My flagging heartbeat

thuds in my ears. "After all your centuries defending it, you'd think you . . . of all people." I turn away from her, rolling my head weakly on the hard ground. "But you aren't a person."

"No. Not anymore." She pulls her hand from my forehead. "But I have a heart. I won't let Romeo become an Ambassador. I've found someone to eliminate him," she says. "For you."

"You've never done . . . anything . . . for me." I'm panting, barely able to form words. The end is close. I can feel it in the electricity that flashes through my brain, causing parts of what make me Juliet to explode. Stars going out, burning, dying.

She sighs. "But my self-interest is also in the best interest of the world. Can you say the same? Juliet . . . I'd hoped for so much more." She grows still, as still as the graves that surround us, some of them empty and awaiting their charges, some of them with bellies full of the dead. I knew some of those bones, loved some of them. Tybalt and Grandmother and my baby cousin Louisa, who died before she was three. Perhaps I'll see them when I open my eyes in the world beyond.

I could let go now. I can feel how easy it would be. But for some reason I can't stop thinking about this other life that Nurse said I could have had if she hadn't interfered, this happiness with a husband and babies and another fifty years of human life. It's hard to imagine loving anyone but Ben, but . . .

Ben. If only I could have held him one last time . . .

My lids flutter and I see his face, and my fear slips away. He is with me. He will always be with me.

"You just need more time." Nurse pulls me from my peace with a firm hand on my side.

First there is pain—sharp enough to make me gasp—but then her power pulses across my skin and the pain abates. I take my first deep breath in many long minutes, but before I can wonder at what she's done, she's lifting me in the air, carrying me the few steps to the tomb, and laying me inside.

Inside. Back inside the tomb. No. *No!*

"No," I choke out. I would scream it if I could, but I'm not strong enough to scream or fight. I'm not even strong enough to lift my hands in protest as the stone slides slowly back into place.

"I will return for you," she whispers through the hole where the friar poured the water. "In a few hours. No more. I will put an end to my business with Romeo and come straight here. I will have a new body, but you will know me. As you always have."

"The friar . . . He . . ."

"He won't hurt you," she says. "He's using you as bait, but I am the one stringing this line. I will keep us both safe, and finally be rid of him. You'll see. We will live on, Juliet, and our next seven hundred years will be different. You will have great power. We will win this world back from the Mercenaries and bring peace to humanity. Together, I believe we can."

And then she is gone. Outside, I hear a muffled *thu-thump* as the body she left behind crumples to the hard ground. Nurse is an old woman, with pain in her back and legs. Without supernatural magic coursing through her, she would suffer from a fall like that. But she doesn't make a sound.

"Nurse," I call as loudly as I dare. "Nurse!"

She doesn't answer. There is only silence outside, no breath, no stirring on the floor of the tomb. I suspect Nurse was dead before the Ambassador used her body to come to me. Only

{253}

Mercenaries are supposed to inhabit the dead. Ambassadors are supposed to be above such desecration.

Ambassadors aren't supposed to steal lives or play judge, jury, and executioner. Ambassadors aren't supposed to plot murders, or bury people alive.

If this is what the "good" side has come to, I fear not only for myself and Romeo—wherever he is—but for the world.

NINETEEN

Ariel

The morning sun floods in through the window, giddy and pure and perfect, like heaven is smiling down on my room, approving of Romeo and me. *Romeo and me.* It's a beautiful morning, but even if it were dark and gray and the sky were pouring frogs and locusts and fire, I wouldn't regret what we did.

I love him. I love loving him. If I thought I could get away with it, I would play sick again, hide Romeo in the closet until my mom went to work, and keep him in bed with me all day. Nothing but tangled sheets and his skin hot against mine, and our Selves spilling over into each other as we whisper beneath the covers.

"Stay." I hold tight to his arm as he lifts the window. "Just for a few minutes."

"There isn't time."

"We've got an hour before school."

He looks back at me, the sun creating a halo around his messy hair, making him look like the world's sexiest fallen angel. I decide right then that I'll paint him just like this—one foot out my window, caught between us and the world. "I can't," he says, but I can feel him wavering.

"You can." I stand on tiptoe and kiss him, my head spinning. I thought his kisses would be easier to take after last night, but it only made his effect on me worse. It's like my entire body is caught up in a whirlwind shot through with lightning. I'm dizzy and electrically charged and alive and so *happy*. I don't ever want to let him go, not even for a few minutes. "Come back to bed," I mumble against his mouth, heart beating faster as his hand slides past my cheek into my hair.

"You're making this very difficult," he breathes as he draws his leg back into the room.

I smile. "No. *You're* making this very difficult."

"I have to go. I'll meet you in an hour, maybe less. But this has to be done. It's important." There's an edge in his voice that wasn't there before. He's worried, maybe even afraid.

"Is this about . . ." I don't know the witch's name, but I wouldn't say it even if I did. I don't want to let her into this morning. This moment belongs to me and Romeo and no one else.

"It's something that will be good for us. For you."

"Then let me help. Wait just a second. I'll come with you." I grab my jeans from the floor—he's wearing the same clothes; I might as well too. I stuff one leg in and then the other, moving so fast, I stumble. He reaches out to grab my arm, making my skin tingle as I button my jeans and pull up the zipper.

"I have to do this alone," he says.

"But I—"

"No buts. Not on this. I need you to stay safe. Go straight to school, then straight to class, and don't talk to strangers." He starts back to the window, but stops before he throws his leg over the sill. "Better yet, don't talk to anyone, not even your mother if you can help it."

"Okay." I cross my arms, suddenly cold, though my cami felt warm enough a second ago. But I remember what Romeo said last night. The man in my dreams is one of the Mercenaries, and could come for me in another form, even in the body of my mom or one of my teachers. If he kills someone I know, he could take them over and I might not find out until it's too late. There's no one I can trust. Except Romeo.

"You really think Mom's in danger?" I ask, heart beating faster. "Isn't there anything I can do to keep her safe?"

He sighs. "I'd tell you not to worry, but . . ." He takes my hand, wrapping my cool fingers up in his warm ones. "Just be careful, and I promise I'll do whatever I can to keep you and your mom and everyone here safe. I'll see you in class."

"All right." I pull my hand from his. "Be careful. Call if you need me. I'll have my phone."

"Take your mother's car if you can. Or the bus. I'm not sure walking is safe." He swings himself out the window, dropping to the ground with a soft grunt. I watch him start across the grass, my heart lifting when he stops and turns back. I'm glad he can't just walk away. Really glad. "Ariel?"

"Yes?"

"I . . . love you."

"You too." Our eyes catch and hold, and for a moment there is nothing but Romeo and me and shining golden light. And then he turns and walks away. I watch until he reaches the fence and climbs over with an easy pull of his arms, and try not to feel like everything good has disappeared behind those faded gray boards.

But when I turn back to my room, the world seems shabbier than it did before. I straighten the bed with a quick jerk of the covers, then pull off my jeans and throw them into the dirty-clothes basket. I've got an hour to kill before I start for school. I might as well take a shower and make an effort to look nice. I grab fresh jeans and a clingy red sweater with a deep V in the front that I've never dared to wear before, and head for the bathroom. I shower, dress, dry my hair, and even take the time to put on the layers of makeup I know Romeo won't care if I'm wearing. Still, I find myself dressed with twenty minutes to kill before I have to leave the house. I pace my room, trying to think of something else to do to keep my hands busy. The busier my hands, the quieter my mind. I'm afraid if I stop moving, I'll drown in the worry flood.

What if I never see Romeo again? How could I let him go anywhere without me? How am I going to get Gemma's stuff from her house if I'm not supposed to talk to anyone? What am I going to do if there's nothing I can do to save the people I love, to save Romeo? To save myself?

I'll die without him. At least, I know I'll want to. Even the thought of spending one day alone makes me sick to my stomach, let alone the rest of my life. Still, I've got to eat something. Maybe pancakes from scratch. Or crepes. Something that takes time and attention and will leave less brain space for all the scary questions.

I head into the kitchen—mentally ticking off the ingredients I'll need for crepes, hoping we have eggs left in the fridge. But as I walk through the doorway, I catch a flash of green at the kitchen table, trip over my own feet, and barely keep from screaming.

Gemma lifts her hands into the air. "Don't freak out. I know where you hide the key, and I was dying for coffee. The shit at the hotel was gross, and I was afraid someone would recognize me if I went through a drive-through. I was going to tell you I was here, but you were in the shower."

I press a hand over my racing heart and stare hard at Gemma. She looks the same—more casual than usual in her green sweatshirt and ripped jeans, with her hair wavy and no makeup except yesterday's smudged eyeliner—but that doesn't mean anything. She could still be the enemy. I can't be too careful.

"What are you doing here?" I stay where I am, too nervous to take another step into the kitchen.

"Wow." Gemma gives an exaggerated one-two blink. "Thanks, Ree. I don't think I've ever felt so welcome." She pushes her chair back. "Do you want me to leave?"

"No, of course not," I say, trying to act normal. If this really is Gemma, I don't want to hurt her feelings. "I'm sorry. You surprised me. I thought I was going to meet you at your hotel at four."

"You are. I mean, I assume you are. I just . . ." She grabs her coffee and wraps her fingers around the mug. "I wanted to talk to you before then, without Mike around."

"Why? Are you two okay?"

"We're great." Her smile lights up the shadowy kitchen. "We're crazy in love, and I am Sesame Street happy. I should have gotten married years ago. My parents could have betrothed me at twelve and saved themselves a ton of money on crappy therapists."

"Right." My lips twitch. "If that weren't illegal. And gross."

"There's nothing gross about love, dear Ree." Gemma hugs her steaming mug to her chest. "Love is happiness wrapped in a sugar-sprinkled burrito and covered with awesome sauce."

I laugh, and the last of the worry seeps from my shoulders. This is Gemma, no doubt about it. I don't know anyone else who wraps things in metaphorical burritos. "You're probably right." I head for the coffee she's made. I don't usually drink coffee, but I'm fuzzy this morning. Romeo and I didn't get much sleep.

Romeo. His lips, his hands, his . . . everything. The sense memories rush through me as I pour half a mug and fill the rest with milk, making me smile my new, silly smile.

"What's up with you?" Gemma asks as I settle into the chair across from hers.

"Nothing. Just happy."

She studies me over the rim of her mug, eyes suddenly serious. "Why? What's made you so happy?"

I cover my hesitation with a long sip of coffee. What should I tell her? The truth is impossible. Gemma doesn't believe in fairy tales or curses. I doubt even her own happily-ever-after has changed that. "I'm glad to see you. That's all. I'm glad you and Mike are so good together."

"Bullshit." She sets her coffee down with a loud *thunk.*

"No one smiles like that because someone they care about is getting laid. They smile like that because *they're* getting laid."

"Gemma!" I blush and dart a furtive look toward the doorway. Thankfully, we're still alone. If Mom walks in on another conversation like the one she heard the other night, I'm going to be on my way to Planned Parenthood for a birth control prescription faster than you can say *safe sex*. The condoms that Romeo and I used aren't enough security for my mother.

"What? I'm right, aren't I? You did the deed." Her tone is flat and ominous, like she's pronouncing a death sentence.

I blush harder and shrug. "Maybe."

"Oh god." She buries her face in her hands, muffling the soft "Shit" that is her next word on the subject.

"What's wrong with that?" I ask, starting to get irritated by the drama. "I thought you'd be happy. You're the one who said I was too ancient not to have seen a boy naked in real life."

And you started sleeping with guys in the eighth grade, I silently add, but know better than to say out loud.

"Yeah. I am," she says. "I would be, anyway. If you'd picked a different boy."

I sigh. I get it. This is about Dylan and how much she hates him. I can't blame her. If he were still Dylan, I'd hate him too. Maybe I'll even hate him again, if Romeo leaves and the old Dylan comes back to brag about what we did last night.

But even as the nasty possibility zips through my brain, I can't stop thinking about the way Romeo held me, like the most precious thing he'd ever touched. No matter what happens, I don't regret my decision. One night with the boy I love is worth a hundred days of torture from Dylan Stroud.

"I understand," I say. "But don't worry. I can handle Dylan."

"Um . . . no, you can't. Sorry, Ree. I love you and you're supersmart and could probably be a doctor or something if you'd wake up and realize your true level of awesomeness, but you can't handle Dylan. He's crazy."

"So am I. So are you." I force a laugh. "Isn't everyone crazy in their own way?"

"Not like him. He's evil, Ree."

"He's not—"

"He's a compulsive liar. He's so good at it, he can make *anyone* believe *anything*." Gemma leans her elbows on the table and gives me a superintense look that makes all my easy protests seem inadequate. This wasn't what I was expecting. "Really. Anything. I think he even believes his lies himself for a while, but then he remembers it's all pretend and he turns back into the same horrible person he was before. Except worse, because he knows he played with your brain and won."

My fingers tighten around my mug. I'm not going to let Gemma make me doubt Romeo, but I can't help but be bothered by what she's said. Really bothered. "Since when do you know so much about Dylan? I thought you hated him."

"Yeah. Ever wonder why?"

I shake my head. "I thought . . . I know you think his band is lame."

"Dude, this goes way beyond something stupid like that." Gemma laughs a sad laugh, and I recognize her "gearing up to say things I don't want to say" face. "You remember when I was hanging out in Santa Barbara a lot? At that bar that didn't card?"

"Yeah."

"Well, I wasn't hanging out alone. Dylan showed up one night after I'd already had a couple beers, and came over to my table." She stares down at her fingers, picking at the skin around her cuticle. For the first time I realize how rough her hands look.

I've never seen Gemma when she's gone more than a week since her previous manicure. Her mom has a woman who comes to their house to do manicures and pedicures and facials every Sunday afternoon, and Gemma always looked perfect come Monday morning. Now, seeing her ordinary hands, I feel closer to her than I have in a long time. But I'm also scared. Gemma isn't big on talking about her feelings or personal stuff. She lets her wall down only when she really, really has to. The fact that she thinks *this* is one of those times makes my skin break out in goose bumps under my sweater.

"Anyway." She blows air through her lips. "I thought he was trying to get me to buy him a drink, but he bought me one instead, and we started talking. He was really different that night. Nicer. Easy to talk to. Damn sweet, really." She shakes her head but keeps her eyes on her fingers. She can't even look at me. It leaves no doubt that this story is going to be as bad as it is familiar.

A sweet Dylan. Nice. Easy to talk to.

A knot rises in my throat, but I force myself to swallow another sip of coffee. I felt Romeo's soul in my body yesterday when the screaming things came. He knows about the lost souls and the man in my dreams, and I *know* his story isn't a lie. Dylan couldn't make up something that elaborate.

"I told him things I've never told anyone, not even you," Gemma continues. "And he told me a lot of stuff too. About his dad and this friend of his dad's who . . . did things to him. Touched him and stuff. When he was little."

She threads her fingers together and makes a tight fist. A tiny drop of red appears near the edge of her pointer finger, where she's ripped the cuticle so deep, it's starting to bleed. I watch the ruby liquid swell, and try not to think anything at all.

If I let myself start thinking, I'm going to think dangerous things.

TWENTY

Ariel

"I know I never told you . . ." She finally lifts her face, but I can see how hard it is for her.

Gemma probably feels as naked and terrified as I did when I told Dylan about the crazy voices in my head. I want to reach out and take her hand, but her body language leaves no doubt that she doesn't want to be touched.

She takes an uneven breath. "When I was in first grade, my parents were having one of their big harvest parties after the fall crush. I was down in the basement in my castle playhouse, and my uncle came down and . . . bad things happened."

"God," I whisper as my stomach collapses. I want to say something more, but I can't. I don't know if I have the words for this.

"I didn't even understand what was happening at first," she says. "He was Uncle Steve and . . . I trusted him. Until it was too late. I tried to call for my mom, but the music was so loud upstairs. No one heard me."

"Gemma." I take her hand. To my surprise, she lets me and holds on tight for a moment before letting go. "I love you. I'm so sorry."

"Yeah. Me too. I love you, too." She smiles and lets out an easier breath. "It actually feels good to tell you. I knew you wouldn't think I was gross or anything, but–"

"Of course not!"

"I know." She shrugs and reaches for her coffee. "I guess old habits die hard. I wasn't allowed to talk about it for a *looonnng* time. Even when I started going nuts and my parents sent me to therapy, they only let me talk to a therapist they trusted not to rat out Uncle Steve. And a therapist on the take is worse than no therapist. It only made me feel worse. So I stopped."

I shake my head, not wanting to understand what she's saying. But I do. And it makes me so . . .

I close my eyes, pull in air, and let it out long and slow. I can't afford to have an episode right now. But if I let myself get any angrier, I know I will. I take a second to focus on my heartbeat, willing it to slow. I imagine my blood cooling in my veins and my breath coming out frosty. I am calm, cold, as still and grounded as those giant stone Buddha statues in China.

When I've got myself together, I open my eyes and say

what needs to be said. "Your parents knew about it, and they didn't do anything?"

"Oh, they did something," she says, her voice so bitter it makes my tongue curl behind my teeth. "They stopped inviting Uncle Steve to parties and made sure he wasn't allowed to drink at Thanksgiving or Christmas. Or sit at my end of the table. Not that it mattered. He could still look at me." She takes a sip of her coffee, sets the mug down a little too hard. "I could tell he never regretted what he did for a second."

"They still . . ." I fight the urge to be sick. "You're not serious."

"I am. I mean, Steve's a *really* nice guy when he's not drunk. It was just that one mistake, and it's not worth sending a man to jail or tainting the Sloop name with child molestation charges." She does such a perfect imitation of her mother's voice, it makes me shiver. I can imagine Mrs. Sloop saying these things to Gemma over and over, heaping shame upon shame until Gemma was buried alive beneath it. "That wouldn't be good for wine sales. Or Dad's Senate campaign."

Deep breath in. Deep breath out.

I won't get angry. Instead I focus on how sad it is that the people who should have protected Gemma have spent twelve years protecting the man who violated her. "You deserved so much better."

"You think?"

"I *know*. You were a kid, and what he did to you was sick. Your mom and dad should have done everything they could to get him sent to jail."

She smiles, a secret smile that I'm starting to recognize. "That's what Mike says."

"He's right." Another deep breath. I keep my hands still

on the table, making sure I stay calm even when I say, "And if they couldn't put him in jail, they should have taken care of him themselves."

Gemma lifts one eyebrow. "Meaning?"

I don't hesitate. "They should have buried the body somewhere you could go look at where he's rotting. In case you ever forgot how far they'd go to make sure you were never hurt like that again."

"Wow." She swallows. "That's pretty intense, Ree."

"So is molesting a six-year-old," I say, ignoring the acid that churns in my guts from just imagining a person sick enough to violate anyone like that, especially a baby who had barely learned to write her name, playing in her princess playhouse. "If you were my family, Uncle Steve would have become Uncle Dead Body a long time ago."

"You really are crazy," she says with obvious affection. Her eyes fill, and tears spill over, streaking what's left of her eyeliner.

I don't know if I've ever seen her cry. It makes my ribs contract until I can barely breathe. "I care about you."

"Me too. About you." She reaches for me, and I wrap my arms around her tight, hugging her with all my strength, so glad that she's here. It's amazing she's lived through this and come out semi-okay on the other side. I'm so glad that Mike makes her feel loved. If I'd realized what heinous people Gemma's parents were, I would have tried harder to make sure she knew I loved her too. No matter how uneven our friendship has been at times, she's always been one of the most important people in my life.

We finally pull apart and reach for the roll of paper towels on the table at the same time, laughing when our hands bump. "Allow me." She pulls a towel for me, and then one for herself.

"Thanks," I say, returning her smile as I mop up my face.

"No problem. I've been crying a lot more lately, but I think it's a good thing," she says, with a shrug. "Mike doesn't mind. His parents are both counselors, so they encouraged the touchy-feely stuff when he was growing up."

"Good for them."

"Yeah. Mike's parents are cool. They live in LA. We went down to visit them when we first left, and they came to the courthouse when we got married. They got married young too, but they're still together, so . . ." She smiles her Mike smile. "I think Mike and I have a good chance. I never thought being happy could be so easy. I love him so much."

"I can tell."

"He's the real thing." She pauses, and in the silence her smile fades. When she looks at me again, I can tell we're back to more current events. "But Dylan is not. He's lying, Ree. I don't know what he said to convince you to sleep with him, but it's a lie."

I lick my lips, hating the doubt I taste there. "No, Gemma. I really don't think so."

"You know what Dylan said to me?" she asks, that stubborn gleam in her eye. "He told me that this friend of his dad's touched him all the time when he was little. He even *cried* about it. I guess he knew that would get to me the way nothing else would."

"You don't think he was telling the truth?"

"I know he wasn't. Or maybe he was and he decided to say it was a lie later. I don't know what goes through his sick head, but it doesn't matter. I know for a fact that he acted one way for the few weeks when we were hanging out at the bar, and an entirely different way after we did it a few times."

Gemma and Dylan slept together. It should freak me out, but it doesn't. I've got bigger things to freak out about. Like whether or not the boy I love is a lie.

"What changed?" Doubt and nerves mix in my stomach, making me feel like I've swallowed poison.

"All of a sudden he wasn't so sweet anymore," she says. "One day I went over to his house and he answered the door but didn't ask me to come in. He said he was bored, and that everything he'd told me about his dad's friend was a lie. He said I was a pathetic whiny little rich girl and shitty in bed, and then he slammed the door."

By the time she finishes, her face is pale and her voice trembling. I can tell she's embarrassed and ashamed and would rather have her fingernails ripped out than tell this story.

I know Gemma. I know how hard it is for her to tell any story where she doesn't come out the big winner. Sharing this has to be killing her, but she's doing it anyway. For me. I'm her best friend, and she doesn't want me to be hurt the same way she was hurt. She can't know that it's too late, and that if what she's saying is true, I'll be so far beyond hurt, I won't understand the meaning of okay anymore. I'll be shredded inside, such emotional raw meat that every feeling will sting like fire.

"After that, every time we ran into each other at school, he was an asshole. I gave him shit right back, but all I could think about was how stupid I was for trusting him." She tugs a piece of her hair hard enough to hurt, a little punishment for something else that wasn't her fault. "I mean, who cares about the sex—I've had sex with plenty of guys who didn't care about me—but I trusted him with the biggest secret of my life. And he proved that I was still too stupid to know the bad guys from the good guys. I don't think he told any of his loser friends about anything other than getting laid, but . . ." She drops her hands into her lap. "It still messed me up for a long time."

"I'm so sorry," I say, not knowing who I'm saying it to. Her? Me? Both?

God. What if . . . What if . . . I can't even think it. I *can't* or I'm going to lose my temper, my mind, my heart, my soul. Everything. It will all be gone. Forever. There will be no coming back, no changing my mind the way I did the night I almost pulled Dylan's car off the road.

"Don't be." Gemma waves a hand in the air, oblivious to the meltdown trying to get started inside me. "I'm so over it. I'm with Mike and I'm great. And you're going to be great too."

No, I won't be. If Romeo's a lie, I won't ever be great.

"You'll find someone amazing, Ree." Gemma nudges my boot with her tennis shoe. I force myself to focus on her face, hoping it will help tamp down the frantic feelings. "You are a kick-ass person, and someone better than Dylan is going to see that. And when he does, you're going to look back on Stroud and feel sorry for his pathetic, sociopathic, evil self. You will. I promise."

"I . . . I . . ."

I can't. I won't. I won't feel sorry for him; I'll hate him. Forever. I'll hate him so much, I'll have to do what your parents should have done to your uncle. I'll have to kill him. Because you're right; I am crazy and I can't take something like this. It will break me, and when I am broken, I will break the world.

I grab my coffee and hold on tight, giving myself a stern shake. I can't start thinking this way. I have to have faith. I take a deep breath and focus on the way Romeo's voice cracked this morning when he told me he loved me. That was real. *He's* real, and it doesn't matter what Dylan did, because Romeo is *not* Dylan. *He's not.*

"I hate what he did to you," I finally manage to say. "But I–"

"Don't, Ree. Don't let him use you anymore."

I squeeze the mug so hard, it hurts my fingers. "I know I probably sound stupid, but I think it's different with us. I think he really–"

"Okay, I didn't want to say this, but we talked about you one time," she says, eyes flicking around the kitchen, landing on anything but me. "I told him you'd never kissed a boy, and we made bets on whether or not you'd have your first kiss before we graduated. I bet no. He bet yes and asked me if I'd put up a hundred dollars if he was right. I said sure. I thought he was joking, but . . . maybe he decided to tip the odds in his favor."

A bet. Another bet. This time with my best friend. For a hundred dollars.

"I'm so sorry," she says. "I don't know why I talked about you like that. I shouldn't have. It was last fall, and I was having a really bad day. I was miserable and too busy with my own mental crap to care about how I affected other people. I used to do that a lot, but I'm trying hard not to anymore. I talked to a new therapist a couple of times while Mike and I were in LA, and I'm going to find someone in Washington. I'll get myself straight, and I promise I'll be a better friend to you from here on out. Starting right now."

She touches my hand, but I can barely feel it. I'm numb, and I'm glad I am. I don't want to thaw out and have to make a decision about what I feel. I don't want to feel at all.

"I'd love to believe Dylan has changed his evil ways and is as in love with you as he's pretending to be," she says. "But I know how scary good he is at pretend."

Pretend. Fairy tales. Witches. Wishes. Curses. Dreams.

How easy would I be to read? With my subconscious hanging on the walls of my room and my weakness pouring out of my mouth every time I let it open? But could he really . . . All of it? Even his kiss? Even that hitch in his voice?

"When you were . . . with him," I say. "Did he say he loved you?"

"All the time." She looks me dead in the eye, her expression as humorless as I've ever seen it. "And I said it back. And for a while there, I thought I meant it, because he was so *easy* to love. He made himself into everything he could see I wanted, and then ripped it away when he knew it would hurt me the most."

That's it. Enough to make the entire story come pouring out. Everything, from learning about his bet with Jason and the other boys, to trying to pull the car off the road, to Dylan's strange change of personality and the even stranger explanation for it. I tell Gemma about the episodes and Dylan's talk about magic and how much better it made me feel to imagine that I wasn't crazy but cursed. I tell her about the witch and the disappearing Shakespeare story and Romeo and Juliet.

Mostly Romeo. Romeo, Romeo, Romeo.

Oh, Romeo, please don't be a lie. Please don't be a lie. Please, please, please . . .

Even as I spill my guts, a voice deep inside me is praying

for a miracle. The magic has to be real. If it dies, I don't know what I'll do.

"Shit," Gemma says when I'm finished. "What a twisted bastard. I would say you're batshit crazy for buying *any* of that, but I know him. He could make being possessed by the soul of another person sound believable."

My "lovely" face crumples. Lovely. I believed that, too. I believed that Romeo thought I was beautiful and valuable and worthy of being loved like a princess from a fairy story, scars and psychotic breaks and all. But there is no Romeo. There's Dylan, the most gifted liar the world has ever known. Dylan, whom I told all my secrets. Dylan, whom I let sleep in my bed and touch every part of me and snatch my still-beating heart out of my chest.

"I can't believe this," I mumble. "I can't . . . I . . ."

"Ree, don't beat yourself up." She gives my limp arms a shake. "A good liar can make people believe all kinds of wild stuff. Like that Scientologist guy who convinced the movie stars they're being spiritually attacked by the disembodied souls of dead aliens or whatever. That's *insane,* but it's a real religion, and there are tons of people out there who waste their lives worshipping something some sci-fi nerd pulled out of his ass in the 1950s. Their *entire lives.*" She shakes me again and tries to smile, but I can see that she's scared. Something in my face must be telling her this isn't going well. "This is just your virginity. You were safe right?" she asks. I nod, and her shoulders drop. "Good. So, really, at the end of the day, this isn't that big a deal."

"It's not that," I whisper, sounding as broken as I feel.

She sighs. "You loved him."

"I did."

I do. I still do. I can't stop myself, even though I know Gemma's right. I've been played. Spectacularly. Stupidly. Hatefully.

I hate him. I love him. I hate him. I'm going to lose my mind. I can feel the threads holding things together starting to pull tight and rip, rip, rip . . . *pop*.

"It's okay. You're going to make it through this." Gemma squeezes my hands. "I'll help you. We'll figure out some way to make that psycho ass-wipe sorry. We'll bring him so low, he'll never be able to do this to anyone, ever again."

"Yeah. Maybe." Revenge. It's cold comfort, but at least it's something to focus on to keep from falling apart. "I have something. He let me take a video."

"What kind of video?" she asks. "Something incriminating and shame-inspiring, I hope."

"I think so. At least to the real Dylan it would be."

"There is no *real* Dylan," she says. "He's just one big ball of stupid and false wrapped in rotten."

"Right." She is. But my heart still hurts so bad, I'm not sure I'll live through it. And maybe he won't either. Maybe I'll kill him.

"Let's start with the video and go from there," Gemma says. "Let me get some more caffeine in me so I can think my most evil thoughts." She grabs her coffee mug and heads to the pot for a refill.

"We should probably go somewhere else. My mom worked late, but she could be up soon. If she sees you, she'll call your parents." I'm amazed that I can think logical thoughts, let alone speak them. And how can I sound so normal when half my mind is busy thinking of ways to get away with murder?

"Right." She ticks her finger in my direction and sets her mug on the counter. "We can get drive-through coffee. You can drive; I'll hide my face. I'll be out in Mike's car, okay? It's an old black Subaru Forrester. I parked around the corner."

"I'll get my backpack and purse and be right out," I say, accepting the hug Gemma hurries across the kitchen to give me.

"Don't worry, girl." She pats my back before turning toward the door. "We'll get him good."

I smile like she's made me feel better. But she hasn't. Nothing can and nothing will. Even hurting him won't make this better. But at least it's a start. First I'll make him wish he were dead. And then, if I still feel this betrayed and horrible and empty . . . maybe I'll make his wish come true.

TWENTY-ONE

Romeo

The Mercenaries have her.

By the time the final bell rings, I'm sure of it, and am just as sure that I'm not going to survive losing her. In my old body, in the mist, in a paradise filled with golden light—it doesn't matter where I spend eternity if I know that I've failed Ariel. The first time I killed her with my own hands, but this isn't so different. I gave the Mercenaries the chance they needed. And now they have her and they'll torture her until they destroy every beautiful, brave, innocent thing.

I should never have left her alone.

I walk faster, pushing past sluggish, stupid children talking about what they're going to wear to the dance and who's picking up whom in what kind of limo. Their happy chatter is more meaningless than ever. Because Ariel is missing, stolen away while I was doing what I thought I had to do to protect her, and accomplishing *nothing*.

Juliet's nurse wasn't as easily conned as I'd assumed she was. She must have seen through me last night. By the time I reached the cave, there was nothing there but a lingering rotten smell, like the inside of a garbage can that had just been emptied.

Empty. Gone. Lost.

Stupid. Imbecile. *Fool.*

I break into a run.

"Slow it down, Stroud!" the principal yells, but I'm already on the concrete path heading toward the parking lot.

I race for the car—no idea where I'm going, but knowing I have to get there fast. I already checked Ariel's house during lunch. No one was home, and her cell rings and rings without any answer. I went back to school hoping she'd end up there, but the afternoon passed without any sign. Now I don't even know where to start looking, but I'll drive every back road in the valley searching if I have—

Wait. By Dylan's car, leaning over the hood, scribbling on a piece of paper. Her back is to me and she's wearing a gray sweatshirt with the hood pulled up over her head, but I'd know those slim hips anywhere. It's her. She's here!

I sprint across the asphalt. "Ariel!"

She spins, blue eyes wide, face so pale she looks like a ghost of herself. Something awful has happened, but at least she's here. Together we'll find a way to keep her safe. She opens her arms, and I scoop her up, crushing her against me. Her body is warm and whole and so precious, it hurts.

"I was so afraid," she whispers. "I thought Gemma might have come for you while I was at her house getting her stuff." Her arms tighten around my neck. I clutch her closer, shaking with relief.

"It's Gemma, then?" I suspected the Mercenaries would come creeping in someone close to Ariel. I curse myself again for leaving her alone.

Ariel nods. "She's one of them. You wouldn't believe the things she was saying."

"You're safe now." No thanks to me. "I promise I won't—"

"I can't believe this is happening," she sobs. "I hate myself."

"This isn't your fault."

"My best friend is dead and an evil *thing* is living in her body," she says, blinking tear-filled eyes. "And it *is* my fault. Why are the Mercenaries after me? What do they want?"

"They want your soul." I look around, feeling exposed. A few other students have reached the edge of the parking lot. There could be more Mercenaries hiding inside them. It's best for Ariel if we aren't seen. "But whatever happened with you and Gemma might give us a clue how to protect you. Let's drive and see what we can figure out."

She nods, but it takes several seconds for her to unwind her arms from around my neck. I know the feeling. Now that I'm holding her again, I don't ever, *ever* want to let her go. On impulse, I bend to kiss her, but she flinches away.

"What's wrong?"

"You're going to hate me," she says, voice thick. "I was

going to do something horrible. To you. At first I believed everything Gemma said, and I—"

I cup her face in my hands. "I love you. I will *never* hate you."

"I'm not so sure about that."

"I am." I kiss her—sealing my promise—and reach for the passenger door. "Get in. We'll talk while I drive."

After a moment, she eases into the seat. I close her door, steeling myself for what I have to tell her. I can imagine what kind of "horrible" thing she was planning. I know how the Mercenaries work, and what they would need from Ariel in order for her to become one of them.

I start the car and swing out of the narrow space, shoot through the parking lot and down the road that will take us to the beach if we drive far enough. "I told you that I used to be a Mercenary," I say, checking the rearview mirror to make sure we aren't being followed. "I know how they can twist your mind in knots until you don't know what's right."

This is the moment when I should confess it all, tell her that I tortured and deceived my wife. Juliet drove the knife through her own heart, but I might as well have done it myself. I killed her. And then I tormented her for another seven hundred years.

But I can't make the words come, even when Ariel covers her face and confesses, "I'm so ashamed."

I ease her hood down and place a gentle hand on her hair, wishing I could soak up her pain and leave her heart as clean as it was before. "Don't be. Don't let them put ugliness between us."

She moans low in her throat. "I was . . . so angry. I wanted to *kill* you."

"But you didn't." I take her hand, squeeze it tight.

"You don't understand. I had a *plan*," she says. "Gemma and I snuck into the cafeteria today, around ten o'clock, when the workers take their break. We wanted to punish you . . . punish Dylan." She swallows. "While we were there, I hid my grandfather's .22 in the storage room they're using for the coat check for the dance. I pushed up one of the ceiling squares and slipped it in. I was going to wait until you were onstage tonight and go get it and . . ." She tries to pull her hand away from mine. When I refuse to let go, her fingers grow limp. "I don't know if I would have done it, but I was so . . ." She sucks in a jagged breath, and when she speaks again, her voice is barely a whisper. "I hated you. As much as I loved you last night."

We drive on in silence. I know what I want to say, but I don't want to rush. I want her to know that she's been heard and understood and that I'm still choosing to keep my hand in hers. I smooth my thumb across her soft skin. "I love you."

"How?" she chokes out. "I betrayed you. Even if I didn't actually *shoot* you, I was *seriously* considering it. I was so sure you were lying, even though you'd warned me about the Mercenaries. That Gemma could change my mind so fast shows that I'm an evil, awful—"

"And what did the *thing* inside Gemma say to convince you I had to die?" I know this is what she should be focusing on. She was manipulated. She didn't go from loving me in the morning to wanting to murder me in the afternoon without help.

"She said that Romeo was a lie," she whispers. "She said you were really Dylan and that everything you said about the curse and magic was just another way to get me to sleep with you and win the bet. She said you told her lies to get her to sleep with you too, and that you and Gemma made a bet about me when you were . . . with her."

I sigh. Well . . . *shit*. "She was telling the truth. About some of it, at least. Dylan did lie to her, and they did make a bet," I confess, wondering if Ariel could be wrong. Maybe Gemma isn't a Mercenary. Maybe she's only a concerned friend incapable of believing an extraordinary story. "I'm sorry I didn't tell you. I didn't want you to be hurt, and I didn't see that what happened with Dylan and Gemma mattered. Because I'm not Dylan, and everything I've told you is the truth. I swear it."

She nods, and I feel her start to relax. "I know. When I finally got away from Gemma, I started thinking and I . . . I couldn't see how the Dylan I knew would be smart enough to make up a story like that. The things you've told me are too incredible *not* to be true. And then, when I was at Gemma's house getting her stuff, I remembered what you said about the Mercenaries and how I wouldn't be able to tell the difference between one of them and the person I loved until it was too late. That's why I was writing you the note. I wanted to meet somewhere and talk before I went to give Gemma her jewelry. Not that I guess I have to anymore." She closes her eyes, sighs a miserable sigh. "The Mercenary inside of her isn't going to need money to go to Seattle."

I slow the car, pulling to the side of the road and shifting into park. What I have to say isn't the kind of thing you share in a moving vehicle. "Ariel, I—I'm not sure . . ." I brace myself. I have no choice but to speak, no matter how much I'm going to hurt her. "I don't think Gemma's a Mercenary."

Her eyes open. "What?"

"We can't know for certain, so it's best to avoid her, but it sounds like she was only concerned about you."

"What . . ." Her pale face grows even paler. "What do you mean?"

"Dylan was cruel to Gemma. It seems like she was trying to protect you from a similar experience," I say gently. "Did she know about the gun in the cafeteria?"

"No . . . she didn't. She was busy with the audiovisual equipment. I—I didn't tell her . . ." She's quiet, and for once her fingers are still. "I wasn't tricked," she finally says, voice flat, numb. "I was going to commit murder all on my own."

"You wouldn't have killed me."

"Oh no. I might have." She reaches for her door, but I stop her with a hand around her wrist.

"Where are you going?"

"Let me out."

"No."

"Let me out!" She slaps at my hand, but I grab her arms and pull her close.

"Don't leave," I whisper, inches from her face. "Please."

"Don't you see?" she sobs. "I'm a psycho. I'm not good enough for—"

"You are the best thing that's ever happened to me," I say, voice shaking. "I don't care if you planned to kill me. I don't care if you'd *done it*. It would have been worth it. *You're* worth it."

"You're crazy."

"I told you that the night we met." I try to smile but can't, not when she's so upset. "I love you. I forgive you."

For a moment the only sound is the rumble of the car idling beneath us. "That's what I always feel like I should say to you," she finally says. "In my dreams."

"I need forgiveness too." I move closer, until I can feel the seductive warmth of her against my lips. "More than you can imagine. Maybe the only thing I need more is to forgive someone else, so that I know that *this* much forgiveness is possible."

"You really . . ." Her hands brush over my heart before sliding up to my shoulders.

"Really. And nothing will change my mind."

"I don't know what to say." Her breath catches as I find her waist and dig my fingers into the thick fabric of her jeans.

"Don't say anything." I lean in, kissing her with everything in me, and she gives everything right back. It's beautiful, terrible . . . perfect.

By the time we pull apart, breath coming fast, our foreheads pressed together and our eyes closed, I'm dizzy and wishing I could keep spinning into her and forget that this is the last day. These are the last few hours, and we will never have a last dance. Or a first.

Or maybe . . . Maybe . . .

"Let's go to your house," I whisper. "Eat something. Get ready for the dance."

"No." She shakes her head. "We can't. When Gemma and I were in the cafeteria today, she messed with the file for the slide show. It's going to play the video you let me take when it's your turn to sing. I don't know how to change it, and I don't—"

"I don't care. Let the video play. You're the only thing that matters to me."

"But what about the real Mercenaries? Shouldn't we be hiding from them?"

"A Mercenary wouldn't kill me in front of a room full of people. They don't like an audience."

She bites her lip. "So you'll be . . . safer at the dance?"

"Exactly. And I have a song to sing. And I want to see the sets you painted all lit up."

"I just want to be alone with you," she says, tears filling her eyes again.

"Me too, but this is important." I brush her hair behind her ear. "I only have until midnight. And I want you to remember—no matter what Dylan says or does when he comes back—that tonight was real. *We* were real."

The tears slip down her cheeks. "It's not enough time." She presses her fingers into the back of my neck until I shiver. Her touch will haunt me forever. Even when I am dust, I will remember the feel of her skin.

"I'm sorry." I am, for so much more than she'll ever understand.

She turns, finding my lips again. "I forgive you," she says, kissing me with the words, making me ache for another night. Just one more. Lying next to her, holding her while she sleeps. But we don't have another night. We have only a few hours, and they're slipping away.

"I hate to say it, but we—"

"Should go," she finishes, a smile thinning her lips. "You're right. And I guess I . . ." She clears her throat, settles fully back into her seat. "You're right. About Gemma. I should run her jewelry by the hotel."

"Let me come with you. In case she's—"

"No. Gemma might not be a Mercenary, but she still hates

you. She won't understand why you're with me." She drops her face into her hands, rubbing her eyes with a tired sigh. "Especially after everything we did today."

"I don't want to leave you alone. All day I thought the Mercenaries had you, and it was my fault. It was torture."

"I'm sorry," she whispers.

"Don't be sorry." I loop my fingers around her wrist. "Let me keep you safe."

She drops her hands to her lap. "Okay. You can drive me to the hotel and wait in the car. We'll find a spot with a view of Gemma's door. It shouldn't take but a few minutes."

"Ten minutes. No more, or I come after you."

She nods. "That should be plenty. I can't stay long anyway. Gemma called the office pretending to be my mom this morning and said I was sick again, but the school might have still called with the absence message. I have to get back and check before Mom gets home. She'll never let me go to the dance if she knows I skipped."

"A fate that must be avoided." I shift the car into drive and pull back onto the road. "I *need* to see you in that dress."

"It's beautiful," she says softly.

"You're beautiful."

"Because of you."

"No, not—"

"Yes. Because of you. Don't argue," she says.

I don't. I drive. Because I'm still a selfish creature at heart. I want to believe I've given her beauty, and that it will be something for her to hold close when the boy she loves is a monster too hideous to show his face at her window.

But if there is any way to manage it, I will be there, hiding in the shadows, doing my best to protect her from the darkness.

TWENTY-TWO

Ariel

Smile and lie, smile and lie, smile and lie. The mantra is a hand to hold as I cross the parking lot of the Knight and Day motel. I can feel his eyes on me, watching me from where he parked in the shade, determined not to let me out of his sight a second longer than necessary. Because he *cares* so much.

Care. *Love.* As if he knows a damned thing about either.

The black cloud teeming inside of me buzzes louder, a furious swarm of feeling that has drowned out even the screaming things. There's no room inside my head for them now. Not when I'm so furious that my heart is on fire, that I move through a thick, suffocating fog of hate as I make my way to room fifty-three and lift my fist to knock on the door.

Almost immediately Gemma appears, squinting against the sun. "Hey! Mike's not here. He drove up to San Luis to grab a few things from his old apartment," she says. "What's up? Did you . . ." Her words trail away and her grin shrivels. "What's wrong, Ree?"

I swallow and try to smile, but I can't. My face has forgotten how to move that way. I can fake it for him, but not for her, not after everything her mother told me.

"Oh god. Something went wrong, didn't it? *Shit*." She sighs and leans past me to scan the parking lot before grabbing my hand and pulling me inside. "Come on. Let me get you a Coke. You can tell me all the gory details."

The room is dark, the curtains drawn against curious eyes. To our left are two double beds, one with the forest-green bedspread still tucked in tight, the other with rumpled sheets and a mound of smooshed pillows at the top center. It looks like Gemma and Mike sleep close, snuggled in the center of the bed. Just like Romeo and I did last night.

My eyes slide shut, and a choked sound gurgles in my throat. The pain is worse than anything I could have imagined, even worse than this morning, a mountain of misery crumbling down on top of me, vast and crushing and inescapable.

"Ree? Ree, you're freaking me out," Gemma says.

I open my eyes to find her standing in front of me, holding my hands gently in hers. I can barely feel her touch. My skin is numb again, a shell, a suit of impenetrable armor I'll use to protect me as I fight.

But first I have to make sure my only friend is safe.

"I'm sorry." I let her guide me into one of the chairs near the small table in the corner. She pops the top on a Coke and sets it in front of me while I reach into the pocket of my hoodie and pull out the plastic bag. "Here's your stuff." I set it on the table and scoot it toward her with a flick of my fingers. "I put it in a plastic bag and carried it out in my pocket. I forgot my backpack."

"Thanks," Gemma says, but she doesn't reach for the bag. She's too busy watching me. "So what happened? Was my dad there? Did my mom catch you or—"

"She did."

"*Shit!*"

"But it was okay." *Because she wasn't your mom anymore,* I silently add, knowing it would be pointless to tell Gemma what's going on. She wouldn't believe her mom's body is hosting another soul—an Ambassador of Light sent to protect me—any more than she believed me about Romeo. But for once in my life, I was right. Romeo *is* real. And my anger when I thought Dylan was pretending is nothing compared to the fury of knowing that everything Romeo said is true.

"Ree? Ariel?"

Except the part about loving me. That's still a lie. The way I should have known it was from the start.

Romeo came here to trick me, and as soon as he realizes he has failed, he'll kill me like he did the first time. I've seen it, felt it, known what it's like to have a bullet push through my forehead and lodge in my brain. I watched his face light up with satisfaction as he fired the gun. He *enjoyed* it. I could see it in his eyes. The Ambassador in Mrs. Sloop's body showed me everything. She took me by the hand and sent visions of Romeo's reign of terror dancing through my mind, saving me from becoming one of his victims a second time.

She showed me all the people he murdered, countless men and women he won over with clever lies, only to turn them into murderers and monsters—like him. He's still a Mercenary, though a cursed one. He pissed off his boss, and if he doesn't find a girl to love him and sacrifice her to the Mercenary cause, he'll become one of the lost souls that scream in my head. He's been seducing me for the slaughter. But unfortunately for him, Juliet's Ambassador reached me in time.

Now *I* will be the one to take revenge. For myself, for Juliet, and for all the people whose hearts and souls and lives Romeo has ripped apart.

"You'd better start talking, Ree," Gemma says, her voice trembling. I glance up, registering the shimmer in her brown eyes. She's about to cry. I made myself cry for him, to make my lies more convincing, but I won't cry for real ever again. I'm too full of hate to feel anything else. "If you don't, I'm going to call your mom," she warns.

"That can't happen," I mumble in a flat, hollow tone. I sound empty, though I'm so filled with rage, I feel like I'll bubble over any second. "That would ruin everything."

"I don't care. What's wrong with you? You're scaring me."

"I'm . . . sorry." I sit up straighter, trying to focus through the haze of fury. But it's so hard. Every time I blink, images of my grandpa's gun flicker behind my eyes. For the hundredth time I wish I hadn't hidden it in the cafeteria. I wish I could go home and get it right now, the sooner to take care of my problem and spare myself the agony of pretending, and the torture of enduring Romeo's touch, his kiss.

His kiss. The fury spikes again, and I'm possessed by the urge to rip his lips from his lying face, dangle them in front of him while he screams. But I can't. I have to wait for the gun. I'm not certain I'm strong enough to get the job done any other way.

Gemma reaches for her pocket. "Okay, Ariel. I—"

My hand whips out to grab her wrist, stopping her from pulling out her phone. "I'm fine," I say, forcing myself to pull it together. "It was just hard talking to your mom. After everything you told me . . . It was hard to even look at her."

Gemma sighs. "Maybe I shouldn't have told you. I've been thinking about it since we got back from the school, and—"

"No, I'm glad you did." I grab the Coke and take a long, sharp, sugary sip, enjoying the way it burns in my throat. "I'm glad I know the truth. About everything. I'm sick of pretty lies. And ugly lies."

"And moderately attractive lies with nice smiles," she says, but her joke falls flat. I'm not in a joking mood. Her eyes meet mine and flicker away. "Okay. Well then, let's see what we've got." She reaches for the plastic bag and peels open the crumpled top.

"It's all there, right?"

"Yeah, I think so," she says, digging through the rings and bracelets and tightly wrapped rolls of twenty-dollar bills. "Let me see if Mom took anything."

I was so out of it by the time I went to get Gemma's things that I can barely remember dumping the box into the white Albertsons bag the Ambassador pressed into my hands. Her hands were shaking by that point too. It was hard for her to show me all those horrible things, and even harder to show me the boy.

She had him tied up in the barn. Like an animal. But that's what he is. A dumb animal with a pretty face, one Romeo will wear again as soon as he kills me. My death will pay his way into the beautiful body of my boy on the hill. Just like Juliet's death paid for his immortality.

"Monster."

"What?" Gemma asks, glancing up from the jewelry she's laid out on the table.

"Nothing." I open my mouth wide and close it again, trying to banish some of the tension from my jaw. I feel like I could chew the diamonds in Gemma's hands in half.

I breathe slowly in and out through my nose. It's going to be okay. The Ambassador is going to hide Romeo's body in the school cafeteria freezer later this afternoon. It will be there, drugged with her magic, tied up and waiting for me. When the time is right, I'll grab it and grab my gun and put an end to Romeo the way the Ambassador told me to. He'll never barter another girl's life for his again.

"It's all here." Gemma sweeps everything back into the bag with a sigh. "Thank you so much. You have no idea what a load off this is."

"No problem. I was happy to help."

She looks up with a wicked grin. "Me too. I can't wait to see Dylan's face tonight."

Right. "I wanted to talk to you about that." This is what I came for. I need to get it done so that Romeo and I can go get ready for the dance. So that I can kill him the way I told him I was going to kill him, and see his stupid lying face when he realizes I beat him at his own game. "I don't want you to come tonight."

"What?" Gemma laughs and pokes the back of my hand with one finger. "Are you crazy? There's no way I'm missing this."

"No. It's too dangerous. Someone will see you and call your parents. They're still pretending you're missing. Your mom didn't—"

"Pfft!" She waves a hand, dismissing my concern. "No one will see me. I'll wear Mike's black hoodie and hide in the curtains backstage until the big moment."

"But—"

"Ree, seriously. When that video starts, everyone will be too distracted to notice little old me," she continues. "I'll slip out, watch Dylan crash and burn, and escape out the back door into the night. Mike will be waiting in the parking lot. We're leaving for Seattle right after. I've got it all planned."

She's got plans. But I have plans too. "No. You have to go. Now. As soon as Mike gets back."

She shakes her head, confusion in her eyes. "Ariel . . . what's up? I thought—"

"I don't want you to get hurt. If you stay here, your life is in danger."

She stills. "What?"

"Dylan's an even worse person than we thought," I say, telling the lie I prepared, knowing she won't believe there are Mercenaries out to invade the bodies of the people I love. "I found out some other things about him today."

"What kind of things?"

"I can't tell you. I don't want to put you in any more danger than I have already," I say. "I couldn't forgive myself if I was the reason you were killed."

"Holy shit." Gemma's voice shakes. "Are you serious?"

"Completely serious. You have to leave. And don't ever come back."

"But what about you? If Dylan's dangerous, then—"

"Don't worry. I'm going to take care of him."

Her eyes narrow for a moment before widening in comprehension. "Ariel Dragland . . . You're not thinking what I *think* you're thinking."

"I can't say any more. Don't ask me any more questions."

"No, no, no," she says, jumping up to pace the small patch of flowered carpet next to the table. "This is *not* okay. I know what we talked about today with my uncle and stuff, but if Dylan has done something worth killing him for, you have to go to the police. If you do something—"

"Gemma, stop!" She flinches at the intensity in my tone. "I'm not telling you anything else. We already went into the cafeteria together. If I get caught, it's best if you haven't done anything else that could make people think of you as an accessory."

"An accessory . . ." She licks her lips, lets out a long breath. "Ariel, I—"

"Go, Gemma." I stand, facing her head-on. "Promise me you'll leave as soon as Mike gets back."

"No," she whispers. "You'll ruin your life."

"My life is already ruined."

"No, it's not, Ariel." She reaches out, fingers brushing my elbow, hesitant, cautious, as if she's afraid even a friendly touch will make me explode. "You may feel like that now, but I promise you Dylan isn't worth—"

"Shut up," I snap.

"Okay, fine." She pulls her cell phone from her pocket,

but I snatch it away and hurl it across the room, gratified when I hear it crack into pieces. "What the–"

"You don't understand," I say. "You'll never understand, so don't talk to me like *I'm* the one who's stupid."

She blinks. Then blinks again. Then starts for the door.

I dart in front of her, blocking the exit with my body. "You can't go out there."

"Yes, I can," she says softly. "I'm going to the front office and I'm calling your mom."

"No."

"Yes. You don't know what you're–"

She reaches for the door, but I knock her hand away. "He's out there! In the car."

She shakes her head. "Who?"

"Dylan."

"Why?" She lifts her hands, fingers splayed in the air above her. "What the hell are you doing?"

"It doesn't matter. I just can't let him see you. Especially upset."

Gemma drives a hand through her hair. "I'm not upset, Ree. I am *freaked. Out.* Really *fucking* freaked out." She swallows, and I can see the fear in the way her throat works. She's afraid. Of me.

"Don't be." My lips tremble. I bite them to make them stop. I didn't want things to end this way with Gemma. "Please," I beg, praying she'll listen to me even as I edge to the left, closer to the bureau shoved into the corner and the lamp on top of it. "Calling my mom isn't going to help anything. If you really want to help, do what I asked. Leave with Mike and be safe and happy. You're my best friend. You're the only real friend I've ever–"

"And you're mine," she says, tears shining in her eyes. "Don't you know that? I meant what I said this morning, Ree. I love you, and I'm not going to let you do something I know you'll regret."

"I won't regret it."

"Yes, you will," she says, with that stubborn look on her face, the one that lets me know she won't be backing down. That I have no choice. "But I'm going to make sure you don't have to." She starts toward the door, and I go for the lamp. The cord rips from the base as I lift it over my head and bring it down.

Hard. Harder than I meant to.

Gemma moans and crumples to the floor and lies there. Still. Not moving. Not talking. Not blinking. I drop the lamp and slap shaking hands over my mouth to muffle the cry that tries to escape my lips.

I kneel down next to her. There's a lot of blood, rushing from her temple, cutting a winding trail down her cheek. But she's breathing—soft, shallow breaths that grow more even the longer I crouch next to her listening. Finally I feel brave enough to put two tentative fingers to her throat and feel her pulse. Slow and steady. Rhythmic. She's going to be fine. Unconscious for a while—which is what I was hoping would happen—but fine.

"Thank god," I whisper, hand shaking as I pull it from her skin. I hurry to the bathroom and grab a few towels. One I position gently beneath Gemma's head. The other I roll into a log and lay over her wound. It soaks up some of the blood, but not all. Some still runs down her face, drips off her cheek-bone, making tiny red splatter marks on the towel beneath her. But it's slowing down. She's going to be okay.

"She'll be fine," I assure myself as I arrange her crooked arms and legs to make her as comfortable as possible.

I *had* to do this. It's the only way to make sure Gemma's safe. If she's unconscious, she can't call my mom. And if she's scared of me, she won't dare come to the dance. She'll leave and get on with her life, and I won't take anyone down with me. I already mailed my mom a long letter, explaining that I have to leave forever but that I love her and want her to be happy. I wish there was time to leave Gemma a letter, but there's not. I've already been in here longer than the ten minutes Romeo and I agreed upon. Pretty soon he'll come looking for me, and I can't let him see Gemma on the floor.

I settle for a quick note on some hotel stationery I find on the bureau. *I'm sorry. Go and be happy. You deserve it. Love, Ree. P.S. Don't ever look back.*

I tuck the note into her softly curled fingers, and whisper, "Good-bye." I stand up, run my hands through my hair, shake my arms until I feel a little calmer, and plaster a peaceful smile on my face.

And then I walk out the door, into the sunlight, through the haze of hatred toward the monster I loved.

The monster I'm going to kill before the night is through.

TWENTY-THREE

Romeo

I stand in the shadows outside the storage-room-turned-coat-check with my hands clasped tight, listening to one of the other show-choir members croon about luck being a lady, while I wait for my unlucky love.

Ariel insisted on wearing her mother's long, black coat over her gown. She even took it into her bedroom when she got ready so I wouldn't get a glimpse of the dress until we were at the dance, until she stepped out into the disco-ball-speckled darkness in all her glory. I appreciate her flare for the dramatic, but standing here, waiting for a flash of white, imagining how beautiful she'll be, is only making me more miserable.

I feel like a groom waiting for his bride, but soon I'll be gone and Ariel will live on to love someone else.

Or she'll die before she gets the chance. Thanks to you.

I trap my cheek flesh between my teeth and bite down, until the pain is sufficiently distracting. Dwelling on my mistakes won't do Ariel any good. I've already warned her—at length and in great detail—about the kind of people who will come for her after I'm gone, and what they'll do if they catch her. I've helped her plot her escape, and shared every survival tip learned in years of stealing the bodies of the dead. All I can do is hope that I've prepared her . . . as well as anyone can be prepared for supernatural evil.

"Nice tux, Stroud." The redheaded boy laughs as he pulls his date onto the dance floor.

"It's vintage." I force a smile as I scan the cafeteria.

On the far side of the press of bodies swaying in the dark, the stage is lit up in soft blue and white. Behind the girl giving her bluesy rendition of "Luck Be a Lady," pictures of the senior class flash on a screen suspended above Ariel's backdrops— giant paisley shapes painted with intricate patterns like henna on the back of an Indian woman's hand. They're beautiful. It seems a shame that soon all eyes will be staring at Dylan Stroud making a fool of himself, instead of her lovely work.

I'm beyond human embarrassment—have been for centuries—but I'd prefer to spend my last few hours with Ariel undisturbed by the drama my striptease will no doubt cause. I want to hold her in the darkness, with the silver stars hung from the ceiling twinkling around us, and pretend this is our eternity, where we will always be no farther than a breath away.

Breath. She steps through the door, and I have none.

She is . . . unspeakably beautiful. Her hair, a shade darker than the dress, falls around her shoulders, each silky curl kissing a bit of bare skin. The thin straps emphasize the elegant architecture of her bones, and the bodice clings tight to her curves before blooming into layers of chiffon that cascade all the way to her feet. The white rose corsage she wears—a cheap thing we picked up at a grocery store on the way—completes the picture, its wilted bloom suddenly magnificent because it sits on her wrist.

She is a goddess, and for the first time in hundreds of years I remember what it feels like to be humbled by beauty. I am unworthy, imperfect, corrupt and full of holes, but when she looks at me, I am something better, something more.

"Good?" she asks, a shy note in her voice that makes me smile.

I shake my head, at a loss for the words to tell her how perfect she is.

"You? Speechless?" She laughs as her eyes drop to the floor.

"Dance with me."

She looks up through her lashes, smile fading. "I've never danced with anyone before. Ever. I realized while I was in the coat check . . . Gemma and I used to play DanceDance Revolution when we were little, but—"

"Don't worry." I hold out my hand. "I'll lead."

"Don't you have to get ready to sing?"

"Not yet. I need to touch you." By the time we dropped off Gemma's things and drove back to Ariel's house, her mother was home. There wasn't a message from the school, so Ariel was allowed out, but the loss of our last chance to be alone felt like a death in the family.

It's already nine o'clock. By the time we dance, I sing, and we hit the punch bowl, it will be ten and the dance will nearly be over. Then I'll have to take Ariel to the bus station and come back to the woods behind the school to confront the Ambassador. Maybe I'll be able to convince her to let me stay here in my old body. Maybe she'll have my specter with her and I'll be able to make contact and take the decision out of her hands. If so, I plan to follow Ariel to Las Vegas, drag my rotted corpse across the desert if that's what it takes, and do my best to protect her.

But if I fail, at least she'll be away from here, on the run, making it more difficult for the Mercenaries to find her.

I suppose. I *hope.*

I'm sick of the uncertainty, of being at the mercy of everyone's desires but my own. Right now I don't want to think about Ambassadors or Mercenaries. I want to be here, with Ariel in my arms.

"Dance with me. Please."

"Okay," she whispers.

I take her hand, keenly aware of every shift of muscle and bone that it takes to thread my fingers through hers. I can't remember being this nervous before. I feel like a boy again, but worse. Back then I had no idea how precious moments like this would be in my many lifetimes of wickedness and pain. Now I do, and it makes my hands shake as Ariel and I find an empty place in the crush of swaying bodies and I pull her close.

The song about lady luck has ended, and now a girl in a

skintight black gown that makes her look like an eight ball with legs wails about finding her love at last. It's a heartbreakingly happy song, with soaring violins and tripping drums, and the girl works every note in a way that gets under my borrowed skin.

Borrowed. Stolen. Almost gone. I'm getting ready to expire, and every moment with Ariel is becoming more precious.

"You smile, you smile," the girl onstage sings. I think about the first time I saw Ariel smile, that night by the side of the road when I was still stupid enough to think I was in control. I hold her tight as I spin in a circle, making her cling to my neck and her breath rush out.

When I set her back on her feet, she ducks her head. "People are staring," she murmurs against my shoulder.

"Let them." My fingers spread at the small of her back, mesmerized by the warmth seeping through the fabric. She's so alive. I can't imagine her any other way. I won't. "Promise me you'll keep moving. No more than a few days in Las Vegas, and don't call anyone. I'll meet you on Sunday if I can. If not, buy a ticket and get on a bus. Don't wait for me. If I'm held up for some unexpected reason, I'll find you later."

She sighs. "My mom is going to be so upset. She's going to lose her mind."

My fingers curl. I know Ariel doesn't want to leave her mother, but there's no other choice. There's no guarantee that I'll be here to protect her. Running is Ariel's best chance at survival. "If you stay, she'll be more than upset," I say. "She'll be dead. And so will you."

"I know," she whispers.

"I don't want to scare you, I just . . ." I force my fingers to relax. "No. That's a lie. I want you to be scared. I want you to be so scared that you never, ever stop running. Even years from now, when you imagine that the creatures hunting you must have turned their attention elsewhere. They won't have. They're ancient. A year, ten years, twenty, is nothing to them. They will hunt you until the day you die. Promise me you'll do as we've planned."

She's quiet for a long, unsettling minute. I try to catch her eye, but she won't look at me. She stares at the disco ball lights swimming like tadpoles across the floor, tension turning her mouth into a crooked line.

"Please." I sway to a stop, sickened by the thought that she has changed her mind. "If I have to leave without knowing you're safe, I don't know what . . ." I *do* know. I'll go mad. "Please. If you love me at all, do whatever it takes."

She lifts her chin, and I see unspoken questions in her eyes, but still she doesn't say a word.

"What's wrong?" Silence, and for a moment she seems flatter, hollow, like a picture of herself instead of the living, breathing person I've known. But then she blinks, and Ariel is back.

"Nothing's wrong. I mean . . . *everything's* wrong, but you're right." She stands on tiptoe and brushes her lips against my newly smooth cheek, the one she helped me shave with her pink razor. "I'll keep to the plan. I promise."

I kiss the skin near her ear. "Thank you."

"You don't have to thank me. Just . . . tell me you love me again."

"I love you," I say, wishing she knew how much more those three words mean to me now that I've met her. "More than anything."

A sad grin licks the edges of her lips. "You'd better go." The girl singing the Etta James number finishes her song, and a boy with heavily gelled hair starts a country-inspired version of "Maria" from *West Side Story*. "You're on after Logan, right?"

"Yes." I squeeze her hand. "Come with me. Stand by the stage. I want to see you when I'm up there."

"Okay." She tucks her chin, hiding her face as we thread our way through the couples paired up on the dance floor.

Some sway stiffly back and forth, but the more daring are dancing in a way that leaves no doubt what they'll be doing later. Hips roll and hands roam, and I suddenly can't stop thinking about last night, about Ariel's long legs wrapped around me. I cast a glance over my shoulder, wondering what she's thinking, but she's still looking at her feet, shoulders hunched.

She's too busy worrying about the future to focus on our last happy moments. But I can do something about that. I've seen the way she looks at me when I sing. I'm going to sing like I've never sung before, then I'm going to pull her back onto the dance floor and we're going to dance like people are supposed to dance, wild and wanton and free, until we forget everything but her and me and the music.

"Don't move." I release her hand at a shadowy spot near the wall—dark enough for her to feel comfortable, but light enough for me to see her from the stage.

"I won't." She accepts the kiss I press to her cheek, but doesn't look up. Her gaze is still fixed on some distant nothing, her arms hanging limply at her sides. Again, I get that sense that she's emptier than she was before.

"Are you all right?"

She meets my eyes, but something is still . . . off. "No. But

I will be." She smoothes the hair away from my face. "Now go. It's your cue."

I nod, but the off-kilter feeling follows me through the curtains into the backstage area, making my jaw tight as I take the microphone Mrs. Mullens offers, and cross to the holding area. I remind myself that leaving one's family and setting out alone in the world is enough to make anyone shell-shocked, but I don't believe that's the reason for Ariel's vacant expression.

Even before the girl in the black hooded sweatshirt slips from her hiding place in the curtains, I wonder if something else is to blame. And then I see Gemma's face, her haunted eyes, and know my troubles are much bigger than I believed.

"What are you—"

"Shut it, Stroud. We don't have time for your stupidity," Gemma hisses. "You're a sorry excuse for a person and I hate you like cancer, but I don't want you dead."

Dead. The word lands in my gut and lays there like a bomb waiting to explode, heavy and full of dreadful potential. Back when I was a Mercenary, I was nearly impossible to destroy, but now . . .

I'm not even an Ambassador. If I'm killed while I'm in Dylan's body, I don't know where I'll go, but I don't imagine it will be a good place. Maybe I'll reach the mists of forgetting and wander there for eternity like the Ambassadors I killed, or maybe I'll bypass the slow rot my Mercenary maker had planned and go straight to being one of the lost souls that howl in Ariel's mind. Either way, I'll be useless, helpless to protect or serve anyone.

"You can't go onstage." Gemma grabs the sleeve of my jacket and holds on tight. "I know you think I'm crazy, but trust me—don't go out there. Sneak out the other side of the curtains, go out the back door, and—"

"Why?"

She shakes her head.

"I'll believe you," I insist. "I promise I will."

She hesitates, but then the music shifts and I see her decide there's no time to argue. The song's almost over.

"When Ariel brought me my jewelry this afternoon, she told me she didn't want me to come to the dance. She said she was afraid I'd be spotted." Gemma pulls in a breath, and continues with obvious effort. "I told her I didn't care, I wasn't going to miss seeing you get what's coming to you. We snuck into the cafeteria earlier today and—"

"I know about the video."

Her jaw drops. "What?"

"I don't care," I say, glancing over my shoulder. "It's no big deal."

Gemma grabs my elbow and shakes it until I turn back to her. "What about this? Is this no big deal?" She tugs the hood off her head, revealing a bloody gash at her temple. The blood has dried to a dark umber, but the wound is fresh. "When I told Ariel she was acting nuts and I was calling her mom, she lost it. She told me to leave Solvang and not come back or I'd end up dead. Or an accessory to murder. And then she hit me with a lamp."

Time slows; the music piping through the speakers goes twisted and strange. I can barely breathe. Ariel said she and Gemma shared a Coke and parted with promises to stay in touch. But she must have been lying. She *has* to be lying, because there's no way Gemma is. The grief and horror on her face are too real.

And there's only one reason Ariel would lie to me.

One nightmarish reason.

"I passed out for a little while. I don't know how long." Gemma brushes the sleeve of her sweatshirt across her nose. "Mike got back to the room an hour ago and woke me up. He tried to convince me to leave, but I told him we couldn't go without warning you."

"Dylan! Get ready, it's time," Mrs. Mullens hisses behind me. The last notes of "Maria" echo through the cafeteria, and Logan slips through the curtain. She's right. It's time. I have to go out there and face the music. And the girl. And the evil that has nearly won the battle for her soul.

I step forward, but Gemma latches on to my arm. "No!" she says. "You can't. I think this is when she's going to do it. Hurt you. Maybe even kill you, I don't know."

"It's all right." The intro music begins to play. "I have to go."

Gemma groans in frustration. "Please! Don't! I'm the one who said Ariel should get revenge on you. If you're hurt, it'll–"

"Don't worry. She loves you, and I love her." I turn and hug Gemma against me, a swift squeeze that shocks her silent. "Leave. Now." I step toward the opening in the curtain. This time, she lets me. "Find Mike, go to Washington, and stay away from Ariel."

"I didn't know she was really crazy," she whispers.

"She's not." Before Gemma can respond, I flick my mike to the on position and step out onstage in time to sing the first words of Dylan's song. I search the shadows where I left Ariel, but I'm not surprised to find them empty.

Devastated, but not surprised.

Ariel's *not* crazy. She's doing what she has to do to earn a position as one of the ultimate bad guys. The Mercenaries have gotten to her. Her lies this afternoon were inspired, so pitch-perfect that even someone with hundreds of years of excellence in the art didn't see through them. The way she colored each falsehood with a hint of truth . . . Exceptional. Even when I said the Mercenaries wouldn't attack me in public, she didn't flinch, though she knew I would escort death to the dance on my arm.

Maybe she plans to shoot me now, as she confessed. Maybe she's going to wait until later, when we're alone, on the way to the bus station. Either way, she played me perfectly, the way I played hundreds of pretty young girls who wanted to believe that love could conquer all. She made a fool of me, a sopping, starry-eyed fool.

But who am I to judge her? I've done what she's done, been what she will become. Even now—as the room fills with laughter as the video begins to play and I wonder if Ariel's out there ready to use this distraction to destroy me—I can't hate her. I still love her. It's hopeless, but it's real.

It wasn't all a lie. For a day or two she loved me and I loved her. She has changed me, and I will never be the same.

I take a breath and keep singing, voice so full that the people closest to the stage stop laughing. "Till I'm buried . . . buried in my grave."

Buried. This would be a poetic time. Ariel is a romantic with a flair for presentation. She's going to bring terrible beauty to her work.

Just the way I did.

"Oh bring it to me." I lift my arm to the side, a gesture of surrender, an offering. "Bring your sweet lovin'—"

The shot cracks through the air, cutting off the music, inspiring a ripple of screams that becomes a wave of terror as the shooter fires again and the disco ball shatters. Slivers of glass rain down onto the dance floor. Students cover their heads and run. Teachers and chaperones scramble to open doors, and couples grab hands and race for the exits. Mrs. Mullens runs by the stage, shouting for me to "Run!" But I don't.

She's done it. It's over. I am Juliet on the floor of the tomb, with a knife in my heart and the person I love to blame. Ariel hasn't hit me yet, but she will, and I can't bring myself to run and hide.

I drop the microphone, the *thud* as it hits the ground echoing through the room. I clench my fists, brace myself for the pain. I'll feel it any second, the slam of the bullet, the fire as skin and organ and bone make way for blood to pour. This is poetic justice at its finest. This is the saddest waste in the world. I loved her, and I stupidly thought that would be enough. I'm still hoping I get to see her again, that she takes the time to look me in the face before . . .

There . . . in the doorway to the coat check. Right where she said she'd be.

She leans against the doorframe, the glow from the room behind highlighting her silhouette through the gauzy fabric of her dress. I can't see her face, but I know she's looking my way. I can feel her eyes on me, inspiring a dizzy mix of fear, misery, and a hint of plain old lust. The realization makes me smile. Seems I haven't become such a good boy, after all. I'm still sick enough to be turned on by a girl who's trying to kill me.

"Are you going to do it?" I shout. "The suspense is killing me."

"Suspense would be too gentle," she calls back.

She's done it, confirmed all my suspicions. She's a trickster and a liar and is holding a smoking gun in one of the slender hands hidden behind her back. Still, I can't believe this will be easy for her, and I can't believe she hates me—at least not completely.

"You're doing a great job." I step closer to the edge of the stage. "Your first murder, and already proficient with the witty banter. Give you a few weeks and—"

"Romeo!" The whisper comes from behind me, the urgency in the woman's tone making me suspect it isn't the first time she's called my name. I turn to find the Ambassador hiding behind the curtains, one brown eye and one white hand peeking through. In the hand, she holds a gun.

A gun. But I thought . . . I . . .

She holds it out to me. "Take it. You know what you have to do."

I stare at the weapon for a moment before looking back at Ariel. She's still in the doorway, a perfect target, all lit up. I'm an excellent shot. There's no doubt I'll hit my mark with the first bullet. I can already imagine the way the red will burst from her stomach, staining the white fabric like a flower eating up her insides to feed its bloom.

"She's beyond salvation." The Ambassador tosses the weapon. It lands at my feet and spins in a lazy circle. "It's better that she dies quickly. We can't allow her to take the Mercenary vows."

"I . . ." I turn back to Ariel. Why is she standing so still? Why doesn't she run or pull her own weapon? Is there a part of her that still cares? That's waiting for me to give her a reason to stop the madness?

There was a time when I would have agreed that Ariel's death was for the best—if she's come this close to becoming a Mercenary, there will be no turning back. But looking at her now, at the graceful lines of her body and the tip of her chin and the rise and fall of her shoulders as she draws breath . . .

"I can't," I say.

"No. *I* can't," the Ambassador whispers. "It is forbidden by my magic, but you can kill her. If you do, I promise I will make you one of us. It will be your final murder, a noble sacrifice made for the greater good."

Noble sacrifice. Greater good. Noble. Good. Sacrifice.

The words swirl through my head, shocking in their resemblance to what the Mercenary who created me said that night on the hill.

Apparently the light and the dark have even more in common than I believed.

I crouch, pick up the gun, and move slowly back toward the edge of the stage, a suspicion forming in my mind.

TWENTY-FOUR

Ariel

I watch his fingers curl around the gun, but I'm not hurt or miserable anymore. I'm not even relieved to see evidence that the Ambassador was right, and Romeo really is a killer with some unseen accomplice behind the curtain.

All I feel is anger. Sharp and deadly.

I lift my chin and clutch my pistol tighter. I have to take care of him before the people who ran call for help, before Romeo shoots me, or whoever's helping him steps out with their own weapon. The Ambassador warned me that Romeo would have another Mercenary watching over him, but that his colleague will abandon Romeo when it's clear that he's failed, when I put an end to him with a bullet through the heart of both his bodies—one borrowed and one so nearly bought.

Dylan is in front of me; Romeo's old body is tied up in the room behind. The Ambassador kept her word and had him waiting for me in the freezer at the back of the kitchen. During the uproar as Dylan's striptease played, no one even noticed me leading the vacant-eyed boy in his tattered clothes into the coat check and closing the door. No one saw me tie him up, or climb the storage shelves to fetch my grandpa's gun from the ceiling. And now all the witnesses are gone. It's just Romeo and me.

It's time. Now. *Now.*

I lift the gun, pulse racing so fast, I can see it leaping at my wrist, throbbing between the muscles straining to hold the heavy weapon.

"Wait!" Romeo shouts. "Please." He jumps from the stage to the dance floor, where puddles of silver are all that remain of the disco ball's racing lights. I hit both the sound system and the disco ball on my first tries. Apparently I'm a good shot. I should be able to kill Romeo before he can lift the gun in his hand.

My finger tightens on the trigger. Tighter, tighter . . .

"Talk to me," he begs.

"I'm done talking. I know what you are."

He lifts one hand in the air, the one not holding the gun. "I've told you what I am."

"I know you're still a Mercenary."

"No, I—"

"When I went to Gemma's, there was an Ambassador in

her mother's body. She told me everything," I say, unable to resist throwing the truth in his face. "She showed me how you killed me. How you *shot* me!"

Guilt flares in his eyes. "Please, Ariel. You don't understand. I–"

"Shut up."

"Please!"

"I told you, I'm done talking."

"Then you don't have to talk." He takes a cautious step forward. I shift my body, blocking his view of the boy hidden behind me. I can't let him see, not until I'm ready to fire on them both. "Just listen. Juliet was inhabiting your body the first time we met. I did shoot her, but only because I had no choice. It was the only way to protect her from–"

"I've had enough of your *protection,* and I don't want to hear your lies."

"They're not . . ." He trails off, fear evident in the rapid rise and fall of his chest. He's finally realizing the truth. That I'm beyond his reach. That he's about to die. Once and for all. "Please, just let me tell you how I feel. One last time."

"Love . . . yes . . . ," Romeo's old body whispers, making me jump and my finger ease off the trigger.

I peek back to see him rocking side to side, his grin so innocent and happy, it makes me want to cry. He's more pathetic than scary. He's as handsome as the boy in my dreams, but empty inside, a damaged thing I didn't think could speak. He was eerily quiet today in the barn, so silent and still that at first I thought he was dead.

The Ambassador told me he's Romeo's soul specter. When Romeo's soul went to live inside the dead, this was what was left behind. Romeo hasn't lived inside this body for hundreds of years, but he wants to. He planned to kill me to earn the privilege.

Instead, I'll kill him. If Romeo's host and his specter are killed within a few moments of each other, Romeo's reign of terror will end. He won't be able to inhabit a new body. He'll be truly dead, once and for all.

But so will this poor thing. Look at it. It's like killing a puppy.

I grit my teeth and turn back to Romeo, taking aim, remembering the way I gave him every part of me—body and soul—while he plotted my death. I think about the shocked, betrayed faces of all the other people he turned or killed. I remember the girl in the tomb, her eyes closing in pain as her blood leaked out onto the floor.

If anyone deserves to die, it's Romeo. And I'm not *really* committing murder. Dylan's already dead, and Romeo should have died hundreds of years ago. This is justice, no matter how wrong it feels to aim a gun at someone's heart.

"I love you, Ariel," he says, voice breaking.

"Gemma's mom said you'd say that. She said you'd never admit you're lying. Because you need me to love you in order to make killing me worth your while."

"Killing you was *never* on my agenda. Never."

"Mrs. Sloop said you'd say that, too."

"Mrs. Sloop . . ." He moves closer with slow, steady steps. "She wouldn't be a redhead by any chance, would she? Pretty? About forty? Wears a lot of khaki?"

His question confuses me, and the gun dips a few inches toward the floor.

"Pale skin, dark brown eyes," he continues. "Smells like vanilla?"

"Yes, but I—"

"She's the witch who sent me here!" His eyes spark with excitement. He really thinks I'm going to believe more of his crap. "She's not a witch, she's an Ambassador, but it doesn't matter. *She's* the one who gave me this gun, and I can only imagine what lies she told you this afternoon. She's trying to turn us against each—"

"Shut up."

"Ariel, please . . ." He looks like he's going to cry, like it's breaking his heart to see how much I hate him. "I can explain everything. I still love you." He lifts his hands at his sides. "I've been where you are, and I—"

"I know where you've been." I imagine all the blood he's spilled dripping from his pleading hands. "I saw all the people you killed. I saw how you *laughed* while you ripped them apart with your bare hands."

"I used to be a brutal, sick bastard. I *told* you that, but I—"

"You didn't tell me you killed Juliet. When you were both young and she loved you. Trusted you." His face pales, but he doesn't stop taking careful steps toward me. I've got a minute, maybe less. I have to focus on the truth, not the hurt in his eyes or the way an insane part of me wants to believe he really cares. "I saw the way you tricked her. *She* would have killed you if she'd been strong enough to pull the knife from her chest."

"You're right. I should have told you that, and a lot of other things, but I . . ." He swallows. "I'm sorry. I needed you to love me. I didn't know it at the time, but I needed to love you, too. I . . ."

Sirens sound in the distance. I steady the gun on his heart. I have to do this. Before he makes a fool of me yet again.

"Please, Ariel," he says, in a voice that mimics caring so perfectly. "Look at me. You know I've told the truth about everything that matters."

He's close enough to touch now, but I can't seem to squeeze the trigger. He leans in until the barrel of the gun is kissing his chest and the smell of him reaches out, connecting with something inside of me. A soft, human something.

I grit my teeth and will the soft places hard again. "This is for the people you've hurt and the people you won't live to hurt." My entire arm shakes; my hand begins to sweat. "This is for–"

"The greater good," he says at the same time I do.

My elbow spasms and my arm goes limp, the gun sagging between us.

"That's what the Ambassador inside Gemma's mother told *me* when she gave me this gun," he says, motioning over his shoulder to the stage. I glance behind him, but see nothing. The curtains are drawn. But still, somewhere deep inside, I start to wonder. What if . . .

"She said killing you would be for the greater good, a noble sacrifice. She thinks it's better for you to die than to become a force for evil. But I don't believe her." He steps so close, I have to tilt my head back to look into his eyes. "I'll never believe that killing you is good or noble. I love you, and I know you're a better person than I am. Don't let the Ambassadors or the Mercenaries turn you into something you're not."

"I'm not–"

"You're not a person who thinks it's okay to knock your best friend unconscious."

My mouth goes dry. "How did you–"

"She came here. To warn me. She's worried about you."

"I was trying to protect her," I say, but I hear the lie in my words.

"You don't believe that. Any more than you believe it was okay to shoot a gun in a crowded cafeteria. Or that it's okay to kill the person you loved," he adds softly. "Not when he's standing in front of you, promising you are the best thing that ever happened to him."

His eyes are shining. I know I should hate him for his fake tears and his false words, but I don't. All I feel is confused and sad and possessed by the almost overwhelming urge to lay my cheek against his chest. If he's a liar, he's too good at it for me to see through him. If he's telling the truth . . .

Well, he's still too good, and I'm as stupid as I've ever been.

"I'm going to put my gun down," he says. "The Ambassador inhabiting Mrs. Sloop says she can't hurt you because it goes against her magic, but I wouldn't risk it. Run out the side door and hide where no one will find you. The police will be here any second. I'll tell them I didn't see what happened." He wipes the gun on his shirt and throws it away. The sound as it lands on the floor makes me jump.

He dropped his gun. He's not going to kill me. He's not even going to defend himself. For the first time since witnessing my own murder this afternoon, the buzzing anger goes quiet and my mind feels like it's mine again.

The first thing I register is relief, and then . . . horror. Complete, absolute horror. "Oh my god." I drop my gun, flinching when it hits the ground by my feet. "I . . . I almost—"

"But you didn't." He wraps his arms around me, and

pulls me against him for a fierce moment before pushing me toward the door. "Now run. Hurry. I love—"

"No. You don't understand." The sirens are loud now, but I can't leave him here. "She told me how to kill you forever. I was supposed to shoot you, then shoot the other boy."

"What other boy?"

"It . . . that . . . It's in there. She did something to him with magic. I tied him up." I point to the room behind us, my arm trembling, the insanity of the day catching up with me, making me feel like I'm literally going to fall apart. Everything is so fragile. My body, my mind, the line between right and wrong and good and evil.

I can't believe I hurt Gemma. I can't believe I shot a gun, or that I almost killed someone. Killed *Romeo*. Who loves me. Whom I love. Oh my god, I—

"Who's in there, Ariel? You have to—"

"It's you. The way you looked on the hill," I mumble. "She said you'd die for all eternity if I shot you, then shot the specter of your soul right after."

Romeo doesn't move, but I see the wheels turning behind his eyes. He looks . . . excited, and I'm more confused than ever. "Has she come out from behind the curtain?"

I glance over his shoulder. "No."

"Come on. Hurry!" He grabs my hand and pulls me toward the coatroom as sirens howl and horns blare closer than ever. The emergency vehicles have reached the school parking lot. The police will be here any second.

"Wait, we have to—"

He wraps his arm around my waist and lifts me off my feet as he rushes forward. "This body is what I was looking for this morning. If I touch it, I can go back inside it and stay with you."

"What?"

"I know it's hideous, and I would never ask you to—" He stumbles through the door, but freezes a step inside. His mouth falls open. For a person who said he knew what was in here, he looks pretty surprised.

"Come now!" The thing on the floor lights up when he sees Romeo. He reaches his arms out like a child, the scraps of clothing still covering his thin body flapping with his excitement.

"I can't believe this." Romeo's arm grows loose around me. "This isn't . . . This is . . ."

"I'm sorry." I don't know what I'm apologizing for, only that sorry feels like the most inadequate thing I've ever said. I'm still half-numb, but once the numbness wears off, I know the mental backlash is going to be awful. I'm even crazier than I thought, a gullible loser who doesn't know who or what to believe.

"You don't understand." He turns to me, a smile stretching his face. "My body is whole. It was rotten and falling apart. I—"

"And it will be again." Mrs. Sloop is suddenly behind us. We spin to see her standing in the doorway, hands pressed together and golden light building between her palms. "I won't let you have this. I don't care how pretty your soul has become. You don't deserve freedom, and *she* doesn't deserve life. It took less than a day to tempt her to murder. You're both dangerous, and I—"

"Ariel, run!" Romeo dives for her legs. For a second, I think he'll knock her down. I imagine grabbing him and pulling him out the door into the gym, but her foot flashes out at the last second, catching him in the stomach, knocking him back into the shelf against the wall.

"Stop!" I beg, but it's too late.

She opens her hands, and the ball of light leaps forward, heading straight for Romeo. He has shoved the heavy shelves off his back and made it to his feet, but he'll never get out of the way in time. She's going to hit him, hurt him, maybe even kill him.

Before I know it, I'm moving, hurling myself into the magic's path, reaching my arms out, out, out . . . I don't know right from wrong, good from bad, but I know it's easier to die for Romeo than it was to kill him.

As the light hits, sending me crashing into Romeo and sending both of us skidding toward the wall where his old body howls in fear, I hope that means something. I hope I'm better than I could have been. Or am at least better than I would have been without him.

I try to turn and look into his eyes, but my chest is on fire. I open my mouth to scream, but the fire spreads to my lungs and throat and mouth, and the world fades in a press of smothering gray.

TWENTY-FIVE
Romeo

Everything collides.

I wrap my arm around her and snatch a handful of my soul specter's tattered old shirt, holding tight to my love and myself as the force of our combined momentum throws us against the wall in a knot of arms and legs and pain.

Maybe it's not too late. Maybe touching the specter will be enough and I'll be able to enter my old body and protect Ariel. The Ambassador said she couldn't kill. Whatever magic she's used shouldn't be deadly.

I still have hope, a little, but then—

We slam to a stop. I look down just in time to see Ariel's eyes close and her spine go limp. I swear I can feel the moment her soul steps away from her body. I try to scream at the

Ambassador, to beg Ariel to come back, but I can't make a sound. I'm falling to pieces, crumbling as the walls melt and the floor beneath us drops away.

I close my eyes, and the barrier of Dylan's skin thins and fades. Ariel bleeds into me, and I bleed into my old self, and everything in the world is malleable and transparent and I finally see it for what it's always been. A lie. A pretty lie made of curved light and faith in the solid nature of things that aren't solid at all. There is no beginning and no end, and the forces separating here and now, then and there, are as fragile as spiderwebs pushed away with shaking hands.

There is only one thing solid enough to hold on to and it is her. I love her. She is my other half, my second chance, the only way in the world I could have learned to be more than a monster. Her weakness showed me my strength, her faith made me believe, her love made me whole. I will never forget her, and I won't let her go.

The air gets hotter and hotter, and matter rearranges itself into flesh and bone and a rough, dirty floor beneath my cheek. But still I hold on, so tight my fingers cramp. And then . . . someone moans beside me.

My eyes open. It's her. Ariel. She's lying next to me, in this room with the coarse floor and the air filled with gray dust. It is . . . unbelievable. I reach out to smooth the tangled hair away from her face, and encounter something even more unbelievable. *My* hand. My *real* hand. I'm back in my own body, the living, breathing, coughing, choking–

I cover my mouth with my sleeve and cough until my throat feels bloody. The gray in the air isn't dust; it's smoke. There's a fire. The building is on fire. We have to get out.

"Ariel!" I cough again as I come to my hands and knees, the rawness in my throat telling me I've been breathing the smoke-filled air too long already. "Ariel, wake up! We—"

The crack of splintering wood explodes behind me, shredding the air. I spin to see a blazing timber crash down onto rows of simple wooden benches. Above them, a stained-glass window reflects the writhing orange and red below. I catch the gaze of a Madonna dressed in blue holding a strange-faced baby, and experience a moment of terrible clarity.

I know this church. I don't know how we've ended up here, but I know where we are. It's the church I grew up in, the one where I fidgeted for hours on those same hard benches, the one where Benvolio and I joked that the baby in the stained glass had the same shriveled face as our great uncle, the church I wished I could have taken refuge in after I tricked Juliet into taking her own life in the tomb not a hundred yards from its front door. The one that burned to the ground with Romeo Montague trapped inside in an alternate version of history. *This* version of history.

"Juliet." A strange feeling, halfway between hope and terror, leaps inside of me.

Juliet might still be alive. She might be in the tomb, close enough to smell the smoke. If I can make it out . . .

I turn on my knees, taking in the rest of the church. The fire is everywhere, blocking the entrance and the lower windows on the left side. The flames haven't reached the front of the church, where Ariel and I lie near the stone statue of Jesus on the cross, but they will soon. We have to get out.

"Ariel! Wake up!" I pull her onto my lap and shake her gently, willing her eyes to open. I don't know how I've come to be back here, and I have even less of a clue how I brought her with me, but I need her to open her eyes. We may be able to get out—there's a narrow path through the benches to our right that hasn't started to burn—but not if I'm carrying her. If we don't stay low to the ground, we'll be overcome by the smoke.

"Please, Ariel," I whisper into her ear, kissing the soft skin near her cheek. So soft and smooth and . . .

The scars. I pull back to search her face. The scars are gone, vanished, along with the glossy lipstick and sparkling eye shadow she smoothed on for the dance. Her face is clean and unmarked, and her hair is longer, falling in waves past the waist of a dress made of a coarsely woven gray fabric. It's unlike anything I've seen in hundreds of years. I look down at myself, a part of me not surprised to see the same cloak I was wearing the day I was supposed to meet Friar Lawrence on the road outside Verona. But there is no blood on the sleeves.

I haven't tricked Juliet. I haven't yet sold my soul to darkness.

I pull Ariel closer, planning to drag her across the floor if I have to, but a flash of movement catches my eye. I turn in time to see a woman with red hair slip behind the metal screen where the priest waits to address his parishioners. It's her. The Ambassador. *She's* done this.

"Help! Help us!" I scream. I point a finger her way, but she remains unmoved. It's no surprise that she wants us both dead, but surely she can see this isn't justice. "If you're truly on the side of good, you can't let her die! It's pointless. She won't hurt anyone here."

You underestimate the girl's capacity for evil. And your own. I hear her voice in my head, a disturbing sensation that makes me wince.

"She's not evil," I whisper, but I know the Ambassador can hear me. "In this time, a woman is the property of her father or her husband or the Church. She won't have the power or freedom to—"

Women have their own power, Romeo. Look how she's made you her slave.

"You're the one who would have made me a slave!" I shout, though I know this argument is pointless. There's only one thing left to say that might move her. "No matter what you believe, it's against your vows to watch two people die and not lift a finger to help."

My vows prevent me from doing harm to any living thing, she says, a sly note in her voice that reminds me of my maker. *But there were no living things in this church when I started the fire.*

I shake my head, more repulsed than surprised.

I'm sad it had to end like this, Romeo.

I ignore her, and gather Ariel into my arms. We'll have to go up the stairs to the bell tower. It's our only choice. The path to the low windows is catching fire, and the Ambassador stands between us and the nearest escape.

If it offers any comfort, I'm going to save Juliet. I will pull her from the tomb and give her another eternity of happiness and light.

"Another eternity of slavery!" I spit as I stagger to my feet. Ariel can't weigh much more than a hundred pounds, but she's dead weight, and the smoke is making my head spin.

Juliet will not be a slave; she will be a savior of the world.

If I weren't choking, I would laugh at the delusion in her voice. She's insane. As mad and murderous as I once was, and I will not allow her to have Juliet if I can help it.

I turn my back on her and stumble toward the stairs, mind

racing with possibilities. The bell tower steps are made of wood, but the tower itself is made of stone. Hopefully the fire won't spread as quickly there. If I can find something sharp, I can cut the rope tying the bells and use it to lower Ariel to the ground. I'll follow her down and hide her somewhere safe. Then I'll find Juliet and—

"Romeo. There you are," a low voice speaks from the darkness inside the tower door, making me cry out and nearly fall in my haste to back away. I know that voice. I know it even before the friar steps from the shadows with the knife we used to murder Juliet held in his hand.

"No."

"Where have you been hiding? I waited for you on the road for hours," he says, leaving no doubt that this is the friar as I knew him, when he was inhabited by a Mercenary and he tricked me into destroying the girl I loved. "I searched all the usual places, but it was as if you had . . . vanished from the face of the earth."

I let out a shaking breath. He's speaking in medieval Italian, and he doesn't seem to know about our past. Or future. Or whatever it is, now that I've looped back upon my long life and come once again to the moment when my eternity of evil began.

"Come," he says, motioning me closer. "We have business. There is still time to get through the flames if we hurry."

"Go away," I whisper like a child to a feral dog met on the road. But this man won't listen any more than a dog would. He is unreachable by reason or pleading or prayer, which only makes the cross swinging from his neck that much more ironic.

His eyes narrow, moving from me to Ariel and back again.

"Juliet was telling the truth, then. You *have* had a change of heart."

"Leave Juliet alone. She's worthless to you."

He smiles, waves a wisp of smoke away with a calm hand. "You're correct. There's no need to bother with Juliet. She isn't the one you love, is she?" He holds out the knife, handle first. "Take this with you to the tower; spill the girl's blood before she wakes. It will be simple and painless. I'll be there soon to administer the vows."

He moves closer, pressing the knife into the fingers I've curved around Ariel's knees. Then he takes my cheeks in his papery hands and leans in to kiss my forehead, inspiring a rush of such pure fear that it clears my head and pumps my weakening body full of strength. If I could run, I would, but he blocks the path to the only safe place. I remind myself that I'm the one holding the knife, but I know it won't make a difference.

The friar can kill with a finger, a thought, a smile. I've felt the hands on my face dig under my skin like razor-tipped worms. He has shot a killing thought through my mind and sent my brain exploding out the other side, and kept me alive to suffer through the aftermath. He is every nightmare I never wanted Ariel to dream, and here he is, close enough for me to smell the bitterness of his breath.

"This one loves you. Her heart is on fire with it," he whispers against my skin. "And your aura glows for her, as bright as it ever did for Juliet. Brighter, even." He smiles and shifts his eyes to a spot over my shoulder. "I once knew a love like that. My wife and I went our separate ways, but she's been putting her finger in my affairs of late. That is not something I will tolerate, Romeo, even in my favorite enemy."

I follow his gaze across the flames to where the Ambassador stands behind the screen.

His wife.

Once this terror and the witch behind me were bound by love. Now all that's left is magic and hatred. I can see it in his face, all the things he plans to do to Juliet's nurse if he can reach her before she finds a way out.

"Please . . . don't do this." I close my eyes for a moment and hope that some true force of goodness will hear my prayer.

"I won't do a thing. You will." He pats my arm and shifts me closer to the stone steps. "Make this sacrifice, and you will be my brother in every way."

"No. I won't."

"You will," he says. "You're a smart boy, Romeo. You are banished. This is your only way out. When the flames reach the top of the stairs, you'll be ready with that knife and will send your love to dance with the angels. Then I will come to take you away. We'll walk to the burial ground on the hill, and I'll show you all my wonderful secrets."

I shake my head, the memory of the horror rotting in the stone-covered grave filling my mind. I clench my jaw against a wave of nausea.

"Go." He lifts his palm, and I feel the force of his will shove at my shoulders. I step back in response, a puppet to be controlled by his power. He can still influence me. Maybe enough to make the choice of whether to sacrifice Ariel no choice at all. I shiver and clutch her so tightly to my chest that she moans again.

The friar smiles. "Get some air, and do your work. I will join you in a moment."

As soon as he turns toward Juliet's nurse, I whirl and stagger up the stairs, all too ready to escape his presence, knowing that every second will count. I have a knife. I'll be able to cut the rope holding the bells and fashion a sling to lower Ariel to the ground. Then I can crawl down after and free Juliet from her tomb. If I can manage it all before the Mercenary finds me again, there will be a chance for us all to escape. If not, I have the knife, and I'll do what I have to do.

I don't want to die, but I refuse to live to hurt her.

"Ariel, please," I pant in English as I climb. "Wake up. Ariel, wake up, wake–"

"Romeo?" she murmurs, her voice scratchy and raw. My arms shake. I've never been so happy to hear my own name. At least now she'll be conscious while I lower her down, and able to run from the church even if I can't join her. And I can tell her I love her one more time. Maybe this time she'll believe me. "Romeo? Is–"

"We're alive, but we're in danger. There's a fire."

"What? I don't understand," she says in perfect medieval Italian. She must have assimilated the language during the shift, the way I always assimilated the language of whatever country I happened to find myself in.

"We're in danger," I repeat in my native tongue, surprised by how natural it feels after so many hundreds of years out of practice.

"What?" Groggily she loops her arms around my neck. "Where are we?"

"We're in a church." I don't want to tell her too much. She's already confused. Mentioning where we are might scramble what's left of her mind. "But there's a fire and–"

"You have to put me down."

"If you think you can—"

"Put me down. This isn't right. Especially in the church." She shoves at my hands, and I have no choice but to set her feet on the floor. I'm careful of the knife, but it catches the hem of her skirt as I pull it away, tearing a rip in the fabric. "My dress!" she exclaims, as if I've committed some unforgivable offense.

I stand staring for a moment, dumbfounded. "Ariel, there's a *fire*," I repeat as patiently as I can manage. "Your dress is the least of our worries."

"But people will think—"

"What are you talking about? What people?"

"Are you mad?" She presses back against the wall. "Where is your head?"

"Ariel, we're going to be burned alive if we don't get out of here." *Not to mention that there's a man downstairs who's plotting to force me to drive a knife through your heart as soon as he finishes torturing his ex-wife.* "We can talk more when we reach the top of the tower." I hold out my hand, but she only cringes closer to the stones. "Ariel, please—"

"What are you saying?"

"Ariel! Listen to me!"

"Why are you calling me that?"

I freeze, my hands hovering in the air as if she's thrown up an invisible barrier between us. "It's your name."

"Romeo, you frighten me," she says, big blue eyes filling with tears. "You know my name. We've known each other since we were children."

My hands knead the air, searching for something to cling to. "I . . . I don't—"

"It's me, Rosaline," she says. "Don't you remember?"

Rosaline. Ariel. Rosaline. Ariel looks *nothing* like Rosaline, but obviously she thinks she's Rosaline DeSare. Or maybe Ariel *is* Rosaline now. Just like . . .

"Benvolio," I whisper, thinking of that day on the street in the twenty-first century when Benvolio was so *certain* he was someone else. What if he . . . What if Ben Luna . . .

"Your cousin?" Rosaline asks. "Is he here?"

What if . . . Could he and Ben . . . Could Ben . . .

"Romeo, please. Let's find Friar Lawrence. He can help. I know he is your friend and confidante."

Her words snap me out of my thoughts. It doesn't matter who's who or what's changed or why. There are some very important constants to consider. Fire rages in the church, and two supernatural creatures want us dead. If we waste time sorting out our thoughts, we'll have no brains in our heads left to think them.

I take Ariel's . . . *Rosaline's* hand and hold on, my grip gentle but firm. "I'm sorry if I've frightened you. The smoke must have affected me. I'm better now."

"You are?"

"I am. But there's a fire downstairs. We'll be burned if we go down the steps. Our only hope is to reach the top of the tower and for me to lower you down to the ground with a rope."

Her eyes fly wide. "All the way down? From the top of the tower? But I–I can't."

"You must."

"It's too far." She tries to pull away, but I hold tight. "I'll be frightened to death."

"Rosaline, please. It's the only way. Will you trust me? Will you let me help you?" I look deep into her eyes and try not to think about how painful it is to see her so . . . changed.

She is earnest and sweet and good, but she isn't Ariel. She's not my fierce girl with her head full of pain and her heart full of passion. She's not the person who listened to my secrets in a way I've never had anyone else listen. She's not the love I held in my arms and memorized the way she breathed. This girl with her hand in mine isn't Rosaline, but she isn't *my* Ariel, either. She doesn't breathe the same way. She won't kiss the same way or love the same way or hate the same way or feel or dream or hope or rage or laugh the way my Ariel did.

It makes my heart ache, but I ignore that, too. The Ariel I knew might be gone, but her body and some version of her soul are still here, and there is no time to mourn what's been lost. "Please. Hurry with me. I don't want you hurt, and I know your parents would be devastated to learn of your death."

"My . . ." Her lips blanche. "All right."

I nod and start back up the stairs, hoping we haven't wasted too much time. I concentrate on the feel of the creaking wood beneath my leather boots and the smell of the smoke drifting up the stairwell, refusing to think about what has been lost.

TWENTY-SIX

Ariel

This time, I am the screaming thing, the intruder with the voice no one else can hear.

I'm here! Please! Let me out! Romeo! I'm here! Please! Please, please, please . . .

I scream and scream, but Romeo doesn't hear me. Neither does Rosaline, this person wearing my body and using my mouth to speak a language I can't understand. But I can understand her thoughts and fears, her stupid worries about her torn dress and propriety and modesty and what her father will think when she gets home.

I hear her thoughts. I even feel her emotions, but it's not

like I'd feel them if they were mine. It's like when your foot falls asleep and the tingling blocks out some of the information traveling from your foot to your brain. I'm still aware of going through the motions—walking and talking and holding Romeo's hand in mine—but the sensation's not all there.

I'm not all here. I'm not here at all. I'm *nothing*. Only a voice screaming in the dark inside a mind that can't even—

Rosaline says something, and my hand flies to my forehead. For the first time I really *feel* my skin. Her fingers . . . *my* fingers . . . are cold. They shake as they press against my temple. She's wondering . . . she's starting to . . .

She . . .

She's not a she. I know the thought wouldn't make sense to anyone else, but to me it's a revelation. I'm suddenly connected—mind, body, and soul. I'm still not in control, but I'm a part of this. Rosaline isn't another person; she's a different version of . . . *me*.

Deep, deep down, where the secrets of blood and bone determine what a person is and what they'll become, Rosaline and I are the same. Rosaline is what I could have been if I'd been born in a different time, raised a different way, taught different things. If my dad had stuck around, if my mom hadn't had me all alone, if we'd had family to help us, if I'd never been burned or stared at like a freak, if I'd never heard the screaming things and learned too much about fear and anger, if I'd spent my time daydreaming about spiritual rapture instead of the flesh and blood kind I had with Romeo.

In a way, it's comforting. I can feel how easy it would be to relax my hold on Ariel Dragland and let myself become a part of Rosaline. She would absorb me like a sponge. It wouldn't be like dying, just . . . forgetting. It would be what I wished the doctor could have done for me when I was little. When I first visited the child psychiatrist, I thought she was going to fix me, erase all the bad things in my head and make me normal. I was devastated when I learned she didn't have that power.

But now I could have my wish. All I have to do is loosen my grip and fall into the welcoming darkness of Rosaline. I could let go and forget, and it would be like all the bad things in my life never happened.

A week ago I would have leapt for oblivion without a thought. But now . . . I can't. Because forgetting all the bad things would mean forgetting all the good things too. I'd forget my mom and how much she loves me. I'd forget Gemma and our flawed, but precious, friendship. I'd forget Romeo and how much I love him. I'd forget everything he meant to me, and how he loved me enough to forgive me when I didn't deserve to be forgiven. I'll never get to tell him that I forgive him, too, and he'll live the rest of his life with that haunted look in his eyes. He's in his old body now, but it's full up with the soul I fell in love with. I *know* it's him, just like he knows the girl next to him *isn't* me.

He thinks I'm gone. Maybe even dead. I can see it in the way he looks at me, feel it when he brushes the hair from my face and begs me to, "Please, keep going. Let me carry you if you can't walk. There's no time."

"I . . . I can't," she says, shivering as I push against the thin wall separating the two of us. I can understand her now, and imagine how my lips would move to speak this language. "I feel . . . ill."

Please. Let me out, I beg. *He needs me.* You *need me.*

I send feelings of strength coursing through our body. She

doesn't have to be afraid of the world or life or growing up anymore. She doesn't have to hide in a convent. She has another choice, and the courage to discover all the things that lie outside the walls of her father's estate, beyond the city of Verona, out in the wide world that's as scary as she's imagined, but also wonderful. There are horrible things in life, but there is also hope and beauty and art and adventure and . . . Romeo.

If she'll take the chance, I can show her magic, the highs and the lows and all the astonishing potential of the human heart. We can paint and laugh and play and dance and make the most of every moment with the boy we love, no matter how numbered the moments are.

"I'm afraid," she whispers, and I know she isn't talking to Romeo anymore.

And that's the only thing you have to lose, I say softly. There's no need to shout. The truth is as loud at a whisper as at a scream.

She's spent her life locked away by fear—her father's fear of her honor being compromised, her mother's fear of losing her only daughter, her own fear of leaving the parents who've loved her too tightly for her to know who she is without them. I can see their kind faces in her mind—a man with a red beard a shade darker than his hair, and a blond woman as pale as my mother. But she's not Mom. She's not.

Mom. I'll never see her again. My gut tells me there's no way back from where Romeo and I have traveled. Even if we survive the fire and I gain control of this body, I will never feel my mom's arms around me, never squeeze through one of our awkward hugs. I'll never be able to tell her that I'm okay, or how much I love her.

Pain and loss twist my heart, and my hold on Rosaline slips. Before I can recover, her fear pushes me away.

She forces me back to the farthest reaches of her mind, until I can't feel our shared body anymore. I can only watch through her eyes as we start to run again. We climb the stairs, circling around and around until we reach the top and a room barely big enough to stand upright in. Ancient, rusted bells hang in the center. There are three of them, all tied with a thick rope covered in a sticky yellow coating.

Romeo leaves me . . . Rosaline . . . by the wall and hurries to the closest bell. He begins to saw at the rope with the knife in his hand, back and forth, back and forth, as fast as he can. He must be planning to use it to climb down the side of the tower. But where did he get that knife? It looks familiar, something I've seen in a dream. The blade flashes like lightning, but the handle is a black so deep, it sucks the light out of the already dim room.

The moonlight shining through the three narrow windows isn't enough for me to see Romeo's face anymore, but I can see his silhouette shake with effort and can hear him curse and pull in a desperate breath. The rope cutting isn't going well. And now it's too late. His plan is going to fail.

Because the man in the robe from my nightmares is real.

And he's just stepped into the room.

Romeo

"I see she's still alive."

The friar. He's already here. I feel like I'm choking on my heart. I've failed. It took too long to get up the stairs, and the damn rope is covered in resin or pitch or something–

"Don't worry, my son," he says in that soothing voice that talks my heart down into my chest without my consent. "It still cuts through skin and bone quite easily."

"Damn you to hell!" I hurl the knife down the center of the bell tower, into the flames beginning to creep up the steps. The friar must have made it seconds before the wood began to burn. Now the bottom third of the tower is impassable. There's no way he'll be able to get his hands on the knife.

It's over. I won't kill for him—or anyone else—ever again. I'll die first. I'll let Rosaline die as well, if I have to. It's better for her to die by a stranger's hand than bleed out knowing someone she trusted was a fiend. The less familiar the evil, the easier it is to bear.

Liar. Torture is torture, and he will torture you both. She'll be better off if you toss her out the window.

I run a shaking hand through my hair. I can see it, the way her eyes would widen with betrayal and her arms and legs would churn as her body hurtles toward the ground. I can't do it, I *can't*. I can't kill anymore, not even in the name of mercy. I've had enough death to last ten men a dozen lifetimes. I'm so full, it rises in my throat like sickness.

"Come to me, Rosaline," the friar says, his mockery of kindness making me even sicker. "Come away from Romeo."

"Friar Lawrence?" Rosaline whispers. "What's happening? Why—"

"Come to me. I will keep you safe."

"No, Rosaline!" I step away from the bells, placing myself between them. "Don't trust him. He's a liar."

"Don't listen to him, child. The poor boy has run mad. I fear some evil spirit has taken possession of his soul."

"Friar! I'm so afraid!" Rosaline sobs.

"Come, sweet girl. I will give you peace."

"Peace," she repeats, her voice breaking in the middle of the word, as if there is nothing in the world she's ever wanted more. He's already gotten to her. With a word. One wretched word!

"Yes, child," he says. "You shall have peace."

She steps forward, but my arm whips out, pushing her back into the wall with all the force of my terror. I hear her head hit the stones and her whimper of pain and fear, and I know I've made a mistake. She'll never trust me now. Rosaline is as devout as anyone else I've ever known. It would have taken a miracle to make her choose me over a man of the cloth, and now that I've hurt her . . .

"Be careful," the friar says, his concern palpable. It would be so easy to believe him, even knowing without a doubt that every word is false. "Romeo is not himself. He's been speaking in tongues and—"

"Leave her alone!" I scream, drowning out the soothing lies. "Please!" I fist my hands together in front of me, begging him. "I'll give you anything. I'll give you my soul for the rest of eternity. You can lock me away and torture me and bring your young Mercenaries to watch. Anything. I'll do any—"

"Come, Rosaline." The friar holds out his arms. "Hurry now!"

I turn a moment too late. Rosaline has already circled around to the other side of the tower. Now she's only a few feet away from the friar, rushing to him as if he holds her life in his hands.

Which he does. And soon he will do with it as he wishes.

Time slows and my thoughts race.

Maybe he'll kill her quickly—the better to move on to lapping up my grief. Or maybe he'll do it slowly, bind me with his magic, and force me to watch her suffer until she begs to die and I beg to kill her simply to end her suffering. And then I'll be committing the same, unforgivable sin all over again. And it will be as it's always been, and I will walk in darkness for the rest of my days, until I can't remember the feel of the sun on my face or the safety and bliss of holding my love in my arms.

My love. Ariel. She's gone and I'm alone, and Rosaline will die in this tower and Juliet will die in her tomb, and this story will have an even more tragic end than it did the first time and— I. Have. Failed.

TWENTY-SEVEN

Romeo

Failed, failed, failed, and she's nearly there, and his arms are open and a demented smile is on his horrible face.

The realization beats me down until the weight of my failure feels like it will force me through the boards beneath me and I'll fall and break and burn in the fire roaring below and finally—

Finally.

Break. Burn.

She's in his arms now, his fingers curling around her neck, but it's not too late.

I don't think anything else, for fear he'll read my intentions on my face. I move. Quickly. I close the distance in the time it takes Rosaline's lashes to sweep down. By the time they sweep back up, I'm so close I can smell the smoke on the friar's cassock, I can count the wrinkles on his brow, I can see the light in Rosaline's eyes.

Ariel. I see her rise in Rosaline, but I don't hesitate or wonder or fear. I smile.

Because I know my sweet, savage girl. And she knows me.

I move and she moves, and our bodies work in perfect synchronicity, as if we're parts of the same creature. Our fingers claw into his robes, our knees bend, and we drop to the ground seconds before the friar's hands sweep over our heads. And then we're tipping him over our shoulders, shoving him out into the empty space at the center of the tower, and he's falling, falling, *screaming,* falling . . .

I turn to watch, but I still can't believe it. Even when I see the shock in his eyes, even when his robe kisses the rising flames and goes up like dry grass, even when the black bulk of his body hits the ground and the outline of a man blurs and begins to melt away, I'm still squeezing my fists together, waiting for him to rise and come for me again.

"Mercenaries can't survive fire. It's one of the few things that can destroy them," I say, as much for my own comfort as Ariel's.

Ariel. I turn to her, terrified that she'll be gone again. Before I can say her name, her arms are around me, her lips on mine. We clutch each other tight, every movement sealing us so close that no one will ever tear us apart.

The thought brings old words rising inside me. "Set me as a seal on your heart," I whisper against her lips. "For love is as strong as death."

She pulls away with tears in her eyes. "Shakespeare?"

"No. A psalm."

"It's beautiful."

"And true. I don't know how else to explain . . ." I cup her face in my hands. "I thought I'd lost you. You thought you were another person, the girl I told you about when I–"

"Rosaline. I know." She lets out a shaky breath. "She wasn't another person. She *was* me. Just a . . . *different* me. At first I thought I'd be trapped inside her version, but then I heard the friar saying the same things he said in my dreams, and I pushed hard enough and she . . ." She pauses, searching for the right words. "She faded. Into me. She didn't love anything the way I love you. She couldn't. She was still afraid."

"And you aren't. Not anymore."

"Because of you," she whispers, eyes filling again. "And I mean it this time. I trust you, no matter what. No more lies. Ever."

"Never." I kiss her, and hope rises inside me in a dizzying wave. The friar is dead. We've won, and now we're going to put all the wrongs right. Me. Her. Juliet, too. For the first time in my life, I have faith. I have faith in love and the magic it can work.

I end the kiss and grab her hand. "Let's get out of here."

"How?" She casts a nervous glance toward the center of the tower. "The stairs are on fire, and we don't have a knife to cut the bell rope."

"Do you trust me?"

"Of course," she says with a humbling intensity. "Always."

"Take off your dress," I say, pulling off my own cloak and shirt.

I take the hem of the cloak in my hands and pull–hard,

harder, hardest—until finally it gives with a great *rrrrip*. I tie the ends of the cloak together and see Ariel's face light up with understanding. She stands beside me in the loose chemise women of this time wear under their clothes, her dress already off.

Because she trusts me. As much as I trust her. The madness of the Mercenaries and the Ambassadors is behind us. When I look into her face—her big blue eyes, her sharp nose, those too-thin lips that feel so perfect against mine—I see everything I was too stupid to want for so long, every simple, miraculous secret in the universe revealed in the magic of her smile. She is mine; I am hers, and this life I've been given to share with her will be filled with more enchantment than the past seven hundred years combined.

"I love you," I say again, knowing I can't say it too many times, and that even those three words will never be enough to convey how much she means to me.

She puts her hand on my cheek, a fleeting touch that leaves me warm to my feet. "Me too. Now tell me how I need to tear this. I want to live to hear you say that a few thousand more times."

I turn back to my shirt, tying the sleeve to one end of the cloak. "If we can get twenty or twenty-five feet of rope, we'll be able to fall the rest of the way," I say. "I'll go down first so I can catch you when you drop."

"So you can look up my shift, is more like it."

"That too." I wink and she rolls her eyes, and I wonder how it's possible to feel so brim full of life with death roaring below us, sending plumes of smoke billowing into the room.

"Rosaline's father is going to be *very* upset to have his

daughter brought home to him in nothing but her slip." She starts where my knife accidentally tore her skirt and rips the dress in a circular pattern, longer and longer until I feel the last of the worry bunching my neck fade away. It's going to be enough. We're going to make it. "I've never had a father before, but I'm guessing someone's head will roll."

I take the end of her skirt and knot it tight to the other end of my cloak. "All part of the plan, my sweet."

"You already have a plan?" She watches me tie the sleeves of her dress around the top of the nearest bell and toss our rope of torn clothes out the window.

"Would you expect anything less?" I put my arm around her waist, and she loops hers around my neck.

"No. I wouldn't." She peers up at me with those old eyes of hers. "But from now on I want you to tell me about your plans. And I'll tell you about mine."

"The second we're on the ground." I pull away and move to the window. "Wrap your leg in the rope," I say, showing her how. "That way, if you lose your grip, you'll still be tangled in it and won't fall as quickly."

She nods. "We used to have to climb a rope in gym class. I'm not afraid."

She really isn't. I wish I wasn't afraid for her.

"See you on the ground," I say with a smile. I don't want to leave her, but this is for the best. She'll still make it to the ground long before the fire reaches the top of the tower. And this way I'll be there to catch her. Just in case.

I shinny down, hand over hand, with only one heart-stopping moment as my shirt rips a bit before catching on a seam. Soon I reach the end of our makeshift rope and risk my first glance down. The fire in the nave of the church illuminates the hard earth below, helping me judge the distance left to fall. Only ten feet. Twelve, at most. It won't be a soft landing, but as long as I keep my knees bent . . .

I let go, and the ground rises up to meet me with a punch that takes my breath away. Even with bent knees, the impact is enough to send me sprawling. I roll through the dirt, coughing, curling my knees, checking in with my throbbing spine to make sure nothing is broken. But I swear it feels like my bones are still rattling, rumbling, *bud-a-bump, bud-a-bump, bud-a-bump.* . . .

The sound gets louder, expanding outside my body, overpowering the roar of the fire in the church. I've only just recognized it for what it is—horses, more than two or three—when a man's voice booms through the crackling night.

"Romeo Montague! You are under arrest, by order of the prince!"

Suddenly the ground is alive with pawing hooves. I look up, catching flashes of gray and purple in the firelight. The prince's livery, his castle guard. I know they've been ordered to escort me to the dungeon if I'm caught violating the terms of my banishment. I killed Juliet's cousin Tybalt. I am an enemy of the prince and his friends, the Capulets, and now his men will take me and hold me until they decide on the particulars of my execution. If I'm lucky, it might be a private affair with only the prince's inner circle in attendance. If I'm unlucky, they'll drag me to the square and hang me until death while the entire city watches.

While Ariel watches, unable to do anything to save me from the sins of my former life. "Please! I was on the road to Mantua!" I shout. "But I saw the fire, and went in to help. Rosaline DeSare is—"

"You more than likely started the fire!" one man shouts, while another voice orders him to—

"Ride! Get every able-bodied man to help. Tell them we might keep the fire from spreading to the trees in the church-yard if we work quickly!"

The man who accused me of arson turns his mount back toward town and takes off, stirring up a cloud of dust. When it dissipates, I get my first clear look at the man in charge. It's Adolfo, an elder guard whose family sat only a pew away from mine in this very church.

"Adolfo! Please! Rosaline DeSare is trapped in the bell tower," I shout. "And Juliet Capulet is alive in her tomb. They need help!"

But he isn't looking at me. He hasn't heard me, or maybe he simply doesn't care to listen to the ravings of a murderer. I look to the tower, hoping to see Ariel climbing out the window, but the clothes rope is empty. My blood rushes faster. Where is she? What happened? Has she been overcome by the smoke?

"Please!" I raise my voice, shouting so loudly that Adolfo is forced to turn my way. I jump on the moment, knowing it might be my only chance. "Rosaline is in the bell tower! She's trapped! And Juliet Capulet has been buried alive in the Capulet tomb. There's been a horrible mistake." I'm on my knees. Begging. Please, *please* let him see that I'm telling the truth. "Tie me up and leave me, but you have to send men to—"

A cry cuts through the night. And then another, and an-other, a chorus of shocked voices echoing from the front of the church, where a few of the men have fetched shovels from the caretaker's shed to fling dirt on the fire that is spreading onto the grass. But by the time I look their way, they're dropping the shovels and backing away from the figure staggering toward them from the graveyard.

"A ghost!" one shouts. But he's wrong.

It's Juliet. In her true body. Out of her tomb. Alive! The blue dress she's wearing is rumpled and filthy, her long brown hair falls in wild tangled curls around her shoulders, and she's so weak she can barely walk, but she's alive! I jump to my feet to go to her, and find Adolfo's boot in my chest.

"Please," I grunt. "She needs help. And so does Rosaline." I turn, stomach pitching as I see the window of the tower still empty. "She's in the bell tower. The stairs are impassable. She'll burn to death if we don't—"

"Bonfilio, Marzio," Adolfo shouts. Two of the nearest men turn, the voice of their leader more compelling than even a girl risen from the grave. Adolfo points to the tower. "There's a girl alive in the bell tower. Ride to the barracks and fetch the ladders. Quickly now! The rest of you, back to the fire!" He begins shouting more names, giving each man a specific task in an attempt to organize the confusion.

I take advantage of his distraction and bolt, racing across the yard toward Juliet, heart doing strange things in my chest at the sight of her. I'm *so* happy to see her alive, so full of guilt and remorse, so frightened that I'll have to break her spirit all over again.

We're married. She loves me. I'm her soul mate. Or at least I was . . . before I fell in love with someone else.

I'll have to tell her about Ariel. No . . . Rosaline. *Damn.* Juliet knows I was courting Rosaline before we met. She won't understand. She'll feel betrayed, heartsick. There's no way she'll believe the outrageous truth, but I have to tell it.

I'll confess everything and hope she believes enough of it to be glad to be rid of me. No one but the friar and her nurse knew of our marriage. Her nurse won't betray her, and the friar is dead. So long as I keep my mouth shut, she won't be ruined.

And I will keep it shut. I mean her no harm. I want only good things for her.

I . . . love her, though not the way I once did.

Still, it's love. Warm and real. Joy that she's been spared the misery I brought upon her in another life makes my feet light. I run faster, reach out to her, wanting to help her to safety, to find her water, to send someone to fetch her father while I get Ariel out of—

"Stop!" Juliet holds up a trembling hand. In the writhing light of the fire, her eyes look positively mad. Of course, she has been *buried alive* for at least twenty-four hours, maybe more, depending on what day it is.

Shame burns inside me, evaporating the joy I felt at seeing her whole. Maybe she isn't whole. Maybe her mind is damaged beyond repair and I am to blame for her ruin a second time.

"Juliet." I stop a yard from where she sways on her feet. She looks as if she's about to topple over. My mind screams for me to get close enough to catch her, but her expression keeps me where I am. She looks terrified, almost as if she doesn't remember . . . "It's me," I whisper. "Romeo."

"I know. I haven't forgotten your real face." Her voice is hoarse, ravaged from her time in the tomb. "You have a living body once more. I couldn't believe it when she told me, but . . . here you are."

My head shakes numbly. No. It can't be. She can't . . .

Yet here *I* am, with all my memories of the past and the future still intact. But I was sent here by Ambassador magic. Could she—

"Did your nurse send you here?" I ask, fresh hatred for the Ambassador rising inside of me for making me believe Juliet was lost. "Did she know you were alive?"

"I don't know who or what sent me here. After you shot me, I was dying. I reached out to my specter, ready for peace. Instead I woke up in the tomb." She startles, clutching her dress as more men on horseback clatter up to the church to join the fight. Her eyes flick back and forth—from the men, to the church, and back again—finally seeming to realize there's a fire, and we are in the way.

"Come," I say, holding out a hand. I glance at the bell tower once more, hope sparking inside me when I see a flash of white hair by the window. Ariel! But she's hiding for some reason. . . . Why?

The urge to run across the yard, to scream for Ariel to climb down the rope to safety, is almost overwhelming. But Juliet is still swaying on her feet, making no move to get out of the way as more men and horses pour into the yard, many of them not watching the ground the way they should, in their haste to get to the fire.

"Come," I say more firmly. "We should move." I back away from the flames. After a moment, she begins to follow, but stumbles on her filthy skirts. I reach out to catch her, but her slick, sticky hands slap mine away, making it clear she prefers to collapse in the dirt rather than accept my help.

"What happened?" I ask. "Are you hurt?"

"I'm fine," she murmurs.

"But your hands. They're—"

"I'm fine!" She lies at my feet, looking so small huddled on the ground that something inside of me breaks.

"Juliet." I go to my knees in front of her, rest my fingers ever-so-gently on her shoulder. "Please forgive me. If I could take all the suffering into myself and spare you, I would."

"Nurse is dead. She was in another woman's body, a woman with red hair and . . . But I knew it was her." Juliet's breath hitches and her shoulders shake, but she doesn't shrug off my hand. "The friar slit her throat, but somehow she made it to the tomb and pushed away the stone. She said . . . She . . . She died. In my arms." Head still bowed, she lifts her hands. They look black in the firelight, but I know they're not. They're red. Wet with the blood of the woman who saved her, damned her. "She begged for my forgiveness too."

"As she should have."

"And then she begged me to kill you, and Ariel. She said you both have to die or the world is lost." She lifts her face, and for a moment I am taken aback by her beauty.

Even covered in dirt and grime, Juliet is extraordinary—with her full lips and soft brown eyes and skin so clear and lovely. Objectively she is three times the beauty Ariel could ever be. But in my heart, Ariel is the loveliest thing on earth. Hers is the face that takes my breath away.

And now Juliet has been ordered to kill her.

"She's innocent," I whisper. "Kill me if you must, but please—"

"You love her."

"I do," I say, hoping she can read the truth on my face.

"Nurse said you would find love and happiness. She said

I would have as well, but . . ." She blinks, as if trying to focus her thoughts through a haze. "She changed things with what she did," she whispers. "Giving you a chance to become an Ambassador."

"I'm sorry."

"It doesn't matter." She stares into the fire, the sadness on her face so profound, it takes my breath away. "He's gone."

"I—" I bite my lip. I can't say I'm sorry again. It isn't nearly enough. "I thought I was doing the right thing, I truly did, but I—"

"Promise me something." Juliet turns back to me, her eyes calm and focused for the first time.

"Anything."

"Promise me you will live an honorable life," she says. "Be good, Romeo. Truly good. Prove her wrong."

"I am not truly good," I say, unable to lie to her. "I doubt I will ever be. But I will be kind. And I will do what I can to bring light to the world. I swear it."

After a moment, she nods, seemingly satisfied with my answer. "Then go. Find Ariel and get out of here before someone remembers they're supposed to take you to the dungeon."

I rise to leave, but stop when Juliet calls out again. "And, Romeo?"

"Yes?" My chest aches as I watch her push weakly to her feet, wishing there was something I could do to give her back what I've stolen.

"I forgive you."

My breath rushes out, her kindness hitting me like a fist in the gut.

"But don't come back. Even if the prince grants you a

pardon," she continues. "I don't ever, *ever* want to see your vile face again."

I smile. Because I am vile, at times. But she forgives me. And Ariel is waiting in the tower and she loves me and—

"Romeo! Are you mad? What have you done?" A familiar voice from the road makes me turn to see my cousin Benvolio's horse riding toward me.

With Benjamin Luna on top, dressed in my cousin's clothes, speaking our native language.

I am simultaneously shocked to the core and not at all surprised. Because where else would Ben Luna be? If the girl he loves is here? I'm beginning to think there is only one truth that matters, and time and space and alternate realities are as insignificant as the metaphorical spiderwebs I pushed aside when Ariel and I traveled together to this place.

Ben shakes his head as his horse trots closer. "Why are you—"

"Ben?" Juliet murmurs, fear and hope and every deep thing she feels for him mixing in his name. "Ben!"

But Ben doesn't slide from his horse. He knits his brow, clearly confused by the intimacy in Juliet's voice. Like Ariel when we first arrived here, and the Benvolio I met in the future, he doesn't seem to know the things Juliet and I know. He has no idea that he loved her so many hundreds of years in the future.

"Juliet?" Even her name is unfamiliar in his mouth. "But I thought . . . they . . . Your parents buried you. Two *days* ago."

"Ben? Don't you . . . It's me." Juliet sways. I reach out to catch her as she falls, half expecting her to shove my hands away again, but she doesn't. She lets me guide her to the ground, too weak to repel my touch.

Ben—Benvolio—is off his horse and kneeling beside us a moment later. "Is she all right?"

"Of course not," I snap, finding I don't care for him any more in this time than I did in the twenty-first century. Thank god I've been banished and won't have to call him "cousin" on a daily basis. "She's been *buried alive.*"

"Good lord." He brushes Juliet's hair from her forehead with such tenderness that I know. I know he will love her, even before he mutters "You poor girl" with such feeling, it brings a smile to Juliet's tired face.

"Ben." She reaches for his hand and holds tight, though it's obvious she's getting weaker by the moment.

"Mother calls me that," Benvolio says, wonder in his voice. "Did you tell her?" he asks me.

"I didn't tell her a thing." I shift Juliet into Ben's arms, knowing it won't be long before he remembers she belongs there. "She needs water. And rest. And a protector. Take her to your parents' estate. Don't let the Capulets get their hands on her until she's well, especially her mother. Don't let anyone hurt her."

"I won't," he promises, eyes still fixed on Juliet's face even when he says, "You should go, Cousin. Take my horse. There's already talk of a hanging. I heard the soldiers on the road."

"I will, but first I—"

"No! I won't go! Let me die!" The scream comes from the tower, high and desperate above the roar of the flames.

I spin around in time to see Ariel—

Ariel

—lean out the window and shove the ladder away, shaking even though it's sweltering in the tower.

That was Juliet Romeo was talking to before the other boy rode up on his horse. It has to be. There was something between them, an energy—love and hate and regret all mixed together. They really *know* each other, even if they hate the knowing.

At least Juliet does. Romeo looked like he was smiling there for a minute. . . .

I guess I should be jealous, but I'm not. I'm sure of Romeo's love in a way I've never been sure of anything else, and I'm just too plain scared to be jealous.

I heard the men shouting when they first rode up to the church. They want to take Romeo to the dungeon. I don't know much about medieval Italy—only a few daily rituals left over from Rosaline's memories—but I can imagine what a fourteenth-century dungeon will be like. Rats and torture and disease and death. Romeo will never make it out alive.

I have to save him, or the future we've dreamed about will never happen.

"Rosaline!" Romeo is at the base of the tower now, helping the men pick the ladder up off the ground. "Please! Let us put up the ladder. I'll climb up and help you down."

I lean out the window and shout in Rosaline's language, so grateful the ability stayed with me when her personality was absorbed into mine, "I *can't!*" I meet Romeo's eyes, willing him to see that I'm up to something, silently begging him to play along. "I'm too ashamed."

"Don't be ashamed," he says, the confusion in his eyes tinged with curiosity. "I love you."

"I love you, too," I sob. "I always will."

"Then come down. Please!"

The men watching our exchange turn to look at him, then up at me, and that's when I lift my leg over the edge of the window and start down the rope, hoping the distracting view I teased Romeo about will buy me a few minutes to plan. As I lurch downward, I gather all the strength Romeo has helped me find, and I focus it. I love him, and I won't let anyone take him. I think I know what to say, the one lie that might save Romeo from the dungeon.

I'm Rosaline DeSare, a girl known for her sweetness and piety, but even sweet girls can fall for the local bad boy. And sometimes, when they fall, they fall hard and fast and far, and there's only one way for them to be redeemed—at least in this time.

As the rope runs out and I begin the stomach-turning drop to the ground, I let myself believe my own story. Tears burn my eyes and clutch at my throat, and my breath comes fast enough to make me dizzy.

My first words as I'm caught by several pairs of strong hands—including Romeo's, which I find and hang on to like they're my last hope in the world—are "Please don't take him away. He's the father of my child."

EPILOGUE

TWELVE YEARS LATER . . .

Romeo

"But you were lying, Mommy. Weren't you? I wasn't in your tummy yet." Gemma leans forward in her little chair, her chubby cheeks red, eyes glittering with anticipation as Ariel reaches the end of the familiar story.

Our girl has my eyes—dark and filled with trouble—but her mother's nearly white blond hair and pale skin. She is strikingly beautiful. I could stare at her all day and never get tired of it. When she was first born, I'd stand over her cradle for hours, dumbstruck by her very existence, by the miracle of this tiny person who was mine to protect. She's perfect, unforgettable, the most breathtaking thing I've ever seen.

Except for her mother.

I catch Ariel's eye. She smiles, as if she knows what I'm thinking. Which she probably does.

"Yes, I was lying," she says. "But I had to, or Daddy would never have made it out of Verona alive."

Gemma lets out a shaky breath and turns to look at me, giving a serious nod that I know is her forgiving me again for not always being the good father she knows. We haven't told her the entire truth, only that Daddy did something foolish and wrong when he was young and that's the reason we can never go back to Verona. We had to tell her something. She'd started to ask why Grandpa and Grandma DeSare always come to us in Mantua, and why we couldn't go to their estate, where there are horses and ducks and the portrait of Mommy when she was little.

Gemma's only seven, but so curious, with an imagination that devours all the stories her mother tells. The ones about fairies and dragons and the troll that lives under the bridge down the lane, and the more extraordinary ones about her mother and me and the future and our journey through time and space. Ariel leaves out the scariest parts, but keeps enough excitement to make our story our daughter's favorite. She knows every word by heart, but asks to hear it again and again. Especially the next part.

"And then what, Mommy? What happened next?"

"I hugged Daddy tight and wouldn't let him go. I told the men that Friar Lawrence had promised to marry us, but when we arrived at the church, he went mad and tried to kill your father," Ariel says, sharing the version of events we've agreed to stick to until Gemma is old enough to be told about the Ambassadors and the Mercenaries. "I kept telling them what happened again and again, and finally the men started to believe me. And so the captain of the guard sent for Grandpa, who came to get us right away."

"Two hours later, your mother and I were married by the pastor from the next village." I gather Gemma into my lap and hug her tight. "Before the sun had even come up."

"We loaded one of Grandpa's carts with the furniture he'd given me for my dowry, and set out for Mantua after breakfast," Ariel says. "We planned to stay with my aunt and uncle until we could find a home of our own."

"Even though your great-aunt Mary was less than thrilled by the circumstances surrounding our marriage," I add.

Gemma scrunches her nose and squints her eyes, making a prune face so completely her aunt Mary's that I have to fight the urge to laugh. I try not to encourage her.

Mostly.

"Right." The grin on Ariel's face leaves no doubt she's seen Gemma's impression as well. "So, we were worried about the reception we'd receive, but still very happy to be together. We thought the worst of everything was behind us." Ariel comes to sit beside Gemma and me on the couch, the soft one stuffed with wool that we made in the studio behind the cottage, having not outgrown our taste for certain modern comforts. "But then, not three miles outside of town, a man on horseback came riding up hard behind us."

"And you thought he was a highwayman!" Gemma shouts, pulling her knees in and balancing her chin on top.

"We did," Ariel says, "but as he came closer, we could see that he wore the Capulet family crest. And in his hand he carried a land deed for a small farm outside of Mantua, signing the property from Juliet's father, Lord Capulet, over to Romeo. There was also a note from Juliet Capulet to me. It said, 'Thank you for the past you gave me in the future. Please take–'"

"'–this as a token of my undying gratitude,'" Gemma finishes with a giggle. "Because she was already in love with Daddy's cousin, and they got married two years later and had hundreds of babies!"

"Not hundreds of babies." I tickle her ribs, turning her giggle to a squealing laugh. "Five is nowhere close to a hundred."

"No, it's ninety-five less than a hundred!" Gemma says.

"Smart girl," Ariel says.

"I am," Gemma agrees with a sigh. "I am so wonderful at math." She oozes onto the carpet at our feet.

I take the opportunity to scoot closer to my wife, tuck her under my arm, and smell that irresistible place where her hair covers her neck. Flowers and paint, just like always. The flowers we mix in our soap, and the paint that's become such a part of our life together. Despite the challenges facing women artists in this time, Ariel has found work painting portraits for a few of the city's wealthiest families. So long as she refrains from competing with the male guild artists–who won't allow a female, no matter how skilled, to join their ranks–for the more lucrative commissions in the cathedrals and palaces, she is left alone.

My father died four years ago, and I inherited his fortune, but in our early days, her portraits of wealthy children put food on our table, allowing me to spend my days tending our garden and animals, and, later, teaching Gemma all the things a girl isn't supposed to learn in the fourteenth century.

Ariel teases me about being the world's first stay-at-home

dad, but I don't mind. Of all the things I've been, a husband and a father are by far the best.

"I wish I had brothers and sisters." Gemma plops her feet into my lap, an invitation for me to pull her little toes, a thing she's loved since she was barely able to walk.

"Then you wouldn't have your own room," Ariel says, not a hint of sadness in her voice. Gemma's birth was difficult, and neither of us were surprised when no more children came. We weren't upset, either. We have one amazing girl, a life together, freedom from all things Mercenary and Ambassador, and each other. It is . . . everything. Better than eternity or superhuman power. This is real magic, and I live and breathe it every day.

"I could share," Gemma says. "I'm small."

"No, you're not." Ariel pinches her heel. "You're the tallest girl on the entire road."

Gemma smiles a sleepy smile. "I am. I am going to be the tallest girl in the entire city when I grow up. And I will be a painter like Mommy, but I will only paint animals. Mostly horses."

"Sounds like an excellent plan." Ariel smiles down at her, that loving smile that makes her even more beautiful. And then she turns to look at me with that same look in her eyes, and I melt the way I always do. I am the luckiest man in any world, a soul transformed, pulled back from the abyss and blessed with love more powerful than evil or death or time or space or any of the rules.

"I love you," I whisper.

She smiles. "Two thousand and twenty-four," she says, and then she kisses me. And it is still the best kiss.

And soon we'll put Gemma to bed, and when she's asleep,

we'll go down to the stream behind the house with a bottle of wine and none of our clothes and remind each other that— even in the midst of so much goodness—there are delightful ways to be wicked. And we'll swim and laugh and kiss, and the stars will shine, beautiful and bright, but Ariel will always shine brighter.

At least for me.

ACKNOWLEDGMENTS

As always, many thanks to the team at Delacorte Press, especially to my editors, Michelle Poploff and Rebecca Short, for their guidance, support, and enthusiasm. Thanks to the Bard for the inspiration, Julie Linker for the critique (you were right, as always), and the Debutantes of 2009 for their friendship and support. Thanks to the booksellers who have worked so hard for my books in troubled times. Thanks to the Ithaca College Theater Department, London Center, for the walking tours of Shakespeare's haunts—the frozen toes were worth it! And even bigger thanks to my readers. You inspire me daily.

STACEY JAY is the author of *Juliet Immortal* and several other books for young adults. She lives in California wine country with her husband and their two little boys. Learn more at staceyjay.com.

DISCOVER JULIET'S STORY IN

Juliet Immortal

Juliet Capulet didn't take her own life. She was murdered by the person she trusted most, her new husband, Romeo Montague, who made the sacrifice to ensure his own immortality. But Romeo didn't anticipate that Juliet would be granted eternity as well, and would become an agent for the Ambassadors of Light.

For seven hundred years, Juliet has struggled to preserve romantic love and the lives of the innocent, while Romeo has fought for the dark side, seeking to destroy the human heart. Until now.

Now Juliet has found her own forbidden love, and Romeo, O Romeo, will do everything in his power to destroy their happiness.